COZENAGE

Book 3 of The Scarecrow Trials

❧ * ☙

Tamara Brigham

❧ * ☙

Cover Design by: Tamara Brigham

Published by:
Tamara Brigham
PO Box 151
Clearlake, CA 95422

Printed and bound in the United States of America

First Edition

ISBN #978-1-7371869-0-8

For Cheryl

For all of the support and encouragement

pushing me to write in uncharted territory

and forcing me to think outside of the box.

It's been a long road…and I've enjoyed every minute of it.

Our indiscretion sometimes serves us well

When our deep plots do pall: and that should teach us

There's a divinity that shapes our ends

Rough-hew them how we will

Hamlet Act 5, Scene 2

∽Chapter 1∽

Heart hammering, hands trembling, he shook the stout form bent and discarded at the bottom of the stairs. The grated walkway beneath rattled and groaned with the weight of the black-clad mass as he shook it but the lump did not move. Did not stir. Did not make a sound.

From the angled twist of his neck, it was easy to guess why.

Nervous fingers brushed aside a long shock of salt and pepper gray hair, tinted pink and blue by the glow cast from the alglamp at the corner of the nearest structure and the flickering pop and sizzle of neon from a vindi sign in a nearby window.

The exploration took only seconds though it felt like an eternal moment frozen in time. A moment disrupted by the thundering shudder of boots on wet metal beneath his feet.

"Oy! Mierdita! Move away!"

He did not need to be told twice. He was a little man, thin from malnourishment and ill-dressed for the atmosphere the earth's womb had birthed him into not long before. He should have remembered this cold, this damp. He should have come prepared.

He should have brought some sort of weapon with him.

Since he had done neither of those things, he scurried backward in his crouched position like a crab, falling ass-flat against the stairs he had forgotten were there in that startling moment of barked command. He had barely enough time to scramble to the top of the rise before the pair of bird-beaked monsters bore down on his position.

Crows!

One stopped to inspect the fallen form at the base of the stairs. The other charged after him, reaching black-gloved hands like talons intent on their prey. Despite now soaked through cloth shoes, he was light on his feet and fast, and more desperate to escape, it seemed, than the hunter was to apprehend him.

Words barked into an ICD. Slang code he did not understand. But the widening distance between himself and the beaked horror was cut short by a similar rumble on the path somewhere ahead. He could not tell where it originated, where the threat would emerge from in this maze of grated paths, platforms, and stairs. The forgotten, ever-present crash of the Four Falls and the surge of the storm-swollen river some distance below distorted the sound of approaching thunder steps.

He swung down, slipping under a guardrail to fall a half-Lev to another path. Instinct told him to go up. Desperation, the fear of being trapped without nearby stairs to make an ascent, pushed him down.

Crowds at an intersection, huddled together beneath awnings or in their best protective attire around a concert display of the sort of music he had not enjoyed in too long, proved an adequate shield from seeking eyes. People snapped and snarled as he pushed through, lost himself in their midst, arms clutched to his chest, shoulders hunched to allow him to hide among those taller than himself. There were advantages, at times, to being a small man.

Being small had gotten him out of the Core when many he knew had not been so lucky. Being small also meant that, with so many bodies pressed around him, his pursuers might not easily detect him.

He waited, the pulse in his ears as his heart thundered so loud that the music exhibit on the external Echo was nothing more than a buzz. He faced the screen too, but the focus of his attention was elsewhere.

His hunters seemed reluctant to bully through the throng. Like the scavengers their beaked masks represented, they circled the crowd, looking. Sniffing out his anxiety and fear. He thought they might linger until the prodcast ended, waiting for the crowd's dispersal to pick off the one who did not belong. The crackle of a nearby ICD tickled his ear as the audience in attendance on the Echo screen rose as one in a wave of applause for the small orchestra they had enjoyed. Those on the street corner likewise clapped and whistled their unheard praise. The too-close voice on the ICD instructed its wearer to return to the nest, resulting in a barked grumble of obedience.

The Crows retreated.

Murder. It was the only word the little man picked out of the commanded summons.

The crowd, made nervous by the recognition of the flock of five around their perimeter, not noticed before, began to warily scatter, doing their best to stay a safe distance from the distrusted shadows.

He moved with one cluster as they drifted away from the Echo.

Across the square. Into a lift that would take him in the direction he wanted to go. Up. Away from the Core. Away from the Crows.

The Crows moved another way.

The lift rose a single Lev and the crowd in the mobile room emptied as one onto the wide platform where more Crows loitered.

He did not want to remain in the lift as the Crows pushed to come inside, and so the little man emptied too.

This was not far enough. He needed to go higher. He needed to get away, to lay low somewhere familiar. Somewhere he could rest, recover his city bearings, adjust to the renewed reality Hebenon thrust upon him. He was barely free of the Core for what? Thirty minutes? An hour at most? And already he was accused of murder.

He had been accused before. He had been guilty. This time, the guilt was not his. Not that they would care.

Until the Crows stopped looking for him, until he found suitable clothes that would allow him to fit into the general population, until a killer was positively identified, he needed a place to hide.

Maybe he should have stuck with Enoch and the children. But they had been a burden he had accepted only as long as they afforded him an escape. Now he was free of them, free of the Core.

Some people followed dreams. Some stole dreams from others.

Switz, the survivor, intended to remain free now that the opportunity had been given, intended to reclaim the dreams stolen from him long ago. Even if he no longer knew what his dreams were.

☙*❧

One after another had fallen, men and women, to be greeted by death in the jagged iciness of the vortex at the bottom of the chasm.

Skelter had cut the cable which might have allowed others to reach the bottom safely, yet some had hoped that the length remaining would be enough to offer the chance of a safe drop into the river. Without an adequate light source, the violence of the whirlpool was hidden and not one who watched their predecessors disappear over the precipice, or those willing to attempt it, knew what to expect at the bottom.

Until tonight, none of them had known this exit was here. Three had gone down and had, it appeared, made it out.

If those three could do it, what was to prevent others from doing likewise?

The repercussions of twin blasts sealed the entrance of the Core mining system, where once ore wagons had moved in and out of the earth extracting salt, usable stones, and a smattering of other useful elements to fill the production needs of Hebenon. With the narrow tunnel the children had passed through closed by the concussive force, there was no choice but to try. Some of the survivors were at that tunnel trying to dig through the collapse, driven by hope or by fear for the children. Others had returned to the main door, picked up what tools remained from the war for release, and began to dig.

But the food was gone, or nearly so, gorged upon in the pre-battle orgy of feasting, and what burnable fuel they had once used for lighting, heat, and cooking, had been expended as weapons in the now extinguished battle. Without those things, the thirteen who remained alive inside the Core were condemned to slow starvation, dehydration, or suffocation when the air systems eventually stopped working.

The black maw might be their only chance.

Six tried. Six fell. Six dead, screaming as the river sucked them under, pulled them out, battered them against stone teeth to be devoured by the flow that crashed and rumbled towards the sea.

Those who remained looked at one another with unspoken fear, anger, and dismay.

Wherever Skelter had gone, whether he had survived or likewise perished in the water, this was no way out for those who remained.

Now what were they going to do?

∽Chapter 2≍

During hours of red and black, body beset with pain, lungs struggling against the remnants of swallowed river water and exertion, Rhyd was only marginally aware of the clatter of steps on the grate outside the flop where they had found refuge, the thunder of a skirmish, the debating voices inside that eventually sent Tox on the search for help. Nor was he aware, as he faded in and out of consciousness, of the later arrival of that help.

As long as he did not move, did not breathe too deeply, the pain remained a dim, uncomfortable numbness that only crashed in on him in the moments when consciousness crept too close. There had been intense bursts of it, in his shoulder, his leg, his head, agony that cut through the black of sleep with blades of red and white, but the oxygen mask stifled his cries and quickly allowed him to slip back into the oblivion of unconscious sleep. He was unaware of comings and goings after that, of voices and decisions made, or the eventual effort to relocate to a more secure location, somewhere warmer than an unmaintained kiomonga without the benefits of heat or running water.

The agony was still there.

This was not the first time he had awoken in pain, not the first time he had dislocated a shoulder or endured a plethora of bruises, lacerations, and cracked bones. Nor was this the first time waking in the care of others, but that was a rare enough occurrence that he remained unaccustomed to it. Nor was he accustomed to the faint perfume of masculine cologne lingering in the air, in the cushions upon which he lay, in the pillow on which his head rested.

He knew that scent.

Jaron's flat.

He groaned and tried to sit without opening his eyes, but the jarring bite in his shoulder made him wince and fall back beneath the assault of crimson storming behind lids he was grateful he had not opened. For lack of a better place to hide, Jaron's flat would do. No one would look for him here. If he had been taken to his flat, Venn would have found them, him, and the questions bound to follow were ones best left unanswered.

That confrontation would arise soon enough.

There were few sounds around him, only the murmur of filtered, drowning voices of a prodcast, the hiss and hum of filt and heating systems, water running through insulated pipes and the dripping from overhangs outside. He was alone, if not in the flat than at least in the room where he lay.

Alone brought momentary panic and the fear of what had become of the others, of Skelter, Tox, or any of those who had been at his side at the river's edge. His last vivid memories were someone tumbling down stairs behind him, the sense of blind, stumbling pain, and the click of a door lock.

Everything that existed after that, until this moment, was darkness, blood, and discomfort.

Words from the prodcast moled into his brain, forced him to crack open his eyes and gingerly turn his throbbing head towards the blurry images on the screen behind him. He blinked, squinted, and stared.

How many days had he slept?

❧*❧

Maemi emerged from Vapors' kitchen to the cluster of patrons at the bar staring at the Echo with the sort of rapt attention that typically accompanied reports of murder, carnage, mayhem, or the death of someone of import, the sort of reports Soleia and Kenneth Ximenez were keen to provide. Such prodcasts, no matter how insignificant in the scope of Hebenon's daily life, made for higher viewing numbers, which meant more ticks spent on the goods advertised between soundbites of news and gossip.

The last time Maemi had seen her guests pay such attention to a prodcast had been when Captain Grainger had announced that

Founder Kemway was alive though in failing health. A living Founder was newsworthy when most believed him dead since the night of the Coup. Before that, it had been one or another of Scarecrow's exploits against the brako, the sort of report that made some cheer and made the brako and bugorra gnash their teeth in frustration.

Thankfully, it was not the Scarecrow on the screen today as Maemi feared, but rather the Founder's face once again. When someone in the cluster at the bar called, "Turn it up," Maemi did so eagerly, expecting to hear that the ill man had succumbed to whatever health issues he had battled, that the city was free of the Kemway dynasty at last.

There was his wife, of course, and their sole surviving child. But tradition would never allow either to fill the role of Founder. Of course, traditions could change. Traditions would not have allowed anyone to leave the protection of Hebanthe Falls to go Outside.

Perhaps it was time to break from the tradition of leadership too. But Maemi doubted either Mam Kemway or her daughter were strong enough to provide the leadership Hebenon required to face an increasing number of new challenges.

The news on display, however, was not the death of the Founder but something more troubling.

"That's right, Ken." Heavy with child, Soleia's expression hovered between calculated neutrality and rabid glee as she repeated the news for the benefit of her viewers. "Sources close to the Captain's Office have confirmed the abduction of Founder Kemway from the medical facility where he was being treated. The identities of officers and medi-staff said to have lost their lives in the assault have not been released pending notification of next of kin. The suspects are said to be Talkers in bugorra uniforms and are still at large and to be considered dangerous to the public."

Kenneth took up his wife's story without pause. "Motives for this crime remain unknown. No ransom has been requested and no one has claimed responsibility for the act. A hunt is underway and citizens are encouraged to come forward with any information about the perpetrators' identities or the Founder's location. It is the primary concern of the Captain's Office to find Founder Kemway to provide the care he requires."

The prodcast devolved into conjecture and speculation, about the Founder's health, about what motives might drive Senior Kal and the Voices of Faith to condone or undertake such drastic action, about what the captain and gorra were hiding with their failure to make a public statement on the matter. The timestamp in the corner of the screen indicated the secondary segment, one of what Maemi assumed would be multiple interviews with members of the Nau and high-tiered business moguls. From the stamp, the news had first aired nearly thirty minutes ago and the prodcast, along with any hearsay and the Ximenezes' own opinions and spins on the story, would repeat until the captain or another suitable bugorra representative clarified or refuted the rumors.

It was too late for that now, however. It would take no more than another hour, maybe three, for the entire city's population to hear the news. True or not, the effects of the report would be difficult, if not impossible, to untangle and erase just because the captain appeared and claimed the story to be a lie.

Maemi wondered, as she turned the station to more neutral programming, a repeat of the recital not been preempted by the Kemway kidnapping report, ignoring the protests and groans of her patrons, if Rhyd knew about this.

Not having heard how his exploits had fared, whether he was alive or dead, she wondered what the Scarecrow could do?

If he could do anything at all.

Born in the Uppers to a family of influence, Feena Wulfe grew up understanding power and manipulation and the cost of each. She had been too young, only three when her grandfather's interests had run at cross-purposes with the Founder's. Her parents had been faced with the difficult and cruel choice to either join him in incarceration or accept familial exile into the Levs. With three children to consider and a wife pregnant with a fourth, familial imprisonment, whatever that meant, was an unacceptable option. Thus the Wulfe patriarch was expelled to the unknown fate of prison, presumably in one of the Factories, while his son Tunon and daughter-in-law Muri took their children into the Levs.

They were never beyond the Founder's reach, however. The Kemways controlled everything in Hebanthe Falls. But with the Kemways' distaste for the Levs, the families were far enough apart that the Wulfes were no longer considered a threat and could conduct their business without direct interference from the Founder.

Making the best of what could have been a crippling change, the Wulfes flourished, although the stress of relocation, of readjustment, and a lung illness brought on by the cold, damp environment cost Tunon and Muri the child she carried. Connections to other Upper families were maintained; the strength and influence of the Wulfe name kept their interests intact. The wine production and other industrial efforts the family had dabbled in and controlled since Hebenon's inception ensured that they thrived and wanted for nothing except the comforts of the Uppers they were accustomed to.

Banished in a city-wide climate of growing dissatisfaction with Kemway and Doctet rule, and the often club-handed tactics of the Crows, the Wulfes earned sympathy from their new neighbors and business associates. If a long-revered family could endure banishment for an insignificant disagreement over policy, what was to prevent the Founder and Doctet from quashing others, from crushing the entire city, for no reason other than spite and desire for more control?

With that sympathy came growing power.

At the height of that surge, the Senior Talker of the Voices of Faith crossed Tunon and Muri's path. In less than seven years, the couple gave the family businesses to their sons and became Talkers themselves, bringing additional influence to the Wulfe name. It also provided renewed access to the Uppers, limited though it was. The professed support for the newly appointed Founder Haythem was not enough to allow the family to regain a foothold in their former home, but it did procure frequent favors that Feena's brothers in particular were quick to take advantage of.

The Wulfes continued to prosper. Their influence grew.

One brother died in a bar fight the year Feena's twin sons were born; he never lived to meet them. Within a year, the second brother developed a virulent strain of throat cancer which took his life within months. Feena, never married to the undisclosed father of her sons, took control of each Wulfe business. The benefits, responsibilities, and influence of connections throughout the Uppers, the Levs, and in the halls of the Voices of Faith, came to rest in Feena's hands.

Her parents had favored the Talker Halls. Her brothers each had their own favored corners.

But this, this was her favorite place of all.

Alone in the Lair that was her refuge, with its pink, white and lavender lighting, soft music filtered through hidden speaks, and shiny polished metal surfaces, alone except for the security agents at the front and back doors, Feena swirled the wine in her glass and stared at the now silent Echo above the serving counter. Her family had prepared her to accept control of Wulfe interest, despite never believing she would need to manage them alone. They had also prepared her for her partnership with the man who, until recently, had been known only as Vanderwall. Through him, she had clawed her fingers into every dealing in the Levs she could reach. Some called her stern, calculating, underhanded and brutal, traits she had to nurture, traits she had to cultivate to succeed.

She was not afraid of dirtying her hands with the risks and had learned to do so without rising to public awareness the way Vanderwall had done.

She still preferred this corner of private solitude.

Remaining beneath public awareness, she knew, as she rose from the stool and pulled on the transparent slicker draped across the empty seat beside her, was largely due to Senior Kal's influence. They had grown up together, traveled in many of the same social circles of power. When the Coup claimed Feena's thirteen-year-old sons and forced her to consider the relationship with Vanderwall more seriously, a man as willing to take advantage of the city-wide upheaval as she was…and a man as equally rooted in the city's underbelly, it had been Kal and his Talkers who provided Feena with the shield that kept her from the notice of the bugorra.

Or maybe the gorra noticed but felt that, without proof of criminality, there were more vital matters to be concerned with.

Like Vanderwall's publically known leadership of the brako.

For all of his backing of her endeavors, for all of the Senior's claims that the Voices owed the Wulfes a debt for every benefit, monetary and otherwise, her family had provided, Feena knew Kal was too slick, too self-interested, to focus on their relationship alone. Ever-seeking power, just as she was, Feena knew Kal had dealings with the Mam after the Coup. There were ongoing efforts to forge a link with the bugorra too, and Feena was aware that Kal had his own dealings with Vanderwall. Perhaps none of those relationships were meant to impact his relationship with Feena, but they existed, part of a political agenda Kal had never kept hidden from her and yet had never spelled out.

Mam's alliance with Vanderwall and his cronies forced Feena to choose a side, to protect herself and her interests. Because of this, Vanderwall had become as much of a rival as he was an ally. Feena knew enough about Mam Kemway not to trust her, mother of the last Kemway heir or not. Kal's continued flirtation with Mam's influence, his courting of Vanderwall, were all undertaken with the hopes of getting a Kemway, the right Kemway, back into power where the Voices could influence the entire city.

It would not be impossible, therefore, for the Senior to orchestrate the kidnapping of Haythem Kemway to further that agenda. He was certainly the one person in Hebanthe Falls with the resources to pull it off. Feena could not accept, however, that he would put the reportedly ailing Founder at risk. Why do so if his sworn purpose was to support and protect the office of the Founder, and the sanctity of the Kemway bloodline, at all costs?

If the reports were true, Feena had to believe the Senior had a plan.

But why, she thought sourly, a determined decision made, had he not entrusted her, and her brako, with the information?

One question. That was all it would take to know if he was lying.

If Kal was aware of the assertions against him, against the Voices, he might be in hiding, planning, strategizing, biding his time. It was what she would do in his place, guilty or not.

But she was confident she knew where he would be. He could hide from the gorra, but he could not hide from her.

The Talkers, when she reached the Hall that was her destination, people gathered for the recitation of prayers led by a tall, dowdy, gangly fellow with soft, pallid features, did not turn their heads or otherwise acknowledge her. She silently strode up the side aisle, following a heavy-set woman whose wide-brimmed hat dripped with the evidence of time outdoors. This Hall, containing one of Senior Kal's residences, had also been home to Feena's parents in the years they had served the Voices. Within these corridors and rooms, they had drawn their final breaths. The Talkers who called this place home were familiar with the sole-surviving Wulfe's regal face, her bearing and stride, and the waft of floral perfume that followed wherever she went. No one questioned her right to be here, though she was not a Talker, nor did they dissuade her from a visit with the Senior.

She doubted any were aware of her varied business endeavors, beyond the production of wine, and she was welcome here. So long as she provided monetary backing and supported, at least publically, the Founder's eternal right to lead Hebanthe Falls, she doubted many would care what she did.

Kal was dictating something into the Echo when she arrived; she could hear his low, solitary voice behind the door before her guide rapped to seek entry. "Enter," he called, and as the pneumatic door whirred open, Feena caught a glimpse of the man's hand shutting off the screen, his task either complete or else one he did not want visitors to see. He stood with a smile and a warm, "Feena!" without allowing her escort to speak, and then waited until the other woman left and the door closed before coming from behind the desk to greet her.

"How lovely to see you. I've been thinking about you." Kal clasped the stately woman by the shoulders and kissed both cheeks rather than compel her to kiss the ring on his hand as he expected so many others to do. Only a handful of people were not pressed into that show of respect, out of either political expediency or genuine respect or affection. "To what do I owe the pleasure?"

Most often they went for weeks without seeing one another, their respective businesses giving them little time, need, or reason to cross paths unless some matter of mutual interest arose or a social function brought them into one another's sphere. Feena wondered why she had been on his mind. She returned his gesture and set a bottle of pink carbonated liquid on his desk, the same gift she always brought, always shared, whether they met here or in the Lair. Strawberry Hemp wine, the only beverage Kal had ever seen her drink, the brew her family had perfected generations ago upon which they had built the bulk of their substantial status.

The Wulfes were the only ones to produce it.

Now that she was the last, Kal wondered off-handedly as he opened the bottle and filled two glasses, what would become of the Wulfe's Head Label when Feena was gone.

"You look good…all things considered."

"All things considered," he agreed with a chuckle, neither asking what she knew that he might not nor offering information she might not yet have. It was a familiar dance between them, both hoping for secrets expressed, both knowing that hope would most likely be unfulfilled. Their secrets were their own, the sort of mysteries that could never be shared with anyone. Not even those they trusted most.

No matter how much they respected each other, they knew each other too well.

"It seems there's been trouble?"

Feena dropped onto the long cushioned sofa, her movements languid and graceful, professional and relaxed though the steel in her eyes read differently. Sweeping back her side-parted strawberry blonde hair with her free hand as the other clung to the glass he had given her, she kept her hooded smile as business-like as it was affectionate. "You know me, Kal; nothing I can't handle."

The news of her rival-partner's death had not yet become officially public, though the rumors of it had produced chaos in the streets as brako fought against brako. Blame and guilt had not yet been placed, had not yet been given a target, but it had, as expected, begun to point towards the woman who served, until recently, as the brako leader's second in command.

Vanderwall had once been a partner, a collaborator. Although she was grateful to have him out of the way and hopeful that his absence would remove Mam Kemway's interference in brako business, Feena understood that she had to appear remorseful and troubled by his loss. She had to appear more concerned about it than she felt.

She would not yet make an announcement about such things to Kal, confirm or deny brako dealings he might not know about. She would say nothing until her control was complete to avoid Kal's pressure towards actions she was not prepared to take. Let him learn the truth about Vanderwall some other way and do with the information what he would.

Kal laughed and sipped the wine with an approving smile. "Don't I know it." If anyone knew what the Wulfes were capable of, Kal certainly did. "What brings you here…beyond a delivery of wine?"

Licking droplets from her lips, tracing the rim of the glass with one finger, Feena hesitated briefly before sharing what was on her mind. "Tell me he is safe. That is all I ask, all I must know. Tell me you have a plan."

"Who?"

A frown tugged at the corners of her mouth before her expression returned to neutral. "I've seen the prods, Kal. No one else has the resources to pull that off…or has the audacity to try. If his health is as poor as reported, I want to know he's being taken care of. I want to know he's alive. I want to see him."

Kal's mirroring frown was deeper than hers and did not vanish as quickly as he capped the bottle and set it on the counter behind him amidst an array of other bottles of varying vintages. "You think I would risk abducting Founder Kemway? You think I would have him here," he gestured around him, "if I had?" He forced a dry chuckle and sank against the back of his chair, expression blank again, refusing to give credence to how the prod gossip was affecting his mood.

To be fair, the thought of abducting the Founder, securing him far from the hands of people Kal was sure were poisoning him as a form of public manipulation, had crossed his mind more than once. Without knowing where the Founder had been held, however, making use of that fantasy had been enough beyond his reach to make honest consideration a waste of time.

"I've seen the report; Talkers disguised as bugorra…"

"Fitting fabrications. Wouldn't surprise me if the captain arranged it now that Neoma's been to see him…a way to move him out of reach." It was a good plan, inviting Neoma in, proving her husband lived, and then abducting him so that he might never be publically seen again. "What do you think they're out there praying for? If harm comes to him, someone will pay dearly for it…and it won't be me."

Feena studied him in the silence that followed his declaration, the calm certainty on his face, the resolve in his eyes. He was a Talker; words were his primary weapon. His position demanded conveying assurance in everything he said whether he believed his own words or not. He could be lying. Perhaps the Founder was beyond the closed door behind the Senior's desk. Or maybe he was already dead.

But Feena chose to accept the words, chose to believe him, because she had known him long enough, well enough, to be confident that she would know if he was hiding something like that from her.

"We will find him," she eventually promised, finishing her drink, setting the glass on the end table, and then smoothing her beige trousers. She had people and resources, eyes all over Hebenon, just as the Senior did. If the Founder was out there somewhere, someone would find him, find the ones who had taken him…if he had indeed been taken and this was not some political ploy concocted by the bugorra captain. With luck, she or Kal would be the ones to find him before Vanderwall's brako, or the bugorra, did.

Letting out a slow breath, toying absently with the stylus on his desk, Kal said, "We will…but we may not need him any longer."

Such words were tantamount to heresy from a Talker and Feena narrowed her gaze as she studied him for clues about his intent. That he had voice those thoughts meant he did have a plan, but it was not necessarily one that involved the abduction of the Founder. "Go on."

"Remember the Kemway that went missing years ago?"

Both Kal and Feena had been younger then, children themselves, when that news broke. The prodcasts had been full for days, and then weeks, with the tales of abduction of the Founder's second infant son. Speculation and rumor had swirled through the city like a storm but as days turned to weeks, and weeks into months, without no ransom request issued and no guilty party found, with no word or trace of the child forthcoming, the storm gradually died into the shadows of rumor and mystery and life in Hebanthe Falls continued.

Nearly a year passed before the body of a toddler was presented, asphyxiated, shriveled, gray, and decomposed beyond identification, bringing with it the claim that the missing Kemway had been found. Murdered. Everyone from the Founder to those in the Hub, every prodcaster and information agent, claimed it to be the missing boy though evidence of who had taken him and why remained elusive. There had been an elaborately staged day of sanctioned public mourning, when every vindi, every production facility, every food growing house and fishery, ceased working in honor of the murdered Kemway child.

No kidnapper, no killer, was ever arrested.

In the deepest corners of the city, suspicions grew like mushrooms in the fertile darkness. Claims that the child had died of some horrible contagion. Claims that the Kemways had killed their child, intentionally or accidentally, or knew who had done so. Some went so far as to blame young Haythem, a shadowy accusation of his first act of murder that had followed him every day of his life. There were claims that the celebrated infant was no Kemway, that the child had been malformed or somehow unviable and thus was kept from the world or destroyed to prevent shadows from falling across the

Kemways continued right to rule the city. Some claimed the child continued to live in sequestered exile in the Uppers or had been hidden in the Levs where there would be no possibility of discovery.

The latter, it seemed to Kal, had proven to be true.

"You found him? Alive?" It was news exciting enough to prompt Feena to lean forward, elbows on her knees, her voice low and eager. She was glad there was no one nearby to overhear them, glad that her monitoring systems were currently turned off. Most meetings with anyone other than the Senior demanded the assurances of recorded or monitored conversation. Meetings with Kal were personal.

This was the sort of material best kept out of anyone else's hands.

"I'm nearly certain it is, yes. He knows it too, I think…who he is. He's got the face…the eyes. I confronted him; he didn't deny it."

"But he didn't confirm it either? Who is he? Do I know him?"

There was no reason she should. Hebanthe Falls was full of people she had never met. But if someone was prominent enough to cross paths with Senior Kal, there was a chance Feena had crossed paths with them as well.

"A dwarf; goes by Enoch LeRoy." It was not a Kemway name, not the name of any passed down through the generations of Founders, and his efforts to research it had proven futile. But all records of the Kemway infant had been scrubbed from the now damaged archives or had been buried so deep that, thus far, Kal had not been able to connect the dwarf to the lost child or find any family by the name of LeRoy.

"A dwarf?" The corners of her mouth twitched. That would explain a great deal of hidden history. A dwarf in the Uppers, a dwarf in the Kemway bloodline, would have been a scandal. A dwarf in the Levs, if allowed to live, while hardly common, would have garnered stares but passed through the masses mostly unnoticed.

Such children were often euthanized to keep humanity's limited gene pool clean, but in the Levs, with population dwindling, often children were allowed to live simply to keep the numbers up, to allow for working hands, to keep ticks flowing into the hands of struggling families and goods flowing in the direction of the Uppers.

So long as those individuals did not procreate.

"You've seen him?"

"Maybe." Feena had seen a dwarf or two. It was difficult to know how many, or if they had instead been children, when most people passing on dark streets were covered from head to foot against the Falls' spray and masked by shadows and the sputtering of neon. "If it's true…if it's him…"

Kal nodded with a sly smile. "If there's another Kemway to fill the vacancy, one we can install, we owe it to the people to do so."

Particularly if doing so would put the new Founder in the pockets of the Voices and the Wulfe faction of the brako.

"Anyone would be better than that snake." Feena had never met Neoma. She had never met Haythem. But she had seen the prods, read the daily media skims in her inbox, had seen enough fake smiles and dictated, rote words, to know that Neoma Kemway was too much like herself. If Feena was anyone else, she would not trust herself either.

Ulynda Kemway, the only other choice, was a child.

Convincing people to accept a dwarf, even with the Kemway name, would be no easier than getting them to accept his daughter.

"What do you have in mind? Will he do it?"

"He will if he thinks the Voices are protecting him from the brako…if I can get him to trust me, and you, as allies. We can coax him to step into the role, make him see it's the right thing to do."

Captain Grainger was not failing the city with his leadership, but he was no Founder. Hebenon needed a Founder, a Kemway, in the place where one had been since the city shut its doors against the poisons of the Outside."

"I can do that." Feena was uncertain Kal's plan would work but he seemed to know the dwarf, better than she did at least. Anyone targeted by the brako would be lucky to have the protection of the Voices and the support of a prominent influencer like Feena Wulfe.

They would be grateful…and gratitude bred favors.

"We'll try it your way…"

"And if it doesn't work," Kal smiled, "we'll try it yours."

Whatever Feena's way would be.

Agreeing on the goal was the first step towards reaching it.

Chapter 3

The two men were similar enough in build, in height and weight, with a breadth of shoulder and body mass that evidenced a life of manual labor, lifting and other feats of upper body strength, for them to have been brothers. They might have even been thought to be twins, except for the differences in their skin tone, hair…or lack of it…and eye color.

Most of those familiar with the one called Vanderwall had not known those details, details kept hidden within the disguise of a Crow hood and rarely revealed to outsiders. Uriah Frankel, Frankie to most, Uri to some, was a face more familiar to his conspirators, a man whose blue eyes never missed a detail of the business that went on around him. His bald pate was as smooth as the thick shoulders protruding past the torn seams of his makeshift tank top and the scars he bore were battle evidence he wore with pride. He should be cold, as wet as he was, dripping on her floor without concern, but Frankie never appeared cold and like the man who had come before, he was not intimidated by the woman who had summoned him.

"No one can prove anything," Neoma purred, circling him with fingertips that traced trails through the droplets on his back, her manicured nails snagging in the fabric of his shirt. He was, in her opinion, cleaner, more handsome, than his predecessor, an opinion expressed through those fingertips and her appraising gaze. "That is why you are the perfect choice. The bugorra presume Vanderwall's dead. I want you to prove them wrong."

"You want me to take his place?" Her meaning was clear enough but he wanted there to be no misunderstanding. If he was to control and lead the brako, he rather than Feena Wulfe, he wanted to be certain he had Mam Kemway's backing, her blessing, her permission to beat Hebenon into submission.

"You are Vanderwall," Neoma replied, emphasizing the second word with a steely smile.

"Mam…please…you must see this…"

The woman known only as Nanny, who served the Kemways as cook, housekeeper, tutor, and childcare worker, bustled into the room and turned on the Echo without permission, thinking it more important that her employer witness the news herself than to remain quiet and later be fired for hiding it. The three watched the prod with varying degrees of horror and disbelief as the faces on the screen repeated the announcement that Founder Kemway had been abducted by Talkers disguised as bugorra.

Neoma's complexion bled from white to red to purple in fury.

"How dare he!"

Assuming the individual in question was Senior Kal, Frankie, now carrying the scourge mantle of Vanderwall, growled, "Shall I deal with him? Find him? Bring him to you?"

"Why didn't you…?"

Neoma's impulse, her desire, was to lay blame on the man in the room with her, or to throw Senior Kal…a man she only marginally trusted…from Hebenon's outer shell into the falls and the river below. Disposing of Blayd likewise, for his part in this apparent betrayal, also crossed her mind. But she would deal with both men herself, in her own way. Her absent husband, however, for all of her presented outrage, only mattered for what his life could provide her.

Perhaps this abduction, his absence, could work to her benefit.

From Vanderwall's expression, as he watched the prod, this development was news to him too.

"He'll turn up."

Noises from another room, tiny steps of hard-soled slippers retreating from the open door between them made Neoma frown and swallow every comment she had been about to utter, every thought she harbored.

"Find Haythem. Find him and bring him home."

Whatever else she did, that was, for Ulynda's sake, the most important thing. Vanderwall would find him. Neoma, meanwhile, had different duties to perform.

Through the closed door, as she removed the traitorous slippers that had announced her efforts to overhear her mother's conversation, Ulynda heard the shrillness of the woman's voice as she shouted into the air, "Blayd! Get here! Now!"

Ulynda did not doubt that her mother's sometimes boyfriend was going to find himself on the striking edge of Neoma's rage tonight.

At least it was not her.

❧*❧

Hunger was the driving force that compelled Switz to emerge from the damp of the drainage pipe where he had found refuge from the bird-faced hunters. Crows, he assumed, for those were the faces that had long ago hunted and caught him for crimes he rarely talked about. Eventually, the streets had cleared of their presence and the normal routine of the citizens' lives resumed as if nothing was amiss, as if the predators had forgotten him.

They would be back. Crows always came back.

Hunkered in the pipe, stiff with cold and wet, he managed to shed enough fear to fall into an uncomfortable sleep, only to have the shift whistle's wail jar him awake again to resume his watch, expecting that the new shift of Crows would be out en masse to claw through humanity looking for him for the crime they believed he had committed. He saw a few, traveling alone, which was unlike any Crow behavior he remembered, but alone did not mean they were less of a threat. It only suggested they had changed their hunting patterns.

He had disappeared into the Core thirty-four years ago, long enough to be one of the mine's longest surviving residents, long enough ago that a lot in Hebenon had likely changed. At a glance, nothing appeared so different on the surface. Still dark. Still wet. The Levs still hummed with the drone of the Four Falls and the churn of the river, with the undermining rise and fall of voices, the clang and clatter of commerce chirps, the hiss of steam-driven gears, and the rattle and ring of boots on metal.

Nor had hunger changed. He knew those pangs too well. The need for rationing resources in the Core had created a perpetual state of gnawing in their bellies. Out here, food was more plentiful if one had ticks for it. From somewhere nearby, the sizzle and smoke of frying fish, an aroma steeped in remembrance, mixed into the steamy mist to fan the flames of his hunger until he decided the risk of procuring something was worth taking.

He should have stayed with Enoch for the promise of a handful of ticks to get him started. Without them, he could not buy a meal, but he knew how to steal one. So long as there were no Crows nearby, it would be a simple thing to do. Maybe afterward he would hunt down Enoch, claim to have gotten separated and then lost, and beg for the ticks the dwarf had promised.

With no hat to cover his balding head, the moisture in the air collected on his skin and ran in rivulets down the sides of his face. It was an annoyance, but also a refreshing novelty. He stretched, body stiff from so long in that uncomfortable pipe, and fell into step behind a gaggle of teens dressed in matching boots, jackets, and hats. School students, he assumed, though from the rear it was impossible to tell more about them.

Their tittering soon identified them as girls, fresh and innocent around twelve years old. A little young for his taste, but only by a year or two, the sort he liked to groom, to suck dry of budding maturity and discard like dishrags squeezed of their moisture.

The temptation to follow them was supplanted by the twisting in his belly and, as he passed a vindi offering kabobs on display, fried fish, potatoes, and onions, he snagged one of the dainties while the vindi owner was otherwise occupied. Switz's eyes barely left the girls.

The need to eat was overridden in turn by three bird-masked terrors who emerged onto the avenue some five yards ahead of him.

Switz ducked sideways onto another path, around a corner between other vindis he did not take the time to study, hoping to give the Crows the slip. They had seen him, however, just as he had seen them, immediately giving chase, shoving people aside, knocking over carts, pushing shoppers against rails and the sides of buildings or into each other without regard.

Not very Crow-like, Switz noted, his ill-gotten meal clenched in his fist, its cooking juices slowly washing away in the damp air.

He could not afford to look back, to see how close they were, thus he did not notice that the three had split to encircle him and cut off his flight. One of them appeared from a passage directly in front of him.

Or maybe it was a fourth Crow. Switz was unsure.

He dodged the blow of a gloved fist aiming for his head as a hand from the other side closed around his arm and spun him sideways. The pain of that grip, the impact against the rail, and his own effort to twist free caused the kabob to drop and disappear over the side of the walk.

"Wasn't doin' nothin'," Switz protested, hoping to talk his way around the crime of theft committed on behalf of his empty stomach.

A digitizer crackled, the precursor to whatever the Crow was about to say, then the masked figure lurched forward and released Switz's arm as a long, reflective blade passed through the Crow's torso, a blade long enough to extend out the front of his body.

A Crow without body armor.

Switz stumbled sideways, eager to escape while his attackers were distracted. There were four of them now, though the one was on his knees, gasping for breath, clawing to dislodge the blade that had punctured his lung. The others flanked the unexpected brown-skinned savior, seeming to have forgotten their original quarry. The Crows carried no buzzers, no injectors, not even thumpers, and the man with the intricately shaved designs in his close-cropped hair still wielded a second long knife and a longer than standard thumper.

A merc. A bodyguard.

A look around while snatching the blade from the dying man's corpse revealed no one of import the merc was likely to be serving. The streets were emptied of shoppers by the chaos and what travelers Switz could see opted for any other route around the skirmish.

The merc looked as if he had the upper hand, looked as if he would win this fight as a second person dropped beneath the concussive crack of the thumper against his skull and the third staggered as if drunk, blood streaming into his eyes from a head wound. The fourth, wilier than his companions, danced from one foot to the other as though he had pugil training and the merc was having more difficulty managing his blows. The Crow managed a grasping strike that wrenched the knife from the merc's hand and when he threw it, the merc was fortunate to dodge its path, lucky that it cut along his exposed neck rather than imbed in his throat as the thrower intended.

It was enough of an injury to produce a shriek of outrage and a gush of blood between the fingers of the hand that covered it. That moment of instinct was the opening the Crow needed to launch another attack but it was a leap cut short by the knife in Switz's hand that sliced through the tendons of both of the Crow's ankles.

The Crow went down.

Switz leaped up.

He grabbed his savior by the arm and yanked, compelling the merc to follow. Up two half-flights of stairs to the Lev above. Through the mist, around several corners, through a row of abandoned vindis, out onto the roof of another half-Lev below. Through another group of students Switz made no effort to study, into a building that smelled of damp, of strong chemicals, perfumed cleaners, and hot, hissing steam.

Switz knew places like this. He had grown up in places like this as his mother bounced from one vindi's employment to another, until her Heb addiction caught up to her and forced her to seek somewhere else each time to continue to provide for her little boy.

He vowed he'd never go back. But here he was.

After snatching a fist full of white cloth strips from a wire that held other similar strips, hemp bandages being cleaned and sterilized for reuse or repurposing, Switz shoved the merc down behind a bubbling vat and huddled with him, both men listening to the sounds of the room for any hint that they had been followed, for the possibility that an employee might have seen them enter.

No voices in the room, however, meant the workers were letting the laundry rest as they shared their shift break. By Switz's calculation, that gave them fifteen minutes at most to rest and be away before anyone would return and find them."

"Here…let me…"

Involving himself in a brako tussle had not been Blayd's intention. He did not recognize the wiry little man, had no compelling reason to help him, except that four brako against this one fellow had seemed like overkill and Blayd hated to see an underdog taken down in such a way. The man might be innocent or guilty of nothing except double-crossing them or failing to pay the protection ticks he knew the brako were prone to charge vindi owners whenever they could.

This fellow did not look to be a vindi owner.

Innocent of crime, however, did not mean that the stranger was trustworthy and as he raised a strip of cloth, folded in a thick square, towards Blayd's throat, the merc slapped his hands away with a snarl.

"I don't need your…"

"You wanna go to a medi like this? Bleeding to death?" Perhaps the wound was not bad enough to result in death, but it was bad enough to warrant care and to attract the attention of people the merc would pass in the streets. "I don't have anything to stitch you, but this ought to help keep pressure on til you're home. I used to be a medi…I know what I'm doing."

Their gazes held for several moments as they assessed one another. "Used to be?"

Switz shrugged, avoiding eye contact. "Run in with the Crows; been in the Core. Continued practicing, but it wasn't the same."

"Core's not real." Blayd knew the rumors, the myths, but he did not believe the place existed. It could not. If it did, someone would have revealed it a long time ago.

The man might be delusional, but the skin beneath Blayd's hand was growing wetter, stickier with each pump of his heart, and he decided that accepting help was not the worst decision he could make.

He had lost his knives but still had his thumper, and he had no doubt he could overpower this small fellow if necessary.

"Oh, it's real…or it was." Switz shrugged again and pressed the folded pad to Blayd's neck. "Hold that."

Blayd did as instructed.

"After tonight, don't imagine anyone's alive in there. Pity any bastard who is." The other two strips were wrapped around Blayd's neck tight enough to hold the padding in place but not tight enough to be a choking hazard. The merc's growl when it approached that point told Switz when it was tight enough. "Dunno why the Crows want me; I ain't done nothin' wrong…so I owe ya for helping me."

Owed him. Blayd liked the sound of that. He continued to stare, his thoughts racing, until a bell clanged at the other end of the room.

"They'll be back. We gotta go."

Growling at the statement of the obvious, leaving blood on the floor and a red handprint on the side of the washing vat, Blayd struggled to his feet, allowing the little man to steer him through the emergency door through which they had entered. They looked right and left, above and below, and, seeing no one who might be a threat, left their shelter and slipped back into the city without anyone's notice. They trudged no further than the end of the treatment building, Blayd's staggering steps growing steadier, his red-stained hand leaving a smear along the wall that the damp was already washing away, before the merc stopped, making Switz stop too.

"Name?"

"Switz. Daniah Switz." What did it matter, the past attached to that name, things he had done years ago? He had been in the Core longer than this merc had been alive. Odds were, he had never heard Switz's name. If he went nosing around in Hub records, learned the truth, well, surely, men could change after so much time.

So many years locked away from humanity would change anyone.

Locked away with humanity's worst would change a man too…just not in a positive way.

On his wrist, Blayd's ICD began to chirp, an insistent emergency tone he knew would only come from one source. He dropped the intended questioning long enough to read the converted message on the tiny screen rather than listen to the woman's voice and reveal any connection to her that his companion did not need to know about.

Blayd grunted at the words and then fumbled in his pocket for a pale green hemp plastic passcard stamped with a quartered circle in red. "Take this…it'll get you into any hostel in the city. Get off the streets; stay put."

As payment for saving the merc's life, an open-ended stay at a hostel was a good start. It would not put food in his belly or put ticks in his pocket, but a bed, a real bed, with sheets and blankets and pillows, and a decent hot shower, were enough.

Switz tentatively took the card, grateful but also wary of the trap that might await him there. Not from the Crows, but who was to say this merc was any better than they were.

Then again, if the merc wanted him dead, he would have killed him already.

"Wait there," Blayd warned. "I'll find you when I'm done." He did not know what use he might have for such a man, but he figured the little fellow owed him and seemed desperate enough for a patron that he would do whatever Blayd asked.

Switz bobbed his head. Odds were, the merc had saved him for a reason. Of course he wanted something. Desperate enough to replace the protection the Core provided, it would be worthwhile to hear the merc out. If he did not like what he heard, Switz could always renege on any debt he owed later.

Right now, the lure of a bed and shower awaited.

Until Rhyd got back on his feet, with no way of anticipating when that would be, Tox and Lash were the best ones to see this duty done before the authorities discovered the evidence and decided to use it as proof of some unspecified crime. It might have been used for fishing, like some of the other gear attached to the railing, but it could have more nefarious purposes and Tox did not want that to be the bugorra's conclusion. There had been a noticeable increase in bugger activity over the last several hours, likely connected to the prodcast playing on every Echo in the city, the claim that Talkers had abducted Founder Kemway, but their activity might have other purposes too.

She did not believe Rhyd had anything to do with Founder Kemway's reported abduction, as he had been here, at the river's edge, and not in the Uppers. But it might only take the buggers finding the winch and cable to start asking questions and somehow formulate a connection where there was none. It would be just like the buggers to fabricate a trail from the Founder to the city's sometimes scapegoat to give people someone to blame.

Besides, as she pushed back the folded metal sheeting of Hebenon's southern shell, her job as kesfek meant she scavenged equipment for repair or repurposing. She was often asked to retrieve equipment for those same reasons, and so coming here would not be suspicious. Mostly she worked with more intricate gears and electronics, jewelry and a variety of buckles, zips and snaps, but she sometimes tackled larger requests and no one was likely to question her taking this.

The winch left the night of Skelter's rescue, still affixed to the rail meant to keep workers from falling into the river, was not so far out of her realm of work to be an unlikely scavenge job. Left as it was with an assortment of fishing equipment, the winch might not seem out of place to others, but she was not willing to take the chance.

Neither was the bruised and battered man waiting for her there, the stump of a keffer between his lips that he flicked into the river as soon as she arrived. He wore no hat so his thin blonde hair clung to his skull, cheeks, and neck, and he wore no jacket to shield his thin, bare arms from the damp. The vest he wore offered little protection, but the cold and wet seemed not to bother him.

Tox imagined he was stoned enough to barely notice. So long as he put neither of them at risk of being swept up by the river, so long as he could help dismantle the significant weight of the winch segments, she did not care if he smoked.

"Let's do this," he muttered as she opened her tooler and handed him a wrench. She, in turn, took out a portable cutting torch and turned on its heating coil.

"Seen Enoch?"

Lash shook his head as they began to break the unit into transportable pieces. "Not yet. Maemi says kids are safe, but he ducked out on them to find Skelt and Rhyd soon as they got clear. No one's seen him since. With the buggers about, he's probably keeping his head down like the rest of us til things dry up."

Tox nodded. While not the reassuring news she wanted, it was a smart precaution on Enoch's part. "Heard anything from up top?" she eventually asked when the silent cutting began.

"Only that a dozen or so made it out. They're isolated to be sure they're healthy while the buggers figure out what to do with 'em. The beating the captain's said to have taken and this business with the Founder's keeping 'em busy. They're combing the streets but not likely to bother us. They haven't started looking into Vanderwall…"

"Vanderwall?" Tox scowled, catching the cut-away piece, dropping it onto the walkway, and shutting off the torch.

Trading the wrench for a pry bar, Lash answered, "That's what's got the brako stirred. Rumor is he's down, but I don't know anything more. Brako are fighting over it; might be the buggers are letting them fight it out among themselves while they deal with the Founder crap."

It had not been hard to miss the increased brako activity when Tox had moved through the city to bring Doctor Tamner to Rhyd and his injured companions. Nor was it hard to miss the increased presence of the buggers. The doctor had first helped them move Colyx and Otta to the closest clinic and, in time, returned to aid in moving Rhyd to Jaron's flat. Her intent to resume her usual routine had been hampered by the opposing traffic, but for Tox, it had been just as well.

Without Xiaodan's company, his assistance, her return to her vindi had not felt the same.

"Assassination maybe?"

Lash shrugged. "Long as they keep it to themselves." The last thing Hebenon needed was a turf war between brako factions.

"Might help Skelt get back on his feet if they're busy," Tox murmured. "People will be eager to see him…and there'll be a shortage of good kaheaos if the brako are preoccupied."

"We can hope," Lash agreed.

Given the extensive nature of Skelter's former business network, contacts stretching throughout the Levs that allowed him to get nearly anything into the hands of someone who needed it, those contacts had suffered over the last two years because of his reputed death. They had been forced into precarious and often unfair deals, deals that benefited the brako more than anyone else. Some had turned to Tox for assistance because they knew her, and she did what she could, but she did not have Skelter's reach, his finesse. Inevitably she had to disappoint and turn away more people than she had been able to help.

The dismantled pieces of the winch were tucked into packs, distributed between them for ease of carrying. The coil of cable was secured last and Lash zipped his pack closed.

"What about those?"

He pointed across the river's churn, the flow diminished as the storm-swollen upper rivers gradually receded to their normal flow. The bolt-eye pitons were barely visible in the spray, without the flash of his torch's light over their metal gleam, but someone with a sharp eye might spot them. No one but the truly mad, however, was going to be able to retrieve them. No one except Rhyd or another like him.

"Maybe they'll think they're from the building time."

The pitons were not corroded enough to be that old, and after more than six hundred years, the likelihood of metal spikes being intact in the gradually eroding stone was slim. But most in Hebenon did not ask questions of such things and that explanation, as mythical as it might be, would be good enough.

Slinging her pack over her shoulder, adjusting its weight as evenly as she could, Tox nodded as Lash pushed up the panel for her to pass beneath. "I'll tell 'em the kids are safe when I see 'em…and Enoch too." It would be better if at least one of them set eyes on the dwarf, but getting information to Rhyd about their successes might allow the bilger the peace of mind to permit a full recovery.

The issues with the brako, so long as they kept their problems contained within their ranks and did not turn their infighting against the city, did not need Scarecrow's attention.

If luck was with them, the brako would implode beneath their bloated self-importance and the need for Scarecrow would fade. If they were lucky, Rhyd would never need to don his alter ego again.

❧*❧

"How did you let this happen! You did this!"

"What?" Blayd asked, the door clicking shut behind him echoing her tirade. The shrill, chair-dragged-across-a-metal-floor sound and her red-faced fury made him wary, but wary was not the same as submissive and he refused to be frightened or cowed by her anger.

"They got him…took him…you promised!"

Outside of her door, the rattle of vindi cart wheels and the clop-clop of goat hooves over the grated path cut her off. "I don't know what you're talking about." 'They' and 'him' could refer to a lot of people, although Blayd could think of few people Neoma thought enough about to warrant this outrage. Without specific details, he preferred not to volunteer information.

"Kal and his Talkers have Haythem!"

Blayd did his best not to react but from the twitch of Neoma's jaw, he knew she read some change in his expression he failed to hide. Hoping to calm her, he began, "Are you sure it was the Senior? You can't believe everything the Ximenezes…"

"Of course it's Kal!" she shrieked "Who else? No one else has the means, the ability…"

Tending to ignore the Echos and the prods playing on them, as most of the time they aired unimportant drivel, rerunning laughies, or sales pitches he cared little about, Blayd did not know what the aired prods said, but he could imagine it. He crossed the room to fill an etched tin snifter with the pale yellow apple wine she kept in a carafe on the side table at all times, expecting that she would stop him before he reached it, before he poured it. Wine was not typically to his taste, but the action of opening the bottle, pouring its contents, and then drinking it, occupied his hands.

"Rumors and sensationalism…"

It infuriated her further that he took her charges, her anger, so evenly. She did not answer his implied question and refused to acknowledge that her accusations might be overreacting, might be based on unfounded, unproven rumor. "You were hired for one thing! You were commanded to do one thing! Stop Kal! Not only have you failed, you've let him get away with murder!"

"Murder?" Blayd looked at her, his head cocked. "You said he's been taken. Taken's a far cry from…"

Neoma stalked across the distance between them and slapped the drink from his hand. The metal snifter bounced across the hemptile like a ball, splashing its contents as it hit.

"If Kal has him, of course he's going to kill him!" It should be illogical for a Talker, for the Senior, to destroy the individual they revered as a god among men, but Neoma had few doubts that once Kal saw the condition Haythem was in, killing Haythem was precisely what he would do. Parade his frailty to the city as a product of Captain Grainger's abuse and then kill him, or let him die, and lay the responsibility for his death on Grainger's, and the Nau's, shoulders. Kal might not have killed him yet, but he would.

He might call it a mercy killing, but it would be murder.

"Kidnapping is not…you told me to…"

"Useless hijo de puta! If you're not going to find him, get out!"

Blayd's eyes narrowed. "I've never said…if you'll give me a chance…" He wanted to explain what he had done, share the brilliance of his plan to frame and destroy Kal and his Talkers, but he was not going to beg to be heard. He would ask her once to hear him, give her one chance, before he changed his mind and did something he would likely regret later. "I did what you…"

"Go! Don't come back! Poq Gai!"

For the span of several breaths sucked between clenched teeth, they stared at one another, Blayd's face darkening with growing outrage at the insult, his eyes narrowing as Neoma's flashed as though firing needles at him. There was much he wanted to say, so many ways he could undo this, undermine her fury and make this right. But if she would not back down, would not hear him, would continue to insult him, he was not going to give her the chance.

When the plan had formed he had never imagined it would result in a flash of disillusionment, never imagined that she might fire him for doing what she had asked him to do…cast doubt on Senior Kal and the Voices of Faith.

Discrediting Kal had not been done publically as she had hoped, perhaps, but that would come in gradual stages. A few more hours and the legal system would have done the work and all of Hebanthe Falls would suspect the Talkers of foul play against the dethroned Founder.

Maybe Blayd should have told her sooner. Maybe he should have realized that despite her tendency towards cool, detached composure, she might react irrationally to the news of Haythem's abduction.

Maybe he should still reveal his hand and put her mind at ease.

But with the insult came the tucking of his cards and the decision to bide his time. Let her lash out at him. Let her throw away the one reliable person she had at her back.

He did not have to submit to insults.

"You'll regret this," he hissed, rubbing the back of his hand that stung where she had struck him. She was good in bed, he enjoyed their dynamic when they worked together towards a jointly satisfying goal, but he did not deserve abuse. One thing was clear. He believed she needed him more than he needed her, regardless of the ticks, the benefits, the prestige she offered.

She growled low in her throat and though he paused long enough to prove that her unspoken counter-threat did not frighten him, he did retreat, allowing the door to slam between them with cutting finality.

The path ahead was uncertain now, his choices less clear, but the sound of shattering ceramic on the door behind him fortified his choice. After everything he had done, was doing, was risking on her behalf, he did not deserve this. He had intended to bring the Founder here, intended for her to be part of his plan so that the Senior was no longer an obstacle to hers.

Instead, Blayd decided to keep the Founder under his control for as long as necessary, as long as it took the city to turn on Kal, as long as it took the bugorra to take the Senior down. Maybe he would then reveal his hand to Neoma. Maybe she would get her estranged husband back. Maybe she would thank him and welcome Blayd back into her good graces, into her bed.

Maybe he would refuse to accept either.

He walked long enough that his hair collected the moisture and directed it into rivulets down his cheeks since he had forgotten to lift the hood of his jacket. Long enough for the shift whistle to blow once, and then twice, signaling the end of one shift and the beginning of another. Long enough for the horde of humanity to surge and dwindle, leaving only shoppers seeking nessies, streeters, and those pursuing after-hour diversions. When he eventually stopped at the café vindi where he and Ilya had shared a drink a few days earlier, he looked at those seated there, sharing warm tea and pleasant conversation, and made a small smile before tapping the side of his ICD.

"Lieutenant Young."

Her reply sounded weary, distracted. He felt briefly guilty for what he was putting her through. No doubt she had slept little since the recital. With the captain reported to be laid up with unexplained injuries, leading the bugorra, the hunt for the Founder, was on her. She was smart, strong, capable, but so much sudden obligation when she undoubtedly blamed herself for the Founder's capture, for everything else that was happening, would not be an easy burden to carry.

Blayd did not feel guilty enough, however, to confess or apologize or try to explain. He believed that, ultimately, his actions would result in making Hebenon stronger, return it to its rightful leadership.

"I didn't expect you to answer…"

"Blayd. What do you want? I'm busy." It was good to hear his friendly voice, but he had interrupted her efforts to nap and when a peek at the Echo revealed none of the answers she hoped to see, her irritability increased.

"I promised dinner, but if this isn't a good time…"

"It isn't."

"Oh…well…later then?"

"I can't."

"Can't? Or won't?" He had not considered that the timing of his work would undermine his hopes of seeing her again.

"Too much going on. You don't know the shit that's gone down here. I don't have time to…"

"You have to eat, Ilya. Everyone has to have time for that. Tell me when and where and you can tell me all about it. I'll pay…"

"I…"

"Not taking no for an answer…I can wait. You sound like you need a break. Whatever it is, it can wait long enough for you to eat."

She would not find the Founder until he was ready for that to happen and he had taken care so that his accomplices could not be easily traced…and not traced back to him. If she had found any of them, identified them, or if there was more going on than he knew about, he was eager to hear it.

Getting in good with the gorra lieutenant was as good as getting in good with the captain and would help Blayd stay ahead of the bugorra for as long as he needed to.

He imagined Ilya rubbing her eyes, her temples, trying to think of a way to counter his demand for dinner. Maybe she was seeking a way to let him down because she did not want to be seen with him. But gentle subtlety was not her style. If she did not want to see him, or be seen with him, she would say so. Hoping her silence was not building to that, he added, "Come on, Illy…what do you have to lose? No harm in a free meal, eh?"

There was an extended sigh on the other end of the commlink before she muttered, "I'll call you when I'm free."

"Fair enough," he agreed, hoping his voice conveyed the smile on his face. "Pick a place and I'll meet you there."

"I will. Young out."

He continued to smile as he turned his back on the café. Her agreement took the sting out of Neoma's rejection and the loss of employment. He did not need Mam. Not when he had Ilya on his side.

❧*❧

The flat was silent, the sounds of breaking ceramic and wordless fury ending with the slamming of yet another door, her mother's, bringing Ulynda relief where she huddled beneath her bed, hands over her ears, eyes squeezed shut. Neither effort had kept the storm out, but they had lessened it. Now that silence had come again, she crawled onto the bed and beneath the blanket that was thrown over her head to block out the world.

She knew her mother's temper. Before, in the Uppers, before the evacuation, before the deaths of her brother and sister, before the loss of her father, that temper had been largely hidden. Her father had not wanted his children exposed to such fits of fury and had done his utmost to shield them from it as often as he could. Neoma had done her best to mask her temper as well and had continued to do so when they emerged from the Factory to the realization that they were the only two Kemways left.

Since learning that her father was alive, however, things had begun to change. Ulynda was too young to name what she sensed, to identify the cause and the nature of her mother's moodiness, but something was simmering there that the girl did her best to avoid. Tonight, the simmering had turned to a bubbling overboil, all because Senior Kal or some other Talker had killed her father.

Maybe not the Senior himself. It seemed the messy sort of work that the man Ulynda knew would never have attempted. But she knew that other Talkers did what the Senior told them to do. Didn't they? He gave orders and people obeyed. It was how grownups worked. Ulynda understood there were grey areas, fringes outside of the typical command and obedience structure. She was mature enough to question why some obeyed obviously unwise and unsound orders. But she was a Kemway, and giving commands, being obeyed, was something Kemways had always done.

It was her understanding that the structure of the Voices of Faith worked the same way.

❧36❧

If Talkers had taken her father, killed him, then it had to be at Senior Kal's order. Her mother believed the Senior was responsible.

The Voices were supposed to be on the Kemways side. The Voices were meant to support the Founder and his family in all ways, at all times. If they had failed to do so, had willfully taken her father's life, Ulynda was never going to trust Senior Kal or another Talker.

She was not even sure, after her mother's cries finally evaporated out of the walls and left the early morning hours still, that she would trust her mother either.

Not after an outburst of violence and rage like that.

❧Chapter 4❧

The primary recorder room in the Archive was abuzz with higher than usual between-shift chatter when he arrived, the recent recital and other excitements of that night remaining near the surface of many people's attention. The blackout and the quakes during the performance, the detainment by the bugorra afterward that kept attending guests in the recital hall for more than two hours, the debate about whether that detainment had been to inspect the stairs and lifts as claimed or had been intended to find terrorists as some suspected, were food for gossip between people who saw each other daily and had little desire to discuss their personal lives.

Novelty was preferred to the mundane.

He avoided eavesdropping as he hung his jacket in his locker, keeping his thoughts about those things to himself while they tangled and twisted instead around the man he had fought against leaving unattended. It was important to keep up appearances, to keep his life, his routine, as near to the same as possible so as not to draw attention to himself and thus back to Rhyd.

Rhyd would be safe in his flat, safe in Skelter's care, but would he be safe enough if the brako, the buggers, or anyone else came looking?

Jaron worried.

During the Coup two years ago, Jaron had kept his head down, avoided the chaos of that day by remaining at his desk, eyes on his screen, making a stoic effort to continue doing his job as the world fell apart. When the power had gone off, when the Hub failed, making the doing of his job impossible, those inside the Archive had been held captive by the failure of the pneumatic doors. It had kept him safe, gave him an excuse for his lack of participation.

At times, he wished he had done more, taken a stand, the way men like Rhyd and Skelter and Lash had done, but Jaron did not deny that he had been relieved that the opportunity, the choice, the risk, had been taken out of his hands.

What he had done not so many nights ago, aiding Scarecrow in a perilous rescue, facing the brako while explosions rang somewhere above, was like nothing Jaron had ever imagined. It had been both exhilarating and terrifying, and in the hours since, his heart had yet to stop pounding.

A loud-voiced fellow Jaron recognized but did not know, dressed as if he had come on shift after some formal function or else intended to attend one after his shift, was surrounded by a gaggle of next shift archivists. He gesticulated wildly as he spoke of the recent prods proclaiming that Founder Kemway had been taken out of the care facility he had been housed in. The report was still a rumor, unsubstantiated by either bugorra or Nau, and without official word, people fell into speculation about what, if anything, had happened. Had he been taken during the recital? Were the quakes explosions and if so, did they connect to the abduction? Were the Talkers responsible? Why would they do such a thing? Why would anyone? If not the Talkers, then who?

Or was the story just so much vapid ratings-hunt journalism of the sort the Ximenezes were known for?

What truth might exist in prods Jaron had not watched, had only heard snippets of as he trekked from his flat to the Archive, was lost in the flurry of speculation spreading like a virus. The possibilities were as varied as the people who gradually drifted out of the locker room towards their desks or towards home as their shifts ended.

Loitering to gossip and speculate could result in docked pay. Keeping others from working might do so too. Each shift since the recital was double-timing to work through a backlog of SCAM footage, ICD reports, prods, and communication chatter from that evening. They sorted, cataloged, saved, and erased as necessary, each archivist not too secretly hoping to be the one to find a kernel of truth to support any of the rumors being bandied about.

As curious as he was, as much as he wanted to know if the rumors were the reasons for Oliver's conspicuous absence from the prods, the reason he had not yet reached out to Jaron, Jaron was not curious enough to draw attention by reaching out to the captain for answers.

The quakes, the power outage, did not concern him. Jaron was certain they had been part of Rhyd and Skelter's agenda, diversions to keep the bugorra busy while Scarecrow breeched the Core from below. The details of those diversions, whatever Skelter had organized on the inside to allow him to get clear of those imprisoned with him, had not been shared with Jaron and he had not asked. He knew as much as he needed to know at the time, enough to track Scarecrow to Lev 1 and be there to bring Skelter and his companions to safety.

Jaron was, however, curious to know if Oliver's attempts to hide the Founder had failed, whether his pointing the captain to the Core's primary door and a threatened breach of that door from the inside had played any part in that failure.

He wanted to know that Oliver was okay.

When his shift ended, he intended to take the host of harvested rumors to Rhyd. If the man was awake, surely he would make sense of them. Rhyd and Skelter could fill in the blanks with whatever they thought Jaron needed to know…or patch the holes over with reassurances if it was best he knew nothing.

Jaron would trust Rhyd either way.

The prevalence of gossip, talk over separation partitions, during breaks, during lunch, made for a tumultuous shift, but the day did not seem otherwise unusual when Jaron settled at his desk to tackle the bits and pieces of data assigned to his station. He hoped the deluge would keep his mind away from the one choking thought he had been unable to shake during the hours he had watched over Rhyd, getting the man to safety without incident, making vague plans with the others to return to a more or less normal daily routine.

He had killed a man.

He had no proof he had done so, had not examined the fellow he had kicked down the stairs. There had been no prodcast proclaiming a death. But Jaron was certain.

Maybe the death was attributed to a fall; they happened often enough and were rarely deemed newsworthy unless the result was particularly gruesome or the victim was someone of celebrity. Maybe one brako less was not worth anyone's notice or worth prodcast time when the Founder's rumored abduction was more newsworthy. Eventually, however, if any of the SCAM's in the vicinity of those stairs gave Jaron up, he would have to face the consequences.

It had been self-defense. He had done it for Scarecrow, for Rhyd, and would gladly do it again if necessary. But the ghosts of those consequences made him perpetually sick to his stomach.

He would be lucky to make it through his shift a free man.

He would be lucky to make it through with his sanity intact.

There was no algorithm to the order in which data was fed to an archivist for processing. Information streamed to the first open archive port it found unless the senior archivists put data flags in place to capture key morsels for closer inspection before it was archived. The faster an archivist was at scanning, tagging, saving with the proper priority codes and labels, the quicker new data took its place. No one monitored who sorted what; it was accomplished automatically within the internal Hub brain according to the day's criteria.

With so much talk centered around Kemway today, Jaron was not the only one hoping for news to share with the authorities. Others were seeking connections between the abduction, the quakes, the blackout. Jaron suspected he was the only one looking for news about Oliver, or news he could take directly to Oliver, in the hopes of keeping his mind off of the man he had killed and the man he had left in his flat. How many days had they hidden there? How many days had it been since he had last seen Oliver? How long had it been since he moved out of the man's suite and back to his own? To his own life?

So much had happened in so short a time that Jaron was no longer sure. The passage of time had become a blur and refocusing on a normal routine proved difficult. What he was certain of was that every archivist on his shift, and every other, wanted to be the one to find some special tidbit of information that might prove to be a vital clue to the apprehension of a terrorist, a kidnapper, a killer.

That was little different from any other day. Uncovering such data was the highlight of an otherwise tedious shift and brought a few moments of prestige to the finder and sometimes a few extra ticks.

Today, the last few days, it was more likely to happen than usual.

It was random luck or fate that this particular data search, initiated by Lieutenant Young, was routed through Jaron's station. Being bugorra business, the parameters set and coded by the lieutenant with bugorra keys, there was little to do except log the timestamp and the nature of the request and clear it for processing. Bugger business was always approved; an archivist needed to do no more than note the official code and allow the Hub to comply.

Hoping the lieutenant's request would provide news about Oliver, Jaron opened the file to skim the contents, to view the faces of the four men pictured therein, before routing it on its way.

Buggers. Talkers disguised as buggers, as the prods hinted. So there was truth to the rumor. Dead men without known faces, none of them Oliver, killed in an attempt to kidnap the Founder. There was no indication if the abduction had been successful. A request for facial matches and identities provided evidence of nothing.

The inference, however, was easy to make.

The Talkers, the Voices of Faith, had taken, or tried to take, Founder Kemway.

As soon as he could escape this desk and make it safely across the city, the man who could do something with this rumor, prove or disprove it, learn the truth and possibly find the Founder, would know everything Jaron knew.

If he did not know it already.

When the prodcast appeared on one of the two Echos he demanded to use as long as he was stuck in the clinic under surveillance, popping up while studying his medi-reports, the impulse to storm the production studio and demand a retraction, demand the heads of whoever had approved reporting Founder Kemway's abduction, forced him to push further up against the pillows. He summoned Lieutenant Young for answers, certain that only she could have provided the prods with that information. But as with every other attempt made since waking, her signal came back as offline, possible for any number of reasons, including avoiding her captain's calls.

Frustrated, Grainger turned his wrathful demand for answers to the next targets on his list: Kenneth and Soleia Ximenez.

He would deal with the lieutenant soon enough and learn what she was not telling him. Written and dictated reports of that disastrous night were one thing. He would see her face as he asked questions and he would have the truth.

Whatever had happened, whatever had gone wrong, Grainger wanted solutions found so that the issue was put swiftly behind him.

He wanted out of this damn medi-bed. At least his arm was no longer suspended in the positioning sling and he could sit with only minor, lingering discomfort.

The duo arrived promptly, together, their matching suits of powder blue proving that they had come from the studio. Their smiles were as insincere as he had always thought them to be on every prodcast he had ever seen. Both had been born with family status and on-air presence and had grown up in a world of cam exposure and manipulated news. They were popular with the viewers, who had little else to compare them to, handsome, pretty faces and outwardly friendly, if dissembling, demeanors. Unlike so many things to change after the Coup, their faces beaming on the Echos had remained, allowing a level of comforting sameness the people needed. No one in the Levs knew the pair, however, knew the plasticity of personality that matched their glued-on smiles. Even the miens presented to their colleagues in the Uppers, Grainger believed every time he crossed paths with them, hid what the husband and wife were actually like.

He wondered if they knew themselves.

"Captain, you look…" Kenneth began, speaking as if he had rehearsed his sentiment, his expression of concern, the way he rehearsed the majority of his prodcast performances.

"Where did you get your information?" Grainger barked, cutting the platitudes off.

"Information?" asked Soleia in a neutral tone colored with the barest hint of surprise and confusion.

"Who is spreading rumors about Founder…?"

"It isn't true then? What they are saying?"

"What who are saying?" Grainger repeated.

Soleia continued, "The Founder isn't…?"

Grainger swallowed the growl, the irritation, that would give Soleia information she hoped for, a tidbit of truth to support the rumors. Grainger only knew what his officers' reports claimed and most of those made no mention of an abduction. Most did not mention or refer to the Founder at all.

Instead of answering her questions, just as the couple refused to answer his, he countered, "Does it look like I've been out there to know what's happening?" The now black Echo screens did not indicate what he had been doing, so it was possible that if an abduction attempt had occurred, the information had not been reported to him in his recovery. "You're irresponsibly creating public panic with unsubstantiated reports, without the permission of…"

"With all due respect, Captain, we do not report to you."

Grainger held Kenneth's gaze, the two men staring coolly, their points made without words. The Founder had controlled the news, what the city heard and saw, what they knew, what they did not. But Grainger was no Founder and the Nau, while managing Hebenon's resources and policies, had chosen to allow the prodcasters freedom in reporting that had not existed in several generations. Rumor, fallacies, misinformation, all were bound to creep in now that the Founder's restrictions were lifted, although, Grainger admitted, they had been the staples of the prods for far too many years with the Founder at the helm. He had never imagined, when laying the groundwork for changes to the sharing of news after the Coup, that the choice would blow back on him.

Smiling disarmingly, Soleia interrupted the staring match with a hand on her husband's arm and a slight clearing of her throat. "We reached out to your staff but no one was willing to make a statement. But I trust our source, Captain. If it's true, if something has happened to the Founder, the people deserve to know…"

"The Founder deserves his privacy!" As well as, he thought without saying so, the chance to be located without Senior Kal and his Talkers being made aware that the bugorra were on their trail.

Of course, if Kal was the mastermind and perpetrator, sending Talkers disguised as bugorra, he had either expected success without casualties or else was aware that he was the bugorra's primary suspect.

Other than the public outcry, the turmoil the news might create, the prod would change very little about law enforcement's progress.

"You will not," Grainger growled, "make further reports about the Founder until I know what is going on." Better he looked as if his injuries had kept him out of the information loop than for it to appear his subordinates were keeping the truth from him.

He did not want to lead by the Founder's example. He wanted to do what was right for Hebenon. He wanted to be honest with those he served. "Not a word until I'm prepared to make a statement."

Kenneth and Soleia looked at each other. A public statement by the captain was what they wanted, a chance to catch him in a scandal that would attract viewers and create support for those reporting it.

"Agreed," Soleia answered, though it was Kenneth who offered his hand to seal the agreement.

Grainger wondered, as they retreated, if one or both of them hoped to climb into a position of power by gaining the people's support.

That, he thought with a growl and shouted, "Get me Tamner!" was never going to happen.

☙*❧

A double shift was something Jaron could not pass up, regardless of his desire to return to the flat, to be certain Rhyd was safe. The man was not returning his messages, which was no surprise, nor was Skelter after the single time the redhead had assured him that there was no change, that everything was fine. The lingering uncertainty refused to leave and left a stranglehold of panic growing ever tighter around Jaron's chest. But he had never passed on double shifts in his history with the Archive except due to illness, and he worried that it would look suspicious if he did not take the opportunity now.

He accepted the extra duty and the ticks that came with it, but his thoughts rarely strayed from the one sprawled on his sofa…or at the bottom of a set of Lev stairs.

Taking the double, he hoped, would make up for his distraction.

Tamner had said Rhyd was in no danger of dying unless his lungs lost the battle against the river water he had swallowed and Skelter was there to make sure the oxygen in his mask continued to flow. Yet Skelter had also suffered at the hands of the river and the wisdom of leaving one weak man in charge of another was debatable, even if Tox frequently stopped in to check on them as she had promised she would.

What if Rhyd's tank ran out of oxygen?

What if his heart gave out?

What if Jaron was not there when Rhyd needed him?

It took effort to remind himself that Ballard was a fighter, a stronger man than Jaron would ever be, a man who had lived through more pain and abuse than some people ever experienced.

But when did it become too much?

Preoccupied with his worries, he took little notice of most of the data that crossed his station, coding it by rote memory without the attention to detail he normally took. A clip taken by a stairwell unit, unfocused and speckled with water droplets, showing seven mostly unrecognizable individuals staggering up Lev stairs could have been anywhere, could have been anyone. In the split-second before he pressed the submission button, the flicker of the timestamp in the upper right corner and the SCAM's identification code sank like a stinger between Jaron's eyes and forced him to pay closer attention.

It was a drunken gaggle with a hook in their midst, supporting each other as they maneuvered the slippery stairs. The SCAM angle only offered a view of their backs. When another figure, larger than the rest, charged out of the grainy shadows behind them, Jaron's palms began to sweat.

One of those in the group turned, planted a foot in the shadow's chest moments before the clawing hands could grab anyone. The figure tumbled back like a dropped sack of nessies down the stairs. Another, supported by the weight of his companions, twisted awkwardly, either pulled around by the one who delivered the kick or else to see what had happened; he struck an iron stanchion and would have fallen as well if not for the hook on his other side.

Unable to breathe, Jaron paused the feed to wipe his palms over his thighs and then clutched the edge of the desk with one hand. Back one frame. Another. Another. Until two motionless faces stared towards the SCAM long enough to be recognizable.

Scarecrow.

Jaron.

He swallowed the bile at the back of his throat and inched the footage forward again. None of the others revealed their faces as they made it up the stairs and stumbled along the walk out of the SCAM's-eye. The figure at the bottom of the stairs never moved. Not long after, another appeared, wearing the barely practical attire of a streeter. He squatted to inspect the fallen figure, the mass bearing a strip of yellow tied around his arm, but was then pursued up the stairs in the direction Scarecrow had gone by the beaked brako, a few of whom remained to share a heated exchange before toting the body away.

Vanderwall.

It had to be.

The tremors in Jaron's hands traveled up his arms and overtook his body as he scrambled to find interconnected footage from any nearby SCAMs that could reveal where the seven had gone, that could expose where Scarecrow had gone into hiding. It would not matter now: Scarecrow was no longer there. But Jaron did not want to take any chances that later footage might have allowed hunters to see Scarecrow leave again, carried by others who might then be recognizable. And he sought any footage that might show where the brako had gone with their fallen leader. With so many SCAMs damaged or destroyed during the Coup, yet to be repaired or replaced, with so many frequently vandalized by tingers, streeters, addicts, or rebellious individuals of other sorts, there proved to be no other data to connect either Vanderwall or Scarecrow…or Jaron…to this snippet of footage.

He was relieved, though not surprised, that the SCAMs in the vicinity of their Lev 1 exploits had been dark, perhaps at Zara's hand, and relieved that no other SCAM had picked up their retreat.

Only that one.

One was enough.

It was not the first time Scarecrow had been caught by a SCAM, but it was the first time, to Jaron's knowledge, that he was seen aided by others, others who could be sought and pressured to reveal the man behind the mask. Though most of those seven could not be identified, Jaron could be, if anyone bothered to try. If Oliver saw the footage there would be questions that Jaron did not want, could not, answer.

If the brako learned that he had been the one to take Vanderwall's life, Jaron would be their target too. An act of self-defense or not, the brako would not likely care. They would come for him and not even Scarecrow would be able to protect him. Not unless the vigi remained glued to his side. Not unless Jaron went into hiding where the brako would never find him.

No such place existed in Hebanthe Falls.

There was only one way to prevent it, one way to keep this information out of the hands of people who must never see it, Oliver and brako alike.

Two keystrokes would be all it took.

It happened all the time. SCAM failures. Glitches in the Archive system or the Hub. Especially after the Coup. It was not supposed to happen, but sometimes it did.

Two keystrokes and he would be free.

It was illegal. If he was caught deleting data without authorization, it would cost his job and possibly more, unless he could convince his supervisors that the act had been accidental. Maybe Oliver would grant a light sentence, show leniency, but if the brako learned of it, they would give no mercy.

It was a risk Jaron was reluctantly, anxiously, forced to take for his own protection…and for Rhyd's.

His fingers hovered over the touchpad, over the only connection between him and the truth.

One keystroke.

Confirm?

Another.

It was done.

He leaned back on the stool, closed his eyes with his hands laced behind his head, and let out a long, slow, squeaking breath, waiting for an alarm, for the inevitable on the off chance that the Archive SCAMs had chosen that moment to monitor his station. If they had, Archive Security would bear down on him swiftly.

One minute passed.

Five.

No one came.

The lunch shift whistle cried.

Maybe Security was waiting for him in the break room. But he could not stay at his desk. Staying here would be admitting to guilt he would be forced to hide the way he had hidden that damning bit of footage. The way he had to hide what he had done to Vanderwall. The way he hid the man in his flat.

He was too nervous to eat but appearances had to be maintained. He would not survive long without them.

☙*☙

He had no reason to be suspicious about the woman's whereabouts when he burst into Vapors to find her absent from the bar counter where he expected her to be. Maemi, like everyone else, had a life outside of her vindi hours. Once she had a nephew to raise, a mother-in-law to care for, a husband to enjoy. And he had been told, by Tox, by Zara, by Maemi herself, that she had done a great deal to keep Rhyd from sliding into despondency after Venn was taken. She had cooked for him, cleaned his home, ensured he had daily nessies and clean clothes. Above all, she had made sure he found a purpose, a reason, to rise out of bed each morning, a reason not to drink himself to death.

That Venn did not approve of, or agree with, the crutch that had given Rhyd purpose and kept him going, the reason that had eventually allowed for their reunion, was not Maemi's fault, any more than it was her fault that Rhyd could not let that purpose go now that he and Venn had found one another again.

Venn was happy Rhyd lived, happy he had not succumbed to despair. But he was not happy about the way Rhyd had done it.

It was that displeasure and the knowledge that Rhyd had not been at the flat when Venn, having left Agnys and Tamner's son Cori in the care of the parah, ventured into the city to find Rhyd, that made him scowl sourly at Maemi when she eventually appeared behind the bar, smiled, and offered him another drink.

He had lost track of how many he had consumed, how long he had waited, for her, for Rhyd, for anyone who could give him answers.

"Glad you could make it," he groused.

She brushed off his sour attitude with, "Don't you start. Been a rough couple of weeks. I don't need your insolence, Venn Weyer. Think you'd be on a cloud after that beautiful recital…"

Appropriately chastised but frowning still, Venn accepted the glass from her hand and stared at it. "You caught it?"

"Some of it."

"Some?"

"Been taking care of a friend. Made it difficult to see all at once, but I heard it. I'll sit with the prod soon as I snatch some downtime."

What little Maemi had seen and heard had been moments gleaned while procuring a hiding place for the Core children, crossing the city, running the little ones to safety before returning to Vapors. In the hours since, there had been a scramble to find them food, clothing, bedding, and other nessies. There had been constant vigilance on behalf of those she worried about. Tox had said Rhyd's efforts were successful, that everyone was safe, but until Maemi saw them with her own eyes, she was hesitant to believe it was true.

Like other popular events in Hebenon, the concert prod would repeat for days, possibly until everyone was tired of listening to it or until something new and exciting replaced it.

The cazzing prod about the abduction was slowly doing that.

Venn nodded but did not meet her gaze. "Friend okay?"

"Will be," she replied, refusing to give details. Who that friend was, what ailment they had, was none of his business. Unlike Rhyd, Maemi did not believe Venn would be persistent enough to follow up on the question to learn the details she did not share.

"Good." He gulped the contents, the burn of it as it slid down and settled in his belly no longer the fire it had been with the first drink. Deciding he had consumed enough, he savored the drops of Zaolei on his lips, Rhyd's drink of choice that Venn had never developed a taste for, and turned the glass upside down on the counter. "Seen Rhyd?"

"He wasn't there?"

Again Venn scowled. "Should have been." Should have been, but Venn had not seen him. "Haven't seen him in days."

After their reunion, that was not unusual, but before the recital, the bilger had made some effort to speak to him, to message him, at least once a day in an effort to rekindle their relationship. Venn should have made the same effort but he had stubbornly left the reaching out to Rhyd, a passive-aggressive means to force Rhyd to prove his interest since he would not leave his vigilante lifestyle behind.

After the last few days of silence, the ever-widening gap was overtaking any progress that might have been made. Venn knew he should try harder. He should reach out more than he had. His efforts since the recital had proven to be too little too late.

"Know where he is?"

"Haven't seen him since early the day of the recital," she admitted as she picked up his glass and wiped the counter. "Wish I could help you, mpenzi." She knew Rhyd had made it safely into hiding that night but she did not know where he was. She had contributed to the night's success, had been happy to do her part, but she felt she should have done more. She would like to do something more than maintain silence and continue this show of ignorance.

"Think he had something to do with what happened that night?"

"With what?" There had been a discussion about a diversion staged somewhere far from wherever Scarecrow intended to be, but Maemi had not been given the details and it was no surprise that Venn knew nothing about Rhyd's activities. Rhyd would not have put Venn's life at risk with knowledge, would not have endangered his efforts, and would have done his utmost to keep what he was doing as far away from Venn as possible to keep the cellist out of danger.

Regardless of their struggling relationship, Rhyd wanted Venn to be safe. He wanted Venn's musical comeback to be successful.

"Didn't feel the shaking? Did the lights go out?"

"The quake?" She shrugged as she put the glass in the bin for cleaning and resumed wiping the counter. The prods were awash with speculation about the tremors, just as they were about the Founder, but no authority had come forward with an official statement about that either. "Lights dimmed a bit, but I didn't think they were connected. It didn't last long and nothing was damaged."

It was Venn's turn to shrug. "Dunno. But the buggers searched everyone while they locked us down to inspect the lifts and stairs. Don't think they searched us without a reason."

"They're buggers," she grunted. "They don't need a reason. They arrested you, didn't they?" Just because the Founder was no longer in charge, it did not mean anything else had changed. The only changes anyone noticed were the changes in facial gear of law enforcement, the increased activity of the brako who now wore Crow masks, commodity shortages, and the new ability to travel Outside.

Day-to-day life seemed little different.

Her candid assessment was valid. Venn had not seen Captain Grainger that night either and had only seen Lieutenant Young before, and then long after, the recital. There had been an overabundance of buggers present, presumably to keep those from the Levs out of places in the Uppers where they were unwelcome. He was unaware of any other reason why they would be there.

Living as a Crosser, rarely coming into Hebenon if he could avoid doing so except for rehearsals with other musicians, Venn knew little of the state of affairs inside the metal nest. Having seen so many buggers on his way to Vapors tonight, having seen group after group of brako huddled in shadows as if waiting for something, maybe Grainger was proving to be no different than the generations of Founders who had controlled the city before him.

"Looked at home? Think he'd be there if anywhere." The flat was no longer Venn's home but it had been once and her tone spoke of hope for reconciliation between two men torn apart by ill-fated events.

"Wasn't there."

"On shift then. Been working a lot lately." The words were true, even if Rhyd's work had not all been as a bilger. "I'll tell him you're looking when I see him," she offered as Venn rose from the stool and offered his passcard for the requisite deduction for his drinks. She would give him the drinks for free but he rarely accepted charity, and so she ran the card through the purchase reader as expected.

Other than the Shed, there was one more place he could try, one more stop he could make. Venn was reluctant to do so but he was running out of ideas. The one time he chose to reach out and Rhyd was invisible. It was as if the bilger did not want to be found.

It was as if he had given up.

Despite the temptation of telling Maemi not to bother, Venn muttered, "Do that. Tell him Agnys is worried. And I'm sorry, Maemi…about Xiaodan. I really am."

Rhyd might not care if Venn worried, and Venn's too-late efforts might not be enough to temper a change, but the cellist continued to hope that Agnys' opinions, fears, and wishes did matter to the man who had gone to such extraordinary lengths to save her life.

Someone's opinion had to matter to Rhyd.

Venn's obviously did not.

❧Chapter 5❧

Propped awkwardly, the aching burn in his side and shoulder making it difficult to find a comfortable position while the medis came and went at random intervals for samples, tests, for inquiries about his pain levels, was pushing Grainger to the snapping point. He wanted to sleep but the pain and over-attentiveness of the staff prevented him from doing so despite the evening hour and meds in his blood. Frustrated, he gave up and shifted his focus instead to something more productive than staring at the sound-absorbent panels above his head.

With the Echos he had been granted open within easy reach, he switched between SCAM footage, ICD stills, witness and officer reports, and any other files thought useful in his efforts to understand the recital-night events he had not been present to witness or direct. As the hours crept deeper into the night shift, slowing the flow of medis and officers, the external focus on work helped direct his thoughts away from his injuries and the continuing indignant glow the Ximenezes had left in their wake.

If Tamner did not arrive by morning to release him from this bed, this room, Grainger had already decided he would get up and walk out on his own, get back to work, medical advisory be damned. The first thing he would do would be hunt down Lieutenant Young and demand to know why she had failed to respond to his repeated summons.

He found nothing out of the ordinary in those Lev reports beyond the unsubstantiated rumors of Vanderwall's demise. The only proof of it was the increased number of skirmishes within the brako ranks that could have any number of other causes. The tremors of that night had shaken the entire city but had been felt most strongly in the Uppers and only a few areas in the Levs had experienced brief interruptions of power as the Uppers had. Neither occurrence lasted long enough to induce panic although the Igraci were capitalizing on both with increased street-corner protests of doom. Only in the Uppers had the power outage been complete, lasting less than five minutes as it had at the Core door, corresponding with the tremors…the explosions…in a way that Grainger knew was not coincidental.

The outage had caused no damage. No one was injured because of it. But it may have contributed to, or assisted, the infiltration of those who had taken Founder Kemway.

He could no longer argue that they had 'tried' to kidnap Kemway. The lieutenant's requests to identify the dead, service reports for the deceased officers and techs provided to their families, and Ilya's avoidance, spoke in support of abduction, leaving Grainger certain that the unapproved prodcast, the leak in the story, were not rumors.

That leak could only have originated in a few places.

Only two people, as far as Grainger knew, could know the truth.

The abduction should have been part of viewable SCAM footage. Generations of Founders had believed it necessary to install SCAMs in any area of the city, including the Uppers, prone to foot traffic. But Grainger's efforts to secure the Founder and move him in secrecy, from and to locations he had not wanted publically revealed had precipitated the disabling of SCAMs in the necessary corridors, and in others as well to give the appearance of SCAM malfunction rather than deliberate tampering, before the move could be made. Other than a short clip of a group of buggers emerging from a stairwell and splitting up under the direction of the tallest among them, there was nothing viewable of note. Those figures could have been his bugorra dispersing to their assigned checkpoints but there was no evidence of that either. There were no clues on the footage as to the fate of the posted buggers, no evidence of the ambush, no evidence of those who had taken the Founder, no evidence where they had gone.

It was as if they had known which SCAMs were disabled, allowing a choice of undocumented, unproven escape routes.

Not even the lieutenant, however, had known about the disabling of the SCAMs. Only two other people had known and he would confront each of them to determine their loyalty and possible culpability in the abduction plot.

Those summons had been issued too, but no one was likely to come until morning.

His focus shifted from the scouring of SCAM footage to a review of the events at the primary Core entrance where he had been. The file had not yet finished loading when the door of his room hissed open and a familiar individual pushed inside, followed by the grappling hands of staff members hoping to detain him.

"Where is he?"

Grainger waved off the medis and orderlies with a weary, "It's okay…let him in," and an internal effort not to be irritated or agitated by the man's demands.

"I've been told the recital was a success, Mr. Weyer. I'm disappointed I could not attend. It must have been…"

Red-faced, Venn charged the bed to loom over the captain though he stopped short of physical contact or coming within reach of Grainger's hands. "Answer me! He's so damned certain the Core exists, that he could get Skelter out…he was there. I know he was. You were there too…"

Venn did not know where the Core was, did not know where the captain had been. He was not convinced the place existed. But Rhyd believed it and there were enough slivers of rumor around Hebenon, bleeding into Marbordo via the Crossers and Prossers who came in and out of the city every day, for Venn to guess that somewhere inside Hebenon the mythical Core might be a reality.

If anyone knew it for certain, the captain must.

Rhyd and Grainger had a history. If the captain had been injured in a fight at the entrance to a place Rhyd had been determined to go, it seemed likely that Grainger's injuries had come at Rhyd's hands.

Not Rhyd's.

Scarecrow's.

Grainger did not have to ask whom Venn referred to. There was only one individual they had in common, only one whom the cellist would be interested in locating. "Why do you think…?"

"Look at you! No single, ordinary man…"

"Who said this was done by a single man?"

The question cut Venn's bluster short; the possibility that there had been multiple combatants had not occurred to him. With no public statements yet regarding the incident in the factory, speculation and details about the captain's injuries, as well as the injuries and deaths of so many officers, was rife. A man who knew Ballard intimately and knew his history with Grainger was bound to make that leap of logic without any facts to disprove it.

When Venn did not offer an immediate answer or retort, Grainger sighed and continued, "I assure you, Mr. Weyer, he is not responsible for this. He was not involved." He gestured absently across his body, indicating injuries that could be seen and those that could not. "What else he may or may not have been doing, I can't say, but I haven't seen him in…"

How long had it been? Grainger had lost track of days while he had been stuck in this bed, and so he settled on, "days…maybe a week…days before the recital at least."

"Find him. Make him tell you the truth," Venn hissed with an insistent growl, retreating towards the door with reluctantly frustrated steps, dissatisfied with the conversation but accepting that, if the captain knew more, he would not share it with Venn. "Make him stop. Send him home. Make him do this before someone gets hurt."

Or killed.

With no opportunity to ask other questions, the one he had asked still unanswered, Grainger sent a message to the subordinate officer who had been with him during the under-Factory fight. Interrogate the Core prisoners who had survived. Find out who Skelter was.

Why he might be of interest to Scarecrow.

He returned to the study of SCAM footage, knowing his nerves and whirling thoughts would not allow him to sleep. Maybe he could find something on the SCAMs that he had missed, something that would explain why Weyer was so afraid for Ballard's safety.

❧*❧

"You'll wanna see this…"

There were too many faces for Uriah Frankle to know them all. Turnover was high in the life they had chosen, or that had been thrust upon them by circumstance. But there were benefits too, and for some, the potential benefits outweighed the drawbacks. Maybe the fellow with the bushy, unkempt graying hair and handlebar mustache had been with the brako since their inception. Maybe he was a new recruit.

Frankie, known now as Vanderwall thanks to Mam Kemway's appointment, did not care how long the fellow had been around. It only mattered that he was useful.

It only mattered that he was loyal.

"What?" he grunted.

The passchip the fellow placed in his outstretched hand was like so many others, a tech rarely used anymore when it was easier to send and receive data, prodcasts, and communications via ICD or Echo. Especially sensitive or private correspondence, things one wanted to keep out of the hands of others, was sometimes shared this way and this sharing now told Frankie that this was something intended only for his eyes.

Though apparently, he thought with a frown, the courier had seen its contents to presume its importance…or someone else had and this fellow had been told of its significance by whoever had sent it.

Already seated at the Echo W model on his desk, the big man closed the array of spreadsheets he had been studying as he inserted the passchip into the aftermarket reader on the side of the unit. It was no longer standard to equip Echos with readers in the hopes of discouraging the copying of information and avoid the sort of secret communication the chips were designed for, but picking up a reader on the streets was easy to do. Most, however, never had the need.

Frankie had that need, just as Vanderwall had before him.

He opened the single file on the card. The grainy quality of the footage and the timestamp in the upper corner identified it as SCAM video hacked from the Hub. Nothing unusual about it, a group of drunkards staggering up stairs somewhere in the Levs. It could be anyone. It could have been anywhere. Only the code in the timestamp would reveal the location to those who knew how to read it.

He did not need to dig for that information. A familiar form, as big and burly as he was, a slight limp evident in the few steps the footage showed, rushed from the shadows in the lower right of the video and attempted to grab one of the individuals. The one at the back of the group turned, startled, and lashed out with a kick.

A kick that sent the assailant sprawling backward, down the stairs, to land in a disjointed heap at the bottom.

The fallen individual could have been anyone, but the armband he wore identified him and revealed where, on which Lev, this footage had been captured.

Frankie had already visited the scene.

"Who are they?"

"Who?" The messenger had remained on the opposite side of the stained, rusting desk where he could not view the Echo screen or the footage. His seeming ignorance suggested he had not viewed the video or that he was a fotzing good liar.

Frankie watched again, looking for identity clues for those on the screen. The four in the front never showed their faces to the SCAM, never turned or slowed or stopped when the attack came. The hook could have been anyone; there were enough of them in the city, tough individuals not easily intimidated, her clothing so common it was unlikely she would ever be identified. The other two, however, the one the hook supported as they struggled up the stairs, was Scarecrow. From the cut of his mask, Frankie would stake his life on it.

Maybe not a drunken cluster then. Maybe this was something else.

He had not heard of any unusual activity amidst a night of unusual activity, but it might be worth digging deeper.

The last individual, the only one to allow the SCAM a glimpse of his face, was a stranger. The quality of the image might not be good enough for an I.D. search, might not be enough to identify the young man, but there was only one way to be certain.

"Find out who he is," he growled, shoving one beefy finger at the face turned towards the SCAM. The messenger came around the end of the desk to see. "Find out who he is, where he is…bring him to me."

"Alive? Or…?"

Alive meant interrogation but there was no need to interrogate the stranger to prove what had happened. It had been an act of self-defense and no law would prosecute him for it.

Whoever he was, his actions, and Vanderwall's carelessness, had resulted in his predecessor's death. Without that set of coincidental actions, Frankie would not be in this chair. Frankie did not care why Vanderwall had died and was content to leave the matter alone.

For the sake of the organization, however, he could not do so. Lower-ranking brako who had respected the man would want to know who killed him and why. The Mam would want to know. Was he working for someone? Was there a reason Vanderwall had targeted him? Or had Scarecrow been the target and this fellow, whoever he was, happened to come between them?

Kill or capture, either way might bring them Scarecrow. That might be reward enough for his underlings, might be enough to put the matter of Vanderwall's death behind them. Knowing the why would seem unimportant compared to that. And removing the Scarecrow thorn from the city's side, from the brako's side, would bring Frankie the prestige he needed to tighten his grip on his new position.

"Whatever it takes."

"On it.

The passchip was returned to the messenger's hand, the tool with which others could track down Vanderwall's killer, and he darted from the room. He knew where to go for this sort of work. With luck, Frankie would have what he wanted within a few hours.

She remembered what she had seen through the medi-bay window when she eked out a few minutes the night of the recital, the night her world had begun to implode. Her captain had been heavily bandaged at the time, his leg immobilized from the knee down, his arm carefully suspended in a collection of straps, cables, and pulleys to limit its movement while the plasts and surgeries set, allowing his arm and shoulder to heal without undue strain. From the looks of his condition at the time, he was lucky to be alive.

Seeing him now, arm no longer suspended, bandages no longer wrapped around his head, leg no longer held immobile by splints, his face as stern as ever and focused on multiple Echos as a pair of junior officers and a medi passed her on their way out of the room made her exhale an uneasy breath of relief. He had not seen her yet, or was ignoring her, and after a few nervous swallows, she cleared her throat.

"It is good to see you well, sir. What happened?" Her words erupted before the trio was out of the room, before the door closed, her anxious attempt to avoid the tongue-lashing she expected. Grainger glanced at her, shaking his head, whatever he had to say seeming to be something not for the ears of civilians or lower officers. With the latching of the door, he motioned her closer, continuing to stare at screens she could not see.

His silence was unnerving.

She should have found the time to come sooner, when he had summoned her and not when it was convenient.

"Where have you been?"

Ilya refused to lower her gaze, bow her head, or cower at his crisp tone of irritation. "I'm sorry, sir. The last time I came you were…and I've been busy."

"Doing what?"

She was his best officer. He would not have appointed her as his second otherwise. He did not want to believe that she was shirking duty, avoiding him, hiding something, but the time spent in this bed, with so many failed attempts to reach her, allowed his frustration to concoct too many negative reasons for her not coming when called.

"My job."

"Tell me…and it better be good."

Not certain what he might consider good, not knowing what he remembered from the night he had been hospitalized or had learned from the Echos set up, she began where she thought it best.

"There were two tremors…or explosions…that temporarily cut power in the Uppers and parts of the Levs. There were no reports of injuries or fatalities, and the recital continued uninterrupted; so far the system inspections have not pinpointed the cause of the failure. We presume it was a quake, as we've been unable to locate a blast site so the assessment is the shaking jarred something loose…"

She had not been beneath the factories, having no reason yet to investigate there and she did not know where the captain had been when he was injured. She guessed he was aware of the shaking, guessed that he had been near the heart of an explosion judging by the concussive cuts and bruises across his face, neck, and hands, but she had been too preoccupied with finding Founder Kemway to investigate something that should have been in the captain's control. Wherever he had been, he had gone without a standard-issue filt mask and those who had been there with him, those who had survived, had maintained whatever order of silence he had given.

"Reports have come in that, during the recital, the blackouts, the quakes, or in the hours thereafter, Vanderwall may have been killed."

"May have been?"

"We have yet to find a body…or be presented one for examination. The brako are fighting amongst themselves and the reports we've gotten say they're blaming each other…but we don't know any more than that. We're doing our best to keep the feud contained, to prevent it from spilling into the civilian population."

Testing his injured arm, the mobility of his shoulder hampered by the stiffness he could feel pulling at the muscles, he scowled. If Vanderwall had fallen into the river, his corpse might not be located until the next time the nets were cleared. By that time, so little would remain that a corpse might never be identified and the cause of death would be impossible to determine. It would be just like the brako, he thought, motioning her to continue without looking at her, to hide the body so that the faceless scourge remained unidentified.

"I've got the…dissidents…you were putting down…" It was the only term Ilya could use for the scurvy collection of people her fellow officers had dragged into holding. She had not had time or opportunity to check on them and no one was willing to explain who they were, where they had come from, what crime they had committed beyond assaulting the captain and his unit. Because they had been the captain's concern, something he had been seeing to privately, Ilya decided to leave them for his dispensation after he recovered.

Finding Kemway was her job. The ruffians in holding could wait.

"They're in quarantine in the closed wing of detention, at Doctor Tamner's suggestion, until you are ready to interrogate them. I've given them clothes…food…but I am not sure what else I can…"

"Leave them there for now." He gauged she had not been to the Core and that the officers who had been with him remained silent. Eventually, he would need to share some of that night's events and details with her, but not yet. Not while he was still so tired and confined to this miserable bed.

"There's talk that Scarecrow had a hand in the explosions, in the resistance your team put down, in the death of Vanderwall, in the…"

"That is a lot for a single man to accomplish in one evening," Grainger snorted, suppressing the cough that rose with the sound, his words trampling hers as she continued speaking. "I thought the conclusion was quakes…?"

"…abduction of Founder Kemway."

He heard the words despite his coughing and stared at her as he gulped a cup of water to soothe the burn in his throat.

He must have seen the prods. She knew the Ximenezes had been here and ordered to retract the unsubstantiated statements, an order that had thus far gone unheeded. Ilya believed, without evidence, that the captain had read her reports and knew as much as she was able to express within the formality of an official report.

"The Founder is…"

"Being sought. I don't know what happened, sir." Ilya rushed to explain in the hopes of tempering the outrage building in his eyes. "We were ambushed in the corridor by Talkers dressed as bugorra. They replaced my sentries at the last checkpoint…and I don't know where they are. It appears they got in, got into place, before the power cut. They killed some of my team…Doctor Tamner's techs…knocked the doctor and me out…left us where we fell. Maybe they thought we were dead too. Two of the culprits escaped with the Founder, but I've got four bodies down for I D; soon as the system pulls them up, we'll find who they are…and we'll find those who've gone missing…and those who have the Founder…"

"Did you lock down the…?"

She nodded. "Everything from the recital hall up was on lockdown soon as I woke up. We searched everyone at the recital, searched every room, residence, and vindi…the stairwells and lifts…but haven't found anything. I extended the hunt into the Levs as soon as the Uppers left us empty, but so far…nothing."

She had done everything Grainger would have done, in the order he would have done it. He had read her logs, the incident reports. What she told him now did not contradict what she had written.

But there was one detail she had not yet spoken of.

"So you thought to make a public statement to the prods? Why not arrest Senior Kal and Mam Kemway and be done with it?"

Ilya took a startled step back. "I haven't spoken with the Ximenezes. I don't know where they got their information but I swear it wasn't from me, Captain." Few candidates could have leaked that story, any of its details, and she had been too busy chasing leads, speaking to witnesses, city structural experts, and technicians, to interview those she suspected could have revealed the abduction.

Doctor Tamner was the only person she had interviewed and she had already dismissed him. She was beginning to think the news leak had come from the kidnappers themselves.

But why?

"Shall I call for arrests? On what grounds?" Arresting the man she believed was behind this outrage was precisely what she wanted to do, but Ilya had been unable to rationalize a reason for doing so that would stick without creating outrage among the Voices supporters.

Grainger opened his mouth, choked on the breath he sucked in, frowned and kept silent. Without evidence, or at least more concrete cause beyond circumstantial suspicion created by people who might have been impersonating both Talkers and bugorra to create confusion, no charges would stick. Unlike the Founder, Grainger did not have the authority to make arrests without cause. The Senior would be released to his supporters, would bemoan wrongful accusation and unnecessary arrest and detention…all sticky, sore subjects that had led to the unrest which had birthed the too-recent Coup.

Hebenon was not ready to turn down that path again, not while the memories and losses remained vivid. Ilya knew that as well as he did.

"And Mam?"

"She was searched like everyone else at the recital, but she was clean. I couldn't hold her without revealing why. We searched under the pretense of possible explosive terrorism so not even the officers know the truth." Ilya hated to lie to those beneath her, hated to hide the truth, but waiting for the captain to return to duty had seemed the wiser recourse. "Gagged word about your condition. Didn't think I could mention it without reporting what happened…how you got here…but everyone knows something's up."

How could they not when the captain had been absent from duty for several days and had now begun making demands from a room in a medi ward?

Her decisions and choices brought an approving nod and made her breathe a little easier before beginning again. "But there is still the possibility that Scarecrow…"

"Crucksake, Lieutenant! Scarecrow could not be everywhere at once!" Scarecrow killing Vanderwall was a possibility Grainger could believe, although he would likely have left the body for recovery. Abducting the madman, however, gained the Scarecrow no benefit. Whoever was guilty of that crime undoubtedly wanted to use the Founder for a political end. Someone like Senior Kal or Neoma Kemway. Politics was not Scarecrow's game. Whatever he had been doing that night, whatever Weyer suspected, it had been personal…and unconnected to the Founder.

Grainger was sure of it.

"Stop trying to blame him for everything and bring me the head of whoever has the Founder…and send Jaron…"

"Jaron? I've not seen him since…" Her surprised expression turned thoughtful. "Not in several days. Not since before the recital."

"Then find him. He hasn't been here. I want to know he's safe…"

"With all due respect…"

"I need to know he's…"

"All our resources are tied up with the Founder…and keeping the brako clashes controlled. We can't afford to pull anyone off for…"

For a personal request on behalf of the captain. Grainger growled and sank into his pillows. She was right. His frustrated-child expression set, but he knew Ilya was doing her duty. She had said there were no reported deaths or injuries…except Vanderwall and those at the site of Kemway's abduction. Just because Jaron was not one of the first faces to greet him upon waking did not mean harm had befallen him. The man had shifts of his own, would have been kept out of the Uppers during the lockdown, had to sleep and eat. The Archives had likely been very busy since the recital.

And with the news on Oliver's condition gagged, it was likely Jaron did not know what had happened.

"Tell them to keep an eye out for him," Grainger relented, willing to concede that. "I'll be back on the job soon as they let me out of here and I want everything, every report not yet made, not yet in the system, on my desk when I get there. Find the Founder while he's still alive…and you'd cazzing well best get Tamner here before morning!"

Guessing that the doctor would not release the captain until he was capable of standing, Ilya bowed and replied, "Yes, sir," as she tried to guess how long his confinement would last, how long she had to comply with his commands. She retreated from the room, determined to fulfill the request for access to any reports not yet into the system. Then she would do her utmost to bring the Founder back.

Influencing Doctor Tamner's ruling was beyond her control.

❧*❧

He did not recognize the man's face, the man with the merc designs shaved into his close-cropped black hair, but Jaron knew the type. They were common in the Levs, men and women tasked with guarding patrons, sometimes for an hour or a day, sometimes longer, sometimes retained to guard possessions, businesses, or homes. Some did so without the identifying hair designs, but guild mercs were typically proud of their positions and reveled in proving how dangerous they were by way of that design. Few dared cross them. Their numbers had declined since the rise of the brako as the guild struggled against being absorbed by either the brako or the bugorra…despite many members having defected from the guild for one side or the other.

Some of those members had presented themselves to Oliver for employment with the intent of stemming the rising tide of crime. Some had come with information that they hoped would lead to the inevitable arrests of brako or other mercs who had abandoned the code of protection for one of lawlessness.

This man, however, Jaron did not recognize.

This was not the first time a merc had come to the Archives for information. Maybe he was looking for a mark or doing a background check of a potential patron. Maybe he was seeking someone or something on behalf of his employer. It did not matter the cause, only that the request assigned to him gave Jaron something to think about other than the man on his sofa, the man he had slain, and the possibility of being hunted and killed.

The data request was a simple one, a request for information about a fellow named Switz, a doctor sentenced for some criminal act unknown to the merc. The request was of interest to Jaron only because he recognized the name as someone Enoch and Skelter had enlisted to remove children from the Core. The name did not sound common enough to make this mention of it a coincidence. If the man Switz had made it out of the Core as expected, if he had already come to the attention of a merc…for either a recent crime or one of those which had originally condemned him…then the odds were good that Enoch too had made it out of the Core.

That was reassuring.

Jaron supplied the material he found, details of a series of murders the once prominent doctor had committed, the time of his arrest and date of his sentencing, how long his sentence had been. There was no proof, however, that he had been sent into the mines. There were no specifics as to where he was to serve out his punishment.

Those details and events had been recorded long before Jaron, and likely the merc, had been old enough to heed such news. Though it was troubling that Skelter had put the lives of children in the hands of such a man, troubling enough to spark renewed concern for Enoch and the children, Jaron supposed that, in the Core, a suitable candidate had been difficult to select.

Skelter had made do.

Thankfully that data packet was the final one of his shift and the merc did no more than glance at him when he delivered the file. There had always been the chance that the merc had come for him and Jaron was relieved that it appeared not to be the case.

As he wove through the between shift crowds, pulling his coat closer for warmth, he remained hyper-vigilant for the possibility that the merc was following him, for the possibility that the brako or bugorra knew who he was and wanted him dead. Hopefully, the merc was more concerned with the fellow Switz instead. Hopefully, his goal was to keep that murderer from hurting anyone else.

Murderers had to be stopped.

Unfortunately, Jaron now counted himself as one of them. Knowledge of that label made him sweat nervously all the way home.

By the time he reached his flat, on the other side of the city, his clothes beneath his coat were soaked with it, his vision had tunneled to the path directly before him, his heart hammered painfully, and his breath came in such loud, rapid bursts that he was sure everyone around him must hear it. His narrowed sight negated his focused attention, pushing his anxiety higher, and when he finally closed the flat door, a little too hard, a little too loudly, he collapsed against it and fought the impulse to scream or give in to terrified weeping.

Thankfully, the slamming did not rouse the man on the sofa and Skelter appeared not to be home. The sight of Rhyd, the continued hiss of the oxygen tank with each breath the blonde took, the twitching of his hands as he fought imaginary foes in the hidden recesses of his dreams, began to bleed away the heights of Jaron's terror so that, with every swallowed gulp of air, he felt a little calmer, a little steadier.

He needed to remain strong. He needed to be strong as Rhyd was strong. He could not fail Rhyd with weakness and fear.

Even if Rhyd did not carry the conviction of emotion that had settled so swiftly and easily into Jaron's heart, the bilger was not going to let anything happen to him.

Rhyd had already proven that.

Rhyd was here. Rhyd was safe. To hell with the brako.

To hell with anyone that thought to cause harm to either of them.

&Chapter 6&

Down the body tumbled, the sickening crunch of breaking bones, of soggy flesh impacting each metal step, of leather slapping the grating as the form it encased continued to roll filling his ears like the flapping of great birds' wings. How many steps? How far beyond his reach did the broken man remain despite his efforts to catch him, to break the fall, to prevent the inevitable end? Each flailing grasp came up empty as the body bounced away, each following step a harrowing attempt not to slip, not to fall along with it. Each impact created a crimson splatter that he could not step over, could only step through, and each step into it spread that red further up the legs of his trousers, up the hem of his shirt, up to his shoulders, his neck, his face, until he was covered with blood.

Still the pursuit continued…until a sudden jarring of hands grasping his shoulders, someone catching him from behind, coincided with the heavy, reverberating thud of the corpse on the walkway at the bottom of the staircase.

Jaron's eyes popped open and he lurched awake, upright, with a scream of panic.

"Hey…easy…"

Rhyd's hands were on Jaron's shoulders. The twisted angle of his reaching arms and the discomfort of the weight on his injured leg were etched on his pale face, but regardless of the pain, he was there and Jaron released a long, shaky breath that needed no digitized speech unit to express relief. He had fallen asleep at the table, his head on his arms, the stiffness in his back and neck reminding him why that had not been a good idea.

There was a familiar flavor to the terror in Jaron's eyes that Rhyd knew too well. Now that Jaron was awake and free of his sleep-demons, Rhyd limped into the kitchen, found the limited alcohol stash the curly-haired man kept on hand, and drew out the bottle of Zaolei there solely for his benefit. Having been in this flat before, long enough to know where certain things were kept, he brought two cups to the table, filled them both, and pushed one across the surface to within Jaron's reach.

"Drink. It'll help."

Zaolei was his tonic of choice to drive away nightmares. He thought it ought to work for Jaron just as well.

Jaron downed the shot in a single gulp and pushed the cup back for more. Rhyd obliged as he straddled the reverse-turned chair with a wince and a grimace. He should have sat like a normal person, but keeping the table and the back of the chair between them like a dual shield was a protective measure Rhyd needed against intimacy.

Waking up again in Jaron's flat had been overwhelming and unsettling with the return of his faculties, although after the first several moments of panic he recalled concluding that coming here had been a wise decision when it was made. But being here, regardless of the logic, surrounded by Jaron's scent and the visual reminders of the other man's existence had filled Rhyd with a host of cacophonous urges that he could not afford to give in to. Getting close to Jaron, letting him in, letting him under his skin, would be bad for them both.

Rhyd would never let anyone get that close again.

Venn had done it…and look where that had gotten them?

The compulsion to keep Jaron at arm's length, however, and the voice in his head that warned him not to speak, were not enough to keep Rhyd from quietly asking, "Wanna talk about it?"

How many times had he wished someone had been there to ask him that same question when the shadows of his dreams brought him awake in terror? Would he have talked? He did not know. But the desire for a sympathetic ear had been there.

Though Jaron shook his head no, the words bled through the speecher as he stared at the refilled glass. "I killed him, you know…when I kicked him…and he fell…"

That kick, that fall, were hazy but present in Rhyd's memory. "Self-defense."

As far as Rhyd knew, he had never killed anyone. Some of those he had fought and injured may have died after the fact. It was a hazard of the life he led, who he had become. He found comfort in not knowing. His conflicts with the Crows, men and women doing their job regardless of how heinous obedience might be, had been fights with people he had wanted to subdue, stop. Not kill. When the fight had switched to the criminal element of the brako, Scarecrow had grown less careful about protecting his opponents' lives. The guilt he suspected he would feel over death, when it came, would be directly proportionate to the identity of the victim.

Rhyd remembered the reaching hands, movement caught out of the corner of his eyes on the stairs as they sought a haven. He remembered Jaron bearing the bulk of his weight when he could not continue, Jaron protecting him with that kick. For those things, Rhyd was grateful, and if Jaron had caused the death of a brako soldier, self-defense or not, the other fellow had likely deserved to die. Rhyd felt no guilt, culpability, or regret for that.

"They won't think so," Jaron whispered. "Killing Vanderwall's gonna…"

Rhyd frowned as he set his empty glass on the table between his hands. "Vanderwall?"

"I saw the SCAMs…I saw the band." He gestured to his arm where the brako leader had been noted, whenever he was seen, wearing a yellow armband that stood him apart from his soldiers.

"You're sure?" Rhyd filled his glass again.

"Sure as I can be." Maybe he was wrong, about the man's death, his identity. But Jaron did not think he was. "Brako's been fighting each other since…blaming each other from what I've heard. When they find out it was me…"

Impulsively, Rhyd reached across the table and grasped Jaron's wrist, ignoring the static pulse up his arm that the contact brought with it, Jaron's nightmare-hot skin warm beneath Rhyd's cool, reassuring hand. "They won't."

"I killed the footage; it's gone, except in here." He tapped the side of his head with the fingers of his other hand but he could not lift his gaze from Rhyd's grasp. He did not think Rhyd had ever initiated that sort of contact between them and though it helped relieve his anxiety, it replaced it gradually with a nervous flutter of a different sort. "No one'll see it unless they already have…but that doesn't mean…"

"They won't get to you." Rhyd did not know how he could prevent it, but doing so had risen to the surface of the sea of his priorities. Awkward in that touch now, he pulled away and grabbed the whiskey bottle to mask the gesture with the need for another drink. He filled his glass a third time and quickly drank the contents.

The need to learn the truth behind Vanderwall's death did not lag far behind protecting Jaron in importance.

Jaron wanted to believe him. Realistically, however, he did not see how Rhyd could protect him every hour of every day when he had his own life to lead.

He drained his second glass and gestured for more. Rather than chastise him for drinking or refusing to give it to him, Rhyd filled the glass and emptied the remainder of the bottle down his own throat.

After several moments of staring at the whiskey in his glass and pretending he did not miss Rhyd's touch, Jaron changed the subject, eager to shift focus away from his nightmare and grateful that Rhyd had not pressed him for details he did not want to talk about.

"Wasn't Switz the name of the guy helping Enoch with the kids?"

Rhyd nodded. The whiskey in his belly burned and he pondered the wisdom of searching the kitchen for anything substantial to counter the alcohol's weight.

"You know he killed four wives…and all five of his children?"

"Assume Skelter knew." Skelter made a point of knowing the secrets of those he did business with. It made for honesty in their dealings, prevented backstabbing and double-crossing when someone knew he had enough dirt to make their lives difficult, or potentially shorter, if they tried.

"Must've made it out okay…him and Enoch and the kids. Some guy named Blayd came to the Archives asking about him…"

"Dark-skinned merc?"

Noting Rhyd's fleeting scowl, Jaron asked, "Know him?"

"We've met. He's…" Rhyd rubbed the back of his neck and sealed the empty whiskey bottle. "Mam Kemway's man."

The shadow that passed over Rhyd's face now ghosted over Jaron's. "You think she knows? About the Core? About what we…?"

"No." He believed she knew of the Core's existence despite what she had previously told him, but knowing what they had done would be a far-fetched coincidence. Switz had not known the details of Skelter's plan thus there was little he could have shared with the Mam, if they had crossed paths in the last few days. Skelter's name would not mean anything to her. Nothing he could have revealed would connect him back to Scarecrow.

The connection between Switz and Blayd, however, the potential connection from them to Mam Kemway, was worth investigating.

"I sent his files to your account…you can read them if you want." The impulse that had prompted him to mention the merc's request had prompted him to share Switz's files. If Rhyd wanted to investigate, it removed the need for a request between them.

"Good."

The whiskey buzz was beginning to take hold, drawing the wheezing rattle out of his chest again. Rhyd stood, swayed unsteadily, and Jaron was there to catch him before his injured leg gave out. "I'm fine," Rhyd grunted defensively though without making an effort to pull away from the appreciated support.

He wanted to, but he would land on his ass on the floor if he tried. His leg was not ready to support his weight, at least not when he had a belly full of whiskey. Rhyd vaguely recalled Tamner's admonition, before returning to the Uppers, that it would take several days before standing, before natural walking, was going to come easily.

Several days without eating, without sufficient water, without moving, made the effort to do both through a Zaolei blur ill-advised.

Three wobbly, uneasy steps later, he sank onto the sofa and pulled the blanket awkwardly around himself. Jaron put the oxygen mask in his hand and flipped the valve, starting the lifesaving flow that Rhyd needed to sleep.

"Thanks." Rhyd might have been expressing gratitude for the oxygen, for the assistance to the sofa, or for the information about Switz he would view when he awoke. He might have been thanking Jaron for the care he was offering or for the help he had given at the river's edge. "Why was Tamner there when we…?" he mumbled groggily as he tried to get comfortable. The doctor had taken a risk in coming to them, and someone had taken a bigger risk to bring him.

Without questioning the leap in topic, Jaron shrugged. "Tox thought it best…you needed care…no one wanted you to die."

Rhyd snorted. He had no intention of dying. But it was sound, if risky, reasoning. He glanced at the dark Echo on the wall, scowling, uncertain if his memory of it being on was real or a dream. Where was everyone else? Why could he not remember everyone leaving him alone with Jaron?

"Was that…is Kemway…?"

Tucking the blanket around Rhyd to keep him warm, Jaron nodded. The abduction prodcast had played on repeat, interspersed liberally between repeats of the recital, news prods, and adverts. Jaron had left the Echo on so that Rhyd would not awaken to silence, but had turned it off before sitting at the table and falling asleep. He had not considered, when the rumor first came to light, that Rhyd would hear it or remember it.

"Taken. Talkers dressed as buggers…but who knows if it's true. Only rumors right now, no official statements have come down…"

"But?" Rhyd heard the word though Jaron did not say it. The blanket still contained some of his body's heat, and being wrapped in it and the alcohol's warmth, at Jaron's side, felt more comfortable than the voices in Rhyd's head argued it should.

"They're looking. They've got dead suspects. If he wasn't taken, there was an attempt to do so…or to kill him. Lieutenant Young's looking to confirm a connection between the dead and Senior Kal…so something happened."

Behind the mask, Rhyd grunted. There was a lot to think about, plans to make, but Zaolei and the oxygen and the dregs of whatever meds were still in his blood refused to allow his thoughts to focus.

When Jaron made one more adjustment to the blanket, his fingers brushed across the hollow of Rhyd's throat.

Rhyd's breath hitched.

"Get some rest. And Jaron…" He caught the dark-haired man's hand, the gesture an intimate one regardless of his intentions. "Don't worry about this, okay? Don't worry about any of it. No one's getting in here…getting past me. I promise you…"

Rather than argue, rather than point out the flaws in that promise coming from a man without the strength to protect himself, Jaron nodded. He lifted Rhyd's hand and kissed his knuckles before quickly releasing it so that Rhyd had no opportunity to be the one to pull away.

Judging by the flash of panic in whiskey brown eyes before they abruptly squeezed shut, a barrier closing between them for Rhyd to hide behind, pulling away was precisely what Rhyd would have done if given the chance.

❧*❦

The tracker signal had not moved since coming to rest several hours earlier and Blayd expected to find the passcard at the bottom of a recycle or compost bin, the man he had given it to long gone into the mist. The stationary signal, however, brought him to a hostel on the Lev where he and Switz had parted, not so far from the street corner where Blayd had last seen him. It brought the merc to a quiet room where no light pushed through the cracks around the cockeyed door and only the bass rumble of deep snoring bled through.

The spidery fellow had stayed put. That was a good sign.

He did not knock or otherwise announce his arrival before using his ill-gotten universal passkey to let himself in, flipping on the lights as he entered. Whether the sudden brightness or the bang of the auto-hinged door snapping shut did the trick, his guest scrambled awake, flailing about for some weapon he did not have or something he hoped he could use for one.

The fellow was nude, his tattered clothes in a discarded pile near the sink, joined there by a dirty towel that gave evidence of some effort to bathe. His scarred body bore witness to every fight he had ever endured, his knees were black and blue from recent crawling and his hands too were scraped and raw from the same. Blayd did not believe in the Core, but it was obvious Switz had crawled some distance to gain his freedom.

That much effort to be free meant he would be eager to remain so.

"If I was gonna kill you, I'd've done it with the lights off," Blayd snorted, tossing the bundle he carried onto the shabby mattress where Switz crouched. The contents of his other hand, a takeaway box perfuming the air with the rich aroma of something fried, was set on the stand next to the bed. Switz crabbed away warily, watching, waiting for the springing of a trap.

"Eat up and put that on. Got a job for you, assuming you want it."

Switz opened the takeaway and pulled out the first fried morsel of meat his fingers locked around. Not rat. Rat had been the primary source of meat to be had in the Core. He would have known if that was what this was. "Who do I gotta kill?" he mumbled around bite after bite of nourishment he expected to be yanked from his hands.

"Who said I wanted you to kill anyone?"

"You read my file." Blayd had not said it, but Switz was sure he had done so in the hours since they had last seen one another. It was what Switz would have done if their positions were reversed.

"You're a doctor…or you were." It was the primary reason Blayd was here. A killer he did not need. A doctor, on the other hand, one who owed him his life, was something he could use. "I've got someone who needs looking after."

"Someone you can't take to a medi." Switz's tone dripped with irony at the offer.

"Taking him anywhere would cause problems he doesn't need. He's got a caretaker, but it's a two-man job; I need a second. He can't be left alone. He's sedated, but it can't be healthy to stay like that."

Madman then. Or terminally ill. Sounded like a simple enough responsibility. "What do I get out of it?"

"Three a day…a roof…a few ticks if you keep your nose clean and do what needs doing, what I say. You stay out of lock-up." Blayd watched Switz eat and did not speak again until the takeaway box was empty. "I know who you are…what you did. You don't want the bugorra to know you're loose…"

"Bugorra?"

"Use to be Crows; not anymore. New name, same job." He had no time or interest in explaining events Switz had missed during his incarceration. Reeducating him was not Blayd's job. "You owe me…but I also owe you." He rubbed the side of his neck, now clean and properly bandaged. "Do this and they'll have no reason to find where you are."

Still crouched, Switz opened the tied bundle and pulled out a woven sweater, trousers, a secondhand hemp slicker, a hat, suitable underclothing, and a pair of tall, waterproof shoes. Nothing expensive, he guessed, but functional, appropriate for the damp, without enabling him to spend too long comfortably outside in it. It would keep him dry enough from this room to wherever Blayd wanted to take him, but he was not likely to run off for extended periods without finding himself wet and miserable.

The offer, however, was a good one, the best a man just out of lockup and without prospects, ticks, or friends, could expect. It would do until he found something better, something more suited to his tastes…if such a job existed.

He pulled the sweater over his head, adjusted it over his boney torso, and quickly finished dressing in the rest of the ensemble, assuming that his acceptance of the gift was answer enough, assuming Blayd would have taken it back otherwise.

"Well?"

Switz cocked his head at the merc with a smirk. Maybe he was not so bright if he missed what Switz considered an obvious answer. Or maybe he wanted a spoken agreement so that there was no mistaking intent between them. A spoken, binding contract.

Easier to get out of, Switz decided, then a written one.

"I'll do it." He did not need to see the patient first to accept the work. He only needed a temporary job to get himself reestablished.

"Follow me…and whatever you see, whatever you hear, keep your mouth shut about it. Understood?" He had another he could trust, but until he found him, Switz would have to do.

The corners of Switz's mouth crooked wryly. "Understood.

⤳*⤲

It was good to see Ginna in Vapors rather than trapped with the Core kids. She seemed to have made it her mission to foster them, to teach them, to recruit them into the Spinks on Scarecrow's behalf, but that was no life for a young woman barely past school age herself. Enoch consoled himself with the knowledge that surrogate parenting and a swiver's job were better than the life of a streeter. And for the rescued children, being surrounded by Spinks who knew how to survive meant that they were as safe as they could be when Ginna could not be with them. So long as they did not venture into Hebenon alone, they would learn to adapt and learn to survive.

They could not remain trapped in the hostel where they were hiding; sooner or later they had to be introduced to the lure of Hebanthe Falls. So long as they avoided the siren calls of Heb, alcohol and a life of crime, their prospects were brighter than they had been inside the Core.

He glanced at his chrono again as Ginna poured another drink from the nearly empty bottle he had requested and smiled. To anyone else, it was the swiver doing her job.

To Enoch, it was a look reassuring him that things would be fine.

But where the cazz was Lash? Where were the others?

Enoch had been told where each one of those he had worked with to save the lives of some from the Core had gone. Two were in Jaron's flat, hiding as they recovered. Two were in Doctor Tamner's care. The others had returned to their daily routines as if nothing had happened. On the surface, only the increased activity of the brako, bugorra, and the Igraci had been changed by the events of that night, but as Enoch pushed his long curls from his face and rubbed the back of his neck, he could feel smaller changes creeping over them like errant drops of moisture trickling along exposed skin.

Lash had said there was news.

So far, the spindly blonde had not arrived to share it.

A shadow passed over him, behind him, and Enoch growled without looking up, hoping to impress on whoever had taken the stool to his left that he preferred to be alone. If it belonged to a hook or random drinker, they paid no attention to his suggestion, and though Enoch did not raise his head, he knew the individual had summoned a drink when Ginna set a glass on the counter.

"Hello, Ginna. How nice to see you. It's been some time."

Enoch scowled at the voice though not at the words or the tone or the man's recognition of Ginna. The man knew a lot of people: it was the nature of his position. But he juddered and forced himself not to look when the voice continued, "I have a proposition for you."

Ginna had moved off, deigning not to speak to the man who called her by name. Whoever was seated on the Senior's other side slid their stool further away. Those closest began to speak in whispers.

The man's words were not for Ginna, but rather for the dwarf.

"I don't accept propositions from kidnappers," Enoch grumbled. "Trying to drink in peace here. Alone."

Kal chuckled, the note of it dark and pained, and shifted on his stool to face the room teeming with patrons here to drink, socialize, or watch the andi floorshow that was, judging by the flicker and flash of multicolored lights across the raised dance platform, about to begin. Kal expected public reaction wherever he went, especially in a place like this since the Voices condemned excessive drinking, Heb use, and the overindulgences found in places like Vapors. The Senior's presence in such places made patrons uncomfortable.

After the earlier prodcast, too many people stared as if he would stoop to kidnap or harm the Founder of Hebanthe Falls, the Founder of his faith, the one at the heart of everything the Senior stood for.

He expected to be given a wide berth but the suspicion and hatred were annoyances he was going to have to live with for now and eventually address.

"A man shouldn't drink alone." He chose not to speak of excess or kidnapping. Those things were not why he was here.

"A man shouldn't drink with people he doesn't like."

Kal shrugged. "You don't have to like me. No one does. Just hear what I have to say."

"How about I don't." Enoch wiggled off the stool, the wait for Lash aborted by the unwelcome company. Kal finished his drink in a single gulp and stood as well, intent, it seemed, on following Enoch out of Vapors. Others were staring, whispering, pointing, and the thought of leaving with Kal, the possibility that there were other Talkers, or worse, waiting outside, or that people would talk about his departure in the Senior's company, made him feel uneasy and ill.

Or maybe that was the alcohol.

"I can expose you, you know…to all of them." Kal made no gesture but Enoch knew what he meant without a waving hand or sweep of his arm. "I'm asking for a minute of your time and for you to give thought to what I ask."

"I could expose you too, claim to have proof you're a kidnapper," Enoch growled, hand on the stool, debating climbing up again, standing where he was, or leaving.

"You don't…"

"I could claim it," he repeated.

Eyes narrowed, Kal hissed, "You wouldn't dare."

Accusations against a Senior were dangerous things. Enemies of the Voices had often been viewed as enemies of the Founder, the Doctet, enemies of the city. Maybe the bugorra, Captain Grainger, and the Nau would not trouble Enoch over it except to subject him to a barrage of questions about what he knew. But the Senior had allies, including the brako, he suspected, that Enoch did not want to run afoul of. He wanted to be left alone.

He growled in irritated surrender. "Fine. I'm listening." It was preferable to leaving the security of Vapors' in the man's company.

"You're the only one now. The only one fit to lead Hebenon."

"You've seen to it, haven't you? In case you haven't noticed…" Enoch gestured up and down his body with both hands, explaining the obvious counter without uttering a word.

Odds were, the people would never accept a dwarf, no matter the blood in his veins.

Ignoring the gesture, Kal lowered his voice so that no one nearby could hear him, although now that the first andi-dancer had taken his place on stage, the blare of music and his movement had reduced the likelihood that anyone was paying attention to the Senior.

"You're the only surviving male Kem…"

"The Founder is…"

"…thus the only one suitable to…"

"Look at me!"

"With our support…"

"Our?"

"…that won't matter…"

"He's alive…and I wouldn't want it, even if what you say is…"

"Every man wants his birthright." Kal had wanted his, had embraced it, from the day he was old enough to understand the promise life in the Voices held. "Only a fool would…"

"…would think you could deliver anything you say, anything you offer…could take you at your word…would want the burden of…"

"As I said, we will support you, back you, protect you…"

"The way you protected him?"

Their heated discussion was attracting the attention of the security detail at the door and of the people around them. Kal was wise enough to know that he would be seen as the aggressor, the threat, to the dwarf he towered over. Whatever the Ximenezes' intent with their prodcast, their accusations had begun to do their discrediting work, discrediting him, discrediting the Voices. To counter the damage, Kal would either have to produce Haythem Kemway or convince the man beside him to take up the mantle the mad man could no longer carry.

Kal handed his passcard to Ginna so that she could deduct ticks for his drink and then pocketed it casually before speaking again.

"Or we can expose…"

A lean, blonde fellow, sinewy as many Heb addicts but without the sickly pall and shrunken, haunted eyes of addiction, entered through Vapors' door and started towards them. Kal found the appearance of the bruised, battered, limping figure to be distasteful, dangerous, and he adjusted his coat in preparation to leave.

"I'd be exposed either way," Enoch muttered, catching sight of Lash out of the corner of his eye and feeling comfortable enough to resume his place on the stool with his back to the Senior. "I don't want it. I don't want any of it."

"Think about it. It's what's best for Hebenon. You know it." Kal paused as the longhaired man sat on the dwarf's right and met his gaze. Kal cleared his throat. "I won't make the offer again.

"Even if you did, my answer'ld be the same. Don't need it. Don't want it. I'm fine as I am."

The corners of Kal's mouth curled as if he carried a secret as he said, "You won't be," and left the two men at the bar.

The dwarf might not want the offer now, but Kal was confident he would welcome it later. He just needed the right sort of push, the right incentive. With Feena's help, Kal believed he knew exactly what that incentive should be.

❧CHAPTER 7❧

The small windowless warehouse, a space insulated from the damp and cold, was fitted with a variety of metal hooks and rings and shelves along the ceiling and three of the four walls, meant to hold anything the user wished to store. No inquiry had been made about the particulars when he petitioned for the use of this unit. It did not matter. As far as the Nau was concerned, the building was being used for storage during a retrofit of a flat. No one would verify what he was using it for, so long as he did not raise suspicions. No one would care unless the bellowing inside did not cease.

The ever-present churning of water purification and waste processing systems and the hiss and groan of one of Hebenon's many steam producing facilities located near this particular unit seemed the ideal cover for his little endeavor as it meant a backdrop of constant noise he expected would mask his comings and goings and disguise the business conducted within. However well insulated the warehouse was, however much noise the surrounding businesses produced, the roar from the backroom was likely to be noticed if it was not quickly contained. Blayd could hear it as he swiped his passcard through the lock and swore to himself with a growl.

He yanked the door open as soon as the lock clicked and he shoved Switz inside before slamming it again in the hopes of containing the volume. The door between the narrow office space was open when he had left instructions with his sole surviving assistant to keep it closed. Feeding time and an occasional glance into the room to check on their charge demanded occasionally opening it, but nothing warranted the infernal screaming…from either his ward or his partner.

A hand extended through the doorway, on the floor, flexing and clawing like a dying insect. Blayd dropped the bag of nessies picked up along the way on the desk, snatched the injector and buzzer from where they lay beyond the reach of the floundering hand, and toed the fellow's arm out of the way. With a wave for Switz to stay back, stay behind him, he pushed the door open further with his elbow, not knowing what they would find inside.

"Said to keep him…" he began in a condescending tone.

He stopped and stared.

His accomplice stared up at the ceiling from where he had fallen, blood bubbling from his lips, from his nose, and from the side of his neck where a good-sized chunk of flesh had been ripped away. If he was trying to speak, if the movement of his mouth was an effort to produce words, the only sound was a sickening sort of death rattle that Blayd had heard before.

"What in the name of…?" He aimed the injector at the only other person in the room.

The man bound hand and foot to rings on the wall with lengths of chain and hemplastic binding ties, head hanging forward but with his face uptilted to watch their entry with penetrating, clear eyes, had been yowling and snarling like a feral beast until Blayd, with Switz right behind him, stepped into the room. He seemed unaware of the blood, spittle, and pink foamy froth that dribbled down his bearded chin as he mumbled to himself.

"What's he…?" murmured Switz, certain the man looked familiar though without knowing any reason why he should be. As long as Switz had been in the Core, he did not think he would recognize anyone in Hebenon anymore.

"Counting." Blayd did a quick visual examination of the bound man, whose wrists bore evidence of bruising from extended toil against the ties, enough so that he might have cracked the bones. Blayd was not willing to get close enough to check. His eyes were wild, bloodshot, his face flushed with exertion. The round scorch mark at the side of his neck suggested an attempt to use the buzzer's charge against him.

To subdue him, Blayd wondered with a frown, or to torture him?

The paunchy middle-aged man on the floor had needed to get close to use the buzzer. Too close, as it had allowed the Founder to rip flesh from the man's neck with his teeth.

If the other man had wanted to subdue their uncooperative charge, the injector would have been a better choice. It seemed the addled Founder was as much a danger to others as he was to himself, just as Grainger claimed. Binding him had been a wise decision. Trying to get close enough to use the buzzer had not.

Now Blayd would be forced to recruit someone else to assist in the Founder's care. There was only one good choice he could think of. If the spidery man stayed on, Blayd doubted he would be able to manage Kemway by himself. He needed to sleep too.

"He's not well…incoherent most of the time…out of his mind the rest." Blayd thought that should be obvious. As he and his henchman now on the floor had dragged the Founder here from the Uppers, dressing him in a bugger's attire as well and claiming he was being taken to a medi whenever they passed someone who might ask questions, Blayd had not imagined the limp, compliant man to be capable of this level of violence.

But he had tried to prepare for the possibility of it; with the truly mad, it was always best to be prepared.

"Let. Me. Go." The captive lunged at the small man who had taken a wary step closer. Blayd caught Switz's arm and yanked him back.

Switz stumbled and landed on the floor.

Kemway uttered a clipped, maniacal burst of laughter.

Nor had Blayd imagined those words interspersed within the rhythm of Haythem's counting or the laughter that followed.

Had Grainger lied? Was there still a man, the Founder, beneath whatever concoction of substances the captain had his medis feeding the man for the last two years?

What other tortures had they inflicted?

Maybe a doctor, a man like Switz, was the best choice after all.

"Wouldn't get too close." Blayd glanced at the dead man, the wheels at the rear of his mind already picking apart the best means for disposing of the corpse. To the Founder, who was now wheezing, snuffling, and growling, he grunted, "Be quiet."

Haythem tipped back his head and bayed like a hound.

"Unless you want the stinger?" Blayd waved the injector in the Founder's direction and the man hissed like a cornered rattler.

"What am I supposed to do with that?" Switz thrust a finger at the bound man as he struggled to his feet.

The threat produced no other reaction from Kemway but Switz's voice made the captive cock his head and stare. The hissing ended in a grumbling growl and he licked his lips with an expression of ravenous hunger.

Believing his point was made, Blayd shoved the injector through the waistband of his trousers. Perhaps part of the Founder was there, but he was obviously quite mad too. That had not been a lie. Any sane man would have complied with the thread of sedation in favor of being unchained. He would make an effort to gain his captors' trust.

But there was no reasoning with the mad.

"You're the doctor. Watch him. Feed him. Help him if you can. Clean up after him. Sedate him when it's necessary."

For a man supposedly out of his mind, the snarl at those last words hinted that they were understood.

"He should be in a facility…"

"He was…but he wasn't safe. Too many want him dead, so I brought him here. If he goes back, they'll kill him…so he stays."

"How long?"

Blayd shrugged. "Long as necessary, for his own good, his own protection. Once he starts coming around, gets back to himself…"

He shrugged again, ignoring the dark eyes that focused on him with familiar intensity. Blayd had seen that look on Founder prodcasts hundreds of times. Kemway was not struggling to be free any longer but the bindings were pulled tight, stretched to move him as far from the cold wall, as close to the other two men, as possible.

"How do I feed him if he's like that?"

Huffing, Blayd waited for an opportune shot and fired the injector at his target. A clean hit made the Founder jerk sideways away from the needle's sting. He yowled. Blayd wished he had thought to close the storage room door. In his thrashing, Kemway knocked the dart from his chest so that it clattered across the floor and stopped at Switz's feet. Enough of the sedative had entered his bloodstream to make him drowsy, to cause his muscles to twitch and grow weak, to make him relax and bring his struggling animal sounds to an end.

Only when he was quiet did Blayd let go of a long groan of relief and frustration.

"You'll figure it out. When he's hungry, he'll comply. We'll break him if we have to…"

"This isn't a dog! This is a man!"

But Switz had seen men like this, broken men inside the Core, broken men outside before his arrest. Sometimes the only way to subdue and contain them was to gain their trust, make them dependent for their survival needs. Sometimes a man's spirit, his mind, was too far gone for that. When the brown eyes turned on him again, narrowing, studying him, Switz did not think that would be the case with this one.

There were life and spirit in there still It would be Switz's job to coax it out of him.

For the sake of some ticks, for meals and shelter, he would try. If he did not like it, if he could not make the man cooperate without torture, he could always leave him for another keeper to handle.

Blayd knew they could not keep the Founder sedated. He did not think it would be healthy and coming up with that much of any strong sedative was likely to raise flags in the Source…unless he went black market. He could not afford the ticks for that without Mam Kemway's support. With free time on his hands now, he could freelance it, trade favors for what he needed, but he did not want to be beholden to anyone, did not want anyone to ask questions, while the Founder was in his care. He could not risk anyone finding the man here.

There was always Heb, of course, easy to come by and plentiful, but he doubted it would work without supplying debilitating doses.

"He doesn't know what he is, who he is, where he is. Keep him alive…and if he gets loud or violent there's this." He waved the now empty injector at Switz. "Stingers in the desk if you need them. Just don't unbind him…unless you want to end up like that." He thumbed towards the body on the floor. "And don't let him out of your sight unless I'm here to relieve you."

"How do I sleep? Eat? Where do I shit?" Switz followed Blayd's gaze towards a corner of the room, empty without a bucket or grate to dispose of waste.

Both men frowned.

"I'll take care of it. Don't let him out of this room…and don't leave the building if I'm not here."

Switz snorted, not quite believing him but having little choice. If he wanted the job, he accepted the conditions, until something better presented itself.

"What do I call him?"

Blayd was already retreating through the middle door, the details of sleeping arrangements and toilet facilities in mind as well as the disposal of the dead. He debated the folly of giving Switz an honest answer but decided that, as long as the man had been a prisoner, in the Core or anywhere else, there was no way Switz would know who this man was, even if he gave a name.

"Haythem."

A first name did not matter. Every Founder spawned a host of children in the Levs sporting the same name. A first name would not reveal anything.

He toed the body aside and closed the door without checking to see if the fellow was alive. There was nothing he could do for him if he was dead, and if he lived still, he would be dead soon enough. Blayd turned on the Echo T2 on the desk, set the volume to the maximum so that the running prodcast would drown out any further noises…and might serve as an explanation for the earlier ruckus should anyone come prying, seeking answers for the screams.

There was no blood on his shoes or clothes. The injector was stuffed with the discarded buzzer into the desk drawer after wiping it clean of prints. The bag of nessies he had brought, a stylus and writing pad, a desk alglamp that offered more light than the neon from the adjoining shed barely visible through the facility's grungy window, and a small potted plant were left scattered on the desk as evidence of an office being set up.

It would look as if someone was arranging new business. He hoped it would satisfy nosy neighbors or curious buggers.

Inside the storage room, as the bound man's head drooped forward against the effect of the sedative and his body sagged in its bindings, a grin slowly crept over Switz's face, a knowing sort of plotting grin.

"Haythem."

He knew now why the man looked familiar. But why, he wondered, was the Founder here, like this, in this condition? What had happened in Hebanthe Falls while he had been captive to warrant this?

The whys did not matter. Ultimately they were unimportant.

The only important thing was the possibility of power and influence that came with that name, that might come to a man who could heal the Founder's addled mind with kindness and care.

"You and me are gonna be good friends," he murmured with a chuckle as he rubbed his hands to warm them and stepped away from the body on the floor.

Very good friends indeed.

❧CHAPTER 8❧

Tamner rubbed his face and tried to look at everyone and no one around the conference table with him, members of the newly appointed and elected Nau that had replaced the defunct Doctet. These men and women, chosen from the leading figures in their fields or because of popular support by the people of Hebenon, served as heads of business and production, just as the Doctet had done and Tamner found himself seated with them where he did not want to be. He was one of the few to have been appointed here, appointed because of both his extensive medical and scientific knowledge and because, of all of those in the city, he was the only one to have gained the trust and support of both Hebenon's residents and the parah of Marbordo.

It was his work with the parah, as physician and liaison, that was called upon now.

"I don't think it is a bad thing…" he began.

"Production is here," Andre Nunn countered. One of the few members of the original Doctet to survive the Factory Plague, his family had been at the forefront of glass production since the city's erection and thus instrumental in the manufacture of the solar systems the city needed to survive. He too had been appointed by Grainger to the Nau, along with Delora Carville, who had been the education officer for so long that few could imagine the city without her. The other six members of the nine-person governing body had been elected and hailed from the Levs. Though many in the Uppers, accustomed to being the sole governing body, fretted about being outnumbered in representation, Tamner agreed with Grainger's decision.

The Levs contained the greatest percentage of the city's population. They deserved greater representation than they had ever had. Grainger had resisted the lure of appointing himself to the Nau; his attendance was strictly for matters of peacekeeping, oversight to keep the city running while the Nau deliberated, and occasionally to break a stalemate when the Nau was incapable of reaching a decision.

He was not here today. Tamner felt the weight of his absence too heavily on his shoulders.

"Production can easily move Outside," he pointed in the direction of the world beyond the city's shell, a world he doubted Nunn had visited or seen except through the windows of the now open dome. At least Delora had gotten up the courage to set foot beyond the walls to witness the world humanity had long ago lost. "It will take constructing infrastructure…"

"It will take too long to…"

"The world is changing, Andre. No one is arguing to cease production here while it does…but for those willing to expand, build a life in this new world, we have to start somewhere…"

"It's dangerous. The parah are dangerous."

"Less dangerous than the brako. Outside is no more dangerous than in here…just the dangers are different. I've not been threatened by a parah…"

"Nor have I," injected a mousy woman whose plain face and basic fashion sense belied the fact that she had risen to the head of cloth production, clothing design, and manufacture since the Coup had claimed her predecessor's life. "Down there, the brako control everything. Have you had to pay protection to do business? To avoid having your goods confiscated? Out there…those I've met…want to learn, want to help."

"How long before that starts out there too?" Some of Nunn's relatives had resided in the Levs where their production facilities were. Many were killed in the Coup. Others had died in the Factory Plague and now the man was cynical and bitter. Each trip he was forced to make into the Levs made him less believing in humanity's continued existence, although he had been lucky thus far to have avoided any clashes, personal or in his business, with the brako. The opening of Outside had killed his bloodline. Remaining inside, as the brako expanded and attempted to claim everything for themselves, seemed better only because it was a familiar world in which to live and die.

Every member of the Nau knew the squabbling had already begun between parah and those from Hebenon as centuries of ingrained superiority to anything that could have survived outside of the city created friction between both sides.

"They're afraid…everyone's afraid…and fear breeds violence. I'm doing what I can to ease the transition, to prevent segregation, territorial clashes…" Tamner began.

"Perhaps we should regulate emigration, allow the parah and those already Outside to adapt and adjust…?"

Delora's suggestion was not the worst one Tamner had heard, but he did not see how the Nau could regulate curiosity, regulate exploration, expansion, and change. Limiting the passage of Prossers and Crossers would, he believed, fan the flames of discontent. After centuries of the Kemways' chokehold on personal freedoms, after generations in a dark, damp world, locking everyone inside, now that the world was open, would likely result in another Coup.

Hebenon would not survive a second.

Better to continue their efforts to manage the interactions between the outnumbered parah and those seeking a new life than to entrap everyone inside Hebanthe Falls.

"That would be a step backward."

"What would the Founder do? Captain Grainger?"

Nunn's bitterness, the man always a steadfast ally and supporter of the Kemway family, was no surprise.

"If the Founder was here, there would be no Outside to explore," Delora gently reminded.

Heads around the table bobbed.

"He wouldn't be missing!"

Those same heads bobbed to that statement as well.

Ignoring the issue of Kemway's absence, having nothing to report and feeling it was not his place to do so, Tamner shrugged. "The captain will return soon." Grainger had made yet another summons of Tamner's time, another demand for release from the medi-ward. If he was healthy enough to continue making those demands, he was likely well enough to resume duty within the constraints of the injuries that would take longest to heal.

Given everything at risk, Tamner did not expect to put the captain's request off much longer.

Given that he wanted to keep hidden his part in the Founder's previous care and location and moving him the night he had been abducted, reinstating Grainger would be for the best. The city, the Nau, wanted his leadership. So long ruled by the voice of a single individual, the effort to distribute power among nine was proving a painful, unsteady thing.

"For now," Delora continued, "we can't allow scandal or slander to rule our prodcasts. We need guidelines, controls, regulations…"

"Go back to a single man's control of news?" someone retorted.

"Someone who can lie to us as they did about the Outside?"

"Never!" exclaimed another. "They can't hide those people forever. Someone needs to…"

"What people?" grunted Nunn.

"Ones in quarantine…brought out of the Factories…"

"The plague has returned?"

Tamner rubbed his face and groaned. After having lost so many lives in the Factories, it was understandably frightening to think the plague had returned, especially since the rumors of such things often burned into a panic before the truth could be told.

"You mean brought out of the Core?" Delora was one of the few to believe in the Core's existence. As chief education officer, she might have had information others did not, but few were inclined to probe too deeply into the truth.

"It's plague, I tell you. The parah have…"

"We should seal the Factories…"

"And kill production?"

"The Core is not…"

"Please!" Tamner raised his voice to be heard over the threads of argument, bringing silence to the room. Fearful faces looked at him expectantly. He too had lost people to the Plague. He was a doctor, a scientist. He had studied the plague, its effect, its cure. If anyone had cause to be concerned, Tamner did.

"There is no plague. I've examined those brought up from Factory East; none of them show any symptoms…"

"Then why are they in quarantine?"

Admitting that they were prisoners, that he had been at ground zero of the explosions that had rocked the city and incapacitated Captain Grainger and killed others, would raise as many questions as it would answer. Questions Tamner had no answers for.

"There was a wall collapse. We don't know what contaminants the dust and rock and earth might contain. Many were injured. It is best, until they recover and we are sure they are healthy, to keep them isolated. The captain will speak with them before they are released; he will be on his feet soon and…"

"The captain is not our authority, Doctor," grunted Nunn. "We need to go in there, see for ourselves…"

"Are you willing to take that risk?" Delora challenged. "If there's a structural problem…or contagion…we'd be risking our lives."

"What if it's plague that hasn't manifested?" charged another. "You should go in, Doctor. Run your tests. Let us know we're safe."

Tamner's eyes narrowed a little, thinking he was being offered as a sacrifice to whatever evil the Nau feared had been released. But because he knew there was no plague, no contagion, no need to be afraid, he let the expression fade without speaking.

"If it's necessary to relocate Factory East because of a structural hazard," someone murmured, "to Outside…it's going to take time. A lot of time. Production will be lost. Contingencies have to be made…plans coordinated. We have to know it's safe, if the Factory can continue operations."

Groaning again, Tamner kept his expression calm. He did not want to be the one to provide these answers, to be the voice the others turned to for reason and wisdom. He did not want to be the decision-maker. He had come to expect it when it came to issues regarding the parah as he had fallen into place as the emissary between worlds. Here, inside Hebenon, in matters Grainger had managed since the Founder's fall, Tamner did not feel competent or prepared. He understood the science, the logistics, the value of it all. He was good with people. But he did not fancy himself a leader.

The Nau wanted direction, however. Wanted guidance. They wanted, needed, a voice they could trust.

By a twist of fate, Tamner had become that voice.

"I'll send someone with a survey team to evaluate the situation, the structural integrity of Factory East, seek evidence of contagion. We will hear their reports at our next meeting. Will that suffice?"

Most bobbed heads in agreement. Nunn grunted and folded his arms over his chest and muttered, "And what about the Founder?"

That was a question Tamner could not answer. He did not have answers, good or bad. He had no idea where the Founder was, who had him, or if anyone would ever see him again.

He did not believe Grainger had those answers either.

❧*❧

"Wait here," the redhead said in a low, awed voice to the man confined to the anti-grav chair, clasping his shoulder affectionately before taking his first steps into a world that he, like everyone else, had only ever dreamed they would see. Rhyd had seen it already, had been here before.

Skelter never had.

The chair was loaned to Colyx when the big man was released from the medi-ward. He refused to use it during most of his waking hours, despite Tamner's admonition that he should. For this venture to the Outside door, Rhyd had resisted using it as well, had resisted leaving Jaron's flat to come here, to face what he knew was waiting. He was reluctant to go near the one person he could not bear to see.

But Skelter could be very persuasive. He had promised a drink afterward and the opportunity to assess the state of the city had gradually convinced Rhyd to accompany him this far. Jaron's desire to see the Outside had been an additional contributing factor to Rhyd's decision. Allowing Jaron to venture alone into a world where he might be a target was unthinkable.

Rhyd would have preferred to walk but his strength had not fully returned and his leg barely supported him. Giving the appearance of weakness by accepting the chair lent credence to his absence from shift and might lull anyone who chose to attack into a false sense of security. Injured or not, anyone who tried would fail.

Despite his curiosity and his desire to see more, however, Jaron elected to remain with Rhyd in the doorway as Skelter and Otta, also released from Tamner's care and eager to see this miracle, stepped into the world of glistening splendor beneath the full moon.

Rhyd wished Jaron would go, would see the world for himself.

He was oddly comforted that the dark-haired man chose not to.

Skelter, being Skelter, wasted little time in procuring what he wanted from the parah who recognized Rhyd in that doorway and welcomed his friends as their own and hastened to offer whatever the redhead needed. The elevated status Rhyd had earned by returning Agnys to them, for opening the city to more extensive trade and the passage of people in and out made him uncomfortable and contributed to his decision to stay where he was, watching from the shield Hebenon provided as Skelter positioned the double-layered fire pot where he wanted it. He lit the twigs and peat beneath it, waited for the fire to rage with Otta at his side staring with fascination at the sea.

Outside had been a story to those in the Core. A myth. Born within the Core, not even Hebanthe Falls had been real to Otta.

Rhyd remembered his awe the first time he had come here. He recalled the stunning moment when the newness of green fields and wide sky had blinded him…and returned what had been too long lost.

He remembered the rawness of that pain, remembered how it had felt to see Venn after so long apart, only to nearly lose him again to the popper shot surely intended for Scarecrow.

That rawness had never healed. Its flame still burned at the center of his soul, keeping him in Hebenon's shadows.

Rhyd could not see him clearly, the figure in the doorway of the home they were meant to share, but he knew Venn was there. If he tried he could imagine Venn's expression, bitter, resentful, full of regret, remorse, and anger. Anger for Rhyd missing the recital. For Rhyd bringing Jaron here. For Rhyd being who, and what, he was.

That was what hurt the most, Venn's resentment and inability to accept who Rhyd was now, who he had become. Could he help that he had changed when Venn was Taken, that the world had changed him?

Did he want to change?

Maybe he should go down there. Try one more time to explain.

He did not move.

The chair kept him where he was, he thought in stubborn self-defense. The grav chair would not work over the grass and soil where there were no metal floors to repel the magnetic system. Rhyd could stand, could trudge around Jaron's flat for longer each hour as his body mended, but he was not yet steady enough to walk so far over uneven, spongey, rocky ground. Crossing between this door and the village over the muddy earth was more exertion than Rhyd felt ready to make. He tried to argue otherwise, but his throbbing leg and unwillingness to confront Venn won the internal argument with his stubbornness.

He needed the chair.

He did not need an argument.

He watched Skelter toss items one by one into the flames.

The cards. The cards and the Spade tokens.

The secretive Spades might still exist in Hebanthe Falls, but the fragment of the organization that had existed within the Core was gone. Skelter was, as far as he knew, the last member.

And Skelter lived.

The ICD on Rhyd's wrist buzzed and he looked away from Skelter, from the rising moon, paying attention to Agnys' arms around his shoulders, the girl comfortable on his lap after having been careful not to hurt him to get there. He glanced at the incoming message, resisted the frown tugging at his lips, and looked one more time at Skelter sharing an embrace with the woman at his side.

Rhyd was happy for him. He was not, however, happy about the figure that disappeared from the hut's doorway, or the man behind him whose fingers brushed accidentally across the back of his shoulder, reminding Rhyd he was there.

Not that Rhyd could forget.

Perhaps not so accidentally.

"Got to go," Rhyd murmured, helping Agnys down. He assumed Jaron had told Tamner that he was awake and mobile. The doctor wanted to see him but Rhyd did not intend to oblige him, for therapy or anything else. "Tell Skelter I'll see him later."

He wanted only to escape and find refuge in the bottom of a bottle of Zaolei. He did not want to wait for Skelter to join him in Vapors.

He did not feel ready for that degree of socialization. He wanted to drink alone…or as alone as Jaron's company in the flat would allow.

❧*❧

It was only snippets she heard, morsels she gleaned from behind the bedroom door or crumbs snatched when her mother answered her ICD before stepping into another room or out onto the walkway outside the flat. It was never enough information to form a picture of events, but it was enough for Ulynda to begin to piece together an ugly, frightening picture of a world she did not know how to process.

That her father was missing from wherever her mother had gone to visit him was evidenced by the speculative prods her mother always turned off or prevented her from seeing by sending her out of the room when they aired. He was not dead, not like they believed before, but missing or dead, Ulynda did not believe she would ever see her father again. There was a glut of ignorance in the prodcasts, rumors, speculation, and made-up details that she could not believe, but Ulynda felt confident of one thing.

Her mother knew where her father was. Knew who had taken him. May have even had a hand in his abduction.

Maybe her mother meant to protect him from people who wanted to hurt him. Ulynda had grown up believing the Founder was beloved of everyone but since the Coup, she had learned otherwise. Some hated him, his family, hated everything the Kemways stood for. Some did not care one way or the other. If those who hated him wanted to hurt him, her mother was right to protect him.

But if that was the truth, Ulynda thought with a frown as the door of their flat opened and closed and the soles of her mother's heeled shoes clacked across the floor, causing the girl to quickly close files on her Echo she was not meant to see, why did her mother deny it? Why did she hide what she knew, the way Ulynda was forced to hide her quest for information and replace it with the open pages of studies she had already completed?

Her door opened. Her mother peered inside, smiled approvingly at Ulynda's studiousness, and closed it again.

He was her husband. She had the right to help him.

He was Ulynda's father. She had the right to see him, to know the truth and expect answers.

Why, if she was protecting him, did she not bring him home?

❧*❧

Duty was duty, and though Lieutenant Young had never been in the Factories or beneath them, and though the order was not given by Captain Grainger, she went where she was commissioned. The Nau's request bore the same weight as the captain's, particularly when he was not available to countermand it. If they had concerns about the underpinnings of the Factories, someone with authority needed to calm those fears.

She was no engineer but the man accompanying her was. Together they passed through the first level of Factory East, to the lift and down into the spread designed as the living arena for those assigned to work the Factories. The walkways and corners and unused spaces of the Factory were still crowded with families who had not yet returned below; they were not impeding production, but Ilya knew they should not be there. Without knowing what she would find, what kept them from going back down, she did not attempt, yet, to make them move.

That would come later, after she learned the state of things.

She could have complained about this duty or resisted it while the Founder was still missing. But there were many nagging questions about what had happened to the captain, where those in quarantine had come from, questions he seemed disinclined to answer, and she hoped that going to the now disclosed sight of his conflict herself would tell her what she wanted, what she felt she had a right and need, to know.

The area below the factories was mostly empty, with only the cafeteria open and drawing the hungry in small anxious groups to either dine at the tables there or else take their meals back up to the Factory floors. Like those above, people cast the lone bugorra and the suited man beside her curious, wary, frightened glances but they did not speak or ask why she was there. They looked to be keeping a secret, more nervous and anxious the nearer she got to the epicenter of the below-ground events.

There was no visual evidence of an uprising. The workers seemed cowed but not battle-scarred. Ilya began to think that, whatever had happened was not what she had been led to believe. Maybe it had not been down here at all.

At the head of the passage where the chain-metal fence was still unlocked, still swung open, the collapsed mound of stone and earth at the far end was accessible to anyone. There was blood spattered across the ground, on the stones where bodies had fallen to later be removed. If someone had carried them away, it meant there were witnesses, witnesses who had not come forward.

The stench of death filled the air as if birthed beneath the collapse.

Bugorra had been killed here. But who else?

Ilya did not need an engineer's report to conclude that what she saw was not a natural collapsing of earth, although she had never witnessed such a thing. It would be convenient to assume a collapse had occurred during the quake. From the patterns of stone and dust, it would also be convenient to assume that the force of collapse had blown outward…from whatever was behind the rubble.

"I don't believe…" began the engineer as he took another step.

Ilya grabbed his arm and held up her other hand to silence him, listening again for something she had not expected to hear.

Something she should not hear.

Knees and hands trembling, she brought her ICD to her mouth, pressed a sequence on the face, and waited.

"Tamner."

"Lieutenant Young. Doctor…you should come down here."

"Why?"

"I think," she murmured in a strained voice, detecting the anxious note in his single word question, "something's alive in there."

❧Chapter 9❧

He had been here the night it happened, to see to the removal of Grainger and the other wounded from the vicinity of the collapse without asking why or how it had happened. He had been here to oversee the collection of the dead, until there were no more bodies to remove. Before his return to the medi-ward where the wounded had been taken, he was summoned to the Levs for an equally important duty. His staff was entrusted with the wounded officers and motley collection of filthy, emaciated people they were given, left with strict instructions that they were not to discuss what they saw, or learned, or suspected, with anyone but him.

They were trusted to do their jobs and obey orders, but they were not trusted with the life of the man he was summoned to help.

Scarecrow.

It had not occurred to him at the time that there could be anyone alive on the other side of that collapse.

It had not occurred to him that those Grainger and his bugorra had clashed with were from the other side, from the bowels of the earth.

There was no reason it should have. The details of those secrets, of the Core, the mines, were things kept from the majority in Hebanthe Falls. Only the Founder and a handful of others had known the truth.

Most of those were dead.

Standing beside Lieutenant Young, listening to the scratching and banging, sounds of something trying to claw out of the earth, into the air, Tamner berated himself for not investigating sooner. For not coming back.

"I want this cleared. All of it. Any workers not on shift are to move all of this until whoever's in there is found." Not what. Who. There was more than one person beyond this debris. He was certain of it.

"What if it's not…human?" croaked one of the three supervisors of the West and East Factories.

"What about production?" asked another with a frown.

"Of course they're human," Tamner snapped as the engineer said, "Shouldn't take more than a day…maybe three at most…to get this cleared…with precautions, of course…"

The third foreman asked, "And if it comes down?"

Tamner glanced at the engineer who had just spoken of precautions, the man looking pale and green under the assaulting stench of death. "That's why he'll be here, making sure that doesn't happen. You'll have whatever you need to shore up the walls, the ceiling, to remain safe. I'll have medis on standby for whoever we find…alive or dead…"

As sure as there were living, there were bound to be dead. "Extra rations and ticks for those who contribute their time and labor. Sooner it's cleared, the sooner everyone can return to their homes."

The Factory West foremen were less concerned about that as their workers' living area had not been affected by the collapse. The sliding doors between East and West residential areas, where the underground facility stretched beneath the rivers, rarely opened except to allow for an exchange of crew when higher production demands were required in one of the three Factories. This collapse, the housing issues it presented for Factory East, would eventually hamper production and thus affect the entire city.

Removing the dead would also prevent disease. The plague had strained the workforce, and the city's nerves, enough.

Tamner was right. With adults and older children working to clear the debris and evacuate the dead, the task should not take long.

Workers from the West would be here to help.

"Captain Grainger?"

The doctor glanced at the lieutenant; her sunken eyes looked propped up by the dark circles beneath them as if she had not slept since the recital.

"I'll deal with the captain," he huffed. The Nau had given him authority to handle whatever he found here so long as he reported to them and assured them that everything was in order, that production would not suffer and the city would be safe. If Grainger had a problem with the decision to reopen this passage and rescue anyone caught behind the collapse, Tamner would face it when it came.

"Go home and sleep, Lieutenant. Looks like you need it."

Ilya chose not to protest. The supervisors and the engineer did not need her. They could carry on without her hovering and there were matters elsewhere she needed to address. Sleep was one of them.

"Yes, sir," she mumbled. She did not know if she could sleep, but she would try to tune out the stressors she was struggling with long enough to rest her body and brain.

Tamner intended to try to sort out the potential disaster on his hands presented by this situation as the supervisors moved away to enlist crews for this job.

He hoped that whoever was inside could wait a little longer.

⚭*⚮

Sometime in the last two or three hundred years of Hebanthe Falls' existence, the Igraci had arisen in opposition to much of what the Voices of Faith stood for. Believing in the equality of all and a future that involved returning to the world outside the confines of the city in the falls, the Igraci had, before the Coup, existed primarily through educating others about what the world had been before Hebenon was built and what it could be again. Their goal was to prepare mankind for that change and teach them a variety of skills that would be necessary on the day of their emergence from their shell. They had been a thorn in the Founders' and Voices' sides as they pressed for proof that the Outside was as contaminated as the Kemways and Doctet claimed. They demanded visual evidence, and when presented with images and SCAM footage of a poisoned world, picked apart every shred of it to prove the data was false to a population unprepared to believe their truth.

The Founder, many had believed, would not lie about that.

The Igraci were peaceful, if persistent, and anonymous, most often waging their war from the shadows. They were the players come to expose the truth to kings who did not want that truth exposed.

After the Coup, with the bandages ripped from the long blinded eyes of the people, with the Outside open at last, the Igraci's claims were proven true and their numbers swelled. They began to distribute digital flyers and prods, to stand on street corners with neon sandwich boards proclaiming that the time had come for mankind to ascend into the world. Membership was no longer quite so anonymous, though many still wore the white hooded jackets, masks, and attire when they took their statements to the street. Recruitment was still most often conducted in secret to avoid persecution by the Voices or the harassment of the brako who found them to be a meddlesome eyesore, in the way of their more immediate pursuit of power.

It was no surprise to find the cluster of Igraci, their neon boards flashing, their voices calling for the Ascension, in the street near Vapors' door when Rhyd shuffled through the beaded curtain for the first time since his battle with the river. Skelter, Otta, and Colyx led the way and Jaron followed behind to protect the injured man and aid him if he stumbled. Jaron's proximity was also out of fear, but they had noticed no brako on their way here. It seemed safe, although the appearance of safety did not ease Jaron's mind.

They ignored the Igraci and the Igraci ignored them beyond trying to shove hemp paper flyers into their hands as they passed. Otta, curious about those paper bits, accepted the flyer and shoved it into the pocket of her knee-length hempleather coat. Her father, on the other hand, drove the Igraci back with a snarl and growl, sparing the rest of the group the need to take a flyer.

"Bout time you showed your faces," Maemi exclaimed as she came around the counter to offer first Skelter, and then Rhyd, a welcoming embrace. Seeing them was more satisfying than hearing it from Lash or Enoch. "Table's ready."

Arm around Rhyd's shoulder in a motherly fashion, she steered the group towards a distant corner where Lash, Enoch, and Zara already waited. Zara began to rise upon seeing them but her smile faltered with the notice of Skelter's eye-patch, the walking stick he leaned on, and finally the unfamiliar woman supporting an older man's weight, a woman who seemed unusually close to Skelter as the group reached the table.

Instead of voicing the questions that sprang to mind, Zara pulled out the empty chair next to hers, hugged Rhyd, and then helped him ease into it, Rhyd serving as a suitable buffer between her and the man who had been a protector, partner, and best friend for most of her life.

"Good to see you both," she murmured. She had spoken to Skelter over the comm prior to his escape from the Core but she had not dared believe she would see him again after having thought him dead for the better part of two years.

"Good to be seen," Skelter agreed with a grin and a hand stretched across the table to her. Her hesitancy was noted but he replaced the momentary scowl with his customary impish grin when she did finally squeeze his hand. "Zara…Maemi…Otta and her father Colyx. Think you know everyone else…"

"Except me." Lash offered his hand to the newcomers as Zara nodded to them both. "Call me Lash."

"Usuals all around?" asked Maemi.

Heads bobbed yes in response.

"Bring the bottles," muttered Rhyd, the tension between Skelter and Zara and the proximity of Jaron's anxiety on his other side convincing him he would need the bottle before this meeting ended. It was as much business as it was social and he was neither happy with the social aspect of so many around him nor with the involvement of so many people in business he preferred to handle alone.

"Curlers too…if you've got 'em." The comfort found in those fried morsels would do him good.

"Of course." Maemi squeezed his shoulder, flashed a smile around the table, and hurried off to the bar to fill their requests.

"So…" Skelter was the first to speak once the formality of introductions and orders were behind them. He wanted to put the business aside so that they could focus on celebrating. "Kids?"

Enoch toyed with his empty glass, eyeing the bottle he and Lash had already finished between them as he replied, "Maemi's got them in her hostel. Seemed a good place for now. Ginna and the Spinks," he side-eyed Rhyd, "are staying too, keeping an eye on them, getting them adjusted. Some made it out up top…"

"But they're locked down so I've not gotten an accurate report of how many survived…or who," Lash finished.

Rhyd nodded. Maemi's family had run a hostel for generations, but she had declined that responsibility after her marriage and the inheritance of Vapors from her husband. With her parents gone, and no siblings to claim it, the hostel had remained in her name, sitting vacant. It was big enough for a score of kids to shack in until permanent housing could be arranged or they moved in with families equipped to provide a better life than being a streeter could offer. In the care of Ginna and the Spinks, they would be safe for now.

"Think there's room for a few more?" Skelter's question came as Maemi deposited three bottles of alcohol in the center of their table and a fourth in front of Rhyd. As the glasses followed, Skelter avoided Zara's wounded gaze. No matter what he said, how he said it, what excuses he offered, she knew him. She would know the thoughts he did not speak.

"Otta and Colyx need a place…we could look after the kids til we can reunite them with any family. They know us…"

"Not a bad idea," agreed Enoch.

"Plenty of room," Maemi assured them. "Come see me and I'll get you passes."

Then she was gone, avoiding the awkwardness around the table.

Enoch pushed his glass forward so that Lash could fill it and said, "I'll keep bringing nessies, whatever I can get, until they're set up. Been hittin' up the herpa for shoes and such, but it hasn't been easy to get what they need."

"I can help with that," Skelter assured him. Meeting people's needs, getting what people wanted, was what Skelter did. Between them, he had few doubts they would get what was required.

"Any word about the captain?"

Zara replied without looking at Jaron, without looking at anyone. Only the bottle she picked up and its contents appeared to interest her. "Banged up pretty fierce, but he'll live. Haven't heard more, but I don't think he's been released back to duty yet."

She did not need to reveal that she had been to see him when he had been barely conscious from his injuries, that she had needed to see for herself that the chaos she had participated in creating had not killed or permanently harmed him. Getting information out of the Hub was one of her many talents; there was no reason for anyone to think she had come by her knowledge differently.

"They lost some buggers, I heard, but not as many as they could have…and no one died in Factory East," Lash added.

"That's something." The fewer innocent deaths on Rhyd's conscience, the better. "You got the line?"

Lash nodded. "Tox and I took care of it…much as we could. Nothing to lead back to us."

"Good."

From the sounds of it, their rescue had gone as planned, with no more casualties or hitches than anticipated. Rhyd should have been relieved. There were loose ends from that night that needed tying off, however, and he was in no condition yet to do so.

At Vapors' door, two of the Igraci were bullied back through the curtain and pinned against the bar counter by a bird-faced brako, the thug shoving a finger in the chest of first one and then the other. His distorted voice was loud enough to carry through the throb of music but the din of patron chatter muffled his words. Feeling Jaron's unconscious shift towards him for security, Rhyd considered interfering in what looked to be the start of a violent encounter. As Scarecrow, he would not have hesitated, injured or not.

As Ballard, however, he could not afford the attention.

Colyx, ignoring his wounds, seeing only that two smaller individuals were being bullied by someone larger than either of them, pushed out of his chair and limped across the room. Otta, too, began to rise, but Skelter caught her wrist and held her back.

The brako did not appear armed. If Colyx could not handle this, others were near enough to intervene without Otta risking the pregnancy Skelter had only recently learned about.

They could not hear the verbal exchange. Colyx said something as he wedged himself between the brako and the Igraci. The brako laughed and tried to shove the unsteady man aside. To his surprise, Colyx caught his arm, twisted him around and clasped his other hand on the back of the brako's neck, and threw him headfirst against the metal doorframe.

The beaded curtain clattered and swayed. The beaked mask twisted on the man's head and he slumped to the ground, half in and half out the door, conscious but groaning and barely moving. Colyx replied to whatever Maemi said behind him and then dragged the assailant outside onto the walkway by one arm.

The pair of Igraci, after glancing towards the table from where Colyx had come and saying something to him, scurried out of Vapors.

"We should go," murmured Jaron, his modulated voice raspy with fear, his knuckles white around his half-empty glass.

"We're safe," Rhyd assured him. Maybe the brako would find their man and send others to harass Maemi and her staff, but so long as Colyx, now standing at the door with his arms crossed menacingly over his broad chest, kept watch, and Rhyd remained inside, he did not think the brako would be a threat.

There were too many witnesses. Rhyd did not believe the brako leadership, whoever was in charge now, would be foolish enough to cause trouble in a place the bugorra had declared off-limits.

Or maybe they would take this incident as an invitation for war.

Besides, the swiver behind the bar, Pietro, had just arrived at their table with the plate of curlers. As much as the press of people made him uncomfortable this deep into the room, Rhyd was not willing to leave until the plate was empty…until he felt comfortable that the brako were not coming back.

Skelter clasped Jaron's back warmly and smiled at Otta. "Looks like he's found himself a job. Don't worry, he won't let anyone in."

Jaron, however, did not seem relieved.

❧*❧

Removing the sealed envelope wedged behind the latch, Ilya pushed the door opened and slid into her flat, the cold and silence the evidence she needed to remind her that Ginna was not here, had not been here since their last fight. Ilya wanted to find her, needed to find her, but so many duties layered onto her shoulders meant no personal time to seek her sister, no time to reach out with even an ICD message in the hopes that Ginna would respond.

She should do it now.

But she was so blasted tired.

Maybe, she thought wearily as she turned on the light, dropped the envelope on the ledge at the side of the door, and shrugged out of her uniform coat, she had not attempted a message, and procrastinated doing so now, because she knew Ginna was unlikely to reply. It would be ironic to say she knew her sister that well, when in truth she did not know Ginna at all.

The younger woman was right about that. Ilya had stopped listening a long time ago. It had been too convenient to let life get in the way. Maybe if she had listened more and made fewer demands, Ginna would trust her the way she had when they were children.

Wet boots left by the door with her dripping coat, Ilya trudged to the kitchen to start a kettle of tea and pull an apple from the bowl on the counter. It was not a substantial meal, but it was more than she had eaten in several hours. A little food in her stomach then she would try to avail herself of the sleep Doctor Tamner had ordered.

There were reports to make; her mind began to whir. Reports to read. Her weariness argued that those could wait for an hour or so. Puttering around the kitchen as the water heated, washing mugs and plates, eating the apple and a handful of hempseed crackers that remained in the cupboard did little to fill her stomach or empty her thoughts of the nagging questions that kept picking at her.

What had the captain been doing at the site of the collapse? Who were those people now in custody? Who had died there…and why?

What was the captain not telling her?

The kettle whistled and she filled her mug before snatching the envelope left for her and sank into her desk chair to see what had been left as she savored the hot spiced aromatic beverage. Nothing was written on the envelope and there were no distinguishing marks on the passchip it contained. She had no chip reader on her home terminal, resisting the lure of questionable tech despite the benefits to her job it would offer. But there was a reader on her office Echo, and so her curiosity would have to wait until she returned to duty.

Whatever was on the passchip, if it was not vital enough to deliver in person or through official channels, it could wait a few more hours.

Sleep. Try to reach Ginna. Then return to duty with the hopes that there would be answers to her multitude of questions when she arrived.

❖*❖

"Twice in so short a time? People will talk."

The woman's troubled expression suggested that people talking was the last thing she wanted. She was considering leaving now and Grainger regretted the teasing as soon as he said the words. There was something on her mind that drew pain lines around her mouth and eyes as she pulled the chair nearer to his bed and toyed with the back of it without sitting.

"What is it?" he asked, reaching towards her, ignoring the wincing pain in his shoulder. She did not take his hand and he let it drop.

"I don't…"

The honest answer was that Zara did not know why she was here. Seeing Skelter with another woman should not have bothered her. They had never been a couple in a relationship sense, had never been intimate, and she had seen him with his share of lovers, male and female, in the years she had known him. She had never felt any desire to be romantically involved with him and he had never expressed any similar desire. Yet seeing him with Otta, witnessing his deep feelings for her, had resulted in an unexpected jealous swirl that brought Zara to Oliver's bedside for reasons she could not explain.

She told herself she was here to see if he was better than he had been when she had last seen him.

But that was not the truth.

Fortunately, she was spared the need to say anything when Doctor Tamner entered. He smiled at her, his expression unassuming, without a hint of curiosity, and said, "Hello, Ms. Peru."

Zara flushed, murmured an apology, and backed towards the door.

"I'll come back later; excuse me," she mumbled before squeezing past the doctor into the corridor.

Tamner looked at Oliver with the same curiosity the captain's face expressed. The captain shrugged without offering answers, without asking how the doctor knew the woman who so hastily departed, without revealing how he knew her.

"I hope you've come to release me. I've got things to do." His eyes remained hopefully on the door as the doctor began the examination routine performed so many times in the last few days that the captain had lost track of them.

"Depends. Think you can stay off your feet? You might be healthy enough otherwise, but your leg is still mending and you're weak."

"Plenty I can do at my desk without hobbling around." They were duties he could do from this bed, but staff meetings required privacy he did not have here. In this bed, in this room, he felt trapped.

"Including reassuring the Nau, I hope. They've been on me about your return…looking for someone to tell them what to do, I think. That someone isn't me."

"Sure you're handling it well enough."

Tamner snorted at the off-handed praise, nodding his head now and then in reaction to whatever his exam was revealing. Grainger eventually growled like a petulant child, jerked away from the hands on his shoulder, and huffed, "Enough. It's fine. Am I clear?"

Tamner pulled the man's clean uniform from the dresser where Lieutenant Young had put it some time before. He tossed it onto the bed before making notes on the digital clipboard he brought with him.

"How'd you think he's doing now? Now that he's not medicated?"

Tamner lifted his eyes from the charts, briefly confused until he met Grainger's gaze.

"Can't speculate," he sighed. "Manic maybe. Comatose. Maybe dead." He replaced the stylus in its storage slot and raised his eyes. "Given how he was that night…"

"How he was?"

Grainger had either not read Tamner's report or wanted to hear the words spoken out loud. Feeling like he was repeating himself, he sighed. "There were traces of lucidity as we moved him. He was hearing, seeing, reacting more than before, despite the meds. It wasn't enough of a response to call him sane, or cured, but enough that…"

"That we ought to be worried." Or at least, Grainger thought angrily, enough that he should be worried. If the Founder recovered his memories from the night of the Coup, if he had any recollection of what Oliver had done…if he shared it with anyone outside of the captain's control and influence, there was no telling what sort of backlash or repercussions it could have.

"You tried using requests and purchases for tranqs to find him?" If the Founder shifted into a manic phase, whoever had him would need a way to control him. An unusual sale of stingers might offer clues about where he was. It was the only hope outside of the already active channels, to locate the missing man.

"Not yet. Haven't had time." He had not investigated that path because he did not expect results, but for the captain, he would try. "Get dressed. Discharge orders will be at the desk on your way out."

Grainger grunted. He had work to do. There was no need for further small talk or pleasantries.

As soon as he could, he would reach out to Zara and learn what she had come for. And as he dug into the details of Kemway's abduction, he intended to also determine where the cazz Jaron was.

☙Chapter 10☙

Sleep failed her and the apple, crackers, and tea did little to soothe her stomach or her nerves. She wanted company, someone who was not bugorra, who had no connection to work and duty. There had been little time to cultivate friendships, not even with Ginna. Ilya had rarely engaged in casual or meaningful conversations with her sister even though they had lived their whole lives beneath the same roof. What dialogues there had been were spent struggling to steer Ginna in directions the younger woman had not wanted to go instead of listening to her, learning her hopes, her dreams, or discussing anything lighthearted or fun. Now Ginna was lost to her.

Only one person came to mind for company, attached to the promise of a meal, and so Ilya was here now, in the café where they had previously met, not believing he would show.

When she saw him duck out of the damp, his grin removed her shroud of isolation and made her smile despite her resolve not to.

"Didn't think you'd come." She waved the swiver over to take his drink order.

"Didn't think you'd take me up on the offer," admitted Blayd, his smile matching hers. The swiver reached the table as he removed his coat and hung it over the back of the chair. "Beer, egg drop soup, hemp-seed toast," he said, glancing at Ilya to see if she wanted another drink or was ready to order a meal too.

She raised a brow, nursing the cup of steaming tea the swiver had refilled from her pot, and said, "Same…minus the beer."

The swiver nodded and disappeared into the building. Blayd sat across from Ilya and looked her over.

"You look wrecked."

"Thanks," she snorted with a roll of her eyes.

"No, I don't mean…"

She waved three fingers around her cup, balancing it between the other two. "Know what you mean. You're right. I am beat. Trying to save my ass, my job, find the malakes who took the Founder."

Blayd's expression did not change. "I thought the Voices…"

"We don't know that. Don't' even know who told the Ximenezes that. Talkers disguised as buggers could be anyone. Captain'll be back on duty soon; he's gonna have my head if I don't get results."

He let out a long breath between his teeth as the swiver returned with the beer, two bowls of soup, and a basket of toasted bread. Blayd side-eyed the swiver until she was out of earshot, waving off the offering of additional spices or grated cheese. Once they were alone again, he said, "I get it. Mam Kemway…she thinks she's being blamed for the kidnapping and kicked me to the curb for not protecting him."

"Like you could do anything without knowing where he was…"

Unless, she thought with a flash of suspicion she quickly brushed away, Mam Kemway had revealed her husband's location to her merc.

But he would not have known the route they would take to move him, or the day and hour chosen, and so he did not seem a likely suspect. He was only one man…and surely he would not have the audacity to do something like this to her.

Mam Kemway would not have fired him for such an act of loyalty.

"Right. Think she wants someone to blame…and I'm her target…or else she wants to keep me from getting too close…"

"You think she knows something?"

Blayd shrugged. "Hard to tell with her. She doesn't have the resources she used to. I was her only…dunno how she could have…but I wouldn't put it past her."

He would have preferred to keep the suspicion solely on Kal, but pointing fingers in Mam's direction meant protecting himself. "I'm not down yet…I've got prospects…but things are a little lean…"

Ilya chuckled. "So you want me to pick up the tab." That sounded like the Blayd she had known. He had always been one for making plans, getting the neighborhood kids into mischief, and then not having a way to cover their tracks. He had always expected others to bail him out of trouble.

Most of the time, Ilya had.

"No. No, we're good here," he laughed. "I promised you dinner, such as it is." Soup and bread did not make a meal for him, but it would do to get into Ilya's good graces.

"Just what I need," she assured him, breaking off a piece of toast and dipping it into the thick, still too hot for consumption, broth. It was rich, creamy, and tasted of salt and curry and some manner of meat she did not question.

"So you've no idea where he's been taken? Who has him? I heard someone clocked you? You didn't get a look?"

She shook her head, wondering where he had heard that. "Not through the disguises. The ones left at the scene are running through the system. If they're officers, Talkers…if they've got records…we'll find them. On top of that, there's this business with the Core…"

"What business?" His question was casual, as curious as anyone's would be who had grown up with tales of the Core that they had never believed to be true.

"Never thought the mines…" Again she shook her head. "There's people in there. Gotta clear 'em out. I'd never been there. The captain knows what happened, but no one's talking yet. Something went down. I'm sure Scarecrow's involved but I can't go after him…"

"Makes sense." Meeting her narrowed gaze, he shrugged. "I mean, that the captain would be involved. Finding the Founder's the priority, right? I mean, Scarecrow's not going anywhere, unfortunately, but the Founder…makes sense to focus there instead of on Scarecrow."

Ilya grunted, seeing his point without agreeing with his assessment or the captain's. Scarecrow should be a higher priority. Find him and she was willing to bet they would find the Founder.

"My priority should be finding Ginna…but I can't even do that."

Putting down his beer, Blayd studied her before speaking. "I'll keep my ears to the ground. She's a good kid, learned from the best. I'm sure she's safe. She'll turn up just fine, you'll see."

"Hope so." Ginna did have a good head and she was a survivor. If not for her association with those Spinks, Ilya would not be so worried.

They shared small talk as they ate, memories and gossip about people they had known as children, what had become of their childhood friends, where the others were now, what had happened to the places the group had frequented. Some of those places had changed ownership, some were vacant as a result of the Coup. Some of their friends had family lost in that same uprising, some had been lost to Heb addiction and alcohol or had been taken by the Crows as so many others had been taken before the Founder's downfall.

Some had simply drifted away from their sphere of acquaintances and neither knew where they were.

Eventually, Blayd's ICD chirped, a summons he only glanced at and wanted to ignore.

"Gonna get that?"

He shook his head, pushed back his empty bowl, and finished his second beer. "Client rescheduling a meet. Like I said…I've got prospects. Guild won't leave me unemployed for long. They don't pay as well as the Mam, but I've gotta eat."

"Maybe…" Ilya finished her nearly cold tea and picked at the last slice of toast in the basket. "Maybe we can help each other."

It was a long shot, but she would not be the first officer to utilize a street informant, a merc. Blayd would not be the first merc to throw bones to the bugorra either.

"What you got in mind?"

"We both want to find the Founder…and think Senior Kal's behind this." Blayd had not said so directly, and he had pointed suspicious fingers at Mam Kemway, but Ilya had heard the intimation in his earlier tone and words that told her his bet was on the Voices. "We share what we learn, find the connections. Find the Founder together and get what we want."

"Your boss wants him returned. Mam wants him in her care," he said skeptically. "Don't see how…"

"They want him out of the Voices hands. They agree on that much. We find him, get him safe, and let them sort out the details."

Blayd appeared thoughtful for the time it took the swiver to come for his passcard, run it, and bring it back. A source of information that kept him ahead of the buggers' search, that enabled him to plant further damning evidence against Kal where the buggers could find it, was better than he had hoped for.

Finally, he nodded and offered his hand. "Got yourself a deal, Lieutenant," he said with a smirking grin. Yes, they were friends of a sort and he was hoping for more. They were helping each other as friends. But this was also a business arrangement and he wanted her to understand that, wanted her to know that he understood it. He would give her information but he expected something in return. He also knew he was expected to provide something in exchange for any tips she gave him.

Even if that something was finding Ginna and keeping her safe.

❧*❧

With Otta and Colyx settling into the hostel, Otta doing her best to keep her father off of his frostbitten legs during the hours he was not on duty as Vapors' new security agent, Skelter was eager to get back to the life he had been robbed of more than two years ago. He did not blame anyone for what had happened, not Venn, not the Crows, not the Founder or the Doctet. He certainly did not blame Rhyd. If he could go back to that night, knowing what he knew now, what lay ahead, Skelter would not change a thing.

Though he might have been more watchful of his surroundings as he and his friends fled upward through the Levs.

There were so many people to get reacquainted with, so many to reach out to, contacts and clients, old partners and sources, hands to shake, backs to clasp, palms to grease. People to let know he was alive. His tale of the Core was a difficult pill for many so he fabricated a new story, something more believable that involved the eye patch he wore to cover his weaker eye and the walking stick he had modified for use on the grated walks. It was a tale of head trauma that had stolen his memory and identity until recently.

Despite clandestine meetings in shadows or tea vindis, in clubs or storage houses, elated greetings evolving into extended conversations with those he had known, worked with, and provided for, he repeatedly came up against the immovable wall that was the brako's presence in Hebanthe Falls.

"Ficken mich," he swore as he plopped into what had been his favorite chair when Zara welcomed him into the flat that had once been his home as well as hers. "Cazzing brako are everywhere. How do I get my life back with those schweinhunds into everything?"

Zara shut the door, surprised to see him. They had worked together for a lifetime; she knew the ins and outs of nearly every business relationship he had, knew most of his contacts and the merchandise they typically asked for. Going to her for help was the obvious choice but this time she did not know how she could help, what she could do, or whether she wanted to step back into that world. She had never completely left it, had continued to offer tech services to the old clients and new who came to her. Outside of that, she had forged her own path with his presumed death.

Sorting out where and how their lives fit together now was going to be awkward.

"I've still got the girls…I could give them back to you…"

Skelter frowned and shook his head, accepting the drink she brought as he slumped into the chair. "No. They're better off with you. You've done right by them, protected them, kept them working, added a third. I don't wanna mess that up." He did not know if Zara was working as a svodnik with the andis, but it did not matter. He had spoken to the girls downstairs long enough to know they were pleased with their current living and employment arrangements and the inclusion of a single male andi in their act.

Besides, Zara needed income too. A single andi was not going to offer her much.

Whatever the future held, he would not take anything from her.

"They're just…cowards…" he eventually muttered.

"Can't blame them, Ivan; the world went to shit that night. We lost the Crows until…and gained the brako. Rhyd's done his best to keep them down…the bugorra too, but they've spread too fast for just one man, just a few men. They have no respect for law, for decency, for order. Everyone was looking for their piece of Kemway's table and some wouldn't take no for an answer. Of course people are scared."

"You're not."

Zara shrugged. "They leave me alone. I don't have enough of anything to offer them, I guess. They don't see me as a threat."

Grunting, Skelter drained his glass and motioned for the bottle Zara had brought over. She pushed it across the long low metal table between them so he could fill his own drink.

"There are still a few; they come to me and Tox when they need something. I haven't said anything to any of them yet cause I didn't know when you'd be jumping back into the business." She had known he would; it was the only life he had known. They had yet to discuss when, however. "I'm sure now that you've put feelers out…"

"Where else can I go? Can't sit around with a horde of children all the time."

"No, that's not your style." She chuckled as she smiled and took the bottle back. He was good with the streeter kids on their turf, generous and patient. They liked him because he had been one of them, knew what their lives were like, treated them with respect, offered them work when he had it. But he was not the sort of person to tolerate a multitude of them for an extended time."

"I can put people I know in touch now…if you want."

"Don't want to kype your business…"

"I'm not kaheao. I'm haikara…and a dancer." Those were the contributions she had made to Skelter's business, developing Echo tech, programs, forging passcards, altering tick readers and ICDs, tinkering with anything computer-related his clients needed. Tox aided in the acquisition of parts, equipment, and tools. The rest of the business, the client interfacing, the hustling, the shuffling of questionable goods and materials, Zara was happy to turn over to Skelter if he was ready for it. She would work as his partner again, never as a rival.

"No reason the business can't go back to what it was," she added softly, "if that's what you want. Your warehouses are still intact."

The business. Perhaps their friendship too. But nothing else would be the same and she would never again trick, for him or anyone else. She did not need that attention or income any longer.

She felt his eyes studying her over the rim of his glass. They knew each other enough to recognize facial tics and body tells, the little things that spoke what words did not need to share.

"Thanks for that." He paused, staring absently across the room. "She's pregnant, ya know," he finally murmured in an awkward voice as if afraid to share the news. "I'm not ready; it's not what I…"

"But it is what it is," Zara whispered after the air sucked from her lungs by his revelation rushed back in to fill the hollow void. He would keep this child because he would never abandon one the way he had been abandoned. He would provide for it the way his parents had failed to provide for him. He might even marry Otta, in time, in the hopes of offering the sort of stability his early years had lacked.

But Zara knew he was scared. Especially since, at this moment, he had no means of providing for himself or anyone else.

Otta could apply for income as a foster for the kids under her care. Colyx had a job now thanks to Maemi. Without the andis, without the legitimate income of a svodnik, Skelter had nothing.

She got up from the chair and crossed to a long table against one wall cluttered with a variety of familiar-looking tech. From the chaotic scatter, she picked some things up and returned to her chair before offering the items in her hand.

The ICD band and tick card were like any other a citizen would receive as a replacement for a lost or damaged, item or if they needed a new passcard due to a name, residence, or occupation change. The other card, worn with age, was the key to every stash of goods he had left behind when he had disappeared.

Skelter met her gaze.

"Been setting some aside, hacking your accrued ticks while you were gone." In the Source, she made certain that Ivan Furrell was never identified as dead. She had the skill to make a host of transactions continue as they would have if he had been alive and using the ticks all along. By masking the transfers, picking up purchases here and there to store in his warehouses, she kept his accounts from being reduced due to disuse while saving the ticks he had not been able to use, thus providing an unusually large sum of ticks he could use now, as long as he did so carefully.

"It's all there…most of it at least."

"Zar…" he choked, slipping the band around his wrist and the cards into his pocket. She had never given up on him. He could not express what that meant to him.

"I'll get the others passcards, get them in the system, get the ticks and hostel passes on the same cards, get Jaron to help with identity files." Colyx would already be in the system under the name he had used at the time of incarceration. Under his new name, however, he could begin life without the shadow of his past looming over him. Otta could be entered into the Archives as one of so many streeters who grew up without an identity but took legitimate employment when they became old enough to do so.

None of it was difficult for Zara to do; she was happy to help.

"Make sure they lay low, low as they can, until I get them done. I'll reach out to those on roster and send them to you…if that's what you want?"

Skelter reached across the table and gave a long breath of relief when she accepted the business handshake that was, for him, so much more than business.

"I'm sorry, Zar…about taking so long to reach out to you…so long to tell you…for all of this." He should have reached out to her months ago through Enoch, as soon as he had regained his health. Until the end of his confinement, however, he had been uncertain about his plans, his chances for survival and escape. Getting her hopes up for nothing would have been devastating for both of them.

"You're here. You're alive. The world is new." New and awkward but she and Skelter had been through too much to turn on one another or let anyone come between them. They could start over and everything would be alright.

❧*❧

"I'm glad the rumors of your poor health were exaggerated."

"Feena."

In his office for the first time in too many days, the roof panels retracted so he could view the blue sky and the mountains to the west that he had dearly missed in the medi-ward, Grainger reached across the desk with a gesture towards the chair in front of him. "I doubt they were exaggerated, but I'm back. I'd get up but I've been instructed to stay off my feet as much as I can."

Feena came around the desk and kissed his cheek as she always did when their paths crossed and then took the seat he offered. "I hope whoever's responsible…"

"Has been dealt with, I assure you." There was no need to tell her more. After a good night's rest in his own bed, without the constant interruptions of medi-staff, he had yet to properly tend to those from the Core. They had not been 'dealt with' in any permanent fashion, but he intended to do so as soon as he felt caught up with the reports and demands of a job left too long undone.

"This doesn't have anything to do with the Founder, does it?" Feena asked with a concern-heavy tone.

Grainger shook his head. "No, it doesn't."

"He's still missing? No one's seen him?"

He understood her concern. When he had met her years ago, as a young Crow assigned to the detail investigating the altercation that had claimed her brother's life, Grainger had uncovered the family's deep connection to the Voices of Faith and their marginal connections to the Kemways. In the years he had known Feena, he had never seen any indication that she shared her parents' religious zeal or affiliations, or their political stances, but he knew that ticks continued to flow from her business ventures into the Voices purse as they had done when her parents and brothers lived.

Undoubtedly there were political and societal gains to be had by those contributions. One did not need to believe in a cause to understand the public benefit of supporting it.

"Believe me, when there is news, all of Hebenon will know." He paused for a sip of water from the glass on his desk before asking, "Have you seen or spoken to Kal?"

The question did not throw her. Feena had known that coming here would open her up to discourse about her connections to the Voices and questions about what she might know about the Founder's whereabouts, especially since she had been the one to bring the Founder up. Kemway was the primary topic of discussion and concern throughout Hebanthe Falls and her family's Voices' affiliation made her a logical point of contact for details about Kal.

"I wish I did. I can't believe Kal would sanction something like this, that he would be so misguided as to believe it would be in the city's best interest. Maybe someone beneath him is responsible. I will encourage him to do the right thing, to find the truth and make sure Founder Kemway is returned to your care. But if I may be so blunt, Oliver…have you considered Mam Kemway's involvement?"

He shrugged. "I haven't ruled anyone out. We're following every clue we can get, to whatever end it takes us. We will find him, and whoever is responsible will be held accountable."

"That's all I wanted to hear. I've heard the most awful things."

"What things?" Grainger frowned.

"Rumors that don't make any sense. I'm sure that's all they are, but if I thought even for one moment they had merit…" She dropped her gaze to the ICD screen on her wrist and got back to her feet. "I've got a meeting to attend, but I promise, if I learn anything, you'll know it as soon as I do. I'm glad you're back on your feet, back on the job. I've been worried."

He did not know her business beyond the craft of winemaking. Everyone knew about that. And she had gotten an elbow into the manufacturing of bottles and the labeling that went with them. She was sure if he knew about her primary sources of income now, he would never let her walk out of his office. Remaining above suspicion was as necessary as maintaining a good rapport with the bugorra.

It was fortunate, Feena reminded herself as she departed, passing a young woman in a lieutenant's uniform as she headed to the nearest lift, that Oliver had not asked how she had heard he had been injured.

Perhaps it was a topic best left unaddressed.

Ilya watched the woman pass with curiosity, recognizing her stately face, wondering why she had been in the captain's office.

It was none of her concern, however. The captain knew many people; others came to him often with business concerns. The requirements of his post brought many people across his path.

The only important detail was the one gleaned which proved the captain was back on active duty. It would not be long before he summoned the lieutenant to his office. Ilya hoped to have good news to report when he did.

◈*◈

The first few feedings did not go as well as Switz hoped but they had gone as well as could be expected for a man bound by the wrists who had to rely on someone else to feed him. Switz presumed he had, until recently, been fed in a near-catatonic state by caretakers with marginal concern for his preferences, well-being, or comfort. His physical well-being, perhaps, but not his emotional or psychological well-being. Switz made it a point to talk to the chained man continuously when he was in the room, to sing in his off-key voice in a friendly manner, to cautiously approach him with respect to keep him clean and as comfortable as his position allowed.

He should be allowed to sit, to lay down, but so far Switz had been unable to arrange that.

He could have taken advantage of the poor man, but he had been taken advantage of himself too much in his life, and while some people deserved it in kind, he did not think Haythem did. Haythem deserved the deference his title afforded, no matter how he had ended up in this state, and Switz intended him to understand that as the basis of a relationship between them.

When mealtime came again, he put the tray on a folding table he had convinced Blayd to provide and pulled out a long bit of metal he had scavenged from someone's nearby recycle bin the last time he had been allowed out of this room and building.

Haythem squirmed away from the length of metal that looked enough like a stinger to be frightening. Switz could see the fear in the man's eyes and hastily apologized. "No, no stinger; I promise." He had not injected the man, had avoided bringing the buzzer into the room to show that he meant no harm. He was glad now that he had not attempted to treat Haythem's wrists with plasts to set cracked bones and assumed, as the bruising gradually faded, that they were not broken after all. Without meds, sedation, or the use of the stunning device, the Founder's eyes grew steadily clearer.

He did not appear to Switz, however, to be in his right mind.

"Just wanna get your arm free so ya can eat."

The bound man stood still and stared. If he had been a snake, a scorpion, a venomous spider, Switz would think him ready to strike.

Switz had seen what had happened to his predecessor when the fellow had gotten within striking distance of this particular predator. Prepared to leap away, prepared to strike to avoid an attack, he carefully freed one of Haythem's wrists from the restraints, expecting to be struck by the now free hand.

Instead, in a sign of understanding, Haythem lowered his arm with deliberate slowness without taking his eyes from his caregiver.

"See? I'm not so bad." Switz took a step back, put the metal pick on the tray in exchange for a partial loaf of bread that lay there. Hemp flour bread was the cheapest to make, plentiful enough, and thus one of the most likely staples for Blayd to provide. It was also the easiest food for Haythem to feed himself.

Switz held the bread out.

Kemway's movement was abrupt, direct, snatching the bread before it could be taken away. The action made him wince, and Switz wondered if his wrists were damaged after all or if the reaction was simply to his limbs being too long bound in an unnatural position.

Haythem ate swiftly but with enough care not to choke, again proving that he was not a mindless beast.

"Can't leave you loose. Not yet," Switz murmured. "But if you cooperate…keep this up…I'll show 'im he can trust you, that you don't need to be chained up like a goat. I'll show 'im you understand."

"His fault."

The words were mumbled around the mouthful of bread, an effort that made the bound man cough and choke. Switz offered water from the nozzled bottle, but rather than give up the bread to take the bottle in his hand, Haythem allowed Switz to provide the water the way he had been doing all along, the bottle to his lips so that water could be sucked into his mouth.

"I'm sure Mr. Blayd didn't do this…"

He was not sure of that at all. Not knowing why the Founder was here instead of in his office in the Uppers, not having had the opportunity yet to learn more out in the city or from the Echo in the other room, he could only guess. Blayd might have been the catalyst for Kemway's condition, responsible for bringing him here. But Switz did not think so.

Reassuring the Founder that he was safe, that he could trust him, was Switz's goal. That meant calming his fears. After a little more water he continued. "We want to keep you safe, help you get better."

"All black. His fault."

There was a clacking sound in the outer room, the door of the warehouse being unlocked and opened, and Switz hurried to get Kemway's arm back into the shackles. The man resisted only long enough to push the rest of the bread into his mouth before allowing Switz to bind him. It was as if he understood the danger, the threat, of not keeping up the pretense of continual restraint.

The water bottle clattered to the floor as the middle door opened.

"There a problem?"

Switz shook his head as he retrieved the bottle. "Just being a klutz," he laughed with feigned embarrassment.

Blayd noticed the absence of bread on the tray and the stray crumbs around Kemway's mouth and nodded with approval. "Looks like you got him eating. Stopped giving you trouble?"

"Getting there; think he's getting use to me now…that he's understanding me." Noting Blayd's scowl, Switz elaborated, "I mean he understands I don't mean him harm. Just had to gain his trust."

"No howling? Violence? Madness?"

Switz shook his head. "Still quite mad; it's in his eyes." He looked at Kemway, the Founder's face angled towards the floor though his eyes followed the movement of the others. He hoped Blayd could not see the spark of indignation in Kemway's eyes that might announce a level of coherency that a madman should not possess.

"Whatever he was getting before, it seems 'bout out of his blood now. Few more days and we might know how mad he really is, how much damage was caused. But I could use a scanner…maybe some plasts…for his wrists…"

If Haythem had been repeatedly injected with Heb or something equally addictive, he should be screaming in the throes of withdrawal. That he was not was a good sign.

Nodding, the information vital if he was to decide how to proceed with his plans, Blayd muttered, "I'll see what I can do. Keep at it."

The gamble taken on Switz looked to be paying off. The man seemed the right person for this job, regardless of the murder convictions on his record. Treating Haythem's wrists before permanent damage set would be smart, humane, but would it be wise?

As Blayd left to attend business, Switz smiled at Haythem.

For the first time in more than two years, Haythem smiled back.

Skelter did not recognize the client name Zara sent to him as he was about to settle into sleep with the woman stretched out beside him. It was a name she had collected from Lash, and as Lash often brought Skelter clients, he lazily thought little of seeing an unfamiliar name. Two years of being out of the business, two years of upheaval in

Hebanthe Falls, and the clientele pool had undoubtedly undergone the same changes the city had endured. Skelter had to get his feet beneath him again in any way he could.

An unfamiliar name was as good a place to start as any.

There was a world of parah outside now, people wanting tools, materials, and knowledge they had never had before. There were those in Hebenon, too afraid to go Out, who wanted to experience the food and goods Marbordo had to offer. There were people beaten down by the brako, people who had lost everything to them or the Coup, and people who saw an opportunity in that loss to rebuild. Everyone wanted something. For the right price or favor, for the right trade or arrangement, Skelter could get it for them.

So long as the client was not brako, was not intending to harm innocent people. It was the only stipulation Skelter had, the only one he lived by.

Lash claimed the client was clean.

Set up the meet, he sent back to Zara, careful not to wake Otta in doing so. *Sooner the better*.

He needed to get back into play.

He needed to beat the brako at this game and push them out of business. He had no doubt he would make enemies in doing so.

But the advantage of friends and allies was that he would be ready for those enemies when they came for him.

Wherever they came from.

Otta, Colyx, Rhyd and the others would make sure of it.

❧Chapter 11❧

Night cycle in the Uppers had come again, synced now to the rise and set of the sun outside. A glow of orange and pink kissed the peaks and valleys of the western mountains as the sun sank behind them, allowing the dwindling trail of people to pass in and out of the city before the doors closed until dawn. Hebanthe Falls had opened to the Outside, but the people within were not yet prepared to allow the Outside unfettered access to come and go as it wished.

Because of this, those in the Levs were gradually beginning to understand that there was a day and a night…regardless of the perpetual dark in which they lived.

The glow of the fires within Marbordo's homes mirrored the glimmer of the stars and tonight the moon sat low in the east where Grainger could not see it from his position. Not a full moon, he mused. There was not enough illumination in the sky for that.

There were so many in that trail now, people from within and without braving the frontier of Outside. The night he had first stood here, facing the man whose family had ground the people of Hebenon beneath their heels for too long, he had never imagined the future that lay in wait. Some argued the world had gone to hell that night. Grainger believed otherwise.

He saw the gates of Purgatory open and those who had paid for late humanities crimes were released into Eden.

The door behind him opened. He looked back, hoping to see Jaron, but instead saw one of the young recruits he had yet to learn by name.

"Last report of the night, Captain. Is there anything else?"

Grainger turned towards the desk. "No, you can go. Good night."

"Good night, Captain."

The pneumatic door hissed open and closed and the officer's footsteps retreated.

He should go to bed as well, follow Tamner's order to rest as much as possible if he wanted to quickly resume full duty. But his bed was empty, Jaron absent from it, and though Grainger was weary, he did not have the heart to face that emptiness.

He compromised with the order by sinking back into his chair, propping up his healing leg, and inserted the digital disk the officer had brought into the Echo for examination. A compilation of further interviews from the night of Kemway's abduction and a collection of statements from those who had witnessed the effects of the shaking and power outage.

The number of statements taken that hinted at, speculated about, or blaming Scarecrow for involvement in the night's events was worrisome, but the SCAM footage Grainger had seen, images still displayed on three open windows on the Echo, gave evidence of Scarecrow being on Lev 1 and 2 that night, nowhere near the Core entrance, nowhere near Kemway's abduction. From the images, Grainger could not tell what Scarecrow was doing, as he was snapped moving past the SCAMs in two of the three clips and engaged in a scuffle with the brako on the other. Grainger studied every detail in that video, every one of Scarecrow's opponents, and not a single one bore the distinguishing yellow armband Vanderwall was known for.

If the brako boss had been killed, it had not been in that fight. Possibly still at Scarecrow's hands, but not on any footage Grainger had received.

On the off-chance that Ballard would confirm or deny involvement in the night's drama, he sent an ICD message, summoning the bilger to his office after putting in orders for his officers to investigate the three areas around those SCAMs in the hopes they would find something he could use.

It would not bring him the Founder, but it might put Vanderwall's death to rest.

He doubted they would find anything. Most of the time, Ballard was too careful. Suspecting the bilger of orchestrating all of the events of that night, coordinating them, was giving Ballard more credit than he deserved. He was good at what he did, but not good enough to be everywhere at once.

The Echo beeped and he opened the new message. It was a simple data string, indicating that none of the four killed at the abduction scene were registered Talkers or bugorra. That was not to say someone had not scrubbed their identities before or after the fact. If the four were anything other than streeters or sikuea, if they received ticks for any manner of work, their faces had to be in the Hub somewhere.

It would take a little longer to identify them.

Rather than send Senior Kal a summons as he wanted, which would allow the Talker to avoid him or concoct an alibi, Grainger decided to pay the man a visit in the next day or two. As soon as he could walk more comfortably. He would ask Jaron to search the Archives for the suspects and if that failed, he would go to the only other person he confidently believed could help him find what he needed to know.

He was uncertain if Zara would help. If she would even want to see him again.

❧*❧

"Late for a house call," Rhyd muttered, turning his chair from the table to face the man Jaron welcomed inside. It was Jaron's flat; he could allow anyone in he chose to. Having ignored the doctor's summons, Rhyd was not surprised Tamner had sought him out, but he did not believe his health was enough of a concern to bring the doctor to him. He was weak. There was residual pain in his shoulder and leg. But none of it was worse than any other injuries he had lived through.

He cast Jaron an annoyed glance but the mop-headed younger man did not see it as he cleared meal plates from the table.

"Always on duty," Tamner countered with a shrug.

"Don't you have a kid to…"

"Cori's with Agnys."

Rhyd thought he heard 'where you should be' tagged to the end of that statement, but since Tamner did not say it, Rhyd chose not to acknowledge what he believed he heard.

"And you're playing down here in the dark."

A one-shouldered shrug was his only reply as Tamner listened to his heart, his lungs, his pulse, and ran his scanning instruments over Rhyd's leg and shoulder.

"Plasts have set. Still wouldn't try anything strenuous for at least three or four days, but no reason you can't work on getting your strength, flexibility, and stamina back.

Rhyd's snide reply, something about not needing a doctor's permission to return to his life, was cut off by the buzz of his ICD. He glanced at it, saw the I D of the sender, and promptly shut it off.

"Important?" Tamner asked as he made one pass up and down Rhyd's leg with his hands to verify the healing the instruments reported. Instruments could be wrong. He felt more assured by testing the healing with his hands.

"No." A message from the bugger captain could be anything, a clue, a claim, a threat, or another attempt to recruit him. Whatever it was, Rhyd did not want to hear it.

Piece by piece, Tamner put his equipment back into his bag.

"That it?"

"Actually…I want to talk to you…"

Verifying Rhyd's recovery made him less reluctant to share one of the two things he had come to discuss. He closed the bag and sat in the other chair at the table as Jaron continued working in the kitchen, listening, the doctor wagered, but giving them as much privacy as the two-room flat allowed.

"Sure you've heard about the Founder by now."

"Taken from wherever Grainger had him." Maybe, Rhyd wondered, wishing for a drink he did not have within reach, that was why the captain had reached out. Rhyd suspected for the last two years that the Founder was alive, but whether he was, what his condition was, where he might be, had been things Rhyd gave very little thought to. It had not been his concern.

"There'd been threats…talks about someone coming for him after Mam Kemway was allowed to see him. The captain thought it best we relocate him where not even she could find him…and despite all of his precautions, we were hit. He was taken."

"You were there?"

Tamner nodded with a grim expression. "You saw the prods. He's not been well since…" The flicker that crossed Rhyd's face suggested he knew something about that night, about how the Founder had come to be in such a pitiful state, but Tamner chose not to ask questions he knew Rhyd would not answer.

"I was supervising the move, monitoring his health." He rubbed the back of his neck and nodded at Jaron when two glasses of whiskey were placed on the table. "He's been medicated, sedated when necessary, for two years. Kept him stable, controlled his mania, easing his comatose periods. That day…I saw it. He was changing."

"How?" Rhyd ignored the presence that leaned too close when putting the glasses on the table and remained hovering behind him.

"More lucid than before. That's not to say he was improving, just that he was different. I'm concerned about his state of health…his state of mind…now that he's been off his regimen for so long. He wasn't an addict, didn't need it to stay alive, but…"

Rhyd nodded. His hand closed around his drink as his brow furrowed. Removing any sort of behavioral stabilizing substance could be bad, even for the sanest of men. "You want me to find him."

Though Tamner shook his head no, his hesitancy belayed his thoughts. "You're not…you shouldn't go back out there. But you can return to work, if you're careful…maybe you'll hear something, see something, that might help us locate him."

While Rhyd did not particularly care about the Founder's fate, he knew there were many in the city who did, many who would use his death, one way or another, use the man if they found him, for political games. The effects on the city could be devastating. It was in everyone's best interest if the Founder was returned to the care of someone without an agenda beyond the man's health and welfare.

Someone like Doctor Tamner.

"If I learn anything, I'll tell you."

Tamner downed his drink. "Thank you." The relief in his voice, in the released hiss of breath, in the easing of tension around his eyes, was palpable. He hesitated, considering another drink, considering sharing the other bit of information he had recently learned about a common acquaintance, but instead set the glass down and decided against both. What he had uncovered was not his secret to tell.

"That it?"

Rhyd could feel that there was something more lurking behind the doctor's eyes as Tamner got to his feet and picked up his bag.

"Nothing important. Just…find him. If you can. And be careful. I don't want to have to patch you up again."

"Can't make any promises." If finding Kemway was a call to lure Scarecrow back to the streets, being careful was a promise Rhyd was not willing to make. Or keep.

❧*❦

Establishments like Vapors catered to a city that never slept and rarely closed because of it. While the Uppers had aligned their sleep and waking cycles with the Outside, the Levs continued to operate as they always had, around the clock shifts of workers constantly moving through the wet glare of neon vindi signs and alglamps on street corners and the fronts of occupied homes. The constant movement of workers meant clients moving in and out of Vapors and other bars, eateries, and entertainment venues during every hour of every day.

Those hours immediately after a shift's end drew the most guests, but it was not that hour when Skelter pushed through the beaded curtain and glanced around to get a feel of the place. There was an older fellow at the counter, snacking on peanuts as he nursed his drink and watched the Echosys above the bar. Near the stage, the andis were huddled together, repairing their dance attire or sewing new outfits as they shared quiet gossip. A couple young enough to be barely beyond school age shared a now empty plate of something and a tall drink with two bamboo straws.

He did not recognize any of them, only Lash who occupied the corner table with an elegant woman of Asian descent. Her stylized bowl-cut black hair, dyed with streaks of red, was held away from her ears by river glass flower clips and her nails were flawlessly manicured though not painted as many women like her favored. She was unfamiliar, but as long as Lash and Zara vouched for her trustworthiness, Skelter was willing to hear her request.

"Eido…Skelter."

"Mr. Skelter." She rose and offered her narrow, bony hand, flashing the expensive jeweled band on her finger that marked her as a married woman. It was a custom many people chose to forego due to the expense. "I've heard a lot about you."

He accepted the handshake, noting the coolness of her skin that hinted she had not been inside long. He sat only after she did so. "No mister, just Skelter…and I hope all you've heard is good things."

"Lash was telling me about your miraculous escape from the river. You're lucky to be alive."

"I am." He glanced at Lash, expecting the man to have been discrete in his storytelling. The news about the Core was barely public and Skelter did not want anyone asking about the world inside the mountain. "You have a proposition?"

"I will have, but I wanted to meet you first. I've known Lash for a long time. He vouches for you, says you can get anything I require for my work…"

"Depends on the work."

She smiled, cool and coy, and took a drag off the keffer that coiled smoke in her other hand. "I'm primarily a teacher, ancient history."

Primarily implied other interests, but Skelter did not ask about those. What his clients needed and why was a concern now that the brako were involved in the supply business. Whatever her business, as a friend of Lash' Skelter expected it to be harmless.

"Half up front, half on delivery…how much and how long it takes to get depends on what you need. I don't ask many questions, but I expect honesty…and expect no one to get hurt."

"No one?"

Skelter shrugged. "You got a beef with the brako, I'm okay with that. What happens between you and the bugorra, that's your business, so long as it doesn't come back on me. Anyone else, civilians, kids…"

He would have a problem with that. He always had. Especially children.

Again Eido smiled. "I'm not out to hurt anyone, I assure you."

Removing a small passchip from his breast pocket, Skelter slid it across the table towards her. "When you're ready, pass this through a reader. Follow the instructions. It'll get to me. I'll relay if I can get what you want and the cost. If you accept, the tick deduction will be automatic. Once I get the order, I'll relay exchange arrangements and make the final deduction."

"Before it's in my hands?"

"Standard terms." He had never scammed anyone, had repaid buyers when goods were lost or stolen, when they were unavailable or were not what the client asked for. He had a clean reputation in the kaheao business; it was the reason he believed he could reclaim his former clientele. He did not need to rely on bullying and threats and theft to do business.

Some transactions were different. Some were product-for-product or favor-for-favor. He did not need a history teacher and doubted she had any favors or products to offer him. She wanted a tick exchange and that was the arrangement he offered.

"This'll bypass the Hub…the Source. Anonymous. Only you, me, and Zara…"

Eido picked up the chip, about half the size of a passcard, and turned it around in her fingers as she studied him. Finally, she slipped it into the bright red clutch she carried, the color matching the streaks in her hair and the smart skirted suit she wore.

"I'll be in touch," she promised, nodding at Lash as if to say she approved of the arrangement. Once on her feet, after adjusting the belt of her slicker around her waist, she added, "I don't want the brako involved. I need discretion. They don't offer that, not even for a cut."

"I've noticed they want their cut of everything," Skelter snorted.

"If this works out, I will have further jobs for you."

"You know where to find me." The card would connect them until it was destroyed or Zara disabled it. Lash would connect them too. The less personal contact they had, the safer they would both be.

The glimmer in her eyes as her head bobbed indicated she understood that too.

Skelter watched her depart, noting the limp that marred the otherwise elegant sway of her step. Her hard edge had been won at a terrible price. He would, if she agreed to his terms, learn what he could about her because of the leverage and security such knowledge provided, but for now, knowing was unnecessary. He instead shifted his attention to the dwarf who skirted around her using her proximity to scrape off the two bulky brutes following too close behind.

Whatever rude words were exchanged between the pair and the woman at the door was enough to prompt Colyx to use his mass to wedge the duo against the bar so that Eido could exit without harassment. Enoch's quick steps brought him to where Lash and Skelter sat as the pair watched. At the other end of the bar, a lone Talker who had entered Vapors during Skelter's transaction did likewise with calculated interest.

Skelter could not tell if the Talker was interested in Enoch, in the brako, or in him and Lash.

"They're like leeches," Enoch muttered, climbing into the chair Eido had vacated and drinking what remained in her abandoned glass.

"Or flies," agreed Skelter. "Brako?"

"Who else?" The pair wore no masks to distinguish them as brako, but since the discourse with Senior Kal, Enoch had noted an uptick in people following him. Maybe they were not interested in him and it was merely coincidental. Maybe he was being paranoid. But the Senior's warning that Enoch would welcome the Voices' protection in time did not seem to be an idle one.

If the Talkers were in league with the brako, if only Kal was, or if the brako had gotten wind of a snippet of a truth they thought best to eradicate, Hebenon was about to become an unpleasant place for him.

"They're everywhere," Lash agreed. "What they want with you?"

There was an exchange of glances between them before Enoch grunted, "Nothing they're gonna get. Figured if I lay low here for a few they'll give up and move on."

He might have given the brako the slip, his small stature enabling him to move in and out of places they could not easily go, but Vapors offered the opportunity of a drink to calm his nerves and, as it turned out, the unexpected company of friends.

"Lookin' for an escort outta here? I've got somewhere to be, but I can take a detour," offered Lash.

"And I should be heading back before Otta thinks something's happened." Skelter grinned, his words a jest. Otta was no worrier. She trusted him to be careful when she was not there to protect him, but Hebenon was much bigger than the Core. If he needed her, she might not get to him in time.

Enoch nodded, taking Skelter's partial drink and swallowing it too, not speaking so his voice could betray how rattled he felt. Colyx had escorted the brako out of the vindi and there was no telling where they had gone, where they might be lying in wait, if indeed they had been pursuing him and not intending to share drinks in Vapors.

But the Talker at the bar continued to stare, to watch until Enoch could no longer see him through the crowd. Deciding it was time to leave, he squared his shoulders, hardened his gaze, and strutted through the beaded curtain with his friends. Senior Kal was not going to get the best of him. He would never give that man the satisfaction of being right.

The men parted ways at the base of a stairwell, Lash heading off to whatever business he had and Enoch going wherever he went when not in the other men's company. The redhead did not know where that was, did not even know if the dwarf had a home, was a streeter, or was a sikuea, one of those who made their homes in abandoned buildings, moving when necessary but appearing, for short spurts of time, to be legitimate home-dwellers. It had never been important to know where he lived. Enoch and Lash were among the elite few in Skelter's life he did not feel it necessary to know everything about.

If there were brako after the dwarf, however, Skelter might be forced to change his policy. Some secrets would prove to be regrettable later; he did not intend to regret anything.

What he felt forced to do was double back in the direction of Vapors rather than return to the hostel. Rather than go into the bar, he climbed the stairs that led to the flat above Tox's kesfek vindi.

"Hello stranger," the dark-haired woman smiled, motioning him inside amidst the clutter of exercising equipment that explained her glistening skin and damp forehead and hair. She had always been keen on fitness and never been one to seek it in any of the gymnasiums scattered throughout the Levs. None of what he saw looked out of place to Skelter.

But she was leaner now than he remembered, more muscles and sinew and toughness than before his disappearance. Whatever had happened when the Crows took her, when Xiaodan had died, it had not been easy on her.

"Heard about the kid," he murmured as she picked up a towel from a chair and motioned him into it. "He was a keeper. I'm sorry."

"He was naïve and idealistic," she said with a sigh.

"Weren't we all at that age?"

"Not all of us." The towel was tossed over the hand bar of the stationary bike after being swiped across her face. "Drink?"

'Sure." He watched her round the kitchen counter. "Whatever he was…or wasn't…he didn't deserve what he got. None of you did." The boy's death had hit Tox, Maemi, and his grandmother hard. Skelter could see it in each of them.

"But it's done now." Tox gave him a partial bottle of apple wine, the only alcohol she had on hand until nessies day, and nursed her glass of water as she plopped onto the stool opposite him. "Zar says you're picking up the business?"

"Trying to. Never been one to sit on my hands. Need the ticks…and it's the only thing I'm good at."

"You mean you're good at a little bit of everything," Tox teased. "I'm gonna need a new apprentice to pick up the slack if you'll be needing my help again."

"That's why I'm here…see if you're still in." He took a drink, savoring the sweetness instead of rushing the alcohol burn down his throat. "Gonna take time to reel 'em back, extract 'em from brako's hooks…and I'm thinking I should see to protection in the meantime."

"Protection?"

He tapped the claw-footed cane on his knees against the bottom of the bottle. "Between this and the eye, I'm not what I use to be."

"You don't need either," she scolded warmly. "I've seen you."

"Need? Maybe not. But the back disagrees. And the illusion of them helps. In there, it was a good stiff pipe that I spent a lot of hours etching. Made me looked important; no one wanted to meet the business end. Doctor gave me this, but it makes me look broken."

"You want something elegant."

"And useful, maybe with a blade or stinger or buzzer if I need it."

"You expect to?"

"If I start tinging my people from the brako, don't you?" With his empty hand, he removed the eyepatch and handed it to her. "I can see with the eye…some but not well. Thinking there's a way to turn this into an enhancement, boost what I have without anyone noticing."

Having incorporated enhancements into Scarecrow's body armor, hood and mask, and having tinkered with her share of alternate use glasses and eye-pieces, what Skelter asked would be a relatively simple thing to fabricate. "I can do it, come up with a stick for you too, but if you're expecting trouble, don't know that a stick and a patch will be enough."

"Got something else in mind?"

"Maybe…something fashionable of course." She knew his tastes. He was dressed plainly now, recently out of captivity and having to settle for clothes he had been able to kype in his first few days back. While Tox had nothing appropriate on hand, nothing like the frock coats of velvet and lace and hemp-silk he was accustomed to, given time she could come up with something he would approve of that would once more make him stand out in Hebenon's sea of bland, similarly-attired individuals.

He grinned. "Surprise me. If I'm to get my prestige back, it's time for Hebenon to know Skelter's back in business."

❧*❧

One by one, as carts of soil and stone were cleared away and taken outside of the city, the bodies within the chasm were exposed.

One by one, as the collapsed passage was cleared enough to see beyond the debris, people were extracted from darkness into the light of the world beyond the Core.

Ilya was there when the Factory crews broke through, when the first grimy, emaciated faces of the weary, the parched, the starving were brought out of the earth. Not many, nine in all, but the report was of others inside, others who had not been strong enough to survive the clawing to freedom.

They were in no condition to give their stories, unable to speak before Doctor Tamner took them away for care, to join the others Ilya believed had also come out of this place. It had once been, she now knew, the mines that had provided salt and more to Hebanthe Falls. She did not know how they had come to be trapped inside but she feared they had been left to die.

Not intentionally, since Captain Grainger had been unable, at first, to order their rescue. Later, perhaps he had believed that anyone alive had already been brought out. More likely, she thought as she read the brief message on her ICD, they had been left behind so that the truth could never be revealed.

She wanted to know what that truth was.

Is it true, the messaged read? *The Core's real? People inside?*

Too weary, too numb, to consider the pros and cons of her reply, she sent back an even briefer message.

Yes.

What else, she thought, rubbing the back of her hand over her teary eyes, was the captain hiding?

❧CHAPTER 12❧

With Jaron and Zara's help, Rhyd remained off the bilger shift roster as he mended. Their interference in the Hub and Archives granted him health furlough that he had not earned, time he was being paid for so there was no need to rush his recovery. But loitering alone in Jaron's flat while the younger man went off for the day, without Skelter or anyone there to keep him company, left Rhyd restless and bored. He had no intention of lying on the sofa, watching laughies or continuing to peck through Hub records for clues about where Kal, or anyone else, might keep the Founder.

The best way, the fastest way, to learn what he wanted to know was to put his ear to the street, ask questions of those with eyes and ears everywhere, probe the street network find and question the Senior.

He did not think the buggers had done so. He could think of many reasons why they might not, but more reasons why they should.

Though stiff, sore, and more unsteady than he liked, it felt good to be back in Scarecrow's skin, to slide through the wet shadows of streets, ducts, and tunnels he called home, listening to conversations amongst streeters and addicts, monitoring the murmured dialogues of Talkers inside cozy Halls, hunched on rooftops or beneath stairwells to pick apart the scraps of gossip the bugorra left behind.

There was nothing useful. Even the Spinks he reached out to for aid, had not seen any trace of the Founder since his supposed abduction. If he had been taken, if he had been smuggled into the Levs, it had been done so carefully, by someone who knew what they were doing, that it was as if he had never existed.

The Spinks, the only reliable informants to report directly to him, the only ones who functioned independently of the law, the Voices, the brako, would let him know if they learned anything. Relying on children might be a risk, but who else but the Spinks could observe others without question? Who else could Scarecrow trust?

❧*❧

"This was left at my door."

It had taken too long for Ilya to squeeze out time to view the footage on the passchip left for her and too long, she feared, to get it into the captain's hands. Not that he would know how long she had it. If what it revealed was accurate, and not some cleverly doctored bit of SCAM footage, he needed to see it and she would need to atone for any harm her delay may have caused.

In the background, the daily prods flickered on the Echo, the voices muted during whatever conversation the captain was having before her entry. "What is it?" he asked without looking at her, one hand out to take what she offered, the other jotting notes or details of his conversation on the digital pad on his lap.

He seemed irritable, out of sorts, but she would be the same if she was forced to sit with one leg propped up most of the time, confined to an office and desk instead of being out in the city doing her job. "Footage of Vanderwall's death…SCAM footage."

He looked up suspiciously. "Thought there wasn't any?" He had searched the Archives, his search of all footage from immediately before, during, and after the recital revealing no hint of brako activity except for that one fight between Scarecrow and a cluster of brako. They had been active that night, he knew, the verbal reports from civilians and bugorra alike attested to it, but whatever they had been up to, they succeeded in staying off the SCAMs.

"I thought so too…until this."

Hacking the Hub, removing data, was not impossible. Stealing SCAM footage and images was not impossible for any determined haikara. Nor would faking footage. This would not be the first time someone had attempted to erase evidence but it would, to Grainger's knowledge, be the first time someone had brought erased footage to the bugorra afterward if it was not fake.

"Why would…?" he muttered, eyes flicking to the Echo screen, his mouth pulling into a familiar frown Ilya had seen too much lately.

"I don't know." Her gaze followed his line of sight to where Kenneth Ximenez was silently speaking about the image inset on the prodcast screen, an image of rubble, an unlit tunnel, dirty skeletal figures supported by others or carried on anti grav stretchers, accompanied off the screen by Doctor Tamner.

Thankfully, Ilya thought as she sucked in a breath, her presence at that scene was not visible from the cameraman's angle. Thankfully, the captain did not know yet that she had been there. So long as she said nothing about it, it would not be obvious that she could see what he was watching.

Someone had leaked the story to the Ximenezes. It had to have been someone on site. She bitterly wondered who.

No wonder the captain was ill-tempered.

This was not the time, she decided to request resources to help locate her sister, particularly since she had advised him against doing the same to locate Jaron.

"You've seen it?"

"Sir?" She swallowed hard.

He waved the object between his fingers in the air. "Vanderwall."

Relieved he was not referring to the Echo drama, she replied, "Yes. I copied it to I.D. those on the scene." The only person she had positively identified other than Jaron was Scarecrow, but mentioning either in the captain's current mood would invite a reprimand.

"Get on it then; I want to know who to thank." His muttered words drifted off as he turned up the Echo's volume.

Ilya retreated with a "Yes, sir," before she was able to hear the prodcast's report.

It had not been Scarecrow who had killed Vanderwall, but Scarecrow knew who had, and she would find out their connection to bring it directly to Grainger.

He may not have been involved in Kemway's abduction, but this was a crime Scarecrow knew. She would find them both…and then root out the one leaking bugorra business to the city before the captain and bugorra could be informed. She hated rats more than she hated Scarecrow, for the same reason.

Both made her job significantly more difficult.

❧*❧

It was the second time since the accusations of kidnapping had surfaced that Kal chose to go into the city alone. The first time had taken him to Vapors in the hope of convincing fresh blood to take the reins of city leadership and rid everyone of a host of problems Hebenon continued to suffer since the Coup.

That would not be an easy task, but Kal was confident it could be done, particularly if he and Feena offered their joint support. That meeting might not have gone as well as he had hoped, but it had opened the door to the possibility of change. Having a Kemway in control would soothe a lot of nerves and ease the need to find a man reported to be mad, incompetent…and now missing. No one needed an unpredictable madman at the throttle of power. What Hebenon needed was someone who could be steadily relied on and believed in.

Controlled.

Since that bar encounter, Kal had busied himself with scores of meetings, personnel evaluations, assignment appeals, and counseling requests from congregation members struggling with personal or familial issues and their fears for the Founder's well-being. Kal was forced to repeatedly confront the claims that the Voices were complicit in the Founder's abduction. Having spent an afternoon listening to those repeated fears, Kal escaped the office, escaped his Hall, for a walk in the damp air, trying to talk himself into a meeting with Neoma.

It had been too long since they had spoken. This animosity between them had gone too far. It was time to reassure her that he had no hand in this messy abduction business, to try to establish a new groundwork for cooperation between them.

He would, of course, keep the news of another Kemway from her. He knew her well enough to know she would take such news badly.

Ahead of him he could hear the chanting voices of protests, echoed and muted by the rumble of the falls. He muttered beneath his breath with a roll of his eyes as he turned the corner, annoyed that a protest might force him to go out of his way to reach his destination.

It would have been preferable, however, to the jarring of the metal beneath his feet as a shadow dropped from above, grabbed him, and yanked him into the nearest unlit alley between silent, abandoned vindis. The face looming near his ear as an arm and gloved fist twisted him around and pinned him against the wall was the last individual Kal expected to see.

"Where is he?"

After their previous encounters, with the rumors circulating about his supposed crimes, the Senior realized as he swallowed his first startled breath, that this was probably the first person he should have expected instead of the last.

"Who?" With both arms held tight behind him, he could not turn, could not lash out, and he suspected if he gave a shout he would endure considerably more pain. Anyone hearing him would be as likely to hurt him as to help.

He knew Scarecrow's reputation. Scarecrow might hurt him, but he was not going to kill him. Others who might follow a cry for help from a man accused of kidnapping might be less agreeable.

The digitized voice growled. "Where are you hiding him?"

Kal scoffed and tried to blow off the water droplets running off the tip of his nose that tickled and made him want to sneeze. "Why would I do anything as crass as kidnapping him when there's someone more suitable?"

❧*❧

"He's an archivist," said the hoarse whisper on the other side of the screened door, masked by layers of cloth and a beaked mask that disguised his, or her, identity from the newest leader of the brako.

Vanderwall rubbed a hand over his head. What interest had his predecessor had in an archivist? Why would such a man kill him except in the act of self-defense? Vanderwall was, as so many who worked for him were, reasonably certain that Feena Wulfe had put a contract on the other leader's head. The rivalry between the first brako king and his second had been strained, the woman too resistant to following orders that did not align with her business sense or vision of the city's future. She was prone to doing things the way she thought they should be done rather than the way the brako boss had ordered.

No archivist would serve as a contract killer. That was ludicrous.

Getting his hands on the archivist, however, might be the leverage he needed to put Wulfe in her place or take her down, if indeed there was a connection.

Killing him would at least soothe his underlings.

But it would be a shame to kill a man for nothing more than that.

"Find him. Take care of him."

"Kill him, sir?"

"Find out his connection to Wulfe…then I don't care what happens to him. Just make sure our people know when it's done. The Wulfe bitch included."

If he was going to make a hit, it would be a very public statement.

When that was done, no one would stand up to Vanderwall again.

❧*❦

"Someone else?"

The stamping and chanting of protestors were upon them as the motley gaggle marched past with an assortment of signs demanding the salt shortage the city suffered be rectified, now that it appeared the mines were reopened. There were other sources for salt, waste processing that pulled salt from urine and waste for non-food purposes, some strained from the river and brought in from the salt processing tables the parah cultivated. But those sources had failed to fill the lack that had come after the Coup.

The citizens of Hebenon wanted more.

The images of miners left to die inside what many believed to be the unused salt mines had prompted a new spate of unrest. Mingled with the fevered rumors that the mines were depleted, or that the Nau was hoarding the supply to control the Levs in the same way the Founder and Doctet had controlled them, the shortage had prompted protests for months, but today's dissenters were the loudest they had been, persistent with their demands and insistent on being heard.

Swept along in their midst, noted out of the corner of his eye when Scarecrow turned his head enough to judge that he and his prey were not visible to the passing crowd, Enoch appeared not to be participating in the protest but trying to mind his own business.

Or rather, Scarecrow noted with a frown, Enoch was trying to escape three figures pushing through the crowd behind him, trying to lose himself so that they could not see or find him.

Even to Kal's eye, the dwarf's effort looked to be failing. To the Senior, the glimmer of blades in the hunters' hands looked less like tools of intimidation than tools that threatened death. Brako, no doubt. Had Feena betrayed him with a kill order on this legitimate Kemway heir? Had Neoma learned the truth and sent her minions to track down the dwarf? Was his plan about to fail?

There was no need for a shout of warning, no need to alert Scarecrow to a threat more significant than any knowledge about Kemway the Senior possessed. As he was known to do, Scarecrow saw a threat to a civilian and acted, releasing Kal to charge into the crowd, grab the dwarf by the arm, and yank him back as the first hunter took aim. The man's knife hand cracked down against Scarecrow's wrist with enough force to crack bone. Scarecrow's wrist was spared only because of the armoring of his suit.

The third hunter was joined by the shouts from two more on the far side of the crowd as the second lunged at the interloper and took the Scarecrow, whose maneuvering ability was hampered by the press of people around him who failed to move out of the way, to the ground. Scarecrow's head struck the grate, stunning him long enough for a fist to come down twice against his face. The distraction provided by Scarecrow allowed the protestors to sweep Enoch along until they reached a four-way intersection where they intended to make their stand in front of two known-to-be-working SCAMs.

From the half-Lev above, a dozen or more children dropped onto the back of Scarecrow's assailants, brandishing rocks and bottles, discarded bits of pipe, broken furniture, or tools against the now four unmasked opponents. The distraction of the children was enough for Scarecrow to get back on his feet but he was dizzy and the fall and subsequent rise laced his body with threads of pain from wounded leg to healing shoulder.

His mask and breather had been damaged by the pummeling fist.

There was no need to continue fighting. At the front of the mob, the bugorra arrived and the brako, thinking better of a clash with the buggers, scattered. The bigger Spinks pulled Scarecrow to the safety of the alley from which he had emerged.

Senior Kal was no longer there.

Elsewhere in the crowd, Enoch made it away in another direction.

Limping, defeated but for a group of children, Scarecrow sought safety and shelter as well, avoiding the pair of pursuing brako by ducking into an open drainage pipe where he would be able to find a replacement mask. The Spinks led the brako away.

He had failed to learn anything from Kal but he had protected Enoch.

He did not know from what.

❧Chapter 13❧

Sitting in this chair was the last place Grainger wanted to be, but the unexpected prodcast that leaked the existence of the Core to the public along with the damning details of people trapped inside of it was a matter he needed to address before the Ximenezes and Hebenon's rumor mill turned the story into something so inflated that he would never regain control of it. It was not the welcome back to business he had anticipated, but he was here, with an easy expression of sincere concern as he listened to the questions Soleia asked.

"I only recently became aware of the situation," he said earnestly. "Such things were under the jurisdiction of the Founder and Doctet, as you know, and out of my purview as Captain of Law. Factory East staff alerted me to sounds…"

"Behind a sealed door," Soleia said. "A door you sealed?"

"Arrangements to close the mine were underway when I took command; I was unaware of it until after it was done. Documentation indicates the mines are no longer viable and…"

"The mines are Hebenon's primary source of salt."

"I would not say primary," Grainger corrected, despite knowing that the rise of salt shortages and protests coincided with the cessation of mining operations. He had not had the opportunity to make that matter a priority, to dig into the connections between the shortages and the mine closure.

Rather than debate the point, with a shadow of triumph on her face as if she had caught him in a damning admission, Soleia changed tack. "You opted to continue the pre-ordained closure of the mines without determining if there were still miners inside?"

Exasperated, Grainger struggled to keep his expression calm and hoped the cams did not notice the tick at the corner of his eye.

"My priority is safety and security…the reestablishment of order, managing the fallout of the Factory Plague, the opening of Outside, and the reorganization of leadership to keep the city running. Second-guessing orders previously set into motion was not at the top of my priority list, unless they involved the emergency welfare of…"

"The miners have citizens' rights too…"

"Of course they do. My understanding was that the miners had been absorbed into the Factory workforce. I presumed, wrongly, I admit, that it had been done. Once aware of people trapped inside, extraction was sanctioned. A number were rescued before the quake sealed the…"

"But not all?"

"Several good officers were injured or lost their lives in that accident. Several we sought to rescue too, myself included. During my treatment, I was unaware that anyone was left behind."

Soleia smiled sweetly with a sympathetic nod. Though he did not think the camera would see it, there was another look in her eyes, something predatory and insulting, that made Grainger uncomfortable and defensive as she continued, "Did you direct Doctor Tamner and the Nau to reopen the passage after…?"

"Doctor Tamner has done precisely as I would have, had I known." Stuck in the medi-ward, out of the loop of politics and daily events, with no desire to know the status of a place he presumed to be empty. Besieged by the abduction of Founder Kemway, as soon as he was fit to begin a modicum of duties, going back to the Core had not been high on his list of priorities.

He was irritated that Tamner had acted without his foreknowledge or approval, but the man had done the right thing. Grainger could not fault him for it. "I praise the doctor for his decisive actions. Teams are working to clear the pass, to find anyone still inside."

"When the entrance is cleared, will salt mining resume?"

Grainger pursed his lips. "It is too soon to speculate. As I said, the reports I have call into question the feasibility of the mine. As soon as structural integrity is verified, we will re-assess the mines and equipment and re-evaluate the matter. Our priority is to rescue survivors and identify and dispose of the dead."

Soleia began to speak again but this time Grainger held up a hand to cut her off. "I've no further comment to make; it is imperative that I return to duty to tend to these matters. You know as much as…"

"You will keep the city up to date as circumstances unfold?"

She rose easily, despite her pregnancy, her movements contrasting significantly with the stiffness of injuries that hampered Grainger's efforts to stand. She made no move to support or assist him and he wondered, as he steadied himself with a hand on the back of the chair, if this was a ploy to make him appear unfit as Hebenon's leader.

"Of course," he replied, an easy promise to make without knowing as he said the words, if it was a promise he would be able to keep.

Soleia's smile, when it followed, suggested how trapped in the lie of his office he was.

"I said scare him, not kill him!"

The presence of the salt protestors had been the only thing that had saved him. Scarecrow's reputation did not include killing, and if he believed the Senior and Talkers held Founder Kemway hostage, he would not have gotten answers from a dead man. But that did not mean the vigi would have refrained from inflicting more pain than the soreness of twisted shoulders, bruised wrists, and the abrasions on the side of Kal's face where he had been forced against the wall.

Using those aches and visible facial damage as a ploy against Neoma was already under consideration. He might have to thank the vigi for that bargaining tool later.

Seeing those unmasked brutes with weapons in hand, Feena's brako agents rather than those doing Neoma's, and Vanderwall's, bidding, bearing down on the dwarf, while also a distraction that pried Scarecrow off him, had been more unsettling in some ways than the vigi's assault. Losing the dwarf would be the undoing of everything Kal was working to accomplish.

Ignoring Kal's bluster, the woman coolly motioned to the empty seat across the table with one hand and to the man behind the bar with the other for an additional glass of the pale pink liquid she was sipping.

Kal tossed a rude, un-Talker-like gesture at the bartender before the man resumed drying and polishing glasses. He was undoubtedly armed with a weapon hidden behind the counter, but he did not view the Senior as a threat since he neither drew it nor gave the older man a second glance. The neon pink light here was dim, the room aswirl with the warm misty air that would soon be infused with perfumes and perhaps kef, and soft guitar notes flowed from the Echo speaks hidden throughout the room.

A classy joint, not loud or garish, it served a select clientele at select hours, unlike most clubs that were open around the clock. This was Feena's place, mirroring her sophistication in every flourish, a more comfortable place to meet than Vapors, a Talker Hall, or any of the places Vanderwall preferred. Perturbed that she had not yet spoken, Kal sat where she indicated with a bitter, "I didn't come to drink I came for answers."

He liked it here but was in no mood for niceties or platitudes.

"You want him scared," she crooned, pushing hair behind her ear.

"Scared, not dead."

Feena chuckled. "There is no intention to kill your dwarf."

Frowning, wondering if she did not believe the man was a Kemway, Kal leaned forward with his elbows on the table. "That's not what I saw."

"They're instructed to be convincing. It's what you wanted. If Scarecrow believed there was a threat, I'd say they did their job."

Kal's frown did not fade, nor did his annoyance, but he had no comeback to give before she continued.

"What's his interest in the dwarf? Think he knows who he is?"

Kal shrugged. "Protecting someone outmatched by thugs, I'd say. five's too much, wouldn't you? They wary about your interest in…?"

"I don't tell you how to do your business, Kal. Don't tell me how to do mine. They do what they're told without asking questions."

Drumming his fingers on the table, Kal ignored the implication in her words. Yes, there were some in his organization asking questions, wanting to know if he had orchestrated and carried out the rumored abduction, if he was holding the Founder somewhere in secret, if he knew and approved of the action by someone else, or if he was being framed. Those questions undermined his authority, both inside the Voices of Faith congregation and outside of it.

The only questions being asked among the brako were who had killed Vanderwall and whether Feena, or the new fellow dubbed Vanderwall, should lead them. The factions continued to follow orders of their leader of choice without needing to know anything more.

The Talkers were less inclined to do so.

"Don't fret, Kal," Feena said with a kindlier smile as she covered his hand with hers. It was an honest gesture without animosity or disrespect. "I have them under control. I always do. He should be here in…" she glanced at her stylish ICD, "thirty I'd say…when we open. I'll talk to him, but I advise you not to be here when he comes. You don't want him to think we know each other…do you?"

Anyone with an Echo and access to the Archives could know the familial history between the Voices and the Wulfes, but not everyone knew Feena on sight, or knew her name, despite the influence she held. A street-level dwarf, particularly one seeking to stay out of the eye of those in power, one seeking to hide who he was, was even less likely to identify her.

Kal wondered what pretense she had concocted to lure him here.

But she would not tell him. As she said, who was he to question how she ran her business. So long as they pursued the same agenda, the same goal, of getting a Kemway, the right Kemway, back in place as Founder of Hebanthe Falls, it was all that mattered.

"Tell me how it goes, and make sure your people know," he repeated as he stood, "that killing him goes against everyone's interests. Our only other viable option, if we don't find Haythem, is his wife…and bozhe moy, Neoma is not here for anyone's interests."

"Except her own," Feena nodded.

Kal nodded too. "Precisely."

❧*❧

The distraction of Outside, of moonlight and the smell of hemp shoots in damp soil, helped Tamner keep his mind off the summons he was expecting and the public statement he knew the captain had made. Tamner chose not to watch it, did not want to know what Grainger had to say about him, about his decision to act. What was done could not be undone and he had no desire to second-guess himself. The world would move forward. He had chosen to save lives and was comfortable with it.

Medi-staff was present in the quarantine zone where the previous riffraff was held and as new survivors were extracted from the Core, they would be taken there for treatment. They would tend injuries and any other pressing needs and were under orders not to discuss non-medical matters with their patients. No one else was allowed access to them, allowed to talk to them, and his staff was not allowed to discuss any of what they saw or heard to anyone outside of the quarantine area.

The captain might feel entitled to circumvent that order. The staff would feel obliged to allow it. There would be nothing Tamner could do to prevent it.

When they had rescued the last survivor, Tamner would be summoned to examine and evaluate them, to piece together a puzzle he could present to the Nau and to Grainger. He predicted a grim presentation but he was hoping to get better news than he expected.

His son and Agnys had been playing tag with a group of children, parah and Crossers alike, when Tamner emerged from the city to breathe the clean air and clear his head. Many of those children had already been called indoors as the evening deepened. Cori, always a fastidious child but even more so after the deaths of his mother and sister, was gathering the day's collection of playthings and stuffing them into the mesh bag where they would await another day's play. Agnys, meanwhile, came to stand beside the man who looked to be studying the hemp crop in the dark.

"Have you seen him? Is he okay?"

Tamner did not need to ask whom she meant. She pestered him for information about Rhyd every time she saw him. He was surprised she had waited to speak to him now as long as she had.

"He's good; he's safe." The bilger had not stepped outside of the city since the night of Skelter's rescue and although Agnys had seen him just a few days ago in the open city doorway, every day that passed without contact made the girl worry.

She would likely worry less, he mused, if Venn stopped doing likewise and simply allowed Ballard to live as he felt necessary and comfortable with. The unresolved tension created by his vigi lifestyle and Weyer's resistance to it were poisoning the girl's peace of mind.

While not a proponent of vigilante justice, Tamner had seen too much good come of Ballard's activities to believe he should cease his efforts. Some wrongs needed to be righted. Sometimes, extraordinary measures had to be used to see it done.

"You'll tell him hello? And come read to us?"

It was his habit since the Outside opened, since befriending the girl's family and the people who allowed Cori to stay with them while his father's work kept him occupied in the city, to be in Marbordo every night he could be, to read to the children before they slept. Other parah children joined them, and sometimes the children of other Crossers; it had become a peaceful daily interlude that allowed some relief from his otherwise stressful days.

Agnys had become Cori's surrogate sister in some ways, and seeing the two together had kept Tamner grounded through the last two years of upheaval.

"I will," he promised, taking her hand as he turned. He hoisted the stash of toys over his shoulder and lugged them back to the collection of tiny village homes. He resisted looking at his chrono, resisted satisfying his curiosity about the time, about whether Grainger's interview was over, about how much time had passed since he had received an update about the Core victims.

All were things he would learn soon enough.

❧*❧

Disoriented by the fall and the throbbing in his injured leg, it did not take Scarecrow long to realize his target had escaped and that, wherever Enoch had gone, he was likely safe beyond the reach of whoever was chasing him. The world lurched and spun, tilted and darkened as he pushed through the shadows, ears tuned to the streeters in the hopes of learning something about the Founder, and about Enoch, as he stumbled towards Jaron's flat. He paused long enough to replace the damaged mask with one kept hidden in one of so many cubbies within Hebenon's filt tunnels. Each step brought clarity back to his head, brought steadiness back to his movement and though his senses felt duller than they should, they were not so dull that he failed to notice the splintered jamb of Jaron's door and the wet boot print planted where a kick had forced it open.

His heart seized and his breath caught with the surety that he had failed to keep the promise he made. Thumper yanked from its holster with one hand, he used the other to push the door open, and despite the muffled stuffiness in his skull, he was quick to detect the sound behind him that announced he was not alone.

The sizzle-hiss of a buzzer sped along the back of the body armor designed to protect him from such things and failed to incapacitate him as the wielder intended. Roaring, Scarecrow spun on one foot, reacting despite his weariness, to land a high kick that dropped the Crow-masked stranger to the ground. The brako groaned and tried to crawl sideways to use the wall as leverage to rise. The second brako, bigger and broader, wielded only a short knife yet showed no hesitation to bull-charge their solitary opponent. The lunge forced Scarecrow back, to fall through the open door of the flat and land on his back to roll with his attacker when their grappling hold brought them down together.

The roll ended with the brako tossed end over end into the small table littered with the remnants of an abandoned meal and brought Scarecrow into a crouch that he held, breathing hard, forcing pain to the recesses of his consciousness. Eyes focused on the one in front, ears focused on the one behind struggling to regain his footing, Scarecrow counted the heartbeats of waiting.

One.

Two.

Three.

On the fourth count, the man he faced charged. Scarecrow dove low and the brako barreled over him, landing off balance and knocking his cohort into the rail across from the flat door. There was a crunch, a scream, and the unsuspecting man flipped backward, over the beam, to land with a wet flour sack sound on the roof a half-Lev below. The remaining brako spun, met Scarecrow's charge with a bear-hug grip, and forced him with a crash against the exterior wall of the flat.

The body armor absorbed the blow but the impact of his head against the alglamp was enough to shatter the hemplastic light and cause a sharp ringing throb to shoot from the rear of his skull to the space between his eyes. With the green luminescence of the lamp fluid dribbling down his head, some of it over the lenses of his mask, he grabbed his opponent by the throat with one hand and swung the thumper with the other.

The hold on the brako's neck turned him sideways as Scarecrow turned, slammed the beaked head against the doorjamb, and hit him on the other side with a controlled blow that made the brako collapse to the walk and stop moving.

Maybe he was dead.

Scarecrow did not check.

He did not think the brako were looking for him or that they had followed after the earlier pursuit. There was no reason for them to expect him here. But if Jaron had been identified as Vanderwall's killer, this opportunistic encounter might link Jaron to Scarecrow and the bounty that was undoubtedly on the vigi's head would bring the brako around to Jaron as a double threat.

Maybe he should kill both men to be certain that did not happen.

They must have hidden in the shadows, on the roof, waiting for the flat's occupant. They had not been here by chance, judging by the broken door. Scarecrow's arrival was the only element of chance in their equation. If Jaron was their target, there was only one reason.

Scarecrow staggered like a drunken man, without the benefit of numbing alcohol, through Jaron's small flat, looking for indications that the archivist had been here, had been assaulted or taken. But nothing was disturbed, beyond the wet footprints trailing here and there and the now broken table and chairs. If Jaron had been taken, he had gone without a fight with people who had been careful to preserve the scene and hide their crime.

Except for the broken door.

Such caution did not strike him as something the brako would do.

Jaron was still on shift then.

"Thing's okay?"

The voice of a Spink was unexpected and made Scarecrow spin and crouch as if to throw the thumper he still carried in one hand. The child was not alone. Four others crowded behind him, their faces alive with amazement and apprehension. Whether they had witnessed the fight, or part of it, or were only witnesses now to the evidence that remained, they appeared eager as always to help him.

The oldest appeared no more than ten.

Though reluctant to endanger them, it was help he could utilize. Help that would allow him to see to business instead of trying to accomplish three things at once.

"I need you to do somethings…"

"Anything," the lead Spink exclaimed breathlessly.

"You know where Vapors is?" They were not far from it. Most familiar with this section of Hebenon would be familiar with Vapors.

All heads bobbed in unison.

"Someone needs to tell Maemi the brako may go there."

"We can do that…"

"And someone needs to go to the Archives; you know where…?"

"Everyone knows where the Archives are," the oldest scoffed.

"Find Mr. Rei." He pointed to the only digital image of people Jaron displayed, Jaron with a woman bearing enough physical similarities to suggest she was his mother. "Tell him to go to the man with the cats. See that he gets there safely. Don't leave him until he's inside…and watch him when he gets there. Tell him to stay until I come for him."

"On it." They did not know the man with the cats; they did not know where that house was, but Jaron would. If the Spinks reached him in time, if they found and identified him, if he was on shift and not already taken, they could secret him to safety and Scarecrow would make sure he stayed that way by removing the threat at its root.

Catching his breath, he waited as the Spinks dashed away, until he could hear no trace of anyone lurking in the area except for the still-motionless brako. Needing to brace himself with liquid courage that he expected would clear the fog in his brain and jar his senses to full awareness, he exposed the lower half of his face long enough to drink from one of the Zaolei bottles in Jaron's cupboard. He ignored the pain at the back of his skull and the burn of the whiskey sliding into his belly. A second swallow was little easier. He repositioned the mask and cowl, made sure his breathing equipment was properly connected, and looped his thumper once more in the holster where it belonged.

He closed the door that no longer latched or locked, stepped over the twitching brako on the walkway, and dropped down onto the roof where the other lay moaning in unconscious discomfort. Satisfied that both lived, though he continued to wrestle with the wisdom and morality of leaving them alive, he slid down the nearest banister, intending to do what he should have done already.

It was time to take the brako down.

The sliding made him dizzy and his stomach struggled against rejecting what he had just poured into it. Fearing what was coming, he slipped into an alley, paying no attention to the risk of spying SCAMs, and dropped to his knees behind a collection of empty recycle bins. He fumbled with the mask but a stabbing burst of hot pain at the base of his skull stole his vision before the mask came free and he crumpled into a heap beneath the drippings from the roof overhang.

❧*❧

Enoch knew he did not belong in a place like this before pushing past the flexible strands of neon tubing in shades of lavender, white, and pink that served as The Lair's door. He preferred gritty and low class. He preferred real, not ethereal, detached and upscale that the delicate jazz oozing into the street suggested this place to be.

He was only here because of Skelter's need to rebuild his clientele and someone within had expressed an interest in his services. Skelter often used his closest acquaintances for initial contact. Today, for this job, it was Enoch's turn.

Why the client had reached out to him, rather than Skelter, was an intriguing detail worth investigating.

In silk and velvet and lace, Skelter would fit into this atmosphere better than Enoch ever would. They would have come together, but too much time had been lost skittering from one shadow to the next to lose the tails who had followed him since he shed the salt protestors. There had been no time or opportunity to have Skelter meet him here. Enoch had to do this alone.

Those tails might have been agents of Senior Kal following through on his veiled threats. They could have been the sort who believed it their place to rid the gene pool of less than pure specimens. They might have been the brako who had chased him before or someone following him out of sport.

Whoever they were, they had fallen back as he drew nearer the Lair until at last he was unable to detect them.

He showed the flickering passcard, with its intricate, ever-changing pattern of light threads moving across its digital surface like termites through wood. The man at the door, armed with a thumper on one hip and a buzzer on the other, passed an electronic scanner over it before ushering him inside. There were few invitation-only venues and vindis in the Levs. Enoch grew more intrigued.

Once his eyes adjusted to the dim room lit by false lavender candles and tubing of pink around the edges of the floor, ceiling, edges of the stage and edges of the bar, he noted the current lack of occupants. Many of the tables were adorned with 'Reserved' signs. He might have been invited here, but he did not presume any of those reservations were for him. He went to the bar instead and waited for the swiver to approach.

"Hemp whiskey," he ordered, requesting one of the lowest class drinks to be had in Hebanthe Falls, just to see if The Lair carried it.

"You deserve better."

The husky purr that followed his request came from a woman in a glittering pink gown that hugged her curves from neck to ankle. She leaned against the bar beside him and tapped its surface with perfectly manicured nails that matched the color of her dress. A mature woman, she was elegant and attractive, a woman aware of her allure judging by the perfumed lavender air about her, her evocative stance, the movements of her hands and arms. A regular, perhaps, Enoch gauged when the swiver delivered both his drink and a tall glass of carbonated rose to his unexpected companion.

"I deserve what I ask for," he grunted, grateful the swiver had not replaced his order with whatever the woman was drinking.

"Simple tastes. I like that in a man. We like what we like." She offered a warm smile of seduction that made him think she could be one of those expensive hooks or high-end andis that came with the territory in places like this for the benefit of the patrons. She motioned to a corner table, one without a 'reserved' sign, and asked, "Join me?"

Familiar with the way such things worked, and that he did not have the ticks to pay for a hook's services, andi or not, he picked up his drink and shook his head. "Waiting for someone…"

"I know." Her smile switched to something elusive and coy when he side-eyed her with an arched brow. "You're not what I expected…I mean that as a compliment…and I imagine I'm not what you expected either. I'd rather discuss business in private and not here at the bar."

Half-expecting her words were a ploy to scam him out of drinks or into her bed, based largely on her unexpected compliment, Enoch shrugged, pretending not to be as surprised as he felt, and followed her across the room. Some other time he might consider taking her up on an offered fling, if that was what this was. Tonight, with his nerves shot after his brush with potential death, he was not in the mood.

Once seated with his back to the wall, with the woman sitting across from him, it elevated him nearer to eye level with her. He felt cornered in this seating arrangement, but at least if anyone threatening entered the club, he would see them coming.

"If you know why I'm here, talk."

"I've heard your man can get me anything I want."

Enoch shrugged. Starting with Skelter was a good way to convince him she was the client he was here to see. "Within reason. Depends."

"On?"

"What you want…how much you're willing to pay…what you're offering in exchange."

"Life for a life then?"

Troubled but not surprised by her analogy, he shook his head, hoping that the smile behind the word was in jest. "No murder for hire…no roughing folks up. You want that, plenty of brako around for the job. We don't go there."

She sighed without breaking the smile. "Yes, there are," she agreed, sipping her drink. "But no, that's not what I need. I want him to find something for me. If he's as good as I hear, as good as you say…if he delivers…I can pay handsomely."

The movement of her fingers seemed to gesture to the room. Some of the tables were beginning to fill with well-dressed and important-looking guests and their restrained, polite chatter. None were familiar to Enoch, but if they were friends or associates of hers, if she had stock in The Lair, then she might be able to offer Skelter the sort of influence and credibility his 'death' had taken away.

Such a client would be a good one to have in his pocket.

Or else this was a ruse meant to knock Skelter out of the kaheao game. Enoch did not see it, did not know; it would be up to Skelter to judge that risk for himself.

"How'd I put him in touch with you? Send him here?"

The woman shook her head. "No. That's not necessary. It would raise questions. Discretion is of the utmost importance."

Her nails traced delicate patterns over the back of his hand and for a few moments, both were silent, her eyes studying him with a tempting glimmer that was gradually eroding his determination to withstand her. Not many hooks came at him with such poise; usually their efforts to win a bedpartner were brazen or businesslike. If she was not a hook, it had been some time since such a woman had shown him such interest. Most avoided the stigma of genetic failure he represented. The few who pursued him were interested in the novelty of a dalliance with someone who should not, by the codes of Hebenon's society, be a risk for pregnancy.

Either way, Enoch was tempted to consider her flirtatious offer.

"No," she finally said again, withdrawing her hand to sweep it through her hair and then toy with the string of pink beads at her throat. Her interest seemed to evaporate except for the continuing glimmer in her eyes. "I'm not ready yet. When I am…where do I find him?"

Enoch shook his head, refusing to give her the satisfaction of expressed frustration, and set his glass down once it was empty. "Leave word at Vapors that you've got a job. Someone will be in touch." Since discretion was important, he did not leave Skelter's name. If she knew enough about him to identify Enoch as a connection, she could undoubtedly identify Skelter without Enoch's help. He was content to play the middleman until Skelter was satisfied this was no sort of trap…as long as it did not run him afoul of the brako again.

"I warn you, he doesn't like games…or people wasting his time. He'll get what you're looking for, if it's out there to be had…or made…but you do him wrong, you'll regret it."

"Is that a threat?" she asked with a chuckle of amusement.

"Only if it needs to be."

Feena watched the dwarf strut away, making no effort to stop him, amused that anyone thought they could threaten her. She did not know the kaheao he worked with, nor did she care to. She had enough people around her already who could bring her anything she desired without any cost beyond possibly a life or two. The only thing this nameless kaheao could provide was the link to this dwarf who had, in every fiber that made him who he was, what it took to be Founder of Hebenon.

He was a Kemway, alright. Feena did not doubt it. Dwarf or not, she and Kal could put him at the pinnacle of power, and with his own effort in addition to theirs, they could keep him there.

There would be nothing preventing her from claiming similar reins of power for herself.

Maybe, she thought with a grin as she finished her wine and licked the last droplets from her lips, she could rule at Enoch's side.

No one, neither Vanderwall, Senior Kal, nor Neoma Kemway, would be able to touch her then.

❧*❧

"Scarecrow? Scarecrow? Wake up!"

The Spinks looked at one another with frowns and pouts and nervous distress. From the hiss of an air tank, they assumed he was breathing, despite his failure to respond to their voices, their prodding toes, their shaking hands.

Breathing meant alive.

But if he would not wake up, they could not leave him here.

Not with the threat of the brako about.

Silently, one by one, they nodded to one another, a decision made.

They knew what they needed to do.

&Chapter 14&

Leaving the Archives in the company of his coworkers was not always possible. He rarely made the effort to do so, as he was content to walk alone. He had never invited a coworker home, had never joined them in theirs. Later, after the Coup, it had become especially important as he had not wanted anyone to know the frequency of his trips into the Uppers, that there was a connection between him and Captain Grainger.

He was not ashamed of that dalliance, but Oliver's position as de facto leader of Hebenon demanded discretion, both for Jaron's sake and to keep others from using him to make demands of the captain.

Despite the importance of safety in numbers, his habit of taking his time in logging out of the Hub, retrieving his belongings from his locker, and preparing to go out into the damp, meant that he again passed through the door alone, pushing through those archivists arriving to replace the previous shift. It had been a long eight hours and he was weary and nervous. He wanted to be home.

Where Rhyd was.

He looked right towards a stretch of residences housing mostly the upper echelon of Archive staff. He looked left towards the stairs, pulling up the hood of his longcoat as he did so. The turning of his head shielded his peripheral vision with the side of the hood and meant that he did not see the sudden movement on his right or the fist that caught him across the temple, striking the speech implant hard enough to cause a jarring stab of pain in his skull and draw blood from his ear. The blow pulled the hood back, exposing his face to the damp again. There was a whistle. Someone grabbed his arm, yanking his meal pack free, the clawed gloves raking over his hand and wrist before jolting the bones and muscles there in a tearing, wrenching fashion.

The black beaks were things of horror and shadow.

Then they were there too, more than a dozen children of varying ages, swooping around him, encircling, driving the brako back with chunks of stone, broken bottles, and lengths of pipe, with shouts and taunts and screams of outrage and challenge. Their ruckus in this typically quiet sector drew people out of the Archive and was enough to force the brako to retreat without their prize. Some of the Spinks swept Jaron along while others remained, advancing on the retreating brako with catcalls and shouts of derision that led the witnesses to conclude that the skirmish was between the brako and the children. They did not know it had begun with one of their own.

"Mr. Rei?"

"Ye…yes…" Jaron stammered.

"Scarecrow says to take you to the man with the cats," said the voice closest to Jaron's ear as the children bunched around him and hurried down the half-Lev stairs. "See you there safe. Know the way?"

Jaron nodded, the startled scatter of his thoughts latching on to the words Scarecrow and cats and connecting both to Lash without effort.

"Why?" he eventually croaked when they turned along one path in the direction he had been instructed to go. If the command was connected to the brako attack the Spinks had just thwarted, Jaron wanted to know.

If he was a target, he deserved to know.

But none of these particular Spinks had seen Scarecrow or knew the answer. They were doing as their network had ordered.

Protect Mr. Rei. Get him safely to the cat man.

"Just told to keep you safe," one of the other Spinks said.

Jaron nodded and continued to stumble along with them.

Floodlights punctured the darkness of a place few in Hebanthe Falls had ever seen. What was immediately visible beyond the now opened doorway resembled the old world imagery of warzones before Hebenon had closed its doors on the world. The debris of living, scattered and broken, intermingled with discarded weapons, scorched remains of wood and fabric, and the rust-crimson stains of blood the battle had left behind. What he could see appeared to be a common room, the staging area for mining carts, for unloading supplies before sending them deeper into the earth. Doors and passages, stairwells up and down, extended in every visible direction. Rail tracks, the sort used by the carts to transport trade goods to the Outside doors and to bring hemp back in, branched in three directions from the primary point of entry and disappeared into the darkness from the place where Tamner stood.

The rails, the dirty cracked tile floor, and the grungy white walls identified a date of construction simultaneous to, or perhaps older than, the Uppers and the birth of Hebanthe Falls.

The mines.

The Core.

There was no denying its existence any longer.

To Tamner, however, it did not appear that its original intent had been mines at all.

The desire to go deeper, to learn, to see with a scientist's and historian's eye, was supplanted by the more pressing needs of the survivors who had been extracted out of this darkness. Instructing the attending workers not to allow anyone inside the mines without his permission, Tamner saw the metal gates locked, now that there appeared to be no more bodies to retrieve, and sent most of the Factory workers back to their primary duties.

He debated demanding that the workers who were temporarily camped in Factory corners return to their quarters below. Until the future of the mines and the Core were decided, however, he chose not to pressure them.

There was little point in instructing everyone to keep silent about the things they had seen. He knew the tendencies of man. Some would talk, some would not. Some would believe the tales, others would scoff. The rumor mills would churn anew.

He looked over the last four survivors the workers had pulled out and the pair of corpses as well. A motley assortment, with only hunger, thirst, and the pallor of exhaustion in common. There were no other similarities between them and no explanation, without debriefing them, for their being here. Why they had been left to die.

That would be for Grainger to suss out and work through. Tamner felt he had done enough. The only duty left for him was one that any doctor would have: heal the injured, the suffering. Examine the dead.

Maybe afterward he would screw up his courage to return to this place and learn the truth.

❧*❧

The Spinks did not have all of the answers or connections. They were children, accustomed to surviving but lacking more mature wisdom and adult experience. Thanks to Ginna, however, the night Scarecrow had reached out to them to aid a group of refugee children, the Spinks now knew that the dwarf called Enoch was an ally, was someone on Scarecrow's side. Those who found the fallen vigi, knowing they could not move him themselves, spread the word in the hopes of finding that ally, finding someone who could offer Scarecrow shelter and could help move him to it.

Those Spinks on their way to Vapors, in the hopes of seeking help from Ginna, crossed paths with Enoch on the stairwell near Vapors door and trusted he would be the man for this job.

Enoch's vigilance since leaving The Lair, an exhaustive awareness that refused to leave him after the brush with the brako hours earlier, alerted him to the threat of moving shadows before the children emerged. Their dirty faces, hidden behind their identifying bandas, were a relief to see but he did not think the approach of such a large group could be a good thing. If the brako were following him, he did not want the children to be in the line of fire.

"He's won't wake up," said the girl leading the charge as she clutched Enoch's hand with unexpected strength and insistence.

Afraid to utter the word, afraid of the answer, Enoch murmured, "Who?" as he continued up the stairs towards Vapors with continuing glances into the dark places around them.

He knew who. The man who had saved his life.

❧ 174 ❧

"Scarecrow," said another.

"Where?"

They shook their heads. "We can take you…"

"But we can't move him," offered another.

"And if we do…if we try…"

"We'll be seen."

Enoch's frown grew. Being seen was precisely what he feared. If Scarecrow had been injured in an altercation but managed to crawl to relative safety, it was as likely that the brako were looking for him as they were for Enoch. Either way, if Enoch went to Scarecrow's aid, knowing he would be unable to move him to shelter alone, he might lead the brako directly to the vigi. That would be a risk of last resort.

He cocked his head towards Vapors. "I'll get help…someone who can move him. Some of you wait here…some of you…watch him; let him know help is coming."

Assuming that Enoch meant he would get help from Ginna, the Spinks bobbed their heads and scattered into the shadows like rodents.

Enoch did not watch them, confident that no spying brako could have overheard the exchange, not even the one descending the stairs several feet away to his left. He was confident that the lone brako had not seen where the streeters had gone and cared little about them.

He only cared, it seemed, about the little man he approached with measured, determined strides.

Enoch ducked through Vapors' beaded curtain door, noting that Colyx was not here, and climbed onto an empty stool at the far end of the bar, gesturing to Ginna as if ordering a drink. He had barely settled when the brako entered and made a sweeping-gazed study of the vindi. His focus lingered a little too long on the dwarf until Ginna set a bottle of hemp ale on the counter before him. Only then did the brako look away and slid through the shadows and flashing neon to sit in a far corner booth. From there he might have been watching the andi dancers on stage or might still have been watching Enoch.

Behind the bird-beaked mask, it was impossible to tell.

Unable to send a message or make a call without looking suspicious, Enoch caught Ginna's wrist with one hand and took the bottle with the other. "Tell Lash to come quickly. He's needed."

As someone approached on his right, he could not say more and abruptly let her go.

Odds were that, to Senior Kal, who bent against the bar beside him and said, "Vodka, please," Ginna," with a shiver-inducing smile and tone, the name Lash meant nothing.

Ginna nodded at Enoch, produced the requested glass of vodka, and then disappeared into the kitchen as if to deliver an order.

"Brako problems, I see."

Wondering if the Senior had been in Vapors when he arrived or if Kal had followed the brako inside, Enoch shrugged and refused to look at him. "Nothing I can't handle," he snorted.

Kal took the time to study the thickening crowd. With the end of shift just announced, workers done with their days were eager for a drink or a meal or a hint of company, while others sought distraction before returning home for sleep, before beginning the daily drudgery all over again.

"I don't see him here to protect you this time."

The corners of Enoch's mouth and eyes twitched. The Senior must have been somewhere in the vicinity of the earlier salt protest, must have seen the brako pursuing him. He must have seen Scarecrow's intervention or else he had spies who had told him about it. It was safe to assume that the Voices had spies to keep tabs on persons of interest and that Enoch was now on that list.

Not only did Enoch have the brako's attention. He had the Talkers' and their agents' attention as well.

Even if Lash needed his help, there was no way Enoch could go.

"Doesn't mean I need yours…but if you want to be useful, you could call off your dogs and tell them to stop following me."

"Following you?" Kal chuckled. "My dear paranoid fellow…" He drank his whiskey shot and put the glass down before standing straight and smoothing the front of his shirt. "We have better things to do than follow you." He paused to adjust his damp coat for departure. "I meant what I said, what I offered. I have the resources to protect you."

"If I opt in with your takeover scheme. I told you…not interested."

No threats made. No offers repeated or pleasantries exchanged. There was only a short, "Good day," offered as Ginna returned to the bar and nodded once to Enoch.

His message had been delivered.

He stayed on the stool, nursing his drink. So long as that brako sat in the corner, Enoch was not going anywhere. Not unless he left in Lash's company.

❧*❧

As was often the case, Agnys was up with the sun, out in the dewy fields before Venn pried his eyes open to the new day's glow. It did not surprise him when she skipped through his door unbidden as he sat down to eat, her little face with its blonde halo beaming as if she was the keeper of some tremendous secret. The sunrise stretched its fingers through his southeast-facing doorway, bathing her in a glow that made her look like the ethereal being Rhyd had once claimed her to be, in one of those too-brief moments when his guard was down and he chose to show the heart beneath his hardened exterior.

He had not always been hard. Venn was responsible for it. He blamed no one but himself for what Rhyd had become.

Venn did, however, blame Rhyd for failing to let him back in, for failing to let things go back to the way they use to be.

"He's okay," Agnys chirped as she took a fresh biscuit from the stone where they cooled and took a bite of its sweet, salty goodness.

"Was he here?" There was only one person she would be speaking about, and for a fleeting moment he hoped Rhyd had returned to Marbordo…for the night, for an hour, or even a few minutes, long enough to have spoken to Agnys…even if he had not come to their home or spoken to Venn.

If Rhyd had come here, Venn had not sensed him.

"Doctor Tamner saw him. He's okay, just busy."

Venn made a noise, a swallowed growl that he did not want to direct at the child who considered herself the bearer of good news. It was a relief to know Rhyd was alive, but not seeing him except for that short glimpse at the door into Hebenon's shell, not speaking to him, gave Venn no peace of mind.

He knew Rhyd had been hurt. Hurt, and had not sent for Venn or alerted him. Even when he had known, Venn had failed to go to him.

There seemed little hope, but perhaps he should give Rhyd another chance. Perhaps he should go and see Rhyd's recovery for himself.

"Agnys! Come see what I found!"

Cori Tamner's voice echoed in the morning air and Agnys took up two more biscuits with a smile before racing out to find her friend. It was a strained smile, however, a reflection of Venn's mood and doubts, but she did not let his disposition prevent her from seeking a day's fun.

Nor should it. The matter between Venn and Rhyd was not her fault, not her problem. She could not undo the damage that was done. Only the two men could do that, if they wanted to.

Venn decided, with a glance at his empty doorway, to try again.

᪥*᪥

Lash entered through Vapors' kitchen rather than the main door, the nature of the summons suggesting caution was necessary; he arrived to see Kal leaving Enoch at the bar, a smug expression on the Senior's face and a pensive, annoyed one on the dwarf's. The Senior did not notice him, although Lash was certain the brako in the corner did. He made an effort to appear inconspicuous as he stopped at the bar, lowered the hood of his rain cape, and called for a bottle of lemon beer to go without looking at the dwarf.

Enoch did not look at him either, but around the mouth of his beer he muttered, "That was fast."

Shrugging slightly, Lash scooped up a handful of peanuts from the counter bowl and asked, "Senior still stalking you?"

"Brako too." He could not say that the two things were related, but he could not say they were not either. He had lived a lifetime with his secret, with no one asking questions or prying into his business. The Senior had somehow learned the truth and so it was possible the brako, and others, had too, possibly from the same unidentified source. While the Senior was looking to recruit an ally, Enoch did not believe the brako intended the same.

"Think it's time we tell him?"

"Gotta keep him alive first. Spink's'll take you. Think he took a hit, but if I go…"

Lash's nod might have been to Enoch or to Ginna when she set the requested beer on the counter and took his passcard to deduct the transaction. If Enoch believed he was being followed, by Talkers, brako, or anyone else, sending him to Scarecrow would be a mistake.

Lash raised the hood of his cape. "I'll take care of it," he said, taking his beer and trudging towards the front door, furthering the illusion that he was nothing more than another tired fellow that life was doing its best to bend and break.

Enoch did not watch him.

In the mirror behind the counter, he could see that the brako had not moved.

❧*❦

"Jonner Willis."

The dark-skinned fellow had once been a mountain of a man, as tall as Grainger with a build that might have bested him in a fair fight. Now, spindly-limbed and lean from the meager meals available in the Core, which he had often been inclined to share with others, he looked more like a ghost than a man. The assistant at Grainger's side pulled up the available Archive data as he had with each of the others, seeking to verify the identities of those brought out of the Core, to determine why they had been incarcerated and decide each person's fate.

Even if the mine reopened, Grainger did not deem it fair, nor did the Nau members seated with him to review the cases of the line of people awaiting their turn for processing, to return these long-suffering people to that place. There were other choices available, from incarcerating the most serious offenders, to sentencing mid-level offenders to work in the Factories, to releasing those lowest on the scale, deemed over-punished for petty offenses, into the city to live out the remainder of their lives.

A cluster of them had already been assigned to the Factories and were given provisions, clothing, housing assignments, and instructions for what their new lives would entail. Though some argued that being assigned to a Factory crew was the same as slave labor in the Core, Hebenon needed the Factories to survive and no one had yet to provide another solution to maintain that workforce. The production of additional andis was out of the question. Workers were treated humanely, no different than others in Hebanthe Falls; only living their lives segregated from the rest of the city set them apart.

Non-residents of the Uppers had never been allowed to pass through those halls every day, trailing between the Factories and the Levs to provide the needed workforce. With people now taking that route between the Levs and Outside, perhaps it was time for a change in the Factory workforce too.

That would not happen today.

It was not ideal, but the need for skilled labor had to be met. For the people who had slaved in the isolation of the Core with barely the minimum of food and necessities, it was Grainger's opinion that the Factories would be better for them…while keeping potentially threatening elements out of the city's primary population…than sending them back to the mines.

Three men and one woman had been taken away for permanent incarceration, their crimes ranging from murder to acts of terrorism against the city, acts the Nau was unwilling to excuse. Another three remained in the care of the medis, still being treated for their injuries. Four clustered at the end of the table, huddled around a pair of archivists, an Echo tech, and the Housing and Labor ministers, all of whom were busy arranging identification numbers, passcards, tick accounts, and assigning housing. Places of employment were suggested to each based on their individual experience and skills.

Thankfully, the Nau had agreed with each of Grainger's endorsements and the decision-making process had gone quickly. There were four more people to process, plus those in the medi-ward, and then this part of this business would be behind him.

With the Ximenezes in the background, recording the process, no doubt with the intent of creating either fluff pieces for airing or else looking for something they could piece together as another slam-cast meant to badly reflect on the captain and Nau, the afternoon was as much a public relations move as it was a necessity. Grainger had not needed Tamner present, but since the doctor was the one to open the mines a second time, thus already perceived as a hero in the public's eye, he was the reasonable choice to have here, to provide medical oversight and provide a trustworthy face to any prodcasts the Ximenezes made.

The Nau also wanted Tamner's presence to assure that these strange, pathetic creatures were not bringing Plague into Hebenon.

"Ah, Willis." Grainger looked over the data the archivist pulled up, wishing it was Jaron beside him doing so. "You were an engineer?"

"Fixed and built steam systems, yes, sir." Unlike many of those Grainger had already spoken with, this man was soft-spoken and polite despite his size. His fifteen years of incarceration had failed to erode those things and turn him brutish as it had done for many of the others.

"This…Bjorn Sorens…do you remember him?"

Jonner nodded. "Damn shame that piston broke when it did…"

"You stand by your statement that the incident was accidental?"

"I never pushed no one. Couldn't have timed a push with a mechanical failure if I'd wanted to. Bjorn was trying a repair when the system seized and…"

"They just needed a cazzing engineer to fix carts," muttered the smaller dark-haired man behind Jonner in a tone of contempt. "Whenever we needed something, a cook, a grower, a medi, funny how someone was thrown in to provide it."

Those three members of the Nau who had once been part of the Doctet exchanged glances, unable to ignore the accusation. They might not remember this particular case…there had been so many over the years…but whatever the Doctet recommended, the choice had always, ultimately, belonged to the Founder.

Uninterested in playing 'what if' with the Founder's orders, Grainger flicked a finger over the screen, reading what little evidential data remained. The Coup, the Hub failure, had cost the city a host of lost data. What he saw, however, was enough to prompt a decision and he nodded at Jonner with a gesture to continue down the table.

Without digging too deeply into data that might no longer exist, it appeared to him that this man had been sentenced for a false crime purely out of a need for an engineer in the Core. An unfortunate workplace accident had provided a right-time footnote to the case file of Jonner Willis' life.

"They'll get you set up. Welcome back to Hebenon, Mr. Willis."

The big man's smile was polite and sincere. "Thank you, sir."

Grainger met Tamner's gaze across the room, noting the approving smiles that passed between the Ximenezes as he did so. Tamner nodded back as the next man in line stepped in front of the captain with a curt, "Molly. Molina Netzer."

If only all of the captain's decisions were so easily made…and came with the same stamp of public approval.

❧*❧

The Spinks, as was common for most of those who lived on the street, were resourceful, particularly in their care of the fallen vigi. Lash admired their ingenuity. They had covered Scarecrow with a tarp, shielding him from moisture and the prying eyes of anyone who came across the alley, as well as to provide him warmth. Several children huddled around him, using his hip to balance a dirty game board and deck of cards for whatever game they were playing beneath a discarded sheet of metal siding propped on recycle bins on both sides of the alley. Someone had brought an alglamp to offer a small degree of heat as well as a faint sizzling blue light by which to play. They looked innocent and unconcerned when Lash's guides brought him around the corner, either because the whistle exchange had alerted them to the arrival of friendlies or else because they believed they had little reason to think their subterfuge would be discovered.

Peeling back the tarp as Spinks kept watch up and down the street and the head of the alley, Lash confirmed that Scarecrow was breathing, muttering in his sleep but unresponsive to Lash's touch. Covered with body armor, he could discern little else about the man's condition. Using the tarp as a convenient wrapping, Lash rolled him in it, secured both ends, and hoisted Scarecrow into his arms so that no one would be able to see what he was carrying.

If Scarecrow's ribs were broken, or there were serious internal injuries, this was not going to help, Lash thought grimly. The position of the bundle looked suspicious, and people might still guess, but Lash did not think he had any other choice.

"Supposed to meet the archivist at the cat man's house," offered one of the Spinks. "Know where it is?"

Lash scowled and nodded, fearing what such a directive meant. With the Spinks and their bird whistles leading the way, directing him along a cleared route, Lash kept to the shadows as much as possible, waiting at crossings occupied by brako or bugorra, jostling the man up and down stairs with growing concern that Ballard might end up dead by the time they reached safe shelter.

The lights in his flat were off as expected. If Jaron had been sent there, he could not have gotten inside. There was no sign of him near the doors at the bottom of the stairs. A disparate collection of felines perched on railings, on the window sills, curled in front of both doors and in an exterior flower box, did not prove which flat was which, but with the lights aglow in the other flat, Ballard's flat, choosing that one was as good as choosing his own.

Either Jaron was inside or Maemi…or possibly even Venn. It did not matter. If thinking that flat belonged to Lash threw off anyone following them, it masked Ballard's identity for a little while longer. The man had grown heavier with each minute of the trek and they needed to get off the streets before the shift change whistle sounded.

"Keep watch," Lash instructed. He would offer the Spinks ticks, or food, or something else if he could later, but his hold on Ballard meant he had no hands free to do so and now was not the time. He kicked the door twice with the toe of his boot since he could not knock and waited with a multitude of potential greetings racing through his head to offer whoever opened the door.

Light peeped around the corner of the window as the shade was peeled back enough for whoever was inside to see out. Then the drawing clatter of Ballard's array of interior locks, added to deter entry after Venn had Vanished…when a simple passlock had proven inadequate to keep the Crow's out…and the door opened far enough to let Lash elbow his way inside.

It was Jaron.

"What…?"

In Lash's arms, Scarecrow groaned as if knowing he was somewhere safe enough to awaken.

Jaron's panic-stricken expression was animated as he tossed piles of laundry, clean and dirty, onto a nearby chair, the sofa table, the dining table, clearing the couch so that Lash could put Rhyd down. As soon as the bundle was settled, ignoring the water soaking into the cushions, Lash opened the secured ends to free the man inside. With Jaron's help, the tarp was pulled away, and as Lash pulled off Scarecrow's mask, Jaron dragged the oxygen tank closer to replace the suit's breather with another.

"No idea," Lash finally replied. "You?"

Jaron shook his head, the pain caused by the damaged implant and the blow that had caused it making him wince. Other than directing him to the cat man's house, a dark place Jaron had not had access to, next door to the one shelter he could get into thanks to the passcard he still carried after previous trips here for clothes and oxygen tanks while Rhyd recovered, Jaron was sure coming here was what Rhyd had intended. He was also sure the order, and whatever had happened to Rhyd, was connected to the brako who had assaulted him outside of the Archives. Anything more was speculation.

"Looks like they got you too." Whoever they had been.

The gesture towards his ear and side of his head made Jaron wipe his hand across the drying blood there. He frowned.

"Jar…"

Lash turned his attention to removing Ballard's boots, his weaponry and body armor, actions that aborted the vigi's weak efforts to speak and extend an arm towards the kitchen and the bottle of Zaolei he desired. Alcohol might not be the best remedy, but as much as everything hurt, Rhyd did not think a drink would make things worse.

"Shouldn't have gone after them in your condition," scolded Jaron, clasping Rhyd's hand in one of his, brushing the man's sweaty hair back with his other. Whatever Scarecrow had done, he had gone after someone.

Lash abandoned the undressing efforts and went to the kitchen for the medicinal beverage Ballard asked for. Rhyd's eyes closed, his body, his soul, finding peace in the hand clutching his although he was unable to look Jaron in the eye to let him see it. He opened them again when Lash's footsteps announced his return. Lash pulled the breather aside and helped tip Rhyd's head enough to pour the whiskey into his mouth. Rhyd coughed at the burn, but the sensation had a calming effect; he nodded once and settled onto the cushions again.

"Can't let him…couldn't let him…you're safe." He freed his hand from the touch he could not tolerate without weeping, a touch he both longed for and feared. He brushed his fingertips over the side of Jaron's face; blood came away on his fingers. "Get that…looked at…"

This time when his eyes rolled back and fluttered closed, it was to follow the path of darkness where Zaolei led.

Jaron swallowed the knot of emotion in his throat, trying not to dissect what Rhyd had deliriously tried to say. He would rather have answers but rest was the best thing for Rhyd…and perhaps the care of a doctor. They would be safe here.

❧*❧

Tamner had been the last person to see Rhyd, but Venn's efforts to question him were thwarted by urgent business the doctor was unable to escape. Frustrated, Venn left a message demanding an audience as soon as the doctor was free.

He returned to Marbordo, shoulders sagged in defeat.

Maybe he should have gone to Rhyd's flat.

What more could he do? His last foray into Hebanthe Falls, to the home they had shared, had produced empty-handed results. Rhyd had not been there in some time, from the condition of the flat, which meant he had likely taken to spending time in Jaron's home.

That was the last place Venn wanted to go. He was not desperate enough, not willing, to risk the humiliation and degradation.

Seeing the flat they had once shared so empty, so abandoned, had filled Venn with a sense of heart-twisting, death-like finality that he did not think he could bring himself to face again.

He wanted proof that Agnys' claim was true. That Rhyd was okay.

Surely Doctor Tamner could give him that.

He wanted Rhyd to know he cared, even if some of his actions of late suggested otherwise. Even if Rhyd no longer cared in return.

That, however, was something Doctor Tamner could not give.

❧CHAPTER 15❧

He could not help himself. Forced clean of addiction during the first several weeks of a seven-year stint in the Core, Molly Netzer was still a slave to his passions, to a need for an altered state that was more mental than physical. Arrested for a foolish assault on a Crow while under the influence, the sort of crime that always garnered the maximum punishment regardless of the severity of the act, those present at his sentencing had judged him unredeemable, an unrepentant addict unlikely to change. The decision was made to lock him away where he would either prove a benefit to society by aiding in the mining efforts or else he would die in the throes of withdrawals when the substances of his addictions were no longer available.

Molly was not violent or dangerous enough to others to warrant permanent incarceration or expulsion to the Outside as part of one of the many experiments conducted to study the outer conditions. He was deemed too uncooperative to be useful in the Factories, where skill and attention to detail were crucial, and his relatively short sentence made trying to train him a waste of time and resources. Ten years of grueling labor in the mines, however, seemed a more than adequate punishment for that single stain on his record, and if he had died there under the physicality of the work, it would have been no great loss to Hebenon or the Core…or to anyone.

He had served seven of that ten years and now found himself set loose into the darkness of the Levs he had once called home. Despite now possessing a home he had never had, a tick account for his needs, and a list of three potential employers to contact, the chance to set himself up for a decent, stable future for the first time in his life, he saw no prospects that amounted to anything worthwhile.

There were only two things he wanted. A Heb score to outshine any other…and to find out if Skelter had made it out of the Core alive.

Skelter should not matter. Whatever the redhead's fate, Molly knew he had been given a second chance. He would be a fool not to seize it. But Skelter had left him to die. Had left all of them to die. Skelter, like Molly, had made a pact with death…and Molly believed it was a pact they should both honor. A man must honor his debts. If the river had not forced Skelter to hold to his bargain, had not taken his life, Molly intended to see that Skelter upheld his pact.

The redhead had spoken often of a place called Vapors. Molly did not remember the place but did not think it should be difficult to find. If Skelter lived, Vapors seemed a likely place to find him, and a likely place to score Hebbies.

It was the first place Molly decided he would go.

As soon as he enjoyed his first hot shower in seven years, a full meal, and a night of long sleep in a good bed.

The travel down the Levs, however, from one lift to another, through wet streets and cold, shiver-inducing mist, worked steadily to erode even that intention.

❧*❧

"You shouldn't have reopened it without consulting me," Grainger grumbled using Tamner's arm to remain steady as he stepped over the explosion debris. Enough of the path was cleared through the rubble that the two men and those of the Nau daring enough to risk what some believed was exposure to the Factory Plague, were able to go beyond the locked gate into the abandoned mine complex. With three of the previous inmates still receiving medical care and a restless night's sleep behind him, coming here for answers to questions Grainger knew others would ask was the prudent thing to do.

Tamner shrugged as he studied the central room from this inside vantage point rather than the outside one where he had stood before. "There was no time." Despite the captain's grousing, Tamner was sure he would have permitted the opening if he had asked. He was too humane a man not to. Exposing the ancient history of Hebanthe Falls would raise questions no one alive could answer, but Tamner did not think Grainger would have left those trapped inside to die.

Even if, in Grainger's opinion, it might have been better to leave the past buried.

Followed by a gaggle of structural engineers, historians, mining experts, and others, Grainger and Tamner moved from unlit room to unlit room, through one corridor after another, identifying sleeping quarters, storage rooms, and mineshafts. There were areas for cultivating what crops could be grown here, areas for the breeding of rats and chickens for meat and eggs. There was machinery designed for recirculating air and for collecting water where it dripped through the rocks, for the repurposing or disposal of waste, for cooking, and the care of tools. There were rooms with still-usable locks used to confine those who needed confining or protecting precious resources. One room contained a narrow tunnel, not big enough for a man to pass, through which no air moved; another had a cable hanging into a well where the violent river's tumble could be heard at the bottom.

The entire complex smelled of dirt, sweat, and death.

People had survived here. As prisoners, as a community of miners. People had built lives, maintained them, even after the doors to Hebanthe Falls had sealed to trap them. It could not have been an easy existence but they had done it. How much longer they could have survived, with the animal cages empty and the growing boxes devoid of foliage, was impossible to judge. Whatever this system of rooms had originally been intended to be, something more important it appeared than salt mines, it had not been that in many centuries. With the Outside open, there would never again be a need for anyone to reside in this underground prison.

The captain could be angry with Tamner's choice if he chose to, just as the Founder would have been angry with Tamner's choice to go outside the night of the Coup.

Tamner believed he had done the right thing. Both times.

With the removal of the people from the Core, it was one more piece of humanity's unfortunate history laid to rest.

❧*❧

Enoch's intention to outwait the tenacious brako in the corner resulted in a long night at Vapors' bar but eventually his stubbornness won out. As soon as the brako exited through the main door where he had entered, Maemi hustled Enoch through the kitchen and Enoch quickly made his way to the hostel Skelter now called home. If Colyx had been on shift, Enoch would have asked him to accompany him. Expecting to find the big man at the hostel, he was tempted, as he rounded the corner of the row of vindis where Vapors was located, to ask Colyx if he wanted a side job as his merc.

"Enoch!"

No one ever called his name across a crowd, not here in the streets of Hebenon. Thinking the startling cry to be a warning, expecting to find brako bearing down on him, he turned, wide-eyed, towards the voice. The filter of the public barter of goods, the clatter of carts, the rustle of packs, vindi music, the drone of prodcasts playing on exterior Echoes, and the constant drip of water and the roar of the falls prevented identification of the speaker's voice. But the man Enoch saw pushing and squeezing towards him from across the intersection was familiar enough.

Of all of the people to make it out of the Core alive, Enoch had not expected Molly Netzer to be one of them.

"You got the kids out okay?" When he reached him, Molly pumped Enoch's hand in an enthusiastic greeting.

"Obviously."

"Switz? Colyx and Otta? Skelter? Anyone? I haven't seen…"

"You're the first I've seen…other than Switz." It was an easy lie, but he knew the type of man Molly was. The man consistently sought angles to score gifts, favors, extra rations or supplies, or anything else he could get his hands on. He had gained the nickname 'Moka' inside for his mooching, and if he thought he could get something out of Skelter, Molly would not hesitate to try.

In time, Molly would find the redhead if he wanted to. For now, Enoch chose to remain a buffer between them.

❧ 190 ❧

"Too bad. Jonner's here…some others…I was hoping for more."

Jonner was a good man. Well-liked and respected inside. Enoch was pleased to hear he was one of the lucky ones to secure a new life.

"You know where I can score?"

Hitting up the Core's source for keffers and other items was expected. Enoch had been there when Molly came in; he had seen the addict's state of mind, his physical condition, had watched him suffer through withdrawals. He watched him scrounge every day for anything to fill the void Heb had left. Enoch was not surprised that Molly's first quest after his release was to score a hit.

He was not surprised to be asked.

"Not my bag, Molls…you know that." How often had he refused to smuggle Heb into the Core?

"Come on. I know you can. You owe me, varon. I kept my mouth shut, didn't tell 'em what I know…and you didn't pull favors to get us all out. Think that warrants a few favors."

Enoch scowled. Without knowing how long Molly had been free, he wondered if the addict had been the one following him, wondered if he had told someone about him, if he had prompted the brako's interest. But if Molly had brako connections, he would have his hands on all the Heb he wanted. The brako liked to keep their sources cooperative through favors and the feeding of addictions.

"Blackmail'll get you nothing. I don't deal Heb…"

The man's shifty eyes darted towards the shadows and he shuffled, his nervous body already twitching as if again in withdrawals for a substance he had not imbibed in seven years. Or maybe he had and was now looking for more. "Can Skelts get it? If I pay? I got ticks. I'm good for it." He patted his breast pocket, ignoring the shaking of Enoch's head. "If you see him…tell him I'm looking…"

"If I see him," Enoch snorted, making no promises despite his seeming agreement. He did not trust Molly, did not trust any addict, any more than he trusted the brako.

The man was a stickler for pacts and promises and spoken agreements. He would take Enoch's words as one whether the dwarf meant it or not.

That adherence to pacts made Enoch frown as Molly moved away. Molly was a Spades, the only one other than Skelter, as far as Enoch knew, to make it out of the Core. What were the odds, he mused as he slipped into the mid-shift crowd without looking back, that the Spades pact, the drawing of the ace, was going to bite Skelter in the ass?

If Molly was as predictable as he had always been, this was likely to bite Enoch in the ass too.

Lash was right. It was time to tell Ballard the truth.

❧*❧

The wide-eyed expression of delight, the smile of welcome, made his first stop worth everything Jonner had endured to get here.

"Weren't sure you'd still be 'round," he said, barely reaching the stool before the woman made her way around the bar, reached him, and hugged him so hard it was like the glue pulling all of his scattered pieces back together and holding them there.

"Where the hell have you been?" Maemi cried, her voice ragged and teary as she pressed her cheek to his. He was older than she was by eight years, but their families had been friends, neighbors, and the two had grown up together, studied together. Their parents had talked about marriage at least once before his arrest, his disappearance and it had been a dream Maemi had clung to for years. As with so many others taken before the Coup, no one had heard from him since and it was impossible for his friends, his family, for Maemi, to learn his fate.

Losing him had broken her heart.

"In the mines," he murmured, his hands clutching at her back as he absorbed the floral scent of her perfume intermixed with the combination of kitchen smells and alcohol that tended to cling to every swiver he had ever met. Unashamed of the tears on his cheeks, grateful that after so many years she was as happy to see him as he was to see her, he did not care if he was making a spectacle of himself.

His parents were long dead. His little brother, exactly Maemi's age, had been arrested for protests and civil disobedience not long before Jonner's arrest…and no one knew what had become of him either. Jonner only knew his brother had not been sent to the Core.

Without family, there was no one else for him in Hebanthe Falls. No one but Maemi. She had been his only hope for connecting to his old life, a hope now fulfilled.

"You're one of those who got out?"

He shrugged and nodded simultaneously as he reluctantly let her go, not surprised that she had heard about the existence of the Core, the salt mines, of people living beneath the ground, outside of Hebenon, for decades without contact to the city.

"Been fifteen years…wasn't sure you'd remember…"

With his face between her hands, she murmured, "'course I remember. I was so sorry when your…that they're not here to see…"

"But you are." He had learned of his parents' deaths from those helping him rebuild his life, although he had expected to have lost at least one of them in the years he had been away. The life of a fisher was a hard one, prone to the sort of accident that had taken his father, and his mother had been in frail health before his arrest.

"Seeing you again is good enough. Can an old man get a drink?"

"You're not old," she chuckled, her voice thick with emotion. She ducked behind the bar, grabbed a bottle of black malt, assuming it was still his favorite, and pushed the bottle towards him with a bright smile.

"Gray says otherwise." He dragged a hand over his close-cropped hair, black peppered with white, and smiled back. "It true? There's no more Founder?"

"That's complicated."

He nodded, took a drink, and sighed contentedly. "Damn that's good. You remembered."

"I remember everything." Everything that had been between them, everything that could have been, everything that had passed in between his arrest and this moment. "I'm on shift; my girl's not due for five hours…but if you want to come up for dinner in six, I'll catch you up on what you've missed." She gestured above their heads to indicate where she now lived.

His expression brightened over the rim of the wide-necked bottle. He imagined she had stories to tell. Stories about the search for his brother, about his parents. About the city and the years of her life that he had missed. Stories about the absent Founder and the events that had precipitated a remarkable shift in the city's leadership.

"I'd like that. I'll be there."

The wrinkled man who shuffled onto the stool beside him as they talked, pushed his glass across the table for a refill and grinned. As Maemi filled it and then moved reluctantly away to fulfill the requests of other patrons, the old man bowed his head, as if to hide his low, conspiratorial voice when he said, "Ain't no bigger change than seeing Outside. Everyone ought to."

"Outside?"

The stranger nodded. "Don't need deks. Don't have to stay in the city anymore. Scarecrow cracked 'er open like a nut. Blue sky…grass…the sea. Real sunshine…not that dekking shit. If you've missed anything, you shouldn't miss that."

Expression bright with wonder, Jonner raised his glass in a toast. Outside. They could go Outside…into a world once believed inhospitable and deadly. What a glorious thing that must be.

"May just do that."

He remained on the stool for nearly an hour, listening to music he had missed, nursing his beer, watching Maemi move back and forth along the counter, into the kitchen, and back again. Eventually, the beer was gone and he could not justify continuing to stare like a stalker. There was time before the end of her shift and since Jonner had nothing to do yet to fill it, he decided to take the man up on his words. Seeing the Outside, if it was real, would be the ultimate fulfillment of time…no waste of it at all. He waved at Maemi, intending to pay for his drink when he met her later for dinner, and left the warmth of Vapors for the adventure of Outside that awaited.

❧*❦

Sinking into his chair was an awkward relief from the pulsing pain in his healing leg. Plasts brought torn muscle and shattered bone together, decreased healing time, and allowed a swift return to daily routines, but the pain of that damage lingered as nerves recovered, a reminder that despite medical intervention, the body had endured trauma that needed to heal. The uncomfortable chair endured during the extended hours of retrials and then the limping tour through the Core had punched holes in any belief Oliver had entertained that he was mending. His resistance to using pain medication to soothe the ache meant that it had now flared full force.

He was second-guessing that stubborn refusal of medication as he turned on the Echo and filled his glass from the bottle brought in with him. It was not a Brompton's, but the neat vodka would suffice and might, if he consumed enough, dull the physical pain.

The Echosys screen reopened to where he had left off when the expediency of processing the Core survivors pulled him away from his desk. The file Lieutenant Young had given him awaited viewing, the file image still blinking on the screen as a reminder, and so he clicked to open it before capping the bottle and taking his drink.

He should consider eating, dulling the alcohol's fire with food, but he did not feel steady enough on his feet to consider rising again. And Jaron was not near enough to fetch something for him.

The file was SCAM footage, time-stamped the night and hour of the recital, showing nothing at first except a stairwell that looked like so many others in the Levs. Stairs with no identifying traits in the SCAM's eye view to pinpoint its location. Only the time counter stamp gave a clue, but beyond identifying it as Lev 2, Grainger had no idea where this location was. With no foot traffic, no vindi sign or street marker, there was no reason to know. He frowned as he wondered why this had been brought to his attention.

Then a group of seven staggered into view, nondescript forms leaning on each other for support. As they ascended the stairs, as those in the front reached the landing above, a large shadow with a Crow mask and a band around his bicep identifying him as Vanderwall…or a Vanderwall decoy…lurched into the frame.

Grainger stopped the footage. Rewound. Played it again.

Scarecrow undoubtedly. Struggling, possibly injured, but that was a silhouette forever burned into the captain's mind. A Scarecrow sighting was reason enough for the lieutenant to bring this to him, as he was aware, despite his admonitions, that she continued her interest in, and pursuit of, the vigi.

It was one of the others, however, the one who turned, kicked, and delivered the possibly fatal blow to the brako boss, which made Oliver freeze the image. He rubbed his face with both hands and reached for another drink before attempting to refine and enlarge the image for confirmation. He did not need it. Did not want it.

He made the effort anyhow.

Was this why Jaron had failed to come back? Did the brako have him? Had they killed him? Had he retreated into hiding and kept away from Oliver to avoid drawing the brako to the captain's door? The captain of the bugorra was surely the best place to seek shelter from this sort of trouble. Oliver had the resources, the might, to protect him.

Who else could do it?

Grainger's eyes tracked to the man beside Jaron, the man whose weight he partially bore as they continued up the stairs.

The only other man who might be able to protect Jaron too.

He downed a third drink.

When had Jaron crossed paths with Scarecrow? Had this been a coincidental occurrence, Jaron in the right place at the right time to help the injured vigi? Or had he known him before, had connections to him, for much longer, without revealing that detail to Oliver?

Why would he?

It did not matter. Whatever the reasons, whatever situation had led to this encounter on the stairs, Jaron's life was undoubtedly in danger, if he was not dead already.

Pain be damned. Grainger staggered to his feet, a fourth glass of vodka enough, he hoped, to dull the throbbing and not enough to make him stumble like a drunkard. He paused to prompt an Archive search for Jaron's address, something he had never bothered to look for before, using his status as captain to gain access to information not often shared with other Hebenon citizens.

It was time to see Jaron's home. Make sure the man was there. It was time he stopped waiting for Jaron to come to him. If Jaron was alive, Oliver would find him.

If Scarecrow knew where Jaron was, Oliver would find him too.

❧*❧

The captive's sudden flailing and shuddering in his chains lurched Switz to awareness, taking his attention from the T2 he had successfully begged from Blayd under the pretense of wanting to learn the history he had missed during his time in the Core. It was not the Echo's primary use, as he quickly shut off the screen so that no one who came in would see the compromising prod, but Blayd did not need to know that. Switz saw no reason why Blayd should care how he spent the frustratingly long, boring, silent hours babysitting.

Thinking the man was having a seizure, not considering the fate of the last man who got too close, or his own safety, Switz dashed from his sleeping cot to Haythem's side, caught him, and tipped his head back to facilitate breathing. When Kemway's eyes popped open, they focused on Switz with a clarity of terror that announced no seizure but the waking from a nightmare. Switz shifted to make his hold an embrace of comfort, standing behind him where Kemway would be unable to bite him if he felt inclined to do so.

"You're safe. S'okay."

"All black…all black. Came once…for me. Not again. Not again."

"Who came?"

"All black. It burns! Gonna kill me!"

Switz scowled but began to gently sway side to side, a motion often used to calm fussing children. It seemed to work in stages as Haythem struggled less in that embrace. Switz did not know the Founder's history, what life had been like for him as a child or before he ended up in Blayd's care. From the few prods he had watched during his caretaking hours, he understood there had been a rebellion, the Levs against the Uppers, after which the Founder had dropped out of the public's eye until recently. The man some believed dead had been revealed to be in a state of ill health and addled mind, but whether he was ill before the rebellion or injured during it, Switz could not tell.

In truth, Switz was more interested in studying medical advances and smutcasts than history.

He remembered the black profiles of the Crows, however. They were impossible to forget. Maybe Kemway remembered someone from the Coup who had come for him that night. Captain Grainger, perhaps. With the captain now controlling Hebanthe Falls, Kemway thinking a man like that to be a threat would make sense. He wore black. Blayd too wore nothing but black, and it was not unimaginable that the Founder believed his cranky keeper intended to kill him.

Maybe the nightmare was simply that.

Men with unstable minds were prone to those. Switz suffered more than his share of them.

"No one's gonna kill you," he murmured. "I won't let 'em."

"Black gonna kill me. I know…I know…"

He sagged in the chains, in Switz's embrace, continuing to mutter incoherent phrases and shake in distress. Switz stayed until he was calm, wondering all the while if he might be able to use the man's nightmares, the delusion of impending death, to his advantage.

❧*❧

From the outside, Jaron's flat looked no different than any other Lev flat. The single exterior window was shielded by interior slatted blinds and the alglamp that should illuminate the door was shattered the way so many others were that should have brightened the doorways of homes, vindis, or abandoned structures.

The broken door, however, kicked in from the outside, was not normal for an occupied residence. Popper in hand, Grainger eased the door open with the other, the lump in his throat cutting off the flow of air as his heart pounded in his chest.

The tiles immediately beyond the threshold were damp where the outside moisture had blown and splattered in.

The lights were off.

Grainger turned them on to gain a clearer view of whatever he was about to find. He expected, feared, he would find Jaron dead.

It was a single man's flat, one room split by a kitchen counter with a bathroom to one side. A tatty brown sofa with a hemp green blanket and an oxygen tank filled the center of the room. Against one wall, the fold-down bed was unmade. What had been a dining table and chairs were smashed, the remnants of a meal scattered across the floor. He counted two cups and plates, suggesting someone else had been here, but there were no clues who it had been or when they had left.

Perhaps the brako had taken them both.

The oxygen tank and mask did not belong to Jaron.

He saw no blood. No sign of a skirmish except for the destroyed table and chairs. That should have been reassuring.

It was not.

He circled the room, peered into the bathroom, but there was no one there either, nothing out of place, nothing to see. There was no indication how long ago the break-in had occurred except for the moisture at the main door and the absence of wet footprints on the floor that meant it had occurred long enough ago for them to dry.

He was only certain that Jaron was not here now.

Swallowing the strangling panic, he holstered the popper and closed the flat door as well as he could before sending a maintenance request to the construction and repair Shed to see that the door and alglamp were repaired or replaced as necessary. He would do that much for Jaron in the hopes that, should he return from a visit, or a shift, the worst he would find would be a broken table and chairs

It left one logical, possible place for Jaron to be, the best place to check before putting out a BOLO for a missing archivist.

Despite the contained nature of Hebanthe Falls, people went missing all the time. They became streeters, tingers, and addicts. They fell into the river. Now, since the Coup, some had become Crossers and moved Outside. Though he did not think any of those eventualities applied to Jaron, before Grainger succumbed to the fear of it, it made sense to make sure he was not on shift.

He hoped he would have to look no further than the Archives to ease his worries.

⊱⊰

The beaked shadows shrunk back from the door. The bugger captain had not found whatever he had come here for it seemed. He did not appear to be looking for them.

They had nothing to fear.

They could wait.

❧Chapter 16❧

Mesmerized, Jonner stood three steps beyond the shell of Hebanthe Falls staring towards the mountains in the west capped with snow the color of the billowing clouds in the azure sky. Salt and hemp and a warm, rich smell that came, he learned, from the damp earth beneath his feet and held crumbling out between the fingers of his left hand. Animals he had only ever seen in Echo images during his studies as a child dotted the landscape, and people…so many people…moved through the rows of growing crops, in and out of buildings, past him into the city and back out again.

No poisonous red sky.

No smell of sulfur or chemical desolation. No howling wind or boiling black sea.

Not a single, hideously twisted parah to be seen.

There was only the pristine newness of what the world must have looked like when it was new, before humanity's rise to prominence and the subsequent destruction of everything that sustained them.

Somehow, the world had recovered to welcome humanity home.

"Spectacular, isn't it?" The fresh-faced individual who stopped beside him was more girl than woman, with a paleness of complexion that indicated a resident of Hebenon instead of one of those golden-skinned people he presumed to be parah. She smiled without looking at him, happy, as he was, to enjoy the view as others moved around them. "So many years we wasted in there…kept from this…"

"Kept from destroying it again," Jonner snorted.

"Don't think we should be out here? Think we should stay in?"

He shook his head no and hitched his shoulders. "I think people have a tendency to destroy things, property, environment, other people. If we learned one thing in the last few centuries, it should be not to squander this miracle…not to waste a second chance. But who's to say we've learned anything except how to adapt to life in there."

He thumbed over his shoulder towards the city as he slowly turned to face the sea, seeing the young woman now in her hemp-beige tunic and breeches, the style worn by so many of those he could see, the style, he presumed, of the parah. She was pretty enough, but there was a hard edge to the set of her jaw and the corners of her eyes that belied her eager, hopeful words. Whoever she was, she had lived a hard life.

"We've been captive too long. It's time," Jonner mused wistfully, "for us to be free."

"Exactly." She smiled again and slipped her hand into his, not a romantic or seductive gesture but something Jonner interpreted as a friendly sign of welcome, of belonging. "Come on. I've got someone you should meet."

He thought she would lead him into the village. Instead, she tugged on his hand and drew him back into Hebenon, her smile one of expectant promise that he had spent fifteen years living without.

Whoever she wanted him to meet, what could it hurt? It was time to rebuild, his life, humanity, and meeting new friends in place of the ones long lost was a reasonable place to begin.

❧*❧

His uniform made people passing on the walkway give him a wide berth as he stood at the street corner nearest to the Archive's main door, watching silently until the shift whistle's wail brought waves of archivist into the building and then out of it as the shift change commenced. Having heard of an earlier altercation here between Spinks and brako, he studied the faces he could see, the cloaks and boots and gloves, looking for the ones most intimately familiar to him. None matched Jaron's, no face matched the one he hoped to see, and as the flow dwindled, Grainger glanced anxiously at his chrono.

Most businesses worked a three-or four shift rotation. Just because he did not see Jaron arriving or leaving did not mean he was not here. He might still be inside, working a double shift as he often did. Hoping that was the case, Grainger swallowed the anxious flutter choking at the back of his throat, making him want to gag, and approached one of the last stragglers leaving the Archives.

Business. It was only business. Asking questions. Something Grainger had done hundreds of times before. The report of violence gave him reason enough to be here.

There was nothing to be anxious or embarrassed about.

"Are you an archivist? Do you work here?"

Despite his efforts, the quaver in his voice betrayed his nerves.

"Yeah." The word came out as an irritated squeak, the sort Grainger expected from someone eager to be on his way who was afraid he was about to be arrested for some secret crime…or for no reason at all.

Grainger presented his credentials to verify his status, as if the epaulets on his coat were not proof enough of his identity. The fellow took a step back and his eyes darted side to side in search of a place to run. Grainger sighed. He had not wanted to frighten the man.

"I didn't have nothing to do with what happened before…I didn't see it…it wasn't me…"

"I'm not here about that. I'm looking for a fellow named Jaron Rei. He works here, yes? Is he inside?"

The tension eased out of his shoulders and a long breath hissed out between his teeth. "Yeah, there's a Rei here. Dunno if he's on shift…have to ask the desk. He's not on my floor."

Grainger looked up at the multi-leveled surface with a frown. The Archives was a large building, half a residential block wide and extending two Levs up and two Levs down from the main level entrance. Each level had emergency doors, and he imagined that workers could enter and exit through any of those if they chose. Some of the archivists likely never saw each other or learned all of the names of their coworkers. Just because the man knew Jaron's name did not mean he knew him. Just because he had not seen him did not mean that Jaron was not here.

Gesturing with his head, Grainger grunted and muttered, "Go on."

Another hissed breath of release and the man with the broad mouth and crooked nose scurried away.

Grainger did not move.

Ask the desk.

He had the right. He had cause. No one would question his reason for asking. Jaron's home had been broken into and there had been an incident here. As bugorra, coming to share that information and ask questions, or to inquire about the violence, was expected.

But he was leery of rumors, of talk, of what people might think, what they might do with knowledge that connected him to Jaron. If Jaron was already in the brako's hands, connecting him to Grainger might mean leverage that the brako would not hesitate to use. The danger of such a connection was too high to risk exposure.

No. He would not go inside, would not ask questions. He would have one of his officers do it. But where, he wondered as he retreated to the street corner where he had kept vigil, should he seek Jaron next?

❧*❦

He could have stopped any streeter he passed, any tinger tucked in alleys, beneath stairs, in open drainage tunnels, in the doorways of abandoned flats and vindis, to get what he wanted. Despite the desperate craving to calm his frantic nerves and racing thoughts, Molly had little trust in people he did not know. He never had. He had been a solitary man since the day he had escaped his foster family. In those days of scavenging through waste bins, stealing from vindis, picking tick cards from the pockets of unsuspecting passersby, he had slowly built a handful of trustworthy contacts. There had been one for food passes that got him meals from any of the Lev herpa when his thieving failed to fill his belly. There had been another who always knew the best sources for clothing, shoes, or other street nessies.

There had been three separate sources for alcohol and Heb.

Always three. In case any of the others were short of product or were unavailable when Molly went looking.

It would take time to find those sources, if they still existed. It would take time to replace them if they did not. Time was something his distressed nerves did not have. He had time to be free, to settle in, to procure nessies and make a new life, but his first order of business was to soothe the cravings that had provided him hope enough to keep him alive through that Core escape.

When that was done, he needed to find Skelter.

Locating the redhead, though not a necessity, had blossomed into a fixation almost as compelling as his spinning brain's need for Heb.

There was one place he knew, a place with an almost certain score. Often there were agents situated around the soaper to handed out product to passersby in the hopes of hooking new clients or enticing a desperate user into a favor exchange for a handful of orange pills. Sometimes there was no one there but even then, Molly knew how to score, how to get inside. It was not safe, not wise, but for those fraught enough for their next fix, those short on ticks, it was worth a try.

It was that path, the railing that ran the length of the soaper on the side overhanging the river, where the third net stretched across to catch debris and bodies the first two nets upstream had not already strained out of the water, where Molly chose to take his chance when no samples proved available. He had come this way many times, enough times to be confident about reaching the windows he could see from the building's edge. They were cranked open over the rushing current, as usual, meaning all he had to do was balance along the rail until he reached the first one, calculate the short leap up, grab the lip of the window, and hoist himself inside to awaited bliss.

"Hey!"

He had just straddled the rail at the building's corner, his eyes set on the targeted open window, when the cautionary voice altered by the beaked mask prompted him to stop. The speaker was not alone, the other two with him similarly attired.

Molly groaned.

"Not doing nothing," he whined, hoping to appear as if he had only been sitting on the rail, watching the river, perhaps contemplating leaping into it but nothing more. Certainly not planning to break into the soaper. Having just gained freedom from the Core, Molly was in no rush to go back in for this desperate effort to satisfy his addiction.

Those he believed to be law enforcement did not seem to believe him. They took no pity, showed no mercy as they charged down the alley, snatched his arms, and dragged him towards the front of the soaper. Their hands, their grips rough and biting, tore at the flimsy fabric of the slicker he had been given upon his release.

The parole agents had given the Core survivors the bare minimum of clothing and supplies but had provided enough ticks that they could tend to their needs and preferences in ways they saw fit.

It was no one's fault but his that Molly had not taken the time to procure more durable clothing.

"You don't belong here," said one.

"Vanderwall wants a word," growled another.

"You'll pay for what you did."

"What? What'd I do?" Molly did not believe he had been out of the Core long enough to break any laws.

If this was Enoch's doing, sending the Crows after him, the dwarf was going to pay.

❧*❧

"Drink."

Blayd glanced at his hostage over the rim of his bottle. He had not had luck finding Ilya's sister, in gaining an audience with Neoma to test the waters of her temper, in tracking down Oslo to pressure him into aiding in Kemway's care, nor in finding Senior Kal's secondary haunts. Blayd had believed the man's calling would necessitate the continuation of duty, but that he would avoid his primary places of obligation as a precaution. Instead, the Senior had become a ghost since the accusations of kidnapping had fallen upon his shoulders, making him impossible, thus far, to find.

His lack of progress and the failure to be productive left Blayd in a foul enough mood that he had been reluctant to relieve Switz of his duties for the promised respite. Kemway was asleep, however, and

Switz was right. Blayd was not paying him enough to make this a round-the-clock job, to hold him as a prisoner in this building along with the Founder. Allowing him to pick up clean clothes, grab a shower in a hostel, get some nessies, allowing him to eat and get a little fresh air was barely adequate compensation for the number of hours he had already spent monitory their captive's care.

Constant company had kept Kemway from howling like an animal. He was eating normally now too, it seemed…unless Switz was eating both men's share of delivered rations. Switz's company appeared to be beneficial for the chained man and Blayd wanted him to be content enough to stay on the job until he found Oslo. A few more days at most, until the heat of the search died down and Blayd believed it was safe to relocate.

With planted clues to implicate Kal when that happened, this would be over quickly.

The madman stared at him unnervingly as he ate, slack in his chains, a trace of spittle on his bearded chin that might have been uncontrolled drooling or a response to hunger. Captain Grainger's claims of near-constant catatonia were difficult to believe with those piercing eyes following his every move.

"Shut up."

"Drink." Kemway lunged as if to free himself.

Thinking the Founder smelled the potent alcohol, that the aroma aggravated him, Blayd closed his flask with a growl. "Not for you."

The Founder's chains went slack as he stopped straining against them and his gaze dropped. While not well, he was not as damaged, it seemed, as the captain's claims and Blayd wondered how he could use that in his favor, whether he, or rather Switz, could convince Kemway to work with them instead of against them.

He tucked the flask into the breast pocket of his black longcoat and picked up the water bottle from the floor at his feet. Compliance should be rewarded. It was the first step, Switz said, to building trust and a working relationship between them.

It was the sort of relationship Blayd hoped for.

"Head up." He brought the bottle to Kemway's mouth.

With a malicious, "Drink!" and clear-eyed viciousness, Haythem charged. Blayd was close enough that the bottle was knocked from his hand. Startled and angry, he struck with one closed fist, catching the Founder across the face as he stumbled back and landed on his ass. Kemway lurched and flailed in his chains, the way he had done in the first few hours of captivity, and though he did not howl as before, the sounds in his throat were feral, primal. He landed two awkward stomps on Blayd's ankle, though the protection of his high-ankled armored boots kept the bones from snapping.

Blayd yanked the injector from its holster but it was kicked away before he could fire it or rise from the floor.

The door of the prison opened behind him; he was marginally aware of it but not paying enough attention to avoid Switz's attempt to throw his arms around the merc and pull him to safety away from Kemway. Angry, registering the effort as an attack, Blayd threw his arms open, causing Switz to lose his hold, hitting the smaller man with enough force to throw him against the wall.

Switz dropped to the floor, groaning.

Kemway took the opening to lunge one more time but Blayd struck him too, a blow across the side of his head that made the Founder collapse against the pull of his chains and hang limp as a mealworm on the end of a fishing line.

Blayd snorted, snarled, kicked at the now mostly empty water bottle so that it skittered and bounced off the opposite wall, before retrieving the dropped injector with a string of curses.

He did not need the injector; the hostage was quiet, subdued, unconscious. Switz lay where he had fallen.

Blayd made no threats. He did not yell or say a word. He stormed out of the interior chamber and slammed its door shut and, with an angry-sounding click, locked it.

He would be damned if he would allow Switz another outing. He would be damned if he showed Kemway any more favors, Founder or not. It was time to double his efforts to find Oslo, to find Kal. It was time for the Founder to become someone else's problem.

Blayd had had enough.

❧*❧

A school teacher of all things.

Jonner had not expected that, had not expected to be welcomed into the Igraci with open arms when his escort made the introduction. He had heard of them since he was old enough to have an awareness of the world outside of his family's walls as a boy. The Igraci's mission of returning humanity to a world touted to be inhospitable had seemed ludicrous then but as he had grown older, more suspect of the 'truths' the ruling voices of Hebanthe Falls espoused, the possibilities, the 'what ifs', began to make a lot more sense to the young engineer.

He was not surprised that the Igraci had survived his fifteen-year incarceration. But he was surprised that their mission had grown from 'what if' to a reality and the goal of prompting their fellow citizens to leave Hebenon behind had become a goal attainable.

A practical man, he did not believe that such a goal could be met in his lifetime, regardless of Eido's hopes. Not without determined promoting. Not without force.

He watched the pair of women, the one who had made the introduction and the other, graceful despite her limp, as straight-lined and focused as the cut of her red-streaked black hair and clothing, disappear down the stairs, leaving him at the tea vindi with his first pot of hot tea since escape from the Core still warm on the table before him. He had made her no promises, but he knew they would meet again. He had tasted freedom, from the Core, from the city.

He was not ready to give up either of those things.

❧*❧

Vanderwall took one side-eyed glance at the scrawny fellow his men dragged into the office and knew, despite the claims, that this was not the man who had killed his predecessor. While SCAM images were rarely the best for facial recognition, and the protective clothing worn to shield people from the damp meant that it was easy to disguise oneself, there was nothing about the way this twitchy, scruffy fellow moved to suggest they could be the same man. This little man's eyes were too wide-set, his mouth slightly crooked, the shape of his face more oblong and egg-shaped, to be the same man.

The way his hands fidgeted in the pockets of his torn slicker, the way he shuffled from one foot to the other, convinced Vanderwall that the fellow would have been more prone to flight, to abandon anyone he was with, than he would have been to fight to protect them.

He had doubts about the man's willingness to defend himself.

"Why shouldn't I cut your hands off for trying to steal…"

Trembling uncontrollably, eyes darting from one captor to the next but refusing to lock onto the man who spoke, Molly stammered, "Just wanna fix…I have ticks…I can pay…"

"Then why come here...?"

"Ain't gotta source…ain't got no one…I just need Hebs…"

"Helluva stupid risk," Vanderwall muttered.

"Why it's not watched; no one's stupid enough to risk the river…"

No one except him, perhaps. The rail, the sill, were always slick with the river's spray. Molly had seen some try it and fall to their deaths, but he had been lucky in his previous attempts, had gotten in and back out with what he had gone in for. There was no reason, except lack of practice, and maybe his age, for him to have failed this time.

As if reading Molly's thoughts, the brako boss grunted, "No one but you." He leaned back to stare coolly at the man, a streeter no doubt, who looked desperate enough to do anything for the fix he was after. If he was desperate enough to brave the river, he was desperate enough for more valuable risks. The organization might be able to find a use for him, if he was willing, until his addiction got him caught or killed.

"Your hands…or your life."

"No…not the hands…" wild-eyed, Molly tried to shove them deeper into his pockets as if that would protect them.

"Then your life." Vanderwall's mien was both snide and bored.

Molly shrieked. "I don't want to die! That's not what I…I…I…I can help you!"

The room was silent, except for the rush and tumble of the river, until Vanderwall leaned his elbows on the desk, steepled his hands beneath his chin, and asked, "How?"

The threat had been enough to prompt an offer of servitude, as Vanderwall had hoped. People willing to trade for services were often more reliable, in his experience, than ones forced into employment. But that did not mean the little man had any usable skills."

Shaking, wiping one nervous hand over his brow before hiding it in his pocket again, Molly made a quick visual inspection of the room as he tried to think of what he had to offer. These were not Crows, as he had first expected, but thugs of some sort with stolen Crow gear. Criminals needed all sorts of skills, but what did a man who had spent too many years in the Core, have that might be worth a trade for the Hebbies he wanted?

There were several Echos of various vintages lined on a shelf behind the boss' desk, stretching from one side of the room to the other, sporting streams of data, providing ongoing SCAM footage of the inside of a number of vindis and a few exterior locations, including the soaper. It was how they had found him there. One screen appeared to accept an ongoing barrage of incoming communiques, another monitored audio files. Two displayed Hebanthe Falls prodcasts, laughies on one and a sporting event on another, while a third displayed the usual spate of news, gossip, and production reports that came from the Uppers as conditions within the city, the Factories, and now Outside, changed throughout the day.

Only the Echo on the desk at the big man's elbow showed a static display of whatever the man had been working on when Molly was dragged into the room. He could not read the documents or the messages coming in, nor get a good look at the SCAM windows, but he did not need to.

"I'm haikara…or I was!" he stammered excitedly. "Molina Netzer…look me up. I'm good. With all these." He gestured to the array. "You need a good tech to keep things working and I…"

"You think we don't have…"

"There…see…!" He pointed at one Echo where the open data stream periodically flickered with a flash of blue across the screen. "Feed's not optimized. I can fix that. Make it better. Upgrade your gear…your softs…I know I've been outta the game for a while, but I can do this. Can make prodcasts…hack the SCAMs…hack your competition if you need it…"

He did not know who the brako were or how much of the criminal element in the city they controlled. But he did know that such endeavors, such power, came with rivals, competitors, enemies. The Crows at least had to have it in for them. Molly had no qualms about squashing anyone, or undermining the Crows, on this man's behalf if it kept him alive and earned him some Heb.

Vanderwall cut him off with a glare and a waving hand. "Put him in the tupik." Locking the stranger up for a stint would give him time to research this Molina Netzer, find out who he was, decide if giving him a shot was worth the effort. Molly had seen his face now, seen this room where he conducted business, so turning him loose without some sort of choke and leash was not an option. It was either use him or kill him. Vanderwall needed to decide which was the better end.

It did not matter to him either way.

The attending brutes began to drag Molly towards a side door and Molly, believing he was about to die, shouted, "I know things! I know about the Kemway…"

Another hand motion from Vanderwall and the brako paused, hands tight around Molly's arms so that he grimaced and squirmed. Vanderwall stared at Molly, wondering if he knew the answer to the one question all of Hebenon wanted to be answered.

If so, that was a conversation to be had in private. He said nothing as he evaluated his captive and then again waved him away. He would talk to Molina again, learn what he knew. The next time they saw each other in this room, or his tupik cell, would decide Molina's fate.

Whatever he knew would have to be fotzing vital to save his life.

꙳*꙳

In the now silent captivity chamber it was impossible to quantify the passage of time. One minute. One hour. There was just the throbbing in his head, the ache in his arm and side where he had hit the wall, a low rumble of hunger in his belly, and the repeating question ricocheting inside his skull.

What the cazz had happened?"

Switz was used to being knocked around. Memories of it formed so many of his earliest imaginings that it seemed such pain and humiliation had been part of his life from his first drawn breath. For a time, there had been no choice, and then there was, and then inside the Core there was none again. Survival had necessitated enduring.

This was no longer the Core. He did not have to endure abuse. He did not have to stay here. When the door opened, Founder be damned, Switz was out of here. He could do better than live like this.

Pushing up on his knees, his elbows, with his head hanging as he waited for the pain to subside and the nausea to pass, he heard a low, terrified sound to his right that made his breath catch.

"Get me out of here."

Switz turned his head to meet Kemway's eyes but said nothing.

"Give you anything you want. Position. Ticks. Glory. Anything. Just…get me away from Scarecrow…before he comes…"

"Scarecrow?

Haythem shook his head. "The black…it will kill me. It will. But not if you…"

On his knees, sore arm pressed to the wall so he could leverage to his feet, Switz shook his head too, an act he immediately regretted as he swallowed the ball of nausea in his throat. "Not in a position to…"

"Know who you are…what you've done…"

Doubting that statement, not knowing how it could be possible, Switz met Haythem's gaze again. This time his blood ran cold; he shivered. It did not seem the Founder could have any memory of who he was, his past crimes. That had been long ago, before this Founder had come to power. But Haythem's sharp gaze was convincing and made Switz cough and swallow past the hard knot in his chest.

"Can pardon you," Kemway continued, "if you get me away from Scarecrow. If you don't…when I get out…on my own…you'll go back to that stinking hole you crawled out of…"

That seemed unlikely too, but how could Haythem know anything about his crawling out of the Core? Perhaps Blayd had said something. If not back to the Core, the tales of horrifying medical experiments done on uncooperative criminals were the stuff of nightmares. If the Founder regained power, Switz had few doubts this man would make his life as miserable as he claimed.

He had come to enjoy his freedom, such as it was. He would enjoy it more without men like Blayd berating him. Perhaps there was a way that, working together, Founder Kemway could help him keep it.

Now on his feet, he wiped the blood from his lips. The brief period of coherent speech and thought seemed to have passed as the steel in Kemway's eyes bled into paranoid panic, the man now muttering, "Scarecrow. Scarecrow. Scarecrow," and trembling so that the chains clanged and rattled.

In the outer room, Switz heard the door open. He heard it close. Leaving, he wondered, or coming back? Had Blayd overheard any of the Founder's words? If he had, could Switz convince him they had been incoherent ramblings?

Switz had said nothing damning, but Kemway's words might be cause for concern.

He waited. Listened for footsteps. He heard nothing.

Leaving then.

Maybe Blayd had been listening. Maybe there was a trap.

What could Switz do?

Staring at his bloody hand, rotating his shoulder to ease the ache, he nodded once. "No promises," he muttered, "but I'll think about it."

There might be no way out of this room, this immediate situation, but if there was, he would find it. He always found a way once he set his mind to something. He wanted Kemway as an ally. Achieving that would require proving his worth.

To do that, he had to help him escape. He had to find a way.

❧Chapter 17❧

The sluggish stiffness of his limbs confirmed how long he had slept, and the pain that induced that extended slumber lingered still, but it did not tell him where he was or how he had gotten there. The fullness of his bladder, the sour pastiness of stale Zaolei in his mouth and the ache in the back of his head demanded a response; without opening his eyes, he peeled off the oxygen mask to rise and address his body's needs. He was inundated by the familiar smells of home, his own scents long embedded in the cushions beneath him and on the blanket spread over his bare skin, the lingering aromas of Zaolei and curlers and clean laundry, the damp smell of hemplastic and the fainter smells of the detergents Maemi used when she came to clean his flat.

He knew where he was by the voice that responded quickly to his movement with a worried, "How do you feel?"

That peculiar digitized voice. Jaron's voice.

The sound brought with it a cascade of remembrances, the broken flat door, the attack by the brako who tried to get inside, the impact with the alglamp, his determination to prevent whoever now led and controlled the brako from ever hurting Jaron. He vaguely recalled Lash, some painful jostling through dripping streets, a hand clutching his…and something that forced him at last to peel open his lids and focus on the worried face hovering above him.

There was no blood there now, the way Rhyd remembered, but the speech unit on Jaron's temple was dark, no longer flickering as it processed his thoughts and waited for the audible command to speak.

No wonder Jaron's voice sounded peculiar.

"Shoulda had that looked at…" He remembered giving the command. It was the last thing he did remember. His throat was raw and dry so that his words came out like cracked bits of glass ground beneath the heel of a boot.

Jaron pressed a cup into his outstretched hand and guided it to his mouth. After a few swallows, Rhyd relinquished the cup, glad it had been water and not Zaolei.

His body needed the water more.

"I will," Jaron murmured, his speech crackling and broken. "Didn't think you should be alone." The cadence of his voice was different, the flow of words, which Rhyd preferred to attribute to the damaged speecher than to anything Jaron was feeling. Hands empty, Jaron raked one through his curls and shrugged. Truth was, he did not feel brave enough to leave the flat alone, even though the Spinks were loitering in the shadows when Lash went out and were presumably there still. They might have accompanied Jaron anywhere, but still, Jaron was afraid.

If he left, what were the odds that whoever was after him would come here for Rhyd?

"Looks like you hit your head…or someone…"

"Brako…outside your flat." Rhyd half-heartedly shrugged as he slowly sat up, the blanket falling away to expose his collection of bruises, new and old. Awkwardly self-conscious, he grabbed for the blanket to cover his hips. He assumed Jaron and Lash had gotten him out of the body armor and mask, so they had already seen as much of his battered body as there was to see, but he still felt a peculiar rush of modesty he did not normally experience.

Noting the alarm and the shadow of something else that crossed Jaron's face at his words, Rhyd eased his feet to the floor and continued, "Busted your door…your table…maybe the chairs…but they won't bother you there." It was why he had wanted Jaron here. The brako would never think to come here, and so long as Jaron was here, they would not find him in his own flat…if they dared show up there again. "Is that…?" His fingers fell short of touching the damaged speech unit.

"Spinks drove 'em off…made sure we weren't followed," Jaron assured him, although he felt little of that assurance himself. "I'm sorry I didn't give you the passcard back…"

"You'll need it until I get to whoever's running the brako." It could not be Vanderwall. That man was dead. But someone was giving orders and Rhyd intended to discover who that was.

Jaron bobbed his head, unable to meet Rhyd's gaze. "Thank you. And I'm sorry…about all of this…"

Those fresh bruises on Rhyd's body were his fault.

"Don't be." If not for stopping Vanderwall the night of the Core rescue, they might be dead. Jaron had saved them all. They could not go back and change those events and Rhyd had no desire to do so.

"Your head?"

Fingering the back of his skull, Rhyd struggled to his feet, one hand on Jaron's shoulder, grateful his undershorts were still on. He needed the bathroom but he also wanted more water. As he fought against the spiraling room, he contemplated which of those needs he should tend to first.

"Cowl took the brunt of it," he murmured. "I've felt worse…"

Jaron nodded. He was worried, he wanted to do more, but he knew Rhyd did not want to be coddled. Rhyd was not that sort of man. "Enoch wants us to meet at Vapors when you're ready." He shrugged. "All of us, he said. Says it's important. Think we should go?"

It was a risk leaving the flat but it would be riskier inviting the others to come here.

As he stumbled into the kitchen, Rhyd pondered the wisdom of Jaron going out where the brako might see him, but it was better he accompanied Rhyd to Vapors than remain here alone, unprotected. He might believe Jaron was safer in this flat but there was always the possibility that the brako knew about it too. That possibility meant that the younger man was safer at Rhyd's side than anywhere else, even if Rhyd was not in peak physical condition.

"Give a time?"

"I told him you were out…would let him know when you're up for it…" He did not mention Tamner's visit, the additional plasts provided to mend fractured bones and strained muscles. If Rhyd did not already suspect it, Jaron felt no reason to tell him.

Two glasses of water later, the drink reminding him of the stretch of a full bladder, Rhyd grunted. "Tell him ninety. I need a shower."

"I'll tell him." As Rhyd staggered to the bathroom door, Jaron hesitantly added, "I'm glad you're okay. I was worried." Worried enough to summon Tamner. Worried enough not to leave him alone until he awoke.

Rhyd nodded once, heart thumping, and disappeared, closing the door behind him, half fearing, after that note of emotion in Jaron's voice, that the other man would be prompted to follow him.

He was irrationally disappointed he did not.

ھ۔*۔ی

"Is that rabbit I smell?" Jonner asked as he hung his wide-brimmed hat on a hook by the door and peeled off his wet coat to hang beside it, his eyes combing one of Hebenon's bigger flats for clues about the life Maemi had lived during the years they had been apart. Multiple generations of the same family had lived here, Maemi's in-laws, she and her husband, and at one time Xiaodan and his parents. Now there was only Maemi and her bed-ridden mother-in-law and the woman who stayed on as a caregiver for the older woman during Maemi's hours below in Vapors.

The walls and many flat surfaces were adorned with digi-images of the family, but none, as far as he could see revealed children in Maemi's life and that made him sad.

She had wanted children once. Maybe that had changed.

Maybe the circumstances of her life had precluded them.

"It is," she replied, calling from the kitchen where she had retreated as soon as she ushered him through the door. "Cost me a case…but it'll be worth it." Rabbits were hard to come by in Hebenon but thanks to the few connections she had made with the parah since her first visit outside, getting a rabbit for this special occasion had been accomplished without much difficulty.

"Roasted potatoes and tomatoes too…"

"Know how long it's been since I had a tomato…or rabbit?" He chuckled as he entered the kitchen and took the tray from her hands.

"Of course I do." She smiled, turned to pick up the basket of biscuits baked by Vapors' kitchen staff, and shooed him towards the table. "Sit…get comfortable…the rest will be out shortly."

"Yes, ma'am."

"Don't ma'am me…I'm not your momma."

Jonner laughed, set the tray of potato and tomato on the table set for two, but rather than sit, he circled the room to admire the photos, learning her life through the images of times and changes he had missed. When she eventually came to the table with the platter of rabbit, he looked over his shoulder and asked, "Nephew?"

The young man in the photo before him looked like the two adults he was most frequently posed with, and a little like Maemi's husband, but not at all like Maemi.

"He was…yes…"

"Was? I'm sorry…"

She shook her head and began to carve the meat. "Altercation with the Talkers."

"Talkers?" He did not remember the Voices being a violent or militant group, but having seen the prods now that Talkers were believed to have abducted the ailing Founder Kemway, he supposed anything was possible. The Igraci had told him about the Coup that had led to the opening of Outside, and he vaguely understood that the Captain of Law now oversaw the city's new governing body, but the details of Hebenon's history were blurry.

"Long story. Let's just say he had big ideas…and there was a girl."

"Isn't there always? A girl that is?"

"Sometimes it's a boy," she reminded him with a gentle, melancholy smile.

He nodded. "Sometimes it is."

As they ate of the biggest, best meal he had consumed in years and shared a bottle of blueberry wine acquired for the occasion, there were stories to tell and memories to pick through. Highlights of Jonner's time in the Core, both harrowing and lighthearted moments that illustrated the years of incarceration and made them sound better than Maemi had feared they had been. There was much he did not share, she knew. It would take a lifetime to regale every tale of those years. Nor could she detail every moment of her life during those same years in the course of one evening meal. She spoke of her husband and his death, of Xiaodan and his family. She spoke of gaining and shaping Vapors into what it was. She explained the years of oppression, of people being taken, disappearing without a trace, that led to the Lev Uprising and the overthrow of generations of Kemway rule, as well as the opening of the city to the world outside, a world not poisoned and deadly as they had been indoctrinated to believe.

"Have you been there? Outside?"

"I was there when the door opened," she murmured, pushing her empty plate back and draining the last of the wine in her glass. "Not just me…I was part of a group fleeing the violence down here…"

"That must have been…terrifying." If he had stood there at the door to the unknown, facing the very real possibility that seeing the outside without protective gear would mean instant, agonizing death, he knew he would have been scared. He had not been too scared to fight for his life and freedom from the Core, but coming back into Hebenon was reentering a world, a life, he had some knowledge of. It was not the same as facing an entire unknown.

"One of the parah children had gotten into the city…we were trying to return her to her family. She raised a fuss…proving that nothing out there was what we were told…they wanted to experiment on her." She shrugged. "There wasn't a choice."

"So you've seen it? You've been out there."

"A few times. Where do you think the rabbit came from?"

"Then I owe them my gratitude." He picked a piece of meat from the partially devoured carcass and sucked it and its juices from his fingers. "I think we all ought to be out there. Been stuck in the dark too long. Humanity's not meant to live in the dark."

"No…but we didn't have a choice in those days, did we?"

"Not then…but we do now. No one to stop it. Only a matter of time, I suppose…" He noted her peculiar expression, something that was a cross between wonder and trepidation. He was unsurprised to see it but the look still filled him with a flutter of disappointment. "You thought about living out there? Starting over?"

"Leaving Vapors'?" She shook her head. "There's talk about ways to move vindis there, how to route power and resources, but this is my life. Out there…it wouldn't be the same. Everyone I know's here…and she…" she glanced towards her mother-in-law's closed door. "She'd never survive the move." She studied his face, the touches of gray at his temple, and asked, "You thinking about it?"

"Maybe. I dunno. Not sure what's for me here…I mean, I could go back to the steam systems easy enough. There's always use for engineers…but they might be able to use me out there too. Trading one prison for another…"

He sighed when Maemi nodded. Hebenon was a big place, with most of known humanity crammed into it, but it had been, in many ways, still a prison, holding everyone in, permitting no option for advancement or betterment. No chance for those in the Levs to graduate into the Uppers. Life stuck in one place. She could not fault him for wanting to spread his wings, experience the new freedom the world offered.

But she was not yet prepared to make that same change, nor risk the other woman's life. She liked Vapors. She liked where she was, surrounded by the comforting reminders of the life she had lived, the family she had lost. There was no denying, however, that Jonner's return brought with it exciting possibilities.

"There's always room for you in Vapors…while you decide," she offered. "You got a place to stay?"

"They gave us flats…I haven't been there yet." The flat he had lived in before had been passed to someone else. Jonner had not had the heart to investigate an empty, unfamiliar flat on his first day free of the Core. There had been Vapors, Outside, his meeting with the Igraci, and now dinner with Maemi to fill his time. He would have to go there eventually, but he was not ready to do so yet."

"Anything you need, I can help get it. I know people…I know where all of the best deals can be had. And you're welcome here any time…and in Vapors, like I said."

"Might take you up on that," he said with a grin. He did not specify which offer he referred to, but the flush and shiver his grin pulled over her skin convinced her he was referring to every offer she made.

For the first time in years, Maemi began to feel that the direction of her life just might change.

❧*☙

There was no other way.

Venn studied the passcard in his hand, wondering why he still had it when he no longer chose to live here, wondered if Rhyd would be angry for letting himself into the flat when no one answered his knock. But going in was the only way to be sure the blonde was not dead or passed out drunk in the shower, in his own vomit, the only way to reassure himself that, as Agnys said, there was nothing to worry about.

If Rhyd was angry, Venn would deal with it.

The flat was dark, smelling of humid sweat as if someone had recently showered, a scent attested to by the damp towel hanging over the back of a dining chair. A pillow and blanket lay haphazardly across the sofa and on the table beside it there was an array of medi supplies, gauze, sutures, antiseptic ointment, and things Venn did not recognize.

So Rhyd had been here long enough to patch himself up after a fight. A fight meant Scarecrow continued to prowl the city streets looking for something Venn was unable to provide.

Someone had been here with him. The nearly empty whiskey bottle and glass on the table suggested it. There was no clue who it had been, yet the sight produced a jealous flare in the cellist's breast and he balled his fists.

It should be him. He should have been here. This was their place.

Or it had been. Even as the thought crossed his mind, Venn knew he would never again live here. This had ceased being home the day he was taken from it. For a time, he had long to go back, but it was a longing he had eventually given up, a longing he had outgrown. He had built a new life, giving up on the possibility of going back while Rhyd clung to the hope of finding him. Venn had made new friends. He had no right to deny Rhyd any manner of company unless…

He stomped around the sofa to the short hall with its three closed doors. An empty bathroom, the mirror steam not yet evaporated, the warmth of showering clinging to the air. A bedroom used as storage and once as a recital space, dark and closed and musty as though the circulating heat and air ducts were closed, the room now unused. The other bedroom, their bedroom, with the photos turned down, the bed neatly made, with only a collection of clean laundry upon it verifying that anyone had entered.

It was too cold, however, cold and flat smelling, to have been used recently. The laundry looked to have been there a long time, its freshness no longer perfuming the air.

Good, he thought with selfish annoyance, banging the door shut as he marched back into the main room.

On shift, he presumed. It was the only logical place for Rhyd to be unless Scarecrow was on the prowl despite his apparent injuries. Venn glanced at his chrono, gauged how long it should be until the end of the next shift, and then sat at the table to wait. Zaolei bottle in hand, he knew it was foolish to stay and wait but he consoled himself with "Just a few minutes," before taking a long burning drink.

Cazz, he hated this stuff.

He could spare a few minutes.

If he was lucky, waiting would bring Rhyd back to him. If not, he would leave the flat alone…exactly the way he had come.

"Ficken mich, you look like shit." Skelter rose and pulled out a chair for Rhyd as the blonde stumbled to the table, refusing Jaron's support as he had done every step since leaving the flat. Skelter had expected reminders of their recent activities to linger on Rhyd's face; it had not been so many days ago when the vigi had finally gotten back on his feet. But Skelter had not expected new bruises, new injuries, and he scowled as Rhyd dropped heavily into the offered chair.

"Don't you think you should give yourself time to…"

Rhyd's sidelong glance at Zara silenced her, the woman sympathetically nodded and said no more. Sitting idle when there was cause for action was not in Rhyd's nature. Not anymore. What that cause was, she did not know, but she assumed this meeting had been called to inform everyone of a new or continuing threat.

The missing Founder business, most likely. Or some matter with the brako. Tox was on shift, Maemi was enjoying dinner with a friend, and Otta had remained at the hostel to watch over the sleeping children, agreeing with Skelter that it was too soon to leave them alone in this unfamiliar city. Rhyd did not typically summon everyone to discuss his business, Enoch had, and thus it could revolve around anything…from the Founder to the brako to the survivors of the Core.

The dwarf looked uncomfortable, particularly as he noted the purple splotches on Rhyd's face. Those injuries had come on his behalf; he was sure of it. Weighing the matter he had come to share, he judged he was not about to make Ballard's life any easier.

"Wanted me?" Rhyd muttered.

Ginna came from the bar, bringing two more glasses and the bottle of Zaolei she expected Rhyd would request, but she returned to the customers at the counter without lingering. Enoch waited until she was out of earshot, tracing his fingers through the condensation on his tall glass, and then sucked in a breath before speaking.

"Wanted all of you to know a couple of things." He cleared his throat. "You know someone's been hounding me…"

Rhyd bobbed his head as he poured Jaron a drink and kept the bottle for himself.

"Thought it could have something to do with the kids…someone thinking I'm up to no good with so many…or hoping to get their hands on fresh meat…but I don't think that's the case. It could also be…" Enoch paused long enough to take a drink and look at Skelter, "Molly's made it out."

The corner of the redhead's mouth twitched.

"Molly?" asked Zara.

"Slippery little fotz…gets by moking off others mostly. Fanatical git…one of the Spades," Enoch replied. "First things he asked about when I saw him was Heb…and you."

Skelter shrugged. "Knows if anyone can hit him a score, it'd be…"

"I don't think he's looking to score off you."

Knowing what Enoch meant, Skelter grunted and sat back with his arm across the back of Zara's chair. "He'll have to find me first. Besides, Spades are done…"

"In the Core, yeah…but out here? If he can hook up with them out here…and doesn't get to you first…"

With Skelter reviving his public social persona, it would not be difficult for a determined individual to find him, Molly or anyone else. Although Skelter did not think they would care, if any exterior member of the Spades existed, if the organization could be contacted, if they wanted to hold Skelter to a pact he had made inside, a queue of potential assassins might line up to complete the rules of the game.

He doubted anyone outside would care whether he completed the pact, whether he lived or died, as much as Molly Netzer did.

"So we find Molly and take care of him." Rhyd did not think he would have to resort to killing the man to convince him to leave Skelter alone.

"He'd've been processed with the others up top," Lash added. "Given a pass, ticks, a residence…a job maybe. Think you can get that?" He looked back and forth between Zara and Jaron.

The archivist, sitting slightly sideways in his chair to hide the damaged speecher, nodded and said, "With his name, yeah…but the more details you can give…."

It was unlikely there was more than one Molly Netzer in the census files, particularly one with an arrest record that had landed him in the mines. He should be easy to find.

The slight delay and unusual cadence of his digital voice revealed what he was trying to hide and Zara, seated next to him, turned his head to look at the damaged unit.

"Think I can fix that," she murmured affectionately, pushing his dark curls behind his ear with a reassuring smile, "but you ought to have a medi do the work…"

Jaron nodded without speaking.

After a lull in conversation as more drinks were poured, Enoch continued, his eyes again on Skelter. "Could have a new client…I interviewed her. Seems shady; I dunno. I picked up the tail before meeting her…but they might have known about the summons, might have been making sure I didn't bring trouble to her door…"

"Those were brako," Rhyd muttered. If this potential new client had a connection to the brako, it would be best if Skelter steered clear.

"I know," Enoch said with a shrug. "Can't think of many good reasons they'd care about me…or bad ones…unless it's the same business Senior Kal's interested in. Could be the Voices tailing me too…or he hired the brako."

Those at the table scowled; something in the set of Lash's jaw suggested to Rhyd that the man knew something that the rest did not. The rest…except Enoch.

"This'll get out soon enough now that he's got his hands on it. He's already threatened me with it, and if the brako know…just don't let it go beyond this table." Eventually, the revelation would spread, even if his friends stayed silent, but Enoch hoped he could control the eruption at least a little.

Another drink, held in his mouth before being followed by a painful burning swallow and deep breath, and he grumbled, "Before I came down here…before I was…me…by birth…I was a Kemway."

"You're…"

He did not know whose whispered exclamation stumbled over his words but it was no surprise that it was Jaron, more well-versed in the city's history due to his work at the Archives, who murmured, "Aldrich Kemway?"

He had not been born during those scandalous times. Others at the table had been children. But as the abduction story cropped up every few years when someone chose to 'remember' the lost Kemway child, an Archivist would have seen that name at least once.

That revelation, Rhyd realized, supported something that the Senior had begun to say the last time he had crossed Rhyd's path. Oddly, it did not surprise him as much as he thought it should.

"But he…" Skelter began, his grip on his glass tightening, his tone expressing a flush of anger with himself that, after so many years of friendship, he had not already known this truth.

Enoch shrugged without looking up. "Obviously…I'm not. Fosters told me…but…well…if I wanted to live…"

If he wanted to live, being a Kemway was the last thing a dwarf child in the Levs would want to reveal.

No one asked how it could be true. None asked how it had come to be, how he could be sure. They knew the case history of the missing, then murdered, child and knew the fate many 'undesirables' suffered. It was only a surprise that the family had allowed the child to live rather than euthanize him. It was only a surprise they had not followed through on the murder story to prevent an eventual scandal, that the fosters had known the truth and were able to pass it on to the child.

No one at the table thought Enoch was lying.

"You don't belong here."

The senior swiver on duty and Maemi's primary partner, Pietro's stern words to the woman in the bugorra uniform who entered amidst a cluster of arriving patrons drew Colyx's attention from the door where he discouraged troublesome elements from finding their way inside. Colyx had seen people wearing that uniform since his emergence into Hebenon though most wore the bug-like face masks for which they had been nicknamed. Enoch had explained the new nature of law enforcement to him, so he understood what she was.

She was the first of her ilk to enter Vapors since his hiring and he was unaware of any reason law-keepers were not allowed in.

Or maybe it was just this one. He watched with a scowl but remained at his post.

"I'm here for…" Ilya began, her eyes scanning the stage where andi dancers entertained the patrons seated. A tip, a hint from a subordinate, had directed her here and so she had come as soon as she could, afraid she would find Ginna on that stage selling herself for the ticks to live off of. While there was nothing inherently wrong with those who chose that life, Ilya believed Ginna could do better.

Relieved not to see her there, Ilya's gaze shifted around the room, towards a corner where a group of men and one woman, or an andi perhaps, huddled in conversation. She might not have noticed them at all, or cared to study them, as most of the faces meant nothing to her.

Except for Jaron Rei. It was the first time she had seen him since the night of the recital, except on that grainy SCAM footage. She should speak to him. She should tell the captain where he was. She should let him know that he was being sought in connection to a crime. She took one step towards the table, shrugging off the swiver's grasp, before another movement out of the corner of her eye, someone coming from behind the counter with a clipped, "Ilya? Why are you here?" stopped her.

"He wants you as Founder." Jaron swallowed the pungent contents of his glass behind those words. If he was part of the Voices, and the Founder was ailing…missing, it was what he would want, someone of Kemway blood in a position of leadership at the head of Hebenon.

Enoch grunted. "Not interested. Dunno how long he's known, but it's cazzing convenient to approach me when Haythem's missing."

Rhyd lifted his head. Zara's white-knuckled grip on the edge of the table and her shift of focus towards the door pulled his attention to where the bugger lieutenant was engaged in conversation with Vapors' youngest swiver. Pietro stood his ground, one hand gesture keeping Colyx from acting as he watched the situation between Ginna and the bugger play out.

If the bugger was here to cause trouble, even if she intended to arrest Ginna, Pietro and Colyx would interfere. The staff in Vapors considered each other family, and family protected their own.

If there was a chance the bugorra knew Ginna led the Spinks, if they thought to use that against her, Pietro would not stand for it.

Neither, it seemed from the stares of many around the room, would most of Vapors' patrons.

Not a single uniformed bugger had entered in the past two years and the patrons had grown used to being where they would not be harassed.

"I should call Oliver," Zara murmured.

Skelter's hand on her arm kept her seated.

Again, no one questioned her use of the captain's first name.

"What are you…?"

"Working."

"This isn't what I…"

Ginna snarled, eyes narrowing, and pulled from her sister's well-meaning but unwanted grasp. "It's not your life. This isn't about what you want…it's about what I want. I like it here…and the pay's good. They treat me right. You should be satisfied I'm not up there," she pointed towards the stage, her words a low hiss that no one else but Pietro could hear, "or out there." She thrust a finger towards the door.

Colyx, interpreting the gesture as an order for the bugger to go, thumped from his post, leaving the door unattended. The stiff gait created by the braces proved him less than fit, but he was big and broad enough, his resting-face expression fierce enough, that his presence at the door had proven a deterrent to most unsavory elements. He was not afraid to use those things against the unwanted law-enforcer.

"I am, but you shouldn't…why haven't you…" Aware of the bouncer on her periphery, Ilya paused to look at him, intending to warn him off.

One of the few to carry an umbra in Hebenon, the moisture cover being considered high class, frou-frou, unnecessary when there were coats and cloaks to wear that filled the same purpose more expediently, Feena knew the bright, multi-colored fabric made her stand out from the crowd as she loitered at the intersection, watching the riff-raff move in and out of the beaded curtained doorway of the place called Vapors. Typically, she did not want to stand out too much, preferred the appearance of one slightly above the common rabble's station but not too far above, but today she wanted to be noticed.

She wanted the one she had come to see to notice her.

She should have left this waiting to someone else, as being in the cold for so long was disagreeable and tedious, but Feena was stubborn and convinced that, at this hour, surely the dwarf would have to make an appearance.

Those who served said he came each day to dine.

Today, however, there was no sign of him. The arrival of the bugorra lieutenant did not trouble her but the arrival of a much taller, unmasked figure in uniform, who hesitated long enough to scan the vicinity in front of the door before pushing aside the beaded curtain, did. If he saw her, recognized her, he did not gesture or approach.

There was no way, Feena thought with a frustrated growl, that she would risk going inside, even if the dwarf did show up. She could not tip Grainger's hand to her and Kal's plan.

This visit would have to wait another day.

Having failed to find Jaron in the places he expected him to be, those known places being noticeably few, driving home how little he had learned about the other man during the period of their acquaintance, Grainger decided to seek the one person he thought might be able to help him, who would at least listen, he hoped, with a sympathetic ear. Not only might she be able to help him locate Jaron through whatever magic she performed with her Echo skills, she might be able to help him identify the still unknown dead men who had been part of the Founder's abduction plot.

He did not know where Zara Peru lived. He only knew where she worked, or where she had worked before the Coup, so that was the best place to seek her out.

Pushing aside the curtain, he did not expect to find Lieutenant Young in Vapors, standing at the bar in what looked to be a heated exchange with a swiver…her sister if Oliver was correct.

Nor did he expect to see Zara at a corner table in Jaron's company.

Ballard too.

When Jaron turned in his chair to watch the budding altercation between sisters, he met Oliver's gaze. From his stricken expression, Oliver was sure Jaron's face lost color.

The internal war between relief that Jaron was alive and safe, confusion at seeing him with Ballard, and a darker feeling of dread mixed with outrage and a jealous spark, were only masked by the distance and shimmer of flashing neon and shadow separating them. Seeing Jaron on the SCAM footage in Scarecrow's company had been worrisome. Now he wondered if Jaron knew that Scarecrow and Ballard were the same man.

How could he? Ballard's vigi identity was a secret kept close, one Oliver had not shared with anyone. Yet if Jaron did not know, why, how, was he with Ballard now?

Oliver's intention to speak to Zara, his fleeting thought of preventing Ilya from drawing further attention, was erased by the unexpected discovery and his feet moved heavily, one step at a time, towards the man he had not seen in too long, who opened a floodgate of longing and emotion only tempered by those other things…and the lure of the platinum haikara and dancer who sat on Jaron's other side.

Unseen beneath the table, Rhyd squeezed Jaron's elbow and watched the captain's approach with pursed lips and narrowed eyes.

Ilya took her captain's harsh glare as a command and his steps towards the corner table as an order to follow him, despite her desire to stay where she was, have a civil conversation with Ginna, and hopefully clear the air between them. As soon as she moved away from Ginna, both the head swiver and the bouncer backed off, one returning to the bar counter, the other to the door. Though they continued to watch her, their primary focus was on the bugorra captain making his way across the room with dragging, determined steps.

Ilya had seen that SCAM footage. If the captain had seen it, he now knew what Jaron had done, self-defense or not, and in whose company he had done it. She hung several steps behind, imagining the captain would want a private conversation with Jaron. The slowness of his steps suggested an additional interest in the gathering around that table, however, one that might require her professional assistance.

Or maybe he felt obligated to make an arrest that would, she knew, be difficult to carry out. It would be for Jaron's safety. He had killed Vanderwall. In custody, the captain could keep him safe.

"Oliver." Zara's greeting was as much to distract him from Jaron, from Rhyd, as it was for herself. She knew he heard her by the twitch at the corners of his mouth and eyes, but he either could not look at her or would not.

It seemed Jaron was all he could see.

Certain that Oliver had come to arrest him, that he had brought the uniformed lieutenant to be his official detention agent, Jaron could only stare as Oliver reached the table and stood over him, a shadow of whom he had never been afraid before.

He was afraid now.

Oliver's lips moved soundlessly. He cleared his throat with his hand over his mouth and started again, his voice gruffer than intended. "Outside. We need to talk."

Releasing Jaron's elbow, Rhyd began to rise with a snarled, "You don't need to…"

Jaron shook his head. He was not prepared for Oliver to know about his relationship with Rhyd. He was not certain, if he was honest, that there was any relationship beyond a friendship born of common goals, shared adventure, and similar interests in the future of Hebenon.

"It's okay," he stammered, looking at everyone seated around him instead of singling Rhyd out.

As Jaron rose shakily, Oliver's gaze moved away long enough to make note of each individual at the table whose reactions appeared angry, frightened, or threatening. Ballard looked to have gotten the short end of a beating and Oliver wondered how the man, or men, on the other side had fared. He would have to look for reports of assault victims when he returned to his office. It might give him an inkling of what Ballard, or Scarecrow, had been up to recently.

Whether it had anything to do with Jaron.

If those seated there knew about Vanderwall's death, if they knew what Jaron had done, maybe they thought the bugger captain was here to make an arrest and were eager to protect him. To prove he had no ill intent and had no unseemly motives, Oliver looked over his shoulder at Ilya, shook his head, and motioned her away.

She frowned, looked at her sister who had returned to the bar, and reluctantly obeyed her captain's command to leave the vindi.

Colyx followed as far as the door to be sure she left.

"Come outside…"

"We can talk, but…not there." Jaron willed his legs to cooperate and moved to the nearest empty table where he intentionally sat with his back to the others, his back to Rhyd.

Rhyd would watch him. He would not be able to hear them over the pulse of the bass and drum and the chatter of patrons, but he might be able to read Grainger's lips and if there was a problem, he might have the opportunity to react before something disastrous happened.

Jaron hoped those around Rhyd could prevent any other unfortunate action.

"How do you know him?" Wondering if any of those at the table had been part of the group on the Lev stairs when Vanderwall had fallen to his death, Oliver thought it was easier to open a dialogue with that gruff, curt question than it was to release the deluge of other thoughts and feelings he was struggling to keep at bay.

"Who?" Jaron knew. He did not, however, want to offer details.

"Ballard."

Jaron shrugged. "Met him through Lash. You know him?"

Grunting, not wanting to answer, Oliver countered, "Lash?"

"Edgar Quincy. We worked topside…before. He covered the speech unit at his throat self-consciously. If Oliver checked, he would learn that Edgar Quincy had left employment in the Uppers long before Jaron had been forced out, but not so long that they might not have crossed paths in their lines of work. They might not have worked together regularly, but Jaron's words were not necessarily a lie.

Oliver huffed, his eyes now focused on Jaron's covering hand. The younger man's head was turned slightly so that the damaged unit at his temple was hidden, so Oliver attributed the unusual note in his digitized voice to strangled emotions that he hoped mirrored his own.

"You haven't been…I've been worried. I've seen…"

"Been busy." Jaron cut off any confession Oliver intended to make. "Extra work since the Archives shut down for the recital…and then the shakes, the Founder, the Core, the riots."

Plausible enough but not quite the whole truth. Not a word about Vanderwall and the brako; there were a host of reasons why Jaron might not want to talk about that. Oliver reached across the table and caught Jaron's hand, not a restraining hold but an affectionate one.

Jaron's fleeting panic shifted from one type to a very different sort.

"Come home with me. We can talk there."

At the corner table, Rhyd growled. Zara slid into Jaron's empty chair and draped her arm around the vigi's shoulder. It settled and restrained him, kept Rhyd from rising while also pulling Oliver's attention away from Jaron long enough for the smaller man to withdraw his hand.

"We can…"

"I can't, Oliver."

Jaron's voice was small, strained, breathy with tension, but it was also, Oliver noted, more resolved than expected. "Can't?"

Jaron tried to keep his hands, clasped on the table, steady as he shook his head. "Wouldn't be right…or fair…to either of us…"

"If this is about…"

Oliver did not know what he might have done to upset Jaron, unless it involved information about the Founder or some detail about the Core that had not been shared between them. It might also be, he admitted with reluctance, that for the duration of their relationship, he had been more focused on taking than on giving. He had avoided most serious conversations about work and asked very few questions about who Jaron was, what his life was like when they were apart, what his dreams and goals and interests were. Too late he had asked Jaron to accompany him out in public, to the recital, when he could have done so much more to include him and make him feel needed, wanted, respected, and appreciated.

He had invited him to the recital and had not even attended.

He wondered for the first time if Jaron had gone without him.

"It's not…" Jaron shook his head and slid his chair back to ease the distance between them. "I don't belong up there…in your world. Haven't belonged there in a long time. I tried…but I don't."

He stood, watching for the expected heartbreak in Oliver's eyes and wanting to be quick to retreat from it when it came, to escape an arrest he still expected. He did not understand the nature of their relationship, but he did accept that he had been an important piece in Oliver's life, even if Oliver did not understand it. "You…me…this isn't right. I'm sorry."

His lungs refused to fill, refused to expel the breath he held as Jaron returned to the other table where both Zara and Ballard got to their feet as if to welcome him before Zara sat again in her chair. Jaron sank too heavily into his. Ballard, on the other hand, did not sit and Oliver could feel the man's whiskey brown eyes drilling into him as if he expected the captain to make some threatening move.

Oliver wondered, on the lacy edges of his twisting thoughts, if he had somehow found himself again on Scarecrow's list of targets.

Under his breath, low enough that only those nearest him could hear, Rhyd growled, "Get him out. My place. Now." He wanted Jaron out of Vapors, as far from Grainger as possible, protected from the bugorra who might intend to arrest him, from the brako who were out to kill him. Rhyd could not take him there himself. He stormed away from the table, past the captain with a daggerous side-glare, towards the restrooms at the back of the building.

He could not see to Jaron's safety. He had something more pressing to accomplish. Something that required the Scarecrow's face.

๏Chapter 18๏

On the off chance that the bugorra captain would lead them to their quarry, the second pair of brako assigned to stake out the murderer's flat followed him to the Archives and then to Vapors, with the captain unaware they were there. The press of people at this early, after-shift hour was great, his thoughts so wrapped around his own pursuits, that he missed their curious, hunting presence. They did not enter the club when he did, preferring to wait, to watch, to see who he was looking for and why he wanted them. Why he had come here.

They did, however, notice the presence of Feena Wulfe.

It was impossible for anyone paying close attention to the area not to see her. But she departed alone shortly thereafter and the pair of brako left her alone. They would make a report to Vanderwall later; right now, she was not their concern.

They melted deeper into the shadows when the lieutenant emerged but she too was alone and marched off about her business without seeing them. Not long after, when two others exited together, the murderer and the redhead they had no interest in, the brako glanced at each other, nodded, and left the captain to his clubbing.

If the captain had come for the murderer, the owner of the staked-out flat, he did not follow him from Vapors. The option of separating, of one remaining to determine the captain's interests, was set aside. Bringing in the murderer was too good of an opportunity to pass. That, more than knowing the captain's business, would net the pair a handsome reward. Such a bounty was more enticing than whatever Captain Grainger was up to.

Another followed as well, from a higher vantage point, his enhanced senses dulled more than usual by residual pain, medication mixed with alcohol, and the battle against self-flagellation and annoyance. He did not deny his jealousy of Grainger's hand on Jaron's. Instead, he asserted that he had no reason to be jealous. Jaron had rebuffed Grainger, had pulled his hand away…and it did not, Rhyd reminded himself, matter who Jaron took up with. He was not angry with Jaron, or with Grainger.

He was angry with himself, that Jaron's connection to Grainger did matter to him. Jealousy was useless, futile, and unwanted, the growing attachment to the curly-haired man likewise. Rhyd did not need, or want, the complication of another potential heartache.

Venn had done damage enough.

Anyone close to him was likely to be hurt…or used against him. Or he would be used against them.

He did not want to take that risk.

It was a necessary one now, however, rolled into play by the pair of beaked brako he detected within the first few dozen feet outside of Vapors' door. The two had not yet made a move against Jaron or Skelter, but Scarecrow could not allow the brako to pursue the pair to his flat. They must never know where Scarecrow called home.

They traveled on either side of his friends, interweaving in the shadows, flanking them in a way that Scarecrow could not easily confront both at once. After an intersection, a corner, a turn, and another intersection, he began to see a pattern to their movement, a moment when their paths crossed each time they exchanged positions.

Knowing this zone, well, he believed he knew their plan.

When his friends reached the next set of stairs, Jaron descending first, the brako made their move. From his high-ground position, Scarecrow dropped between them and Skelter as one of the brako grabbed for the redhead's arm.

Skelter turned, startled, lashing out with his walking stick, striking first Scarecrow and then the brako holding him, with Scarecrow taking the brunt of the blow. Behind him, Jaron stumbled on the stairs.

The cane's impact hurt but the body armor absorbed the impact. Scarecrow dodged back and followed the other brako who leaped over the handrail onto the rooftop a half-Lev below, ran, and jumped to the walkway where Jaron was trying to get to his feet. Skelter exchanged blows with the brako left behind but the cane was knocked from his hand. His fighting skills were adequate against a single foe but he was less well-versed than either Scarecrow or the beaked shade trying to fight past him. Lacking protection, Skelter could only swing with all his might to give Jaron a chance to escape, to survive.

The kick the first brako landed into Jaron's ribs was met with a filtered roar and broadside charge that forced him across the walkway, against an alglamp post from which several wires stretched to the corners of nearby buildings. The brako started to go down, stunned by the impact, but Scarecrow caught him in the chest, an arm around one leg, the other beneath an arm and around his back so that the fellow was hoisted off his feet. A turn cracked the brako's skull against the pole and then he was thrown as far as Scarecrow could manage.

The rail he struck proved in need of repair. When he hit, the weld of the stanchion gave way; the rail swung, collided against the nearest building with a bang that produced cries of outrage from the occupants while the brako disappeared over the edge, the echoes of every impact reverberating beneath Scarecrow's continuing bellow of outrage.

Jaron clutched his ribs but had not yet tried to get up.

Faces peered from behind parted blinds, watching Scarecrow defend the innocent against the troublesome brako.

Still on the platform a half-Lev above, Skelter, despite the blood dripping from his nose and lip and the swollen red flesh around one eye, had maneuvered his opponent to the top of the stairs. He threw another punch with an abraded fist as Scarecrow charged from below and caught the brako around the waist. The punch knocked the brako backward and Scarecrow, expecting it, rolled down the stairs with him, his hold around the brako's torso unbroken.

"Get him out of here!" Scarecrow shouted, releasing his opponent so he could land in a crouch on the walkway, the protective position of his body allowing Skelter to struggle to Jaron's side. The walking stick was abandoned. There was no time or chance to retrieve it.

The remaining brako dizzily pushed up, intending to reach Jaron before Skelter did. But Scarecrow leaped, using the alglamp pole as leverage, so that he again landed between the brako and the other two men. The brako's wobbly-footed charge caught Scarecrow mid-torso; though he stumbled back, his one-handed hold on the pole kept Scarecrow on his feet. He caught the brako's arm with his free hand, let go of the pole, and rabbit punched him, driving him away from where Skelter pulled Jaron to his feet.

Dancing side to side, Scarecrow half-listened to their retreat, trusting they could make it to safety without further help. He could have ended the fight with a single blow, knew he should save his strength and flagging endurance. But fury and determination gave him enough impetus to throw and receive several more punches, keeping the brako engaged until he knew Skelter and Jaron were gone.

With a single fist to the brako's temple, Scarecrow threw his beaked opponent backward through the same opening in the rail where his partner had fallen.

The same echoes of collision accompanied him as he fell.

Though he could not be certain, Scarecrow believed both were dead. He should feel sick. He should feel remorse.

All he felt, however, was anger as he retreated, staggering, into the nearest alley, seeking refuge in the closest utility tunnel. He would be safe there long enough to catch his breath…and then he would make sure that Skelter and Jaron were safe.

❧*❧

A degree of guilt, for locking him in, for striking him when Switz had tried to protect him from the Founder's rage and, perhaps, tried to protect the Founder from his, prompted Blayd to allow Switz another venture into the city, sending him this time to pick up their next meal while he tended to business on the Echo. Switz had been reluctant to comply, worried that Blayd's intention was retaliation against the Founder for that earlier episode. But the merc promised he had no such intention, that he regretted his overreaction, and to prove himself, he gave the passkey to the inner door to Switz to take with him.

There was no guarantee he did not have another, but Switz chose to trust his sincerity, just as Blayd was trusting him not to go to the buggers to expose their location, their captive. Blayd had a plan for the Founder, one that would not be served if the man was dead. Whatever Blayd intended, Switz knew he needed Kemway alive.

Just as Switz was only going to benefit if the Founder remained alive to keep his promises.

Arms laden with takeaway and nessies, his thoughts circling his decision to learn how the man had come into Blayd's care, Switz was on his way back when he, like a handful of others, happened upon the split-Lev clash between two beaked thugs and three other men. The beaked horrors had chased him once; sure they were still hunting him, Switz held as far back as he could where he could watch but hopefully not be seen. They paid no attention to the miscellaneous onlookers.

It was recognition of the red-haired man in the skirmish that kept Switz from fleeing.

So Skelter had made it out alive.

Switz wondered how.

It was the other primary combatant, likewise adorned in a mask more like a system worker's than a Crow's, who interested Switz. Covered top to toe in black, Kemway's words came to him as he watched the lone man take out both opponents with skilled precision as Skelter and the other escaped to safety.

All black. Going to kill him.

Was this Scarecrow?

The pair of beaked thugs had dropped over the edge of the walkway and now the vigi in black was gone too, evaporating into the shadows; Switz had no idea where he had gone. Curious, he descended the stairs to look over the broken rail, but wherever the two had landed, they were far below out of sight. When Switz turned, his foot struck something and sent it skittering, creating the tinkling of metal upon metal. He followed. Careful not to spill his sacks, he picked the object up as a nearby door creaked cautiously open.

The occupants stuck their heads out to look around.

"They gone?"

"Think so." The sharp-edged circlet in his hand looked like the same emblem he had seen scrawled on buildings around Hebenon, an inverted toxic symbol used to designate hazardous materials. None of the combatants had worn that symbol, but he had seen something fall out of the solitary fighter's belt during the scuffle. There was nothing else he could see that could be it.

Switz was not one to chat with strangers, but he wanted information. "Who was that?"

"Brako," said the face hidden behind a cloth mask and knit cap, the speaker guarding his identity in case the brako were still nearby.

"And Scarecrow," said another behind the first, an awed voice eager in its youthful worship of the spoken moniker.

"Scarecrow?"

"Where you been, varon?" asked the man in the doorway. "Without him, Outside wouldn't' be open."

"We'd still be suffering under the Crows and Founder," said a third voice deeper inside the flat.

Heads bobbed. "He's the only one standing up to the brako," said the second. "Not even the buggers…"

"Brako?"

The man in the doorway pointed to where the two had fallen. Switz frowned. He thought they were Crows.

Rather than appear more ignorant than he already must, since it sounded like knowledge of the brako and Scarecrow was commonly known, Switz casually pocketed the shuriken and kept his questions to himself. "Well…say safe.," he said in response to the sound of running steps that accompanied the shaking of the platform. He hurried in another direction, intending to avoid what was likely to be law enforcement arriving too late to the scene of the fight.

The people in the flat closed the door.

Whoever, whatever, Scarecrow was, whatever side of the law he fell on, he was lethal…and someone the Founder feared. Whether he was the 'black one' Kemway rambled about or whether that was Blayd or someone else, Switz believed the vigi could be used to his favor, either to control Kemway or to win their freedom from Blayd.

He just had to figure out how it could be done.

❧*❧

Ilya slammed her cubicle door and dropped into the desk chair, glowering at the message on her ICD that had not been the good news she had hoped for. Emotion was impossible to read in a simple line of text, but when her message to Blayd, asking for a meeting, was met with, 'Can't. Busy,' Ilya believed she could read the cold brush off between the words. The perceived rejection and his failure to hold to his bargain made her angry.

Perhaps it was her imagination, fueled by the annoyance at other things that saw a brush off there. Yet it seemed that his interest in her only arose when he wanted something, and not the other way around. A meal, Sympathy. Information. He had given little in return, not even her sister's location, which Ilya had finally discovered on her own from other sources.

A man like Blayd was surely familiar with a place like Vapors. How had he not known Ginna was there?

It had been good to see Ginna, good that she was off the street and away from the influence of streeters and the children who called themselves Spinks. Maybe the death of her friend had frightened Ginna into being smart about her prospects, her future. While not the safest of jobs, swivving was better than slumming amidst the city's criminal element. As Ginna said, it was a steady income, if she stayed with it, and if the people there treated her with respect, that was important. The income might allow her to manage a home of her own, but Ilya did not know where that was.

As a bugorra, she could find out.

If she wanted Ginna's trust, she would not. She would rather Ginna come home, but Ginna looked healthy, well-rested, and well-fed. She looked happy, at least she had until the moment Ilya butted into her business.

Another day then. Ilya would go back to the club and try again, in a calmer, more respectful way, to have a conversation about the future. They were the only family each of them had. It was important not to burn the bridges between them. In the meantime, though the captain had put the club off-limits to the force, she could set patrols nearby often enough to keep an eye on Ginna and make sure she was safe.

Glad she had left the lights off, she rubbed her eyes and leaned back in the chair with a sigh. She should have gone home. Gone to bed. She should have waited for the captain to come out of Vapors and made sure he was okay. Was he arresting Jaron? Was he offering protection or advice? Whichever it was, doing either alone would not be easy for him given his emotional involvement with the suspect.

But tonight, Ilya decided it was not her problem unless he asked it to be. She did not care. She wanted all of them, and all of her problems, to go away and give her peace.

Peace was the only thing that would allow a decent night's sleep.

❧*❧

Molly did not know what time it was, did not know where he was being taken, his head covered, his mouth gagged, when he was finally dragged out of the tupik where he'd been cooped up without food, water, or the Heb he had come for. He was sure his destination would be nowhere good. He and his escorts traveled up and down stairs, back and forth across Levs, in and out of lifts, to confound him or to avoid law enforcement. He had lost track of any sense of direction long ago.

He was so convinced that his final destination would be death that his fear blanked any effort to think beyond the counting of every dragging step.

There was a knock on a door when they eventually stopped moving, the sound of a door opening that allowed a burst of warm air to send shivers across his cold skin, and a final series of dragging stumbling steps into that warmth. The door closed. He was left standing between the two brutes who clutched his arms, neither caring about the bruises they left nor that his breathing came in short, fast gulps and gasps.

He imagined if he passed out, they would simply kick him awake.

The room smelled of baking and the distant sound of a child singing tickled his ears, a perplexing combination that agitated more than soothed him. When the hood was finally yanked off, he could only blink fearfully at the brightness of what appeared to be the living room of a flat and try not to hyperventilate behind the gag.

"This is the man?"

He knew the woman's face although he had never met her. A man like Molly, a Lev baker by familial trade, a haikara by practice, would never have a reason to cross paths with the Kemways. Like her husband, however, Neoma's face had been periodically displayed on Echos throughout the city when she delivered some message intended to evoke goodwill and favor for the Founder and his family. Having come into this room from the damp, he knew they had not traveled into the Uppers and he could not fathom why the Mam would stoop to come down to the Levs to meet with someone like him.

But he had no doubt it was her.

"Haikara…thinks he can be of use to us."

Neoma, reclining on her chaise with one leg exposed through the side-slit of her rose-colored banyan, barely looked at the dirty, emaciated fellow Vanderwall had brought before her. "Can he?"

"He's got a history of it…before he went into the Core."

"So…" she motioned for the brutes to remove the gag, leaning forward a little to expose the valley between her breasts so that Molly could not help but notice when she locked gazes with him. "You're one of those. How long?"

Relieved to be free of the gag, he licked his lips and shook his head. "Seven years," Molly replied with a nervous swallow, hoping he was not speaking out of turn.

"Echos, systems, have changed in seven years." Neoma was sure there had been more changes made after the Coup, efforts intended to strengthen Hub and Archive security, to replace damaged files and programs, attempts made to pinpoint where the Coup had started and what the igniting incident had been. Efforts towards more efficient Echos had been ongoing since the building of Hebanthe Falls.

"Basically the same at the center," Molly assured her. "Tech changes, coding changes, but stays the same at the root. Give me a day or three and I'll run, repair, or jack into anything you give me."

The woman snorted as if she did not believe his bold claims; she got up to walk a barefoot circle around him, studying him as she did so. His efforts to shift away from her were prevented by the vice grips of the brako's' hands. The efforts made her chuckle.

Vanderwall cleared his throat. "Also says he has information about the Founder." That detail, as much as the potential of utilizing a knowledgeable haikara, was the selling point to keep Molly alive and the only reason for bringing him here.

If the Mam decided to kill Molly anyhow rather than use him, Vanderwall would not care. But he did want the man's secrets, if they were worthwhile, to be exposed before that happened.

"About the…?" Molly squeaked. "No! That's not what I said!"

Vanderwall scowled and balled his fists, ready to strike him if his claim had been a lie.

"You said…"

Molly rushed on, interrupting out of fear rather than rudeness, his head turning so that he could lock his wild gaze on the woman who would be his judge, jury, and possibly executioner. "Not the Founder! His brother."

Neoma stopped moving. Vanderwall glowered. The other two men blinked in surprise. They could not have heard correctly.

"We didn't know at first…in the foster…but later…I learned it like he did…and he never denied it. I know him. I can…"

"The Founder has no…" Vanderwall grunted.

"That's what they wanted us to believe," Molly said emphatically. "Couldn't very well have people knowing…"

"Who is he?" Neoma's complexion was paler than before, the lines around her mouth and eyes tight. "Where is he?"

She moved to his other side on her path to circle him and then stopped behind him where he could not see her as he replied, "Goes by Enoch. Dunno where he lives, but I can find him, bring him…"

"You know nothing about Haythem? Where he is? Who has him?"

There was no reason he should if, as he claimed, he was one of the unfortunates recently released from the mines. Maybe the Kemway sibling had been in the mines as well. That would make sense, would explain his absence for all of these years, would explain this dirty little fellow knowing him.

Instead of allowing him to reply, however, she barked to Vanderwall, "Find him!"

"The brother?" he asked for clarification.

"Haythem! Post a prod! Post a reward! Find him!"

"That will take time to…"

"I can do it." Neoma and Vanderwall glowered. "Need equipment, details…we can set up here if you want, give it a personal touch…"

A sound from behind a closed door to the right made Neoma scowl and shake her head. "Not here." No doubt, Ulynda had already heard too much and would ask questions Neoma could not answer.

Haythem's brother was supposed to be dead. Neoma knew nothing about him, what he was like as an infant. If he lived, with Haythem missing, a male Kemway heir posed a threat to Ulynda's claim on the Founder's seat, as well as to Neoma's influence on the highest position of power in Hebanthe Falls.

Mad or not, Haythem had to be found. He had to be alive. So long as he lived, Haythem was the rightful Founder.

"Get him out of here. Give me time. I'll be in touch." She needed to assess her resources, settle a reward amount, find out just how likely it was that the haikara's claim of a living Kemway brother was true.

She did not need this host of wet, smelly men cluttering up her living room as she did any of those things.

Ulynda waited for the opening and closing of the front door twice, and the departing measure of steps each time, before cracking her bedroom door open to peep into the main room. Her mother, it appeared, had gone out with the others, or had gone out alone. Or else she had retreated to her bedroom. The girl pushed a wisp of soft brown hair behind her ear and listened harder, but other than Nanny's movement in the kitchen, there were no other sounds in the flat.

Ulynda was alone.

She was used to that. Once there had been a sister and brother to fill her days. Now there was only her. Alone was better than her mother's fits of anger, better than the subterfuge that drifted in and out the door, big men, frightening men, and a faceless rabble who came to do her mother's bidding for endeavors she never shared with Ulynda.

Yes, she was a child. But she was not stupid. Only ignorant of a world she would never be allowed to view except through the windows of their flat if her mother had her way.

Ulynda did so now, expecting to see her mother on the path outside, sharing secret conversation with the man called Vanderwall and whoever else Vanderwall had brought with him this time. No one was there, however, except for a woman and three children that Ulynda sometimes saw or heard going into or out of the adjoining flat. She waved to the nondescript children in their nondescript waterproof coats and shoes. One of the three waved back, only to have the woman grasp a small arm and usher them into their home.

Sadly, Ulynda sank to the floor, her back against the wall beneath the window, her chin on her knees.

She had an uncle.

She had never heard mention of other family, aunts or uncles or cousins, only grandparents on both sides that she had never met. Her mother's older sister had died in childbirth before Ulynda was born, taking the infant with her. Ulynda had not heard the tale of an uncle dying as a child and she wondered why that would have been kept quiet, if there was some reason she was meant not to know.

A crime?

Why else would an uncle be hidden?

Her mother would never tell her. Her mother would refuse to talk to her about it. Grownups were strange like that.

But maybe, she thought with sudden determination, marching back to the T2 on her bedroom desk where she did her studies each day, there was another way to learn the truth. Some information was blocked because of her age, but surely, she thought with her brow furrowed as she turned the unit on, information about an uncle could not be so bad as to require that.

❧*❧

Rhyd's failure to return from the restroom told Zara and Skelter where he had gone, what he was doing. He had used that departure route many times. The admonition to see Jaron safely out had not been directed at anyone specific, but those remaining at the table knew Enoch, too, would be harassed if he went out the door with little means to protect himself. It was decided that Lash would accompany the dwarf in one direction and Skelter, despite Molly's presence in the city, believed himself capable enough to keep Jaron safe for the short distance to Rhyd's front door.

Their departures left Zara alone, watching Ginna's sporadic, frustrated glances at the door, and Oliver, who had not moved since being abandoned at the nearby table. He looked lost, devastated, unaware that she was watching, unaware of the drink Ginna had brought, unaware of anything except the empty chair across from him.

Sighing, Zara swept back her platinum blonde hair, decision made, and went to the bar. A few minutes later, bottle of whiskey in hand, she came to Oliver's side and put her hand on his shoulder.

Startled by the touch, he looked at her.

She held up the bottle. "Come up; have a drink with me."

As with the last time they had met in this place, he hesitated, no doubt remembering the betrayals that had followed that encounter. Whatever his internal arguments were, he gave in to the inevitable, took her hand, and followed her as he had before, through a rear door, up the stairs, into the same room they had once shared.

He did not think she lived here. Wherever she called home, she would not want the bugger captain to know it. That was a step deeper into intimacy than she was willing to take, and for that, Oliver was glad. It was a step deeper than he wanted to make too.

There were two cushioned, armless chairs in the small room, positioned near the wash vanity just inside the door. He did not remember if they had been there before. She guided him to one and poured a drink in one of the small cups by the sink. The chairs were safer than the bed, less leading, and by pointing him there, she let him know that she had not invited him here for another sexual encounter.

This was a private place to talk, if he wished, to break down safely, if he preferred, or simply to collect his thoughts, his wits, out of the public eye. She poured herself a drink as well and sat in the other chair, staring across the room at the flashing neon signs of nearby vindis visible through the window rather than watching him and making him uncomfortable.

"How long?"

She looked at him when he eventually spoke, meeting his gaze, noting he had not yet touched the drink in his hands.

"How long?"

"Have you known Jaron?"

She shrugged. "Years. I don't know. Since he came down, I think. Since we helped him get the speecher." Oliver did not ask who 'we' were. "You?"

"After the Coup." His brow knit together and he frowned. "Did you…you didn't send him up…?"

"No." Maybe there had been some dialogue between Skelter and Jaron before the Coup that prompted Jaron to cross the captain's path in the hopes of him becoming a conduit for information. Maybe their meeting had been coincidental. Zara did not know where the two had met; she only knew she had no hand in it.

Oliver's head bobbed as he accepted her answer. "Ballard?"

He knew about Rhyd's dual life. Zara had been there when he had seen the faces of both man and vigi. Where the others fit into that picture, how many others knew the same truths, was a question he knew she would not answer and so he did not ask.

He was not asking how long she had known him, however. He wanted to know the connection between Jaron and Rhyd.

"Recent…couple of months." Her shoulders hitched as if to say she knew no more. "Through a client, I think."

Of Scarecrow's? Or hers? Through the Archives?

Oliver's head bobbed again and he resumed staring into his glass. "It shouldn't…it doesn't…it's not…" He drained the contents and set it on the vanity counter. "Once he was there…I never thought about what it might be like…when he wasn't."

His ragged voice was small, stretched thin with pain he had not expected to feel, emotion she judged he had not felt before. Had he been married? In love? Had he ever allowed himself, in the pursuit of his career, to care about anyone?

The answers, when Zara reached for his hand, appeared to be no.

His hand turned and lifted to take hers as if of its own volition, without him looking. There was a gentle tug to draw her nearer and she got up, stepped towards him, and let him wrap his arms around her, to press his face against her belly. His tight shoulders twitched, his body trembled as if he was weeping, or trying not to, and so Zara returned the embrace, offering the comfort he did not know how to ask for. It was an act that came easily to her after years of having provided it for ticks, but this was an act of genuine empathy.

She felt similar grief, similar emotion, about Skelter, about Otta. Her years of relationship with the redhead had been considerably longer than Oliver's relationship with Jaron, but it had lacked the physical intimacy she guessed Oliver and Jaron had shared. Until this moment, comforting and gentle, she had not allowed herself to fully feel the losses she had experienced, first in Skelter's presumed death and then in his moving on to Otta.

The tilting of Oliver's face to look at her announced his awareness of the shudder of emotion that passed through her. Whether he thought it a sympathetic reaction, one of arousal, or one of private grief, he began to nuzzle and nose against the fabric of her blue gossamer blouse until it lifted to expose flesh, the act a distraction from mourning he did not want to succumb to.

Her fingertips dug into his shoulders and her head dropped back with a soft, gasping sound. His hands slid beneath the cloth at her waist and traveled over the contours of her hips, her waist, her back, urging her to straddle his lap.

Without considering the consequences, she did so, moving little by little until their mouths met. Jaron, Skelter, Otta, Rhyd, and the rest of the world melted away.

❧*❧

"Good. Good plan. She can't be Scarecrow forever."

"She?" Switz set the man's empty meal container on the chair and then wiped his face with the hemp cloth that had come with the serving of steamed cabbage, potatoes, and fish. Blayd had not stayed in the building long after Switz's return but rather had taken his portion of the meal with a gruff snort that might have been gratitude or insult and elbowed past Switz in his rush into the city on some urgent business he did not identify or share.

It did not matter. His departure meant that Switz could share his first inkling of a plan with Kemway.

The Founder's eyes seemed unable to focus on anything in the room, his gaze shifting and darting with the continual arcing and turning of his head. The more he rambled about Scarecrow, the glassier his eyes became. It was good to hear the increase in dialogue versus the animalistic grunts and growls that had been his primary means of communication a few days earlier, but those lucid periods did not last very long. It was as if his mind was an Echo trying to reboot, with each pause in between coherency and madness accompanied by limp vacancy or else an incoherent effort to pull free of his chains. The clarity of his speech came and went, fading from logical discourse into ramblings that made no sense almost as often as Switz drew breath.

Switz clung to the belief that, before long, the periods of making sense would grow longer and the nonsense would diminish. It would make what he had planned much easier.

"My wife…know it's her. She didn't think I knew…but I do…I do. Scarecrow came…she's the one. All black…wants to kill me…"

Rather than correct him, rather than point out that Scarecrow was most certainly a man, Switz tried to fit Mam Kemway into the picture as he put Haythem's free hand back into the restraints. Haythem did not resist as he continued to mutter nonsense words about his wife, Scarecrow, the black shadow of his nightmares, and his vivid certainty of his own death.

It felt like putting together a puzzle into which someone continually dropped new pieces of color and shape that were unlike any of the pieces he already had. Switz doubted Kemway would remember the details of his partial plan, but that, he mused as he collected the remnants of their meal for disposal, was a good thing. He wanted the Founder's cooperation, but the less Kemway remembered, the less he could accidentally reveal in his ramblings to Blayd.

It was only important that Switz had a plan. Once it was set, it would be a matter of awaiting the perfect opportunity. Then both he and the Founder would be free to see to their fortunes.

❧Chapter 19❧

The light in Rhyd's flat was on when Jaron stumbled through the door but in his frightened fog and physical pain from ribs that sent jolts through his body with every haggard breath, he could not recall if it was turned off when he and Rhyd left for Vapors. Skelter escorted him as far as the top of the stairs that led down to Rhyd's flat and kept watch from the higher ground, nursing injuries but stoically refusing to give in to them. Jaron looked at him with a half-wave before unlocking the door, and again before stumbling inside, bidding the redhead safe passage back to the hostel. Otta would be waiting for him, would tend to his wounds as long as he made it home.

With no idea where Rhyd was, whether Scarecrow had come through his fight alive after so many recent beatings, Jaron was left to nurse his bruised ribs alone.

"What are you doing here?"

Jaron blinked, startled, frightened, staring at the man who emerged from behind the kitchen counter. It took his addled mind several moments to acknowledge that this man was not his enemy, not in the way the brako were, but he was the last person Jaron expected to find here.

"Waiting for Rhyd." It was a struggle to wiggle out of his coat since each twist of his torso, the stretching of his arms, pulled at his ribs and brought to light other aches from injuries received in his fall. It was equally difficult to remove his boots. He was cold, his trousers soaked, and he wanted desperately to be warm and free from pain.

How did Rhyd stand it?

"You mean Scarecrow."

Shrugging, Jaron left his boots at the door and trudged far enough into the room to sink onto the sofa. The blanket hanging over the back smelled like Rhyd, a comforting smell that soothed his nerves. He would have wrapped it around his shoulders if Venn had not been there, his looming displeasure rubbing Jaron like sandpaper over his skin. He winced and grimaced as he pulled off his long-sleeved tee, exposing the wide, darkening patch along one side where the brako's boot had struck him.

He wondered if anything was broken.

Venn frowned and concluded that Rhyd, Scarecrow, had been part of whatever altercation had produced that contusion. He glanced at the door at the sound of steps on the walk, expecting it to be Rhyd, or Jaron's assailants, but no one came. The footsteps passed.

The panic birthed by that sound was slow to leave Jaron as he stared at the door, breath held so that, even though his voice was synthesized by the units at his throat and temples, it came out as an uneasy squeak. "Told me to meet him here."

"Sure." Venn sat at the table, glaring at the man who was making himself at home in the flat Venn and Rhyd had once shared. Our flat, Venn thought. "What do you want from him? You don't belong here."

"You're the one who left him," Jaron muttered without looking at him. He did not want to look at Venn. He did not like feeling like the intruder in this place. He did not feel that way when Rhyd was here, but he felt that way now.

The accusation stung. "At least I'm not taking advantage of his celebrity."

"Celebrity?"

"You're only here because of Scarecrow."

"Here because we share a common vision of…"

"Death and chaos and destruction…"

"That's not…at least I accept who he is." Arguing hurt and he wished it would stop, but the compulsion to defend Rhyd would not subside now that Venn had lit a fire beneath it.

"He shouldn't be…"

"Who are you to say what he should or shouldn't…I'm not out to change…"

"He's going to get himself killed!"

Although it was a fear Jaron nursed even now, one he felt every time he and Rhyd were apart, he snapped, "You don't have much faith in him, do you?" as he rose from the sofa. He eluded the hand that tried to close around his arm as he staggered into the kitchen hoping for one of Rhyd's bottles of Zaolei or anything else that might dull his senses, numb his anxiety, ease his pain. Drown out Venn's voice. He opened the cupboard, listening to the creak behind him as Venn stood to pursue him.

"He's just a man, not some sort of…"

Though he did not know what words would have been next, Jaron felt a peculiar burn in his chest, as though he was the one bearing the force of those intended insults.

"He's what you made him," he spat, thrusting a finger at Venn's chest, the trespasser in a life, a home, he had abandoned. "You made the choice. If you can't accept him, you don't belong…"

"You're the one who doesn't…"

"He still has nightmares! Of the night you were taken! He still wakes up calling your name, screaming." It was a painful thing for Jaron, the reminder that Rhyd could not let Venn go, could not move past that dark moment of history, that Venn would always be a part of Rhyd, a part of Scarecrow.

Perhaps he would let go of Venn when he set Scarecrow aside. Maybe it would take giving up Scarecrow to make the nightmares stop. Without Venn, there would be no Scarecrow. Venn and the darkness that came with him, from him, had made Rhyd who he was, and nothing Jaron or anyone else could do would erase that. Whatever their future, the two men were anchored to each other. Jaron did not see that changing any time soon.

The retort Venn intended to make, something heated and insulting and unnecessary to accompany the force of a clenched fist, was cut off by metal clattering on the floor behind them. They turned to find Scarecrow lowering himself into the central room, the heating and air filtration duct grating on the floor at his feet.

"Don't."

The command was made more menacing by the voice alteration the hood provided and Venn, having never seen Rhyd in full uniform, startled with a start at the intimidating visage silhouetted by the lamplight behind him.

"Rhyd. Thank the stars." Venn's fists uncurled but his strained voice and feet's unwillingness to move proved more powerful than his relief and the impulse to embrace his former partner.

Jaron, knowing the foe Scarecrow had last faced, was equally relieved but remained silent, his head drooping, his shoulders sagging as if he had been chastised by that command. He might not have heard the vigi's entry, but he was certain Rhyd had heard most, if not all, of the argument in the flat. There was no need to compound the situation with unnecessary words.

"You don't belong here."

Venn blinked, took a gulp of air as the feeling of being punched subsided, and snapped, "This isn't his…"

"Isn't yours either." The Scarecrow cowl and mask came off. Rhyd's matted hair framed his face and the dark circles beneath his eyes expressed dehydration, fatigue, and pain. "You've made it cazzing clear you don't want to be here. This is my home. You should go." He pushed past Venn to get to the kitchen.

Venn, thinking Rhyd was going to Jaron, grabbed Rhyd's arm. The blonde froze, cast him a glare that made the hand fall away, and Venn murmured, "Rhyd, I only want…"

"I'm not that man anymore." Rhyd snatched the unopen bottle from Jaron's hand, wrenching Jaron's arm so that the archivist winced and took a step back.

"You could be…"

Rhyd spun so fast, throwing the bottle, that the cellist stumbled to the side, tripped, and fell. The bottle burst when it hit the wall, its contents splashing to perfume the air with its pungent fragrance.

"I'm not changing for you…for anyone! Get that through your cazzing thick head or get out!"

The two men stared at one another, years of anger, hurt, frustration, and bitterness expressed through the flashing of eyes and the ticks of facial expressions that both had once known intimately. There was longing there too, but the resentment on both sides was too powerful to allow anything good to come of this moment. When Venn, once again on his feet, opened his mouth, wanting to speak, no sound came forth. He was met with a single, emphatic word laced with unmistakable finality.

"Go."

Behind Rhyd, now with his back pressed to the kitchen sink, as far out of the reach of the confrontation as he could be, Jaron shook with emotion and looked at his feet, hoping to make himself invisible to the warring men. Rhyd stared at Venn as if he did not recognize what he saw but trembling as Venn drew back his shoulders, the first to break the stalemate. He said nothing as he retreated from the flat without looking back. Neither Rhyd nor Jaron could see his final expression, but they did not need to. The boulder-weight of so many lost years, unrequited longing and grief, loss and frustration, hung in the air as if wanting to crush them both.

"Rhyd..." Jaron immediately regretted the word that squeaked through the speecher.

Rhyd did not want sympathy. He did not want words. He wanted to be alone. "Go back up top where you belong," he spat.

Jaron's breath hitched. "I don't belong..."

"Don't belong here either."

Rhyd thundered into the other room without looking at the man he wanted desperately to push away. No one belonged at his side. Anyone beside him got hurt. Venn. Tox. Skelter. Jaron. The deepening purple over Jaron's ribs had been noted, and the smoke of Venn's dejection, his rejection, lingered in the flat in the man's wake. They were the only evidence Rhyd needed.

Regretting the breaking of the bottle, he peeled out of the body armor with abrupt, angry motions, ignoring his body's protests of pain.

"I don't belong there either."

"Never told you to leave him for..."

"Didn't leave him for you," Jaron snapped, taking a glass from the cupboard and filling it in the sink. "Left him because it was the right thing to do. I was tired of him being the only one to matter…tired of being invisible." He brought the glass into the main room and set it on the sofa table within Rhyd's easy reach. "I want to matter."

To Rhyd. To Hebenon. To someone. To anyone.

"You don't."

The words burned hotter than Zaolei and Jaron narrowed his eyes, staring at Rhyd's bruised back, noting the way the other man refused to look at him, noting the strain in his voice, the lingering hurt and resentment and fear in his tone. Jaron had witnessed Scarecrow's fury when he had fallen to the brako's assault.

Despite those words, Jaron knew better.

Rhyd could lie to himself but he would never convince Jaron he meant those words.

"You don't mean…"

"You don't know anything about me." Stripping down to his shorts, the pieces of Scarecrow dropped haphazardly on the table, the floor, the nearest chair, he absently picked up the glass of water and drank it without acknowledging gratitude or appreciation. Not thinking about the dangers that awaited Jaron outside of his door, dangers that had twice tried to kill him, Rhyd barked, "Get out and leave me alone. You shouldn't be here…don't want you here…"

Jaron did not move as the battered blonde man stomped out of the central room into the bedroom he had not used in over four years. The door slammed behind him. The tears pricking Jaron's blue eyes slid down his cheeks but he dropped his head back, squeezed them shut, and took a long, cleansing breath before muttering to the air, "I'm not going anywhere. We both know it."

➮*➭

Oliver stared at the hemp panel ceiling tiles for so long that he lost track of the passage of time. His only awareness was of Zara's even, measured breathing beside him, the balm breathing of someone comfortable in slumber who did not fear him.

When had Jaron last slept so soundly, peacefully at his side?

In the beginning, perhaps, when their relationship was fresh and new. Oliver could not recall such a time, only frequent nights of tossing and turning and soft sounds of frustration even in Jaron's deepest hours of sleep.

Had that been his doing?

Irritated, he swung his feet to the floor, leaned his elbows on his knees, and rubbed his face with his hands. Zara did not stir.

She had been a calming palliative over the sting of losing Jaron, but Grainger knew he should not be here. They had used each other before, had used each other again, a pattern that could not continue. It was an unhealthy thing. She had to know it as surely as he did.

So long as Scarecrow was between them, nothing they shared would be right or good or honest.

She had a life, a purpose, people who loved her, people she loved. People who depended on her.

He had a city that needed him.

Unfortunately, he thought with a bittersweet sigh as he dressed and left the room, this duty was something he had to shoulder alone.

The door opened. The door closed. The floor trembled beneath the weight of retreating footsteps. Zara opened her eyes and sighed.

It was for the best.

So why did his leaving feel so hollow?

So wrong?

❧*❧

Each piece of Scarecrow's identity was picked up, dried off, cleaned of blood and more, and hung over the backs of the dining chairs, over the table, over the kitchen counter, across the sofa table. The discarded undershirt was added to the now collected dirty clothes and the broken bottle was swept up for recycling.

Rhyd did not emerge from the bedroom.

For several minutes after his efforts were complete, Jaron stood at the bedroom door, listening for sounds of distress, sounds of upset or need that he might be able to soothe or fill. Rhyd had not taken an oxygen tank with him but there might have been one inside that forbidden room. As angry and hurt as Rhyd had been, Jaron did not dare to disturb him.

Those words, the command to leave, might not have been uttered in malice, might not have been meant, but Jaron did not want to push his luck or hear them again.

Hearing only deep snoring, the sound anyone might make in the clutches of exhausted sleep, Jaron contented himself that Rhyd was okay and returned to the main room.

He was too unsettled to sleep. His reflection in the dark screen of the Echo, the frantic flashing of the speech units at his throat and one temple, reminded him of something he had yet to address. Going to Zara, someone he believed would have a sympathetic ear, might enable him to deal with two things at once. The speecher and his restless, troubled thoughts.

It was dangerous to go into the city. Twice that truth had been proven. But twice he had been in the company of others and that had barely protected him. He did not have far to go to reach Zara's flat. If he was careful, if he stayed alert and in the shadows, there was no reason he could not reach his destination unharmed. He had made such journeys for years.

No reason…unless the brako were watching Rhyd's flat. Or hers.

With only a few hours remaining before his shift, it was best to do this now. By the time he came off shift, Rhyd would be awake, would have had time to calm down. He would either regret his harsh, hurtful words or he would stubbornly stand by them.

If he thought Jaron would give up so easily, he would find himself on the wrong side of an equally stubborn man. Maybe Jaron did not know Rhyd well, but Rhyd did not know him either.

It would come down to a battle of time and stubborn wills…and Jaron's conviction that Rhyd needed someone in his corner who accepted who he was, who would not try to change him.

No matter how much danger it put him in.

❧*❧

The plucked notes of the cello bled through the walls of the flat, muffled and distorted, discordant in a way that dragged Rhyd out of his slumber. The sound was wrong. All wrong. Not the way it should be. There was another sound too, like sobbing, like words bubbling from beneath too-thick water, a sound that pulled him from the bed on hands and knees, the bedding tangled around his legs and feet. He knew the smell that hung like a fog in the air, sticky, heavy, metallic, like the scent of so much in Hebanthe Falls. This smell was close, close enough to taste, and he clamped his mouth closed to avoid it, clenched his jaws, and continued to crawl.

The bedroom door was open. It was always open. The song the same. Always the same. But the notes did not come on the smooth flow of a bow over strings. The foreboding created by the bedding he could not shed, a butterfly unable to be loose of its cocoon, suggested a wrongness more powerful than the jarring cello notes.

Venn at the table where the dream always took him, eyes black holes that failed to see Rhyd even when his face tipped in Rhyd's direction. The rim of a red pool gathered at his feet and Rhyd expected to find the man's eyes in the puddle of blood. But the pool was spreading from the sofa, where the cello bow stood upright as if embedded in the cushions. Rhyd crawled, leaving crimson handprints and a trail of red streaming behind his tail of blanket and sheet.

The labor of breathing strangled him, each gulp of air faster, shallower, until he saw what he somehow knew he would find. A head of tousled black hair resting on the arm of the sofa.

He tried to say the man's name as he used the sofa side to claw to his knees, but the fight for air and the sight of the bow driven through Jaron's chest, through his heart, robbed him of the ability to form sound. He curled his fingers in Jaron's hair with a strangled gasp of overpowering grief.

As ever in his dream, the door crashed inward, slamming against the wall behind it. Captain Grainger, flanked by Crows and now bugorra, burst through, this time with poppers drawn, aimed not at Venn but at Rhyd's head. Behind him, Venn lurched to his feet, scattering an array of orange Hebbies from the table into the blood on the floor. This time the cello did not fall, no strings broke, as Venn raised the instrument to strike him as if it were an ax to split wood.

The cello came down.

The popper spat its seed.

One hand found the mask, the other the knob. Much needed oxygen flowed from the tank into his lungs and he collapsed, gasping, back into unconscious slumber.

৵*৽

"Sorry it's late…didn't know if you'd be up or…"

Zara motioned Jaron inside and closed the door, her smile and expression of relief indicating her gratitude for the interruption of friendly company. "Couldn't sleep either," she admitted. She had been home long enough after her interlude with Oliver to shower. Seeing Jaron now, she was glad it was the first thing she had done. However he felt about Oliver, or did not feel, the scent of him on her skin would have been awkward for them both.

"Looks like you had some trouble."

There was bruising on his face but it was the stiffness with which he moved, a result of his bruised ribs, that spoke loudest of the fight he had been caught in. "Scarecrow dealt with it…and Skelter's fine. A little banged up too, but okay."

He assumed Skelter had made it to the hostel without further incident. He had not heard differently.

A breath of relief escaped her. "Want a drink?" The offer was meant to blanket the concern for Skelter she had not realized she felt.

"No, thanks…thought you could help me with this." He tapped the unlit unit on the side of his head. "Hoping it's just mechanical and not…" Not something that required surgery.

Motioning to the table with its overhead neon lamp, the brightest spot in the room at the moment, she said, "Sit," and gathered a collection of tools from her workbench. She pulled another chair closer, her bare knee pressed against his leg as she bent in and turned his face for better lighting to gingerly open the unit.

"Only worked on a few of these…and not when they're attached," she admitted.

"Just…see if it's a short…something you can fix without…"

She nodded to the unspoken word and continued in silence.

Unable to watch her except for the hand that swapped tools on the table or what he could see of her focused expression out of the corner of his eye, Jaron instead kept his closed and concentrated on the sound of her breathing. His thoughts kept circling to the same place, however, until he groaned in frustration, a sound that bypassed the speecher and bubbled in his throat.

"Looks like the central power module. I should be able to replace it, but I don't have one on hand…and I'd feel better doing it if there was a medi here to supervise." The power module was no bigger than a grain of rice and required delicate, steady hands to remove from where it was attached to the nerve endings beneath it and then to insert a new one. Replacement was designed to be a non-invasive procedure, but this was Jaron's brain, his ability to speak, on the line. If Zara was going to handle the replacement, she wanted someone there to intervene if something went wrong.

"I trust you."

"Good to know." She closed the unit without removing the damaged morsel. "Will take a few days to get another." Not many speechers existed, but such power modules were used for many other purposes. Nearly everything in Hebenon was designed to be multi-purposed. It could take weeks to find one, but with Skelter's skill, Zara was confident that timeframe would be reduced to a handful of days.

"Let me know." While not a pressing issue, as the other unit functioned well enough to allow him to speak, Jaron depended on the set to sound like himself, with the voice he had grown accustomed to years before when he had been robbed of his own. He nodded and leaned against the back of the chair. "Think I could use that drink unless you want me to go."

"Not necessary. I could use the company." Something was on his mind, as it was on hers, and if he wanted to talk she would welcome the chance to avoid dwelling on her thoughts for a while longer.

She dimmed the table lamp, brought two glasses and a bottle of apple wine from the kitchen, and put them down as she sat. "Afraid that's all I have. Skelter drank the other the last time he was by."

"That must be hard."

Zara shrugged and poured the wine. "We've never been a couple, it's not our thing. But when I found out he was alive…I'd hoped he'd come back to the way things were. Never thought he'd…"

"Meet someone?"

"Be a father," she said with a corrective headshake. "He loves kids, but he's never been inclined towards his own."

"Maybe nearly dying changed that." He took the glass she slid across the table and murmured his thanks. She and Skelter had known each other a long time. Long before he had come to the Levs, long before he had met Skelter, and then her.

"How long have they…did they…Rhyd…and Venn?"

Her expression grew thoughtful, her gaze distant. "Years. After he came to Vapors the first time and met Maemi, Skelter, Tox. Was never Venn's scene. But he's Tox's cousin; she introduced them. Didn't take long to be inseparable. Ten years…before he vanished."

She shrugged again and toyed with the rim of her glass. "They've never been…no one thought they'd…" She sighed. "Rhyd's hands-in. Practical. Get dirty and get it done. Venn's heart is in his music. He lives in his dreams, in his head, always had ambitions, idealistic aspirations…and it was hard on him taking so long to get there. Think that's what started the Hebs…the waiting. Think he felt on some level that Rhyd's anchor to the day-to-day was dragging him back, though he'd never admit that. The addiction to Rhyd was supplanted by the Hebs…and then some little mistake, saying or doing that got him noticed by the wrong people…he was Taken…and you know the rest."

Though he nodded, her tale did not give Jaron the assurance he wanted as to whether Rhyd might eventually go back to Venn, whether

Jaron had any chance, any future, with him. Was he a dreamer too? Were his ambitions too lofty? Was he unrealistic?

He had been ambitious once, rooted in science and the study of the data recorded about the world beyond the walls. That was taken away with his exile and the loss of his voice. Since then, his only aspirations had been survival, blending in, day-to-day drudgery that hid him from those in power who wanted to suppress people like him.

The opening of Outside, meeting Oliver, and gaining a toehold in the Uppers again had not awakened any desire or dreams for anything different…except to see more of Outside. Meeting Rhyd, meeting Scarecrow, had birthed a desire to help, to do more for the city from where he was, to be a service in any way he could.

As an archivist, he did not know what that service might be.

It did not mean he could be what Rhyd needed. It did not mean Rhyd could be what he needed.

But Founder's breath, Jaron was determined to try.

❧*❦

Blayd returned. It had to be now. As he had done every other time recently when feeding the man in his care, Switz released one of Kemway's hands from the bindings. He hoped the man's trembling was a sign of anticipation and would not result in the plan's failure.

"Okay," he murmured against the Founder's ear. "Now." He jumped back and scurried to the other side of the doorway.

Haythem's bellow of fury and force and Switz's subsequent screech of horror did what Switz expected, bringing the merc barreling into the chamber, thumper in hand, expecting to beat Kemway into submission. What Blayd did not expect was a crack across the back of his head that splayed him face-first onto the cold floor.

What Switz, likewise, did not expect was for his partner to yank his cuffed hand free of the band that detained him, dislocating his thumb in the process and drawing blood where the cuff bit into his hand and wrist. He leaped, knocked Switz against the doorframe with enough force to stun him. Eluding the flailing hands that tried to apprehend him, Haythem slipped through the open door that could not close with Switz sprawled through the opening.

Haythem swiped the T2 from the desk, swung it at the side of the scrambling man's head, and as Switz sank into unconsciousness amidst a shower of hemplastic parts and electrical sparks, he heard the cracking crash of a door being slammed…with the fleeting thought of regret for what he had just unleashed.

The shuriken fell free of his hand.

❧Chapter 20❧

For the first time in more than two years, Grainger walked the wet grated streets of the Levs alone, watching people with a well-practiced eye that picked up details most others would miss.

A group of blossoming Heb addicts there, not yet so absorbed by their cravings as to have moved into the glassy-eyed, barely functioning stage. Truant schoolchildren playing some manner of dice game with two streeter kids wearing the increasingly familiar black bandas around their neck, wagering over a sack of something that he knew would cost the schoolchildren their wager and win the streeters theirs. A little bent woman in white, removing something again and again from the pocket of her waterproof apron and dropping it into the bags, pockets, or hands of everyone she passed who did not immediately rebuff her. Grainger judged her to be Igraci, though she said not a word and carried none of the signage many Igraci did. A tinger caught swiping a crate of mixed berries by the vindi owner, and the subsequent negotiation that allowed the tinger a chance to work off his crime and keep the much-needed nourishment. Two men, big and pale-skinned, leaning against the corner of another vindi with their cloaks raised to mostly hide their faces, men Grainger was sure were brako though they did not wear the stolen Crow masks.

He contemplated a confrontation, sending the pair on their way, but since they were not breaking any ordinances, and he had not come with backup nor equipped for confrontation, he left them alone.

The ache in his leg reminded him his injuries were not yet recovered and he was not in a mood for a fight he was unlikely to win.

He passed a second group of banda-wearing Spinks with the inverted haz symbol painted, sewn, or drawn over their mouths and nose in bright red or yellow. Footage of that symbol left by vandals throughout the Levs crossed his desk every day, the symbol that had come to represent Scarecrow. When and why the streeter kids had adopted wearing it, Grainger had not heard; he could not recall a single report on the matter.

The next time he saw Lieutenant Young, he would ask what she knew about it. If anyone knew anything, she certainly would.

There was only so much distraction the city streets, the shadows sliced by needles of flickering colored neon, could offer, however, before little things, an animated digital dancer, the spicy herbal smell of cologne, the throbbing bass line of someone's music pumping through an open window, a scrolling lightboard offering a promising career as an archivist, began to drag things he did not want to think about to the surface of his thoughts until pushing them down became impossible. Contemplating a return to his suite and a few hours of sleep before duty summoned him back to his desk, he turned a corner that would take him to the nearest lift only to be confronted with an exterior Echo on the corner of a men's clothier. Kenneth Ximenez's mouth moved soundlessly, the Echo's sound either muted or broken as there was not enough foot traffic to block the audio.

There was no need for audio. Founder Kemway's face was inset in the upper corner of the screen, alternating with a cycling bit of footage of Senior Kal, groups of Voices followers attending a service, and some bygone clip of a clash between Talkers and herpa that could have come from any time in Hebenon's history.

Grainger growled, the annoyances in his personal life lending fuel to an action he already should have taken. To hell with concrete evidence and proof. He was only going to get answers from Kal if he confronted the man he had not seen face to face since the fellow's audacious appearance in his office.

"Lieutenant Young," he barked into the ICD, not caring if anyone around him heard. It was time the people saw their captain in action.

There was a pop of distortion and then, "Sir?"

Her quick reply was a welcome surprise. "I want every officer we can spare to begin door-to-door searches of every Talker Hall in the city…and have four meet me at Hall Prime."

"Sir?"

He could almost see the young woman's scowl.

"I want Senior Kal found and brought to Interrogation. Today. No matter what it takes to get him there. I want anything that even looks like evidence brought in for inspection."

"Yes, sir. I'm on it."

"But keep it quiet; don't give him a chance to run." There were plenty of places other than the Halls for a man like Kal to hide and Grainger did not want to have to scour every business, every home, to bring the Senior to justice.

"We'll find him, Captain."

Ignoring the side-eyeing glance of two weary-looking men in heizer gear, doubting they were the sort to raise an alert that might prompt Kal to go deeper into hiding, Grainger took the lift he had intended, to exit on the level where Hall Prime was located instead of his Upper level suite.

Surrounded by food vindis, deks, and a variety of public entertainment venues, the wide plaza before Prime Hall was a place where one could sit at sheltered tables, on benches around light shows or amidst colored fountain displays and planters of ferns, marsh marigolds, pussy willow, and other flowering foliage that thrived in Hebenon's perpetually moist environment. The atmosphere encouraged visitors from which the Talkers could pluck potential adherents. In a place like this, there was no need for Grainger to hide.

He chose a bench with a good view of Prime Hall's main door after casually asking a young woman if Senior Kal was in today. Without deeming his question a cause for concern, despite Grainger's uniform or the accusations of kidnapping currently leveled at the Senior, she smiled and said that he was before sashaying off to join a group of other women seated in one of the tea vindis. Grainger made a show of checking his ICD as if he was due for an appointment, the action covering his failure to immediately enter the Hall. He moved to a second vantage point, out of the woman's line of sight, with an equally good view to allow him to monitor who came and went through the main door.

If Kal left, Grainger would know, unless the Hall had exits he was unaware of. If anyone suspect went in, Grainger would know that too.

The Senior could not have vanished into the mist of the Four Falls. If Kal knew where Founder Kemway was, Grainger would know soon enough as well.

❧*❦

The reason behind the order was unimportant; Grainger was in command and if he believed there was cause for action, that was all that mattered. Ilya was eager for progress, for any lead in the hunt for Founder Kemway and was willing to do whatever was necessary to find him. Bugorra were sent in threes to the ten Halls with the command to bring the Senior in for questioning, to bring in any documents that looked as though they could be evidence of collusion or clues to the Founder's whereabouts. Another four were sent to Prime Hall as the captain requested.

She felt she should be there. She should be dirtying her hands with this much-anticipated arrest. But coordinating the capture effort would have to suffice. If the Senior was at Prime Hall, there was no point in duplicating the captain's effort or going there to steal this win from him. If his intel had led him there, he had every right to see the arrest made. He deserved the score.

Only when she had every requested piece in play as instructed, the web spread wide enough to snare their suspect, did she reach out to the one person she knew to have an equal stake in finding the Founder…if not necessarily in Senior Kal himself.

Three tries later, however, with no response received to any of them, she gave up trying to reach Blayd. Maybe he was asleep. Maybe he was indisposed. Either way, he was again failing to respond to her efforts to contact him. He had her messages, she thought bitterly. If he missed the spectacle of the Senior's arrest, it would not be her fault. If he wanted the Founder, if he wanted Kal, he knew where Ilya was.

She was not going to plead for the merc's attention. Arresting the Senior was her priority, if it would bring them Founder Kemway.

❧*❧

Three glasses of apple wine later, the bottle empty and a heady buzz making his movement unsteady, Jaron knew it was time to go or else he would not make it to Rhyd's before the blonde awoke. A walk in the cold mist would sober him up. If it did not, he would then be late for his shift and would find the strain of staring at an unending flow of data on the Echo-screen to be mind-numbing enough to put him to sleep at his station. Having filled his duties flawlessly for more years than most managed to endure the job, Jaron did not think he would be docked ticks for being late, or for dozing at his desk, but he had no wish for this to be the first black mark on his record.

A bracing cup of hot cinnamon and cilantro algtea, purchased at the first vindi he passed, sparked his brain out of its alcohol fog and seeped into his bones to ease the chill weighing in his belly.

The fight with Venn, over Rhyd, might have been explicable, but fighting in Rhyd's home so that they were overheard had not been the most appropriate thing Jaron had ever done. He felt guilty. He felt sick, raw, and sad. The moroseness caused him to stop under a corner awning, beneath the flicker of a struggling alglamp, long enough to reach out to Rhyd, to apologize, to say something that might make everything right.

But there was no answer. The shift whistle squealed in the distance and he sighed. He was not going to make it back to the flat.

"I'm sorry," he murmured into the ICD. "I shouldn't have…we'll talk later…after shift…"

What would result from that talk, what would follow, he miserably mused, certain he would find the flat door barred when he returned, would have to wait. It was possible they would never talk at all.

❧*❧

The big man, and perhaps Mam Kemway, were not done with him. There were watchful eyes everywhere, following him as Molly trudged to his assigned flat with a takeaway bag and sack of nessies clutched in one hand. They might be watching him, but at least they had not continued to hold him captive. If he was in their position, he imagined he would watch himself too, see what he would do, learn what his first move after release would be, whether he would go to the authorities or try to cause them some other manner of trouble.

Given where they had caught him, what he was caught doing, in addition to anything they had learned from the arrest records they had undoubtedly searched, it would come as no surprise that the first thing he did, after buying nessies and a meal, was to trade his remaining balance of ticks for a stinger, a bottle of liquid Heb, and a small sack of Hebbies. It had been the entire stash the seller had on him.

Molly did not care that the seller made out on the better end of that trade. He did not care what Vanderwall, Mam Kemway, or their agents thought of his transaction. Behind the closed door of his flat, he only cared about what awaited at the other end of the stinger's needle, a taste of forgetting he had not enjoyed in more than seven years.

❧*❧

On this side of Hebanthe Falls, so near to this river's limb, the constant roar of rushing, dripping, growling water, from the air, from the river somewhere beneath his feet, clawed into Haythem's head like boring beetles chewing through hempcloth, disallowing him to focus, to think to make sense of this world in which he found himself.

Hell. It had to be hell. Everything was wet and cold. The blue and greens of alglamps and the flash and burn of vindi neon seared the darkness. The light hurt his eyes and so he escaped into the shadows after snagging a rain cloak from a hook outside a vindi and a wide-brimmed hempcanvas hat treated to repel the damp that had been left on a diner table. Already soaked to the skin, however, the coverings did little more than retain a sort of sticky, uncomfortable, humid body heat beneath the heavy fabric.

This had to be hell.

Why, he thought as he inspected his throbbing hand again, did his useless hand hurt? How and where had he dislocated his thumb, cut his wrist, bruised and twisted the bones underneath?

He remembered white halls. He remembered warmth and the laughter of children. He remembered, fleetingly, a windowed glimpse of blue unlike anything he ever imagined he would see. But none of those remembered things existed in this place…wherever he was.

Maybe those remembrances were but the shadows of a dream.

There was no solid recollection of Uppers, of Levs, of what had been before chains, except for those fleeting images, sounds, and smells detached from his current reality. With nothing to anchor those snatches too, he could not attest to their accuracy, but some small cupboard in the recesses of his brain clung to the hope that they were not dreams, that they were real, and that he would find his way back to that place…if only he could figure out where he was.

A wraith, joined by another, and then another, tall and sinister, with long black beaks, strode past the alcove where he had taken refuge long enough to struggle into his stolen coverings, a task made awkward by the injury to his hand. Those faces brought back another, a black face, a towering figure, a woman's icy laughter of derision, a piercing gaze of sharp eyes, and a single word.

Scarecrow.

Were they Scarecrow? All of them? Were they looking for him? Did everyone in this hellscape want him captured, want him dead?

Believing it was so, Haythem pressed against the wall and hid his face, determined to melt into the shadows, to become one with the darkness. He was not safe out here, but there was no going back.

There was nowhere to go back to.

❧*❧

It was not the first time Rhyd had regained consciousness on the living room floor. Sometimes it was where alcohol and exhaustion left him. Sometimes it was the result of falling off the sofa or out of the chair in the aftermath of a nightmare. This too had been a nightmare.

He remembered that much. He lurched up, propelled by the horror his foggy brain expected to see sprawled on his sofa.

But the cushions were empty and as clean as a ten-year-old sofa subjected to water and whiskey could be. There was no bloody smear trailing from his feet, tangled in bedsheets, towards the bedroom, no crimson handprints on the worn-smooth hemptile floor, no scatter of Hebbies in a pool of blood or broken cello. The door of the flat was closed, intact, undamaged.

Everything was as it should be.

Except that Jaron was not there.

Rhyd frowned as he pulled the oxygen mask from his face and freed his legs from the tangled bedding, ignoring the evidence of sleeping in a room he had not slept in since Venn's Vanishing. The harsh words last night, words between himself and Venn, himself and Jaron, pounded like tiny pneumonic hammers inside his skull, making him draw his knees to his chest and clutch his head between his hands as if that would make the sound stop.

The severing with Venn was regrettable but it had been a long time coming. Both men had known it. The writing had been on the walls of their lives longer than either of them wanted to admit. Fate had begun to pull them in opposite directions before Venn's arrest and no amount of shared history was going to undo what their world had done to them. Rhyd's life was here. Venn's was in Marbordo. It was done now. It was time to accept the inevitable and move forward.

Rhyd regretted, however, the sharing of violent words and emotion that had laid waste to the final strings binding them.

He also regretted the words spent on Jaron, the effort made to push him away. But there was evidence of the archivist here still, a shirt over the back of one chair, the tidy care taken with Scarecrow's protective skin, dishes washed and in the dry rack, the T2 Jaron often carried still on the table, its diode blinking the need for recharging.

Rhyd glanced at his ICD. Jaron was not gone. The hour reassured him that the younger man had gone on shift, nothing more. He had not taken the demand to leave seriously, but had left his belongings as the traces of life that would bring him back.

Damn stubborn archivist.

Oddly, that thought made Rhyd warm. Reassured him. He needed someone in his life who supported his calling but he also needed someone to push back when he behaved like an idiot. Jaron, it appeared, had the making of those things.

Relieved but still feeling guilty, he got up, scooped up the sheet and blanket, and staggered into the bathroom to shower, pausing only long enough to toss the bedding into the room it had come from. He had slept in that room, in that bed and it had not killed him. It had given him one helluva nightmare, but it had not broken him as he had believed it would.

Letting go of Venn was not, as he feared, a world-ending thing.

❧*❧

The throbbing at the back of his skull, the heaviness of bruising on various places across his body, pulled Blayd back to wakefulness. The stickiness of blood, when he felt for damage and looked at his hand, forced him to his knees with a groan. His eyes had difficulty focusing around the flashes of bright, searing pain, but there was one detail that was impossible to miss.

The chains hanging on the wall were empty.

He lurched to the side to look behind him towards the unexpected moaning there, hoping he would see Kemway. It was not the Founder, however, but Switz, sprawled half in and half out of the room, his clothes torn. The blood upon them both attested to a struggle the merc could not recall. Switz's knuckles were bruised, his lip cracked, his cheek dark and swollen, enough evidence to give Blayd a good idea of what had happened.

"I told you not to let him…!"

"Let no one do nothing," Switz spat earnestly, his grogginess slowing his efforts to rise. "He tried to…and then you came…and he was there…right behind you. Tried to stop him…"

"Who?" Blayd did not remember anyone else present, did not remember where Switz had been when he burst into the room, but he recalled the incapacitating blow to the back of his head.

Exasperated, Switz threw up his hands. "I dunno! Never saw 'im before. Like a Crow…but not. A bugger maybe? He must've taken…"

His wild-eyed expression landed on something shiny on the floor that glinted in the pale illumination of the room. "Look! I told you!"

The circular, multi-edged disc was within Blayd's reach and he gingerly picked it up.

Like a Crow but not.

Bugorra?

No. The evidence in his hand gave the attacker's identity away.

Not bugorra.

Scarecrow.

Scarecrow had found them. Ambushed them.

Scarecrow had taken Founder Kemway.

"Get out there and find him! Find them both!" Blayd snarled, rising abruptly despite the pain and ignoring, for the moment, the blinking on his ICD that told of an incoming message. "If we don't find them, he'll kill him!"

Blayd did not think that was true, given what he knew of Scarecrow's pattern. But Switz did not know it, did not need to know. Switz needed to be prompted to quick, desperate action. Better the little man felt the added urgency. Blayd's main concern was what Scarecrow's interference meant for his future with Neoma…for Senior Kal…and for the leadership of Hebanthe Falls.

❧CHAPTER 21❧

The list received two nights prior was hardly the most peculiar collection of items he had been paid to procure over the years but it was, in Skelter's experience, an odd collection for a school teacher. Perhaps not a teacher of sciences, but what could a history teacher need with under-the-table cutters, torches, and welders?

Part of Skelter's allure as kaheao was that he was not prone to asking questions. Perhaps she side-lined as an artist. Perhaps she was renovating her flat or classroom without Source consent. Perhaps she was building play equipment or study aides for her students.

It did not matter to Skelter.

It had taken twenty-four hours to reach out to the sources he had once used to obtain such hardware. Sometimes Tox could acquire it, but not always. Heavy equipment and tool purchases were monitored by the Source, and once by the Founder and Doctet, as a way of weeding out potentially subversive elements from the Levs. Although the Founder and Doctet were no longer in control, the Nau continued to oversee such sales in an effort, they claimed, to adjust Hebenon's limited manufacturing capacity to fill the city's needs most efficiently.

Because of the Coup, Skelter wagered they had other reasons too.

But there were plenty of people in the Levs who, like Tox, made a living repairing discarded items or repurposing them when possible, transforming things into something with uses other than those originally intended. This allowed an undercurrent of obtainable goods that anyone could access for a fee without alerting the Source. With a set allotment of ticks per individual and family monitored as well, the trade of illicit goods had to be recorded as some innocuous item or else were carried out on an exchange basis through people like Skelter.

He had been, until his disappearance, one of the best.

Some of his prior contacts resisted working with him, their reluctance to cross the brako a reasonable fear. Well-versed in manipulation, in getting his way, with a charming smile, well-placed word, compliment or promise, sometimes Skelter's efforts required more. A sumptuous meal of the sort few rarely enjoyed, the guarantee of an advantageous favor or trade in return might also be required.

Gradually he was able to obtain everything the woman Eido requested, a good two days of work of which he was very proud. As he secured the items in a warehouse location and sent the location and retrieval code to her ICD, in an encoded message she would only be able to access when her payment was processed and received, he was satisfied that his success had proved, to himself at least, that the lost two years had not cost him the ability to survive.

His new family would not suffer due to a lack of income.

They might, however, suffer at the hands of the thugs who had filled the vacancy he had left, who had pushed others like Skelter out of business or absorbed them into theirs. They did not approach him, did not make themselves known, but he could feel their eyes following him every step of the way. It was why he chose to personally take up watch over this transaction, this warehouse, until Eido came for it.

The brako would take the contents if they could. They would try to turn his contacts against him, possibly by brute force. How he could protect them, his family, himself was a growing concern.

Eventually, the brako would come down hard on their new rival. He did not want to form a protection host around him as Vanderwall had done, but Skelter was beginning to feel that there would be no other choice if he was to stay alive. He would become what he…and Scarecrow…hated.

He checked the warehouse door, the lock, once more and stepped away with a reluctant sigh. How he could counter that, stay alive, was the first problem he had ever encountered, except for the river that had nearly drowned him twice, that he did not know how to solve.

⁎*⁎

The missed messages on his ICD made Blayd scowl when he paused his Founder hunt for a hot tea and sandwich. Three attempts in a row from Ilya meant important news, each attempt timestamped during his unconscious period after the Founder's escape. He hoped, when he finally replayed the only message left in those attempts, that the Founder had come to be in bugorra custody. It would not be the best solution, as it would abruptly corrupt his plot against Senior Kal and his plan to get back into Neoma's good graces.

But it would remove suspicion from him, and Ilya and the buggers picking up Kemway was better than Scarecrow having him.

The Founder's returning, if sporadic, cognitive functions was a worrisome detail. If he remembered anything about Blayd's involvement in his abduction, in his care, if he shared what he remembered, if anyone believed the ramblings of the certifiable madman, there would be a price to pay.

The concern that Ilya was reaching out as the prelude to his arrest prompted Blayd to read her words with a hammering heart and trembling hands.

Arresting Kal. You in?

Blayd swallowed the bile at the back of his throat. Arresting the Senior before Blayd had Kemway in place would ruin everything as surely as the Founder's absence would.

"Cazz!" he swore, punching his fist through the fabric back of the chair beside him.

The swiver who brought his tea and sandwich glared.

Now he would have to pay for that too, Blayd groused as he bitterly flexed his aching fist.

Without putting the Founder somewhere that would implicate the Voices when he was found, Blayd believed there was little other evidence to condemn the Senior, to make charges of treason, conspiracy, and kidnapping stick. He would probably be out within a matter of hours.

Unless the Founder had already fallen into the Voices' hands.

Perhaps this was something else. Maybe there was another crime Blayd was unaware of that could be manipulated in his favor.

The message had been received hours ago. Kal was either still in custody or else released back into the Levs. There was no news about him, an arrest or anything else, playing on the citywide Echo system. Whatever had been done, was being done, there was nothing Blayd could do to help or hinder it.

The only thing he could do was continue seeking Kemway until news came that he had been found. As with every hour of his search thus far, however, Blayd had no idea where a man without memory, or very little of it, would go.

❧*❦

Agnys watched the methodical efforts Venn undertook to throw Rhyd's few belongings into a heap in the mud outside of the door of his home after his return to Marbordo. She tried to speak gently, afraid that this display of anger meant something bad had happened, but Venn snapped at her, told her to leave him alone, and then resumed his efforts, muttering words beneath his breath that she was not meant to hear. He paused occasionally to hit something that either broke under the assault or met the blow with enough resistance to leave his knuckles bloody and bruised.

Her lips trembled; her eyes teared. She did not know how to help.

Without his answers, with only her fears to fuel anxious thoughts of harm befalling Rhyd, the girl picked up every discarded item without Venn's notice and took them to her own home. Clothes were folded with care and tucked around other items within an empty hemp crate. Rhyd would either want them back, or she would have them as remembrances of what he had done for her.

Cori's arrival meant extra hands for the retrieval, cleaning, and storage efforts. The boy spoke little as he helped, not knowing what he should say, and when the last item was secured in the crate and the crate pushed beneath her bed, he sat beside Agnys on the stone stoop of her home, his hand on her back as she hugged her knees and stared at the city's door.

"Doesn't mean anything's wrong with Mister Rhyd," Cori finally murmured. "My mom used to throw dad's things outside when they fought. A few hours later, everything would be back to the same."

"If he's hurt…"

Cori patted her shoulder. "Can't think like that. Worrying makes you sick." At least, that was what his father often told him when he fussed over something he could not change. "Thing's'll be fine. You'll see. He'll show up."

When Agnys shook her head no, as if she was unconvinced, he decided a distraction was needed. "I have a surprise I was saving…but we can do it now, if you want…"

She gave him a skeptical, side-eyed glance.

"I know where Ulynda lives. I found it in the Hub. We can go see her. She'll be happy to see us."

In the Uppers, before the Coup, Cori knew the Founder's children had led very structured, protected lives, having limited contact with other children their ages. The Kemway children had relied on each other for company. Cori felt certain that, with her siblings gone too, Ulynda felt as alone as he did. Unlike Cori, however, who had Agnys and an array of parah and Crosser children to play and study with, Ulynda had no one.

He was sure the company of friends would be welcome.

He had persisted in looking up her new residence until finally locating it in the Hub, with a little help from his father's lab partners, his tutors, and other adults with whom he had contact. Now that he knew where she was, he believed that, with Agnys' familiarity of the Levs…more familiarity than he had…they would be able to find Ulynda and pay her a visit.

Ulynda would like it. He believed Agnys would too. It would get Agnys' thoughts off Rhyd.

The girl sniffed, wiped her eyes on the back of her hand, and got up. "It'll be good to see her," she said, her voice rough and small.

Her agreement made Cori smile. He had done something good.

❧*❦

Though not treated with any modicum of the respect he believed he was entitled to as the leader of the Cult of the Founder, the Voices of Faith, the only officially sanctioned religious organization designated as such in centuries long past, Kal bit his tongue when the buggers bullied him this way and that along streets, into lifts, through the glaring white halls of the Uppers, into what he perceived to be an interrogation room. He had never been inside of one as advisor, confessor, or witness.

He had certainly never been inside one as a criminal.

Judging by the cuffs on his wrist and their silence, and the brief glimpse he had gotten of Captain Grainger when the bugorra had dragged him into the square, he knew what crime he was accused of. He had done many questionable things in his life, but this time he was innocent. He had no involvement in, no connection to, the abduction of Founder Kemway.

He almost wished he had.

Confident there was no proof against him of a crime he had not committed, he wondered, with the calmest, most-assured expression he could muster in the efforts of not expressing the annoyance and insult he felt, what grounds Grainger had for his arrest.

Officers of varying ages, genders, and ranks came and went in the hours he was held, asking the same questions, sometimes stepping into the room only long enough to assess his condition, his well-being, before ducking out again. No one offered food or drink or the use of a toilet, no one badgered or bullied him, but the metal chair on which he sat was uncomfortable and the cuffs that bound his wrists to the table prevented him from standing to stretch. It grew more difficult to control his irritability as the minutes dragged by.

By the time the door opened again, bringing him a familiar face, his morbid hope was that the captain would come in abluster and act in a fashion that Kal might be able to use against him. The hope was undercut by Grainger's calm demeanor. The uniform he had worn before had been changed for a clean one, and though he limped, his fresh-faced expression spoke of a meal and possibly sleep, or stimulants, to refresh his outlook.

All were things Kal had been denied. He would have given almost anything for a cup of tea.

"Where is he?" Grainger asked as he sat across the table, toying with the cuff key in his hands. "And please…don't lie to me. I've had more than my share of lies today. Thing's'll not go well for you if that's all you have to offer."

"It would help if I knew who you're referring to," Kal countered with a smirk. He was visibly uncomfortable, a condition undoubtedly reported to the captain more than once over the last several hours, but Kal chose not to mention it in favor of evaluating Grainger with the same focus Grainger evaluated him.

The table between them, a flat, oversized Echo screen, came to life unexpectedly, prompting Kal to draw back his elbows to see the images on it. The faces, dead men he knew by the wash of their pallid features, were men he had never seen before.

"Are these the men who abducted Founder…" Too late, he realized he had revealed his understanding of the individual the captain was inquiring about.

"These are the men who didn't," Grainger grunted with a satisfied expression, seeking a trace of familiarity or emotion in the Senior's face and finding nothing. That did not mean Kal had no involvement in the abduction; it only meant that he had not hired or selected the kidnappers himself. It would have been a wise precaution for an experienced leader to make to claim no knowledge of them later.

"You realize that, without care, by now he's in desperate shape. Holding him without treatment is permitting his…"

"I'm not sure your definition of treatment has been in the Founder's best interest, Captain…"

"Then you've seen him." Grainger leaned forward. "You know what I…"

"If I'd seen him, if I had him, don't you think I'd've used him to my advantage by now?"

"Only if he could be turned into a public spectacle…if he's not grown worse or you haven't…"

"Killed him?" Kal chuckled, leaning against the back of his chair. It caused his cuffed arms to stretch but it put distance between himself and Grainger, the only indication he made to reveal his discomfort with the captain's perceived threatening posture. "Worse would be to my advantage, you know…"

"But not…"

"Even his death could be twisted…if that was what I wanted, which it isn't."

The two stared at each other suspiciously, neither seeing what they wanted in the other's eyes.

"Captain, if you intend to charge me with something, you would already have done so. Either release me or…"

"Or?" Grainger knew of no threats Kal could use against him except for unsubstantiated claims meant to smear his reputation. "By now, your arrest is displayed on every Echo in Hebenon. They know about the raid on every Hall…"

"And you've found nothing…"

"It doesn't matter. The Voices are already accused of the Founder's kidnapping. Some might call this harassment," he waved the key, "but others are going to come down on my side. Sooner or later, you have to give him up, come clean…"

"Believe me, Captain, I would give him to you if I had him. I want the Founder safe as much as you do."

"Even if it displaces the other Kemway you're backing?" Grainger did not know if that other Kemway was Ulynda or Neoma, had only heard the vaguest rumors of the Voices favoring a new candidate, but which one it was did not matter.

The office of the Founder was dead. Neither mother nor daughter would ever rule Hebanthe Falls.

"Because finding him will prove he's unfit to lead us…if he's as bad as you say," Kal said without blinking. "Now…release me so I can continue doing your job, so I can find him and get him safely back where he belongs."

Grainger snorted, pushed away from the table, and left the interrogation room after several quiet moments with only a growled, "You will tell me where he is."

The door closed. The room was left with only the buzz of the overhead lighting and the static hum of the Echo screen in the tabletop.

Kal remained, staring at the faces of dead men, bugorra, meditechs, and kidnappers alike. He waited.

Hours passed before another came, undid the cuffs, set him free.

It was impossible to know who had won that round without knowing what Grainger might have found in those still, late hours. But Kal knew that his release came with surveillance, with the captain's hopes that Kal would lead the bugorra to the Founder…or to the people who had him. A single, faltering move, a wrong word, and Kal would be back in this room. Lie or not, the Voices would be charged with kidnapping even if Grainger could not prove it…unless Kal located the Founder first.

It was time for a very public plea on the Founder's behalf.

❧*❦

The warm, damp smell of recent showering did not mask the fetidness of long-disused rooms. The dull gray of the walls, however, was plain enough to keep her location safe from threats, a privacy concern she was convinced would be crucial as soon as her offer was broadcast into every home, vindi, and public venue in Hebenon. It was not her first choice of locations, but Vanderwall was right.

The more non-descript the location, the better it would be for everyone involved.

She had more faith in the anonymity of the location than she did in the glassy-eyed, jittery man behind the cam and Echo set up prepared on a long table on the side of the room opposite a lone metal chair. A single man's flat, she assumed, but there was not even a bed here. If this was his home, if this was all the Nau had offered after the years of hardship he must have endured in the mines, it was no wonder he had turned to Heb for solace and was willing to do anything she asked for some bit of security.

"You're high." She looked him over derisively and snorted. "I'm not doing this with…"

"No. Wait…I promise I can do this." Molly rushed to her side, caught her by the elbow with his other hand at the small of her back to steer her to the chair. Her brako escort, men without masks to hide her affiliation with them, growled and stepped forward as she made a similarly hostile sound. If Molly heard it, he either chose to ignore it or was too calm in his high to detect the threat. "I can do this in my sleep. It's not…won't take long. Just…sit. Please…and when I say start, talk to the cam as if you're talking to a friend. That's easy, right?"

She shuddered at his efforts to assist in removing her coat but as neither of the brako looked inclined to help, she reluctantly accepted Molly's aid. "I've addressed the public before."

The public, yes. A friend…did she even have those?

"Yes, right," Molly muttered apologetically, releasing her so she could sit, eluding the hands of the brako prepared to pull him away but not help her out of her coat.

"We need more light." She was accustomed to brightly lit interview rooms with cams from a multitude of angles for things like this, with booms and enhancers positioned to create the most flattering image and sound possible. The single bulb hanging above her, its light dispersing fixture long broken, and the small fluorescent lamp illuminating the Echo's touchpad and solitary cam beside it hardly seemed sufficient to film by.

Neoma waved the brako away. They retreated to flank the door to be out of the camera shot but continued their wary surveillance as Molly took his place behind the table.

"It'll be fine. You'll see."

Knobs were turned, a series of keystrokes made on the Echo that produced a soft whirring and clicking from the cam, and then he signaled for Neoma to speak.

Well-versed in the art of public presentation, Neoma's expression morphed into a look of dismayed worry that it had not expressed moments before, a look of fright and desperation as she began to speak, her off-camera hands obviously wringing in her lap.

"People of Hebanthe Falls. You know my face. You know my name. You know the desperate times facing our cherished city. How many months have we endured without true leadership? How many days has it been since the abduction of my dear husband? And yet, the bugorra do nothing. They've failed to find him, to arrest those guilty of this horrific act. Our beloved Founder languishes without the care he needs and no one is willing to find him, to bring him home to a daughter who cries for him every night, to my devotion and care, to a city desperate for legitimate, qualified guidance.

"Captain Grainger and his bugorra may be content to do nothing. They may be content to allow Hebenon to fall to riots, to commodity shortages, to the hands of the thugs menacing our streets. I am not."

She paused for a breath of emphasis, ignoring the scowls of the brako at the door. Let them be annoyed. She doubted either of them understood the subtle intricacies of politics.

"For the love of Hebanthe Falls…for the love of the Founder, help me bring him home. If you have seen him, if you know where he is, if you can provide information to the code on the screen…a reward of two thousand ticks shall be paid to anyone who comes forward with information that contributes to returning Haythem to his rightful place in his family's life."

There were tears. There were cracks in her voice and choked sobs and moments of wavering gaze that supported her pleas with the emotional weight they needed to impact those seeing and hearing her message. The moment Molly signaled that the recording had stopped, however, her expression abruptly grew as cool and dispassionate as it had been when she entered the flat. She dried her eyes and face on a kerchief without meeting Molly's gaze.

Two thousand ticks was more than most in the Levs could earn in a year, no matter what job they held. For that sort of payment, anyone holding the Founder would be foolish, in Molly's opinion, or else some sort of political idealist with crazy plans, not to bring him forward, send him home.

That many ticks would supply Molly with several years of Heb. If he knew where the Founder was, he would turn him over without hesitation.

"Good. That's good." He crouched to eye level with the Echo screen since he did not have a chair, his fingers flying over the pad as she stood up with a stretch.

"Well?"

"Fifteen minutes. Give me that. Won't be disappointed."

Neoma glanced at the door. She did not want to loiter in this room any longer than necessary. The drabness and dampness made her skin crawl and she felt as if the Heb in the man's body was trying to ooze over her skin, beneath the fabric of her plain yet tasteful blue blouse and slither into her pores. But she did not want to be outside in the mist and moisture either, even protected by her coat and hood. If she went out there, someone might recognize her.

Frustrated, she retreated to the kitchen, intending a drink but finding no cups. Given the layer of grime and dust in the sink, she would not trust any water that came through these long-unused pipes.

"There! Come see! Come see!"

Molly had not timed the minutes of his efforts and luckily, neither had Neoma, or if she had, he had fallen under the fifteen minutes he had begged for or she chose not to call him out for a delay. He turned the Echo around so that he could play the message for her to see.

Whatever enhancements he utilized, whatever filters and tricks he used, he had produced a seamless creation that gave every appearance of being filmed in any of the production rooms she had ever been in. The hues were flattering, the light and shadows lent a depth of reality to her tearful plea, and the sound quality, to her ears, came across as more conversational than she had expected, as though she were speaking to herself in a mirror rather than speaking to a mic.

Neoma nodded, impressed that, despite his high, the fellow had held to his claims.

"When can you release it?"

"Depends on the Hub. An hour…maybe two…maybe less." Having been beyond the city's influence for so long, Molly did not know what changes had been made within the Hub's software and framework. He had heard talk while gathering this equipment from what the brako had to offer, that the Hub had suffered a massive data loss during some sort of citywide upheaval, damage that might prove formidable against his efforts. Molly was still confident he could succeed. Claiming two hours provided sufficient leeway to thread his way through the data channels and plant this prodcast where it would be sure to air on every Echo in the city.

Neoma pulled on her coat and closed it protectively, shivering as she armored herself against that feeling of a Heb invasion. "Two hours," she agreed. "Any longer than that," she glanced at the brako, "and they know where you live."

Gulping with a nervous tittering that hinted that he did, indeed, live here, Molly bobbed his head. "Won't be necessary. I can do it."

He dragged the chair into place behind the table and was already pecking away at the touchpad keys before the clatter of the closing door announced Mam Kemway's departure.

He did not know what she was paying him for this job, but letting him live another day was a good start.

❧*❧

He was so very tired.

He could not remember the last time he had walked for more than a few dozen steps. With so few solid memories before he escaped the chains and cuffs that had bound him, he could not remember walking at all. Each step was a reflex driven by something inside that told him he had somewhere to be, something to do.

If only he could remember what that was.

His stumbling, aimless steps brought him into range of a melodic sort of chiming, something comforting, beckoning, that prompted others of his ilk…the shabbily dressed, dirty-faced, stoop-shouldered masses…to follow it to a well-lit, open set of double doors. Beneath the striped corner awning of blue and white, a vindi table was erected and covered with small hemp paper bags waiting to be handed to each individual in the shuffling, snaking line.

He thought there would be pushing and shoving, a free-for-all he thought typical of the people who lived here when offered something without cost. To his surprise, that was not the case. The drab rabble stood quiet, inching forward like a factory assembly queue. As the supply of bags on the table was depleted, more arrived from within the building to take their place. No one in the line expressed panic or dismay as if they knew that no matter how depleted the supply became, there would always be enough.

He smelled potato. He smelled roasted nutmeats. He smelled boiled eggs and the pungent scent of pickled fish. His stomach churned. The closer he got to the table, the more he struggled to remember how long it had been since he had eaten.

With no chrono, no ICD, no brightening or dimming of artificial light to signify night and day and the passing of hours, he did not know how much time had passed since he had come to be free.

Long enough to be ravenous.

Keeping his head bowed, hiding his face, he snatched the offered bag from the herpa's hand with a muttered, "Thank you," before clutching it against his chest as though someone would steal it.

Herpa. Why did he remember that word and not others?

"You're welcome," the herpa said with a gracious smile.

No one tried to take the bag. No one stopped him as he moved away. No one asked questions. No one said anything beyond those two simple words. As he ducked into the first unoccupied alley he found to devour his prize, it was with equal measures of disappointment and relief that no one recognized him.

He thought they should. Despite the impulse to hide, to hide his face, he wanted to be recognized. He wanted to be known.

But the memory holes and the certainty that someone wanted him dead were reminders that recognition might not be a good thing.

Someone. She? Someone in black, in a mask…wanted him dead.

It was safer if no one knew him, no matter how much he craved the limelight of recognition.

❧Chapter 22❧

It felt good to get back into the routine of normal shift hours, to resume life in the comfort of familiar shafts with predictable labor as if nothing unusual had happened during his absence. There were, as always, vents and filts and lines to maintain, to replace, instruments to inspect and repair, the city's need for functioning life systems continuing to hum as it had for hundreds of years.

In the shafts, he was nobody. Part of him preferred it that way.

Supervisors and coworkers greeted him with grunts and nods, a few words of welcome, or an occasional handshake, but no one he passed in the Shed or the tunnels as he made his way to his assigned section, asked where he had been. Whatever Zara, or perhaps Jaron, had done within the Hub and Shed records, his extended absence had been so expertly covered that no one thought to question it.

Maybe most had not noticed his absence. If they saw the bruises on his face and neck, the stiffness of his movement, no one inquired. Those they were accustomed to seeing. Those types of injuries had been part of his appearance for so long, he doubted anyone realized it.

Or they simply gossiped about it behind his back.

What everyone noticed was the dearth of brako scouring the tunnels. Coarse and insolent, they pushed workers out of the way, asked questions in a curt, petulant air, while having enough respect for the necessity of systems' workers not to rough them up or harm them.

That and the knowledge of the tunnels calculated in their movements again suggested to Rhyd that Vanderwall had been a systems worker too.

Rhyd's knowledge of the tunnels kept him out of their paths while enabling him to creep near enough to overhear their business as often as he could. Why they were seeking Founder Kemway in the tunnels was unknown, but their search suggested possible knowledge of

Kemway's abduction that Rhyd did not have or else the increasing desperation to find him.

He memorized mentioned locations where the brako claimed, or hinted, the Founder was not, holding onto those details for the hunt he would undertake after his shift. Haythem Kemway might no longer be Hebenon's governing head, but he was still the Founder and it did him, and the city, no good if he was held by someone who intended to use his life, or his death, for some nefarious gain.

The most disturbing detail repeatedly mentioned was the name of a dead man, a name spoken of as if he was still issuing orders, still pulling the strings of power behind the brako's street-level ranks. Rhyd had not seen the video of the fall, had only Jaron's word and the ongoing hunt for the archivist to suggest that the brako leader had been killed. What if he was not? If he lived, why the ongoing efforts to remove Jaron from the picture?

Unless they intended to use Jaron to get to Scarecrow.

It was all the more reason not to go home. All the more reason to go on the hunt as soon as his shift ended rather than face Jaron. It was better for Rhyd to keep his distance until he knew Vanderwall's fate. How else was he going to keep Jaron safe?

☙*☙

Neoma's face was the last thing Blayd expected to see on every external Echo viewable from the vindi square where he stood. Her plea for her husband's return appeared heartfelt enough that he could hear murmurs of pity and empathy from the people around him, see them shaking their heads with sympathetic expressions. They pitied her, it seemed, but not enough to prompt most into action.

They might believe her, misplaced from her former life, with only a child and her mad, abducted husband to give her purpose and meaning, but Blayd did not believe a single forced tear or tremble of her perfectly painted lips.

If she cared about Haythem enough to double her efforts to find him, to offer a reward for his return, it was because some other threat, to her, her position, or her daughter, had prompted it.

Senior Kal's arrest and subsequent release might have been enough to do that. But Blayd's failure to answer Ilya's messages when she tried to reach him, as good as his reasons had been, and her refusal to respond to his messages now, prevented Blayd from gaining further reliable information on the status of the search and the details behind Kal's arrest and release.

If he was going to find Kemway, he would have to do it on his own, with only Switz's assistance in the search.

Perhaps it was time to plant that last piece of damning evidence. Time to push the Senior to the wall. Time to claim Neoma's reward. He might not be able to take credit for the Senior's downfall, but the reward was more important. He could live comfortably on that sum for several years if he was frugal.

His body's failure to react to Neoma's face as he had done for so long proved to him that he no longer needed her for anything, but the money would be a boon he could not pass up. His plans had to change. He would find Kemway, take down Kal out of spite, earn the reward, and maybe a place once more in Neoma's security detail.

He no longer wanted to share her bed.

That was a complication he did not need.

❧*❧

Several Levs above Blayd, following what he believed would be Kemway's instinct to go up, to travel in the direction of the life he used to lead, Switz paused to watch the same hackcast. The woman was lovely enough, in a regal, refined sort of way, but he did not know her face. If she was who she claimed to be, a truth supported by the mutterings of the people beneath the vindi's outside awning, Switz could imagine why Haythem was afraid of her.

She was not Scarecrow. She was not dressed in black, did not move the same, did not have the physical build to be Scarecrow. Yet, despite her ostensibly honest grief, there was something cunning and cold, like a sliver of steel poked into his skin, that Switz did not trust.

Haythem did not trust her. Haythem thought she meant him ill. And she was a woman. That was reason enough not to trust her.

For that amount of money, his distrust was not enough to refuse to turn her husband over to her if he found him first. With Kemway's good word, he might even be able to stay on as the Founder's caretaker and servant until Haythem was at full health and mental capacity. Between the reward and the pledge of glory and pardon, and with a little extra effort on his part, Switz would be set up for life.

As long as he kept his hands clean and made no more mistakes.

࿔*࿔

He would not do it.

He would not go.

Haythem squeezed his eyes shut and clutched his head between his hands, shaking it back and forth with jumbled mumblings that drew stares from the passersby who noticed him at the base of the stairs.

Even with the hackcast's plea for his return and a generously offered sum, those faceless shadows drifting past barely looked at him, barely stopped to notice the wealth they were passing by.

"Scarecrow can keep his reward," Haythem mumbled. Whatever she wanted, Scarecrow did not intend to treat him kind or fair. He remembered those eyes, icy and dispassionate. He remembered falling blows and pain and the injector's sting…and then snatches of the passage of time he could not quantify.

He would remain hidden. He had to find his way home and hide. Only then would he be safe. Only then might all of the disjointed fractures in his head make sense.

<h1 style="text-align:center">❧Chapter 23❧</h1>

"Cori! Agnys!"

Ulynda had never had visitors before, at least ones that had not been prearranged and preapproved by her parents. In the Uppers, when her life had been whole, her routine was filled with family and fellow students and the type of social engagements demanded of one of her station. Others coming to see her unannounced was simply not done, not permitted. Finding these two, nearly her age, at her doorstep while her mother was out on whatever business had taken her away this time, and Nanny was out picking up the week's nessies, filled the girl with so much joy and relief that she did not consider the dictates of propriety as she welcomed them inside.

"I thought it'ld be nice to visit," explained Cori, looking around the flat as he entered, a much different sort of residence than Ulynda once called home, or than Cori called home now. "Agnys did too."

"Come in! Come in!" Ulynda grabbed Agnys' hand and pulled her inside. She accepted their sodden coats and hung them on hooks over the drip boards by the door. "There are sweet biscuits if you want? Sugar tea? There won't be much else until Nanny's back with nessies."

"Know how long it's been since I've had sugar tea?" It was one of those delights his father did not often allow. He followed Ulynda into the kitchen, a space that was typically its own room in the Uppers or an integrated part of the living space in the homes of Marbordo. Here in the Levs, it was most often separated from the living area by a single wall or a half-wall counter.

Ulynda's kitchen could not be seen from the living room.

Agnys followed, bobbing her head without knowing what sugar tea or sweet biscuits were or if the offer was made to her as well.

Only after setting a plate of geometrically shaped flat biscuits on the counter, the treats golden brown from baking and sprinkled with crystalized sugar, and then pouring three partial cups of tea from what remained in a pitcher in the icebox, did Ulynda notice the damp muddy trail her visitors' shoes made from the door to the kitchen.

"Oh…you should take off your shoes. Mother will be furious."

"Sorry; we just came from Marbordo." When Cori began to remove his shoes, Agnys did the same.

"Outside? You've been Outside?"

"I live there," Agnys explained.

"You're a…" Ulynda gaped. Hearing the tales of monster parah, it was startling to see that Agnys was little different than herself.

"Parah," finished Agnys with a shrug. So far, the derogatory meaning of that word had been kept from her.

"You don't look…"

Cori laughed. "There's no monsters there. That's just stories grownups tell. I've not seen a single monster." He carried both pairs of shoes to the door while Agnys brought his cup, and hers, and Ulynda carried her cup and the plate of biscuits to the sofa table in the living room.

"You should come up with us. Come and see," Agnys urged when Cori took his cup from her hands.

"You can see the ocean, rivers. You can see the falls. There's mountains and trees and flowers…goats and…"

Sighing, her eyes wide as she tried to imagine such wonders, Ulynda munched the biscuit she had taken. "Mother will never allow it. She says it's dangerous."

Agnys shook her head. "Not more dangerous than here." She knew the dangers of both firsthand.

"I want to see…want to go there…maybe one day…"

"You can come with us any time," Cori promised around his second biscuit. "You can come with my father. Oh…we brought something." His side-glance made Agnys leap up and scurry to their hanging coats. After fishing through her pockets, she rejoined them and offered Ulynda a shiny, lumpy bit of gold-colored stone. "Father says it's pyrite…looks like gold but it isn't. Agnys found it by the river. We thought you'd like it."

Ulynda had never held a rock, precious or not, had never seen an object like the palm-sized chunk in her hand. It was heavier than she expected, some of its facets smooth, some of it rough, and it still held warmth from being in Agnys' pocket. "This comes from Outside?"

"Father says it washed from the mountains. They can be magnets, can be used to build Echoes, and were sometimes found in the mines."

Before the mines closed and the salt, stone, and minerals it provided stopped coming. Cori had not been aware of the mines, of the politics of them. He was too young to care but knew it was important. His father would not be involved with it if it was not.

"Thank you."

A rock was not the sort of gift most in the Uppers would have exchanged. Precious stones meant nothing unless carved into a decoration or molded into some manner of jewelry. But she found this to be a more meaningful gift than the boxes of candied fruit Senior Kal had now stopped bringing. "I don't…"

Her eyes lit up. Gesturing for them to wait, she dashed into her bedroom. By the time she returned, Cori had eaten the last biscuit from the plate and the cups were empty.

"You're still drawing?" Ulynda remembered some education event where Cori's drawings had been on display. They had been better than others done by children of similar ages and Ulynda remembered the grownups discussing Cori's potential as an artist.

"All the time," answered Agnys.

Ulynda pushed a set of coloring pencils across the table towards him. "I've too many," she explained earnestly. "You can draw me something…something like Outside…"

"I don't want…"

"I've got more. I'm sure. You can have them." Or her mother could get her more. They were only pencils. Cost that had been irrelevant in the Uppers, before the Coup, meant nothing to her.

From her other hand, she produced a beaded necklace of speckled white river stone, the type gleaned from the water in the fisheries or caught in the straining net. She did not know what sort of stone it was but imagined it was valuable enough to be given to her by some member of her parents' entourage on one of her birthdays.

Someone with a son most likely, who had hoped to begin the tedious process of currying favor and winning a coveted match with the Kemways through a marriage of their children.

"You should wear this."

Though also about to protest as Ulynda moved behind her to fasten the clasp around her neck, a glance at Cori, who bobbed his head once, made Agnys swallow her objection.

"It's pretty. Thank you," she whispered, turning her head to view her reflection in the black Echo screen across the room.

Without warning, Cori leaped onto the sofa, pulling both girls with him, shrieking, "Don't touch the floor! The river will sweep you up!"

It was a familiar game, one Ulynda's brother and sister had often played and pulled her into whenever they could, whenever her studies and eldest child responsibilities permitted. A game she had not played since she had lost them. She squealed with delight and Agnys, apparently also familiar with the game, did too as they bounced and leaped from sofa to chair to table. The biscuit plate became a boat, allowing them to move around the room until most of the moveable furniture was drawn together in the center to expand their area of play.

Soon the game morphed into mock battles between Scarecrow and the brako, the children taking turns being the hero, the villain, the victim, stopping frequently in fits of laughter that Ulynda had not enjoyed in far too long.

No one could recognize her, covered as she was from head to toe in an expensive coat, gloves, and boots, but still, she felt eyes on her as she made her way through Hebenon's streets, having left her brako escort some time ago to make the last half of the journey alone.

Where was Blayd when she needed him? Why had the fool disappointed her and made her terminate his employment? She needed him to fend off whoever followed in the shadows, to find Haythem, find this rumored Kemway brother, to keep her daughter safe.

Whoever they were, the following eyes, the people who stepped aside to watch her pass, they might not see her face but they knew who she was. They knew and pitied her. Laughed at her. Sought a weakness they could exploit now that she was alone.

If Blayd was beside her, they would not dare.

She watched for anyone who looked like they might attempt to take away her hopes of reclaiming her life, anyone who looked like the husband she had abandoned the night the Lev uprising had destroyed Hebanthe Falls' way of life. But the people she passed were as faceless as she was and she suspected that she could pass Haythem in these wet, dreary streets and never realize it.

She could not be certain the rumor, the story Molly told about the lost Kemway, was true. There could be an imposter afoot, hoping to take advantage of the city's upheaval. But on the off chance that it was, that a Kemway thought long dead still lived, Neoma had to act on the assumption that he was a threat.

For Ulynda's sake.

For her own.

Imposter or not, she had to find Haythem before it was too late.

The sounds within her flat as she came up the stairs nearest to home, the shouts and crashes, cries of injury and triumph, filled her with such palpitating dread that she did not make note of the ongoing laughter beneath it. The door and window were closed, unbroken, but the sounds inside were those of a fight, of intruders, her only living child in danger. Neoma fumbled with the passkey and struggled to open the door, expecting to see carnage, expecting to see blood.

She should not have stayed away to view the airing of her reward offer in a place where Ulynda would not see it. If she had come home immediately after the recording, she would not now find her living room furnishings in disarray, cushions scattered around the room, some chairs turned on end such as the one Ulynda was balancing on the rungs of. She would not find two other children, hair disheveled, clothing askew, children she did not recognize, wrestling and trying to push one another off the sofa table onto the floor.

"What are you doing?" Neoma howled, face crimson, hands balled though her manicured nails were too sharp to allow fists to form.

Ulynda froze, the color draining from her face as she tried to formulate a reply. Startled as well, Agnys and Cori abruptly released one another. Agnys plopped backward onto the cushionless sofa and Cori stumbled in the other direction, falling against the chair on which Ulynda balanced. She fell too and hit her head against the displaced end table that had been pulled nearer as part of their game.

"Get out!"

Cori was closest and was wrenched up by one arm with enough force that he wailed in shock and pain before being shoved outside through the still-open door. Ulynda leaped to her friends' defense as Neoma caught Agnys by the neckline of her simple dress. With a yank, Neoma tore the fabric and broke the string of stones while simultaneously lashing out with her other hand towards the movement she saw out of the corner of her eye.

The flat back of her hand struck Ulynda across the face, making her fall to the floor again.

"They're my friends!" Ulynda protested with a furious, frightened, injured cry.

"We don't have friends!" Neoma dragged the blonde girl to the door and pushed her outside beside Cori.

"I do! I want them here! I want…"

"Filthy beasts don't belong…"

"They're not…"

The door slammed, the shoes and coats of the expelled pair still in place near the door where they were stashed. Neoma did not notice.

Listening to encroaching steps on nearby stairs, frightened by what had happened without understanding it, afraid of being found by brako or being punished by buggers for whatever they had done wrong, both children looked at each other in alarm. Cori pulled Agnys up by the hand, both ignoring the pain their falls, and the woman inside, had inflicted, and ran barefoot through the wet chill in search of the one person Cori knew could fix this and protect them.

His father.

Face purple with a fury she had never felt before and the pent-up frustration that had been building for months, Ulynda barked, "You can't keep me alone here forever!"

Neoma jerked her to her feet, heedless of the breaking of furniture it created or the injuries it caused her daughter. Haythem had challenged her. Haythem, as her husband and the Founder, had gotten away with it. But she would not tolerate such challenges from anyone else, especially an insolent child, not even one who was her own flesh and the heir to the title of Founder. "I can and I…"

There was a double knock on the door. "Be gone!" Neoma shouted, certain it was the neighbor children she had just expelled from her home or perhaps their parents come to learn the cause of the commotion heard through the walls.

The knock came again.

Prepared to rage in the faces of those who would not heed her command, she grabbed the handle and repeated, "I said…"

"Mam…a word."

Senior Kal.

Hissing in frustration, not the voice she expected, Neoma snarled at the girl still in her grasp and pushed her away. "Go to your room."

It was bad enough Kal would see past her to the state of her home. He did not need to see this crying, disobedient child as well.

The thrust towards the adjoining doors made Ulynda stumble but she did not fall. "I hate you!" she spat, not caring if Senior Kal heard her. She was far enough away from the second attempted strike to elude it and her bedroom door crashed closed behind her.

Hearing Neoma's shrieks before he reached her door was only marginally surprising. Kal had been aware of her volatile temper since their first meeting years ago, before the Coup, when the Founder's family had been intact and in the supreme position of power. That temper had lifted ever nearer the surface over the last two years, and he watched carefully for it as they worked towards the mutual goal of restoring Kemway rule to the city. He had avoided her wrath in the past. With the rash of chaos of late, the news that Haythem lived, his abduction, the death of Vanderwall, it was little wonder Neoma's temper had reached a breaking point.

He suspected his attempts to clear his name had not helped.

Kal expected to find Nanny, or perhaps the merc Blayd, at the receiving end of the tirade, but when she flung open the door to glower at him with red-faced fury, revealing the chaos of her living room, she was alone and the Echosys was dark.

An ended call then. Or Nanny was sent out of the room in deference to the intruder she now faced with blistering disdain.

She noticed the abrasions on his face, presumed evidence of a fall or a fight, but it did not soften her rage or indignation at seeing him on her doorstep. "You've got some balls coming here."

Kal ignored her bitterness and strutted past her, taking the open door as a welcome although she had not stepped back or asked him to enter. Showing fear would not benefit him and he chose not to do so.

"If I had Haythem," he said coolly, removing his gloves, "I would have made a move already."

"Not while the heat is on you. Not if you think it will give you leverage over me."

He laughed. "I don't need leverage…but I agree we need to find him." He had another ace in his hand, the other Kemway on his chessboard, but that was a play he was not ready to reveal. She had friends still, particularly within the brako, contacts they had groomed together. He did not want word of his plans with Feena to be revealed while Neoma might be able to stop him.

He had no reason to believe she already knew about the long-believed dead Kemway.

"The captain let you…"

"As you know, the bugorra have no proof…because there is nothing to prove. I swear on my oaths. I do not have him. Whoever does, whoever took him, they weren't Talkers, weren't any of mine…"

"I don't believe you." Like herself, Kal was a polished speaker, showman, and tactician. He seemed sincere in word and expression, but seeming did not make him so.

"Believe what you will; it's the truth."

"You didn't come here to plead for…"

"No pleading. We're beyond that I think. I came with an offer. If I find Haythem, return him to you instead of to Grainger and the bugorra, the three of us will make a plan together to end this strife and put your family back where you belong, the way we intended…"

"Before you betrayed me." They held each other in solid, determined gazes until she shrugged, her initial fury faded enough to ease her hotheaded words. "The only deal I will make with you is, you bring him home to me from wherever you're hiding him and I won't press the captain to lock you down for treason."

After that, she would see. When Haythem was safe, she would reformulate her strategies and decide her next step. Only when Haythem was at her side would she be sure that the secret Kemway could not be a threat and that Kal could never interfere again.

A truce. It was the best he could hope for until he proved he was not the villain she believed. He nodded once.

"When I bring him to you, you will have your proof that this has nothing to do with me. You have my word."

Neoma grunted and opened the door again, intending to usher the Senior out but instead finding Nanny on the outside about to knock for entry with the toe of her shoe. She let Nanny in, waited for her to pick her way through the upended furniture and disappear into the kitchen, and then motioned for Kal to leave.

"My word, Mam. You'll see."

"Goodbye," she huffed, noting for the second time that he used her title rather than her name as he once had.

There were several minutes of silence as she faced the door, one hand clenched around the latch, the other balled at her side. When her breathing was calm, she turned to face the disaster in the room and bellowed to the empty air, "I want this put back the way it was! Now!"

She would not lift a finger to do it herself.

❧*☙

Ulynda made no effort to overhear her mother's conversation with the Senior, to learn if the man brought his usual treats or was here to discuss her or her father. Trapped in her room with no way to release the unfamiliar surge of dark emotions, she wildly sought anything that might make her feel better, less isolated, might make her feel that she belonged here. That might make her feel like her world had not just erupted around her once again.

Losing her father had been bad. Losing her sister, then her brother, had been bad too.

Now there was this.

Her mother had never struck her. Ulynda had known the potential was there, had realized it at a young enough age that she had lived in ways that avoided the darker side of her mother's personality. Her father had been a shield then, but he was not that anymore. Her arm hurt where her mother's hand had left bruising prints, her leg hurt from where she had struck and broken the rung of the chair, various other places on her body ached after her multiple falls, and her face stung from her mother's backhanded strike.

She had to get away. But how?

Not through the front door. Not while Senior Kal was here. Not while Nanny bustled about righting the furniture. Not while her mother was holed up in her bedroom slamming drawers, the closet door, smashing a mirror and any other breakables within reach.

No. Ulynda would never make it through the door unless her mother left or went to sleep. That would be hours from now, and Ulynda was afraid of the host of horrors her imagination concocted for what could happen in the meantime.

She expected her mother would lock her in the house and never let her out. Several times she twisted the latch of her bedroom door to reassure herself that she had not been locked into her room.

She had to leave. She had to find Agnys and Cori and apologize for her mother's rudeness. She would go with them Outside where her mother would never go to find her.

Their game still fresh in her mind, when her wandering gaze fell on the wall grate through which warm air circulated and contaminants were filtered out, her eyes grew wide.

Some people said Scarecrow traveled through the streets and vents like a mist. She did not know how that would be possible, knew nothing about the miles of ducts and tunnels and inner workings of Hebanthe Falls. But if Scarecrow could do it, so could she.

At least if she got inside, it would be a place to hide where her mother's striking, clawing hands could not reach her. Where her mother would never think to look.

If her mother heard the scratching and clackings and other sounds made as Ulynda worked the grate filters from the wall, she did not come to investigate. As focused as Ulynda was on her efforts, she knew her mother could have left the flat without her notice. When the grate finally came free, she paused long enough to pull a warm sweater, a cap, and her gloves from the armoire, change into the one pair of trousers she owned, and then crawled into an opening just wide enough for a moderate-sized man to fit through.

For a child her size, it was easy.

She could not pull the grate into place. She wanted to leave it where it was. She hoped her mother would find it, hoped she would know that Ulynda was gone and was not coming back.

There was a world outside of her flat, a world full of people, things to do and see, experiences she wanted to have. She would not stay in this flat where she was punished for having friends.

She would not stay to be molded into a future role she had no desire to fill.

Ulynda wanted to live.

❧*❧

"If you do not do something about that woman, I will!"

There had never been an occasion for Doctor Tamner to burst into the captain's office unannounced, or the Founder's office either to Grainger's recollection, in the red-faced manner he did now. Seated with his chair tipped back, his healing leg propped on the corner of the desk, Grainger felt the position put him in a place of weakness before the doctor's wrath and so he reluctantly put his foot on the floor and turned the chair to sit properly at the desk that served as a barrier, a shield, between them.

He did not think Tamner was likely to attack but the barrier offered a few moments in which he could calm himself before he reached the captain.

"Which woman?" His voice was weary with the weight of so many urgent issues that made him appear slump-shouldered and older than he was.

"Mam Kemway attacked my son!"

Grainger's brow furrowed. "What was he…?"

"That doesn't matter! There's bruises! On him and Agnys both!"

"Agnys?"

"The parah girl. The," he emphasized the word so that Grainger knew which girl he meant, "parah girl! Mam can't be trusted with…"

"Again…please…Doctor…what was he…?"

Frustrated, believing the captain was looking for an excuse to let Mam off with a warning or less, Tamner stomped back towards the door, opening now to allow Lieutenant Young through it. "If you're not going to do something," he spat, "I will!" Hurting children, especially his child and one he considered his, would not be tolerated.

Tamner pushed past Ilya without apology. She looked from him to Grainger, perplexed.

"What was that…?"

"I honestly don't know." The doctor had not provided enough details to give a clear picture. Either way, Grainger supposed he must speak with the Mam to find out what had happened and prevent it from happening again, before Tamner did something unfortunate.

Cazz, that was a conversation he did not want to have.

"You want something, Lieutenant?"

"I was preparing to go off shift when …you should turn on the prods, sir. You'll want to see this."

Reluctant to learn what bad news awaited, he turned on the Echo as she suggested, switched it to a live feed, and was presented with the Mam's impassioned plea and reward offer for the return of her husband, complete with accusations of incompetence against Grainger and the bugorra for not doing enough to find Founder Kemway and bring his kidnappers to justice.

"They're working on shutting down the hack…"

Grainger rubbed his face. This warranted a discussion with Mam Kemway all on its own.

"Tell them to keep at it until it's off…and send a summons to Mam Kemway. I demand to see her here first thing in the morning."

Ilya nodded. "Yes, Captain."

The message would be sent at once but both doubted that the woman would deign to appear for such a summons without force.

❧Chapter 24❧

y the time several glasses of wine and a short restless slumber took the edge off her rage, morning had come again and as she sipped her cup of hot citrus tea, Neoma realized she had not seen nor heard from Ulynda since sending her to her room the previous afternoon. She realized she had not thought about her daughter at all, which brought a frown of consternation to her perfectly made-up face.

"Ulynda. Come eat breakfast." From the smells emanating from the kitchen, Nanny had the meal almost complete and the few more minutes it would take would allow mother and daughter to have words about the episode from the day before.

There was no reply from Ulynda's room.

Rolling her eyes, wondering again if the girl was more like her or more like her father, Neoma set the teacup down, smoothed the front of her skirt as she stood, and then crossed the living room to knock on the girl's door with a single rap.

"Ulynda. Breakfast."

No sounds came from behind the door, and with the constant hum and whirr and rushing air sounds of the filt and heating systems, the ongoing drip of water from the eaves over the door, and the sounds of cooking and Nanny's cheery, mumbled singing, Neoma could not detect sounds of sleeping breath without opening the door.

Asleep was what she expected, or else Ulynda engrossed in her studies with her sound buds in her ears since there was light spilling through the space beneath the door. But Ulynda was not at her desk, not sitting in bed with the T2 in her lap. The blankets looked as if the bed had not been slept in. The armoire door was slightly ajar but it had not properly closed in the months that mother and daughter had been forced to live in this flat. At first glance, nothing appeared amiss.

Nothing except the empty desk, the empty bed, and the open grate on the other side of the bed Neoma noticed when she peeped beneath it…a place she knew Ulynda often hid when upset.

The open grate on the wall separating their flat from the neighbors.

Neoma's first rash conclusion led her to bang on the neighbor's door shouting, "Send out my daughter at once!" She knew little about the shaft system, little about the neighbors, but it was a sensical guess that Ulynda might have gone through the vent into the neighbor's flat to resume playing with the children Neoma had sent away. Furious at being disobeyed, with the audacity of Ulynda's betrayal, she was about to pound on the door again when a frazzled-looking woman opened it to stare at this early intrusion with bleary eyes.

"What are you…?"

Heb user, Neoma judged with a haughty huff as she pushed inside. That the early hour, the care of multiple children, or other life circumstances might contribute to the younger woman's unkempt appearance never occurred to Neoma.

"Where's Ulynda?"

"Who?"

The three children, the same number Neoma sometimes saw coming and going with the woman who was her neighbor, clustered around a small table picking at their day's first meal, stared at Neoma with wide, wary eyes but did not speak. Each had the same curly black hair and mid-tone complexion, indicating that none of these had been the two children in her home.

Neoma barely noticed as she stormed towards the vent roughly equivalent in location to the one in Ulynda's room. The rusted clips holding it in place had not been tampered with in quite some time and the dust that covered the grating had been there nearly as long.

If Ulynda had come here, it had not been through the vent.

The flat's security system would not have allowed the girl to leave through the front door during the night.

"I'm callin' the buggers," the other woman threatened, following Neoma as she charged from room to room, frantically seeking any sign of the child she believed was hidden here.

"Have you seen her? Have you seen Ulynda? Where is she?" Neoma shot back, the threat meaning nothing to her.

Every head in the room, mother and children, shook no.

"If you see her, if you hear from her, send her home."

As rudely as she had forced her way inside, Neoma thundered out. When she threw open her door, which had not closed properly on her way out, it was with an unnecessary wail of "Nanny!"

The matronly woman was already standing in the doorway between the kitchen and the main room.

"Mam?" she asked, drying her hands with fretful wringing.

"Have you seen Ulynda?" She grabbed her coat from the hook and shoved her wet feet into her boots, noticing only then the pair of coats and boots the expelled children had been forced to leave behind.

"Not since before nessies, Mam. She did not come to dinner…"

Neoma's frown deepened. She had not realized that.

"She's gone. Where would she go?"

"I…"

"Tell me!"

Nanny shook her head. "She doesn't know many places." Neoma had only taken the girl out once, to Nanny's knowledge, the night of the recital. The poor girl was a prisoner in this flat. "She's been out with me a few times, to get nessies." Taking her had never been forbidden, and Nanny had felt sorry for the trapped child. But she had also never been expressly permitted to do so, either and Nanny waited for the expected backlash.

"Then go there! Anywhere you've taken her! Find out who was here yesterday…and find her!"

Nanny bobbed frantically and mumbled, "Yes, Mam," before scurrying back to the kitchen long enough to turn off the stove and shove the partially prepared meal into the icebox. By the time she returned to the main room, with her rain shawl around her neck and shoulders, her rain bonnet secured beneath her chin, and her clutch in her hand, Mam was gone.

❧*❧

The Levs was a bigger place than Ulynda had imagined it could be. After their time barricaded in Factory West 2, the time of losing her father and watching her siblings die, she barely remembered the trip down the lift and the hurried march to the flat that was now home. She remembered cold, damp darkness. She remembered fear and confusion. But she had paid little attention to other details of her surroundings that day…or had it been night…and had little concept of where she was within Hebanthe Falls. She did not know which Lev she lived on, how many were above her, how many below.

Other than occasional walks out with Nanny for new clothes, for nessies, and once to experience the novelty of a dek for the first time, Ulynda had barely been out of the flat for two years.

Even in the Uppers, her exposure to the world was limited. Ulynda had spent her short life like a caged animal with little practical knowledge of the world.

She followed the vent system, ignoring unfamiliar smells pulled in from other homes and the acrid chemical odors dripping from occasional fissures in the pipes that lined the walls. Eventually, slurred voices and a cold draft suggested a way out and coaxed her down an unlit passage towards the light of an opening at the end. Two figures with long dirty hair and dirtier clothing huddled beneath a moisture blanket at the mouth of the passage where water dripped around its edges. Ulynda watched them for a long time, judging them to be women, assessing their threat level. When they failed to lift their heads to her tentative, "Hello?" she guessed they were not aware she was there or did not care. The growl in her stomach prompted her to approach, to carefully pick her way around them, and still they did not lift their heads or look at her as she squeezed past and climbed out of the tunnel and into Hebenon's streets alone for the first time.

Blinking at the neon, her nostrils inundated by the cooking smells from vindis collected at the head of the alley where she stood, Ulynda again crept forward. There were nessies carts, the crackling sign over a herpa door, and voices. So many voices. The intersection looked little different than the one Nanny had taken her to, and yet it was not the same. The one Ulynda was familiar with had no herpa hall, had a club with a neon dervish along the left-hand threshold, and a portable stall with a vindi selling fish, rat, and chicken kabobs.

She was glad she did not have to smell that, as it would have made her hungrier than she already was, but the familiar cooking aromas would have been reassuring.

She could not have traveled far in the vents. As her route had remained level for the unmarked duration she had been inside, she felt certain she was still on the Lev where home was. Home was far away from the Falls and so she tried to gauge the direction of the tumbling water. If she traveled away from the roar, it would take her home.

But home was the last place she wanted to be.

She wanted to find Cori and Agnys, but by now they would have returned to their families, to the Outside Agnys called home and the Uppers where the Tamners likely continued to live. Ulynda looked up into the crisscrossing maze of walks and lifts and structures that stretched like spider webs so far that she could not see the top. Maybe up was where she needed to go. Up would eventually bring her to the world she was most familiar with, the world of white walls, the world where people she once knew would surely help her.

They would also, she thought with a scowl, take her to her mother.

Here in the Levs there were others she could seek. Her father, if he was alive. If she found him, she could warn him away from her mother. She could stay with him, take care of him as he took care of her. Or maybe she would bring him home to protect her.

Maybe if she brought her father home, her mother would be easier to live with.

There was also an uncle she had not known about. He was only a name to her. Enoch. A man without a face. How could she find him then…and who was to say he was actually kin, that the story had not been concocted to appease or anger her mother? Who was to say he would be interested in one girl's plight, in the family who had abandoned him? Why would he want to help her, or know her?

There was a third as well.

Scarecrow.

He would be as difficult to find as the other two, and maybe he had more important things to do than protect her from her mother or help her find her father.

She needed to get out of the damp, find somewhere to think. To plan. To weigh her options.

Spotting a stooped, shuffling woman browsing a vegetable vindi, a woman who reminded her of Nanny's friends they sometimes met and shared tea with, Ulynda started across the street, narrowly avoiding a collision with a grave cart laden with the covered lump of some poor soul, and a small goat wagon that turned from one corner at a too fast clip.

"Watch out," shouted the goat wagon owner.

"Move," barked the grave cart driver.

He might have been barking at the goat man or at Ulynda. Likely he was barking at both.

Hands caught Ulynda's shoulders and pulled her back as the two carts narrowly avoided a collision. It was the gloved hand of a beaked brako that made her shriek and jerk away with a shrill, "Let me go!"

Her raised voice turned heads but the person behind the mask seemed unperturbed and made no effort to pursue her.

Maybe he had tried to save her life. Maybe he was one of those brako who knew her mother. Maybe he intended to either take her home or assumed that her mother or Nanny were nearby and planned to keep her safe until her guardian appeared.

Ulynda would not take the chance.

"Want some? They'll make it better," promised a scantily dressed, androgynous individual with violet hair and eyes who held out a handful of orange pills. "Pretty thing like you; I can get you all you want. Food and dry clothes…if you take 'em and come with me…"

"I…" Ulynda stepped back. She was hungry, but not hungry enough to trust a stranger. But the promise of dry clothes was a temptation. She did not know how little orange candy-like pills could solve that though. She had never encountered anyone who looked like this, knew nothing about andis or hooks or exotic dancers. The allure of the unfamiliar, the strange, of being warm and dry left her uncertain about accepting the offer.

The doddering woman she had seen across the street was suddenly there, wrapping a motherly arm around her shoulders with a sneer at the pusher before turning Ulynda away from temptation.

"There you are, dear…I told you not to wander off. You don't want those…trust me."

The andi-pusher, if that was what she was, shrugged at the lost fruit and set her sights on another target.

"Stay away from that sort…and those Hebbies. They're not safe. Where's your family…"

"I…" Because it seemed smarter to lie rather than admit she had run away, Ulynda stammered, "I'm trying to find the dek. My mother and I were going…but I got lost…"

"She's gotta be frantic." The woman flashed a mostly toothless smile. "Why don't you come along with me and I'll help you find her. We can message her from my place while we get you out of the rain. I have to take these nessies…"

The woman propelled her across the street towards two scrawny fellows who looked as emaciated and toothless as she was. They might have been siblings or children; it was impossible to tell. Their leering faces, the twitching of their hands with each step nearer Ulynda came, the spittle on their scruffy-haired chins and their matching expressions of anticipation mimicked what Ulynda had seen on the man Blayd's face when he came to stay with her mother. The expression made her balk, freeze, and then twist away from the tight grip on her shoulder.

They were not safe men. They were not friendly.

The woman was in no condition to pursue the fleeing child and the men who tried promptly aborted their effort when the silhouette of a tall, thin bugger stepped between them and their quarry. They slunk into the shadows with crestfallen expressions of disappointment.

"Looking for your mother at the dek?" the bugorra said, any kindly tone of voice twisted into something unrecognizable by the filters of his mask. "I can take you there."

Believing in the trustworthiness of buggers, even if her mother swore they were not doing enough to find her father, Ulynda nodded, unable to speak at first past the hammering of her heart that squeezed the breath from her lungs. When he motioned down the opposite intersection, she nodded and followed. The direction was away from the noise of the falls, but it was also away from home.

"What's your name?"

"Ulynda," she stammered.

"Nice name. I've a daughter 'bout your age. Name's Margaret. You know a Margaret? You attend classes on this Lev? Maybe you…"

"I school at home." She longed for the company of other children instead of only the company of her mother and Nanny, but as long as she was the Kemway heir, she knew it would not happen.

It was another reason to find her father. To find her uncle.

"I see." They passed another street on this row of clothing vindis, a street Ulynda was excited to recognize. The bugger pointed ahead.

"There's the dek."

The one Nanny had taken her to. Ulynda breathed a sigh of relief.

"Do you see your mother?"

There were nearly a dozen people in a queue outside the dek, waiting their turn to enter the building for their brief taste of a world, an experience, they would never have. Another six were visible through the windows, each expecting to enter bliss or exhilaration as soon as the current users emerged from the deks. Not one of them, thankfully, looked like her mother.

"Probably looking for me."

"What's her name? I'll find her."

"You don't need to do that. I'll wait right here until she…"

"I'll at least enter your name and location in the system, in case she's looking or has posted a missing…"

"You don't have to…"

Ulynda imagined that, behind his bug-faced hood, he was scowling at her skittishness, imagined he judged her to be a truant, a streeter, a troublemaker. His grip on her arm as he studied her, noticing the bruising purple across her face, seemed suddenly threatening.

Frightened, she kicked his unprotected shin and when he reacted to the pain, his hold on her released.

Again she ran.

The dek had seemed a safe place to collect her thoughts, but now she realized she had no ticks to gain entry even if she wanted to. No one knew her face and the name Kemway would likely gain her nothing except derision or a swift return to her mother's care.

Ulynda was on her own. She had no idea, as she scrambled down the nearest stairs, where she would go or what she would do.

❧*❧

With her thoughts tangled and twisted around fears for her daughter's safety, her mind awash with the possible fates and causes for Ulynda's absence, by the time Neoma stalked into Grainger's office, she had not bothered to view the previous night's message that had summoned her there. Though he looked up at her expectantly, as if he had news of his own to deliver, she marched to his desk, leaned over it with her hands gripping the edge, and demanded, "I want you to find my daughter!" before he had the opportunity to speak.

"Good morning to you too, Mam. Please…sit…tell me what…"

"He took her! I want her back!"

"Someone took your daughter? When? Who?"

"During the night! It has to be him! There can only be…"

"Mam, please." Her intensity was giving the headache spawned by a too-early Brompton's a sharp run.

Neoma took a breath, her only pause other than those caused by his interrupting words, and then continued with a less pointed tone. "The vent in her room is open and she's gone! Someone's taken her."

"When?"

"Last night. She went to bed…and now she's gone." The other details about the fight, the failure to show for dinner, the fact that she had not seen Ulynda since afternoon, did not seem important to share.

"Who do you think…?"

"Scarecrow!"

Grainger cocked his head as he leaned back. "Why would he do that?" Never, to his knowledge, had Scarecrow abducted anyone, despite his Lieutenant's belief and the persistent rumors that Scarecrow was involved in the Founder's abduction. Such acts did not fit his M.O. and Grainger could think of no reason for the vigi to risk it, unless the Mam knew something Grainger did not.

"I…because it's what he does! Comes in the night and…"

"Fights brako…use to be Crows." He smirked, having been on the Crow-end of Scarecrow's wrath. "He doesn't take children."

"Well someone did!"

Grainger studied her expression for tells, for some indication that she was lying or hiding something. While she was undoubtedly hiding something, the Mam had always kept secrets, he did not think she was lying now. Her daughter was missing.

"Could it be someone else? One of your enemies?"

Neoma frowned, the implication of his words undercutting the certainty of Scarecrow's guilt she had constructed in her head. Someone in her position always had enemies. Before the Coup, there were none; after the Coup, it felt like everyone was an enemy.

She could think of only two acquaintances who might know how to access her flat through the duct system. One of those was on her side more than most, unless Kal was manipulating Vanderwall against her and her appointed brako boss had turned. Having been the one to elevate Frankel to his current position, Neoma did not want to believe he would dare be so disloyal as to take her daughter.

Her connection to Vanderwall was not worth mentioning. Too risky. Too dangerous. She would see to that conversation herself.

"Blayd."

"Blayd?"

"Halder…a merc…used to work for me."

"Let me guess; you parted on less than amicable terms." It seemed that most people who forged relationships with the Mam ended them on bad terms.

Her frown deepened as he typed the name into the missing child report he had pulled up on the Echo.

"Anyone else?"

There was only one other who might have the nerve, the contacts, to attempt such a thing, particularly after her public reward plea and their face-off the evening before.

"The man who has my husband."

Kal. It oddly made sense to Grainger as he entered that name too If the Voices of Faith believed they were protecting the Founder's bloodline in abducting Haythem, securing his only surviving child made sense too, especially if the Senior was at odds with Neoma.

"He came to my home, offered to find Haythem, return him…"

"For the reward, no doubt." Grainger rubbed his eyes and added, "I want that hack down, today. It's been running all night and…"

"…and I want you to find my husband! My daughter!"

"We're working on it…but you're not making it easier. We're examining the evidence and…"

"You know Kal did this…or you wouldn't have arrested him! Now he has my daughter." Converting her suspicion, her certainty of Scarecrow's guilt over to Kal was a seamless thing. "If you won't find him, I'll do it my way."

"Hacking the prods is causing confusion; it's not helping. If you want to broadcast a reward, you should have come to me…"

"You'd never approve…"

"You don't know that." He thought that offering a reward was a good idea but the city did not have the resources or the authority to do it, not without going through the Nau's debate process. A private reward through the Founder's family, however, might prove to be the incentive needed to get information on the Founder into the bugorra's hands. "What about your daughter? We should broadcast a statement, circulate her picture…"

"I will not put Ulynda's face out there for every…"

"How else do you propose we…?"

"She's a child! The Founder by birthright! Can you imagine what someone might do to her, with her, because of that? To get to me?"

Grainger rubbed his eyes to mask the twitch there, not surprised the situation had come back around to protecting Neoma as much as it was about protecting her child, her husband. But she was right. There were elements within Hebanthe Falls who would use a child to their own ends, just as they might use her father. Haythem was a madman, yes, not in his right mind, but he was an adult.

Ulynda was a little girl.

"At least allow me to distribute her photo to my officers so they will know her if they see her."

With some reluctance, after the passing impulse to protest that made her face twitch and flush, Neoma nodded.

"In return, you will do a couple of things for me."

Her eyes narrowed.

"You will take that hack down. Today. If you want to continue to run it, give it to the Ximenezes and they can schedule a rotation. I want you to give thought to making a statement about your daughter…the right way. Taking over the prods for personal use has to stop."

Between Kal and Neoma, he felt there was a growing need for stronger prod security measures.

"And?" If he was willing to allow legitimate prod time, she would take the offer. But she would not make her daughter a thing for public ridicule, slander, or manipulation. And she would not promise never to hack the prods again.

"You will not strike Doctor Tamner's son, or any other child, ever again."

"I did not…"

"I saw the bruises. On the girl too." Though Tamner had been furious when he blustered into the office and provided little information, he did later submit a report complete with images of the bruises on both children and their torn clothing. Grainger had seen them when he had first come on duty not long before Neoma's arrival.

Whatever Neoma's thoughts were, whether she had known the boy was Tamner's son or had thought him some stranger threatening her daughter, Grainger could not tell from her eerily blank face. Lips that had been pursed as if she had eaten something sour were relaxed now as she shrugged and stood up.

"I won't."

The same eeriness, the sudden stillness of the air, followed her out the door. To Grainger, it appeared that, in that moment of mentioning Tamner's son, Neoma had forgotten her daughter's predicament.

He shuddered, shook his head, and turned to the Echo to issue new orders to his officers. He was almost grateful that Founder Kemway was in no position to see the sort of woman his wife had become.

Then again, remembering all he had seen and heard in this very room over the years, Grainger imagined that Haythem already knew.

∾Chapter 25∾

Hour after hour he searched, returning periodically to the scene of the man's captivity in the hopes that the largely delirious fellow had meandered back to the only home he had known in recent days. The upsurge in bugorra activity, instigated by Neoma's reward to anyone finding and returning her husband to her, had made his search difficult, but as long as that hack ran, the higher Blayd's certainty was that Haythem had not yet been found. So long as no one else found him first, Blayd still had a chance to pull his plan together.

Then Neoma's face disappeared from the Echoes and Blayd, defeated, sank onto the stairs he had just descended and wearily wiped his hand over his mist-soaked face.

That was that then.

His efforts to bring down Senior Kal had failed. He would have to devise a new plan, something that did not hinge upon the Founder. Something that hinged on Kemway not knowing his face or his name.

At least the kidnapping would not be traced back to him. If Kemway did remember his face, Blayd had an explanation for that. It might require getting rid of Switz, or paying him significantly more for his cooperation, but Blayd would sort that out if it became necessary to do so.

The walk stretching out before him was dark, lit only by the sporadic glow of unbroken alglamps and the Echo on the corner of the vindi behind him at the top of the stairs. His search had taken him through the busiest portions of the Levs above and below the holding room, in the hopes that the smells of food and sounds of people would attract Kemway. It had not taken long, however, to decide that the tumult of voices and the bustle of heavy foot traffic might be overwhelming for a man who had rarely, if ever, set foot in the Levs.

Or he could have fallen into the river. He could have been coherent enough to take a lift to the Uppers.

Whatever the case, though no public confirmation had been made, it seemed Kemway was located. Dwelling on what might have happened, where he was found, where he was now, was pointless.

Movement midway along the path caught his attention. He assumed it was a streeter, judging by shabby, mismatched attire that was barely adequate for outdoors in the mist. Seated in shadows himself, it did not appear the streeter saw him as he rummaged through one discard and recycle bin after another. He moved like a crab, like a feral animal, crouched and sliding, slinking and startling at unexpected sounds, like a thing who had been apart from humanity so long it had forgotten how to be part of it. Blayd considered offering the poor fellow his coat, or perhaps taking him to the nearest vindi or herpa for a decent hot meal.

Then the fellow turned.

Blayd could not see his face clearly through the mist. Nothing else about him was recognizable. But he would know that profile, that silhouette illuminated by the blue alglamp's glow, anywhere.

He had not returned home after his shift but had watched it for a time from the black alley across and a half-Lev above. The flat was dark, with no signs of movement inside. Lash's neighboring flat was the same. It was logical to believe that, after a long day's shift, Jaron had come back and gone directly to sleep when he discovered Rhyd was not there. Or perhaps he had accepted a double to distance himself from the one who so callously ordered him away for offering a show of heartfelt, respectful support.

There was no easy way for Scarecrow to learn if Jaron was at the Archive, as vast and multileveled as the facility was. He could ask Zara to hack the duty roster but he wanted no one else in his business, wanted no one to question his concern for Jaron. Instead, leaving the flat without entering, Scarecrow went to the next logical place Jaron might have gone, intending to either rule out that location or ease his fears for Jaron's safety if he found him safe and secure in his flat.

After the recent break-in, the threat of them loitering nearby to capture Jaron if he returned to his flat made going back seem a foolishly dangerous decision for Jaron to make.

Men dejected, rejected, often did foolish and reckless things.

Scarecrow knew it first hand, even if he did not want to admit it. Nor did he want to admit that his words, his actions, could have hurt Jaron enough to warrant such foolishness. Why should telling him to go away hurt at all?

Suspecting the answer without such words having been uttered, brought an unwelcomed tearing in his breast.

He hated that feeling.

From the rooftop perch on the flat nearest Jaron's he watched, noting that the splintered door and broken alglamp had been replaced, an indicator that someone had been here. Jaron, most likely, for who else…unless some city maintenance worker had seen the damage and called in the repairs or undertaken them on his own. As with Rhyd's flat, the lights inside were off and there were no aural indicators of movement, of life, inside. His enhanced hearing, at this range, could not detect breathing behind sealed walls. All he could easily hear were the roar of the Falls, the rush of the river, and the variety of life systems that kept flats and vindis livable.

He noted the figure on the stairs, a dejected-looking man making no efforts to hide though he was partially hidden in shadows. Scarecrow identified him by the stylized cut of his coat he had encountered before. The merc did not appear to be watching Jaron's flat, seemed to be resting or waiting for someone or killing time before he had somewhere else to be. There was no reason to be interested in the merc and so, other than giving him an occasional side-eyed glance to make sure he was not falsely judging the man's intent, Scarecrow kept his attention on Jaron's door.

He would wait a little longer in case Jaron had stopped for takeaway or nessies on his way home from his shift.

Then came movement, the anxious skittering of someone fearing for their safety. As the figure was alone, Scarecrow thought at first it might be Jaron, skirting the shadows to reach his flat without being followed. But as the individual moved from one rubbish and recycle box to another, Jaron was ruled out.

Only a streeter looking for food.

Only a streeter, Scarecrow thought, until he noticed the merc's interest in the scavenger, the tension of his body as he prepared to rise. Scarecrow tuned his senses to the streeter too, now directly beneath him; his incoherent rambling words making little sense.

The words were unimportant.

It was the voice that mattered.

What in the cazz was Haythem Kemway doing here?

The merc erupted from his perch and bounded towards the Founder, determined to catch him and take him to the second hiding place he intended to use against Kal. The clatter on the metal stairs and the wobble of a loose railing announced him and Kemway spun, startled. His sideways movement away from the attacker brought him directly behind the frightening wraith that dropped from the rooftop to land between him and his unexpected assailant.

Pinned as he was between nightmares and rubbish bins and the moisture-slicked walls, there was nowhere for Haythem to go. He pressed against the wall, wailing, "No! Neoma! Stop! Not him! The other! Stop him!" as the terrors clashed and punches flew.

Yet to regain his full capabilities, the pain of recent injuries not fully receded except in moments under the influence of sleep or Zaolei, it took little time for the merc to pin Scarecrow to the wall. His fist, raised for a throat punch that would, unless the body armor protected him, crush the vigi's windpipe. Scarecrow's knee jerked up into Blayd's back with enough force to thrust Blayd away as a simultaneous blow of a recycle box to the merc's head toppled him sideways, raining its contents over both him and Scarecrow.

The Founder dropped the bin with a jarring clatter and ran.

Scarecrow delivered a kick and two punches to the man who grabbed at his ankle to pull him down to the walkway and prevent him from chasing his prey. After a second fist to the side of Blayd's head and a stomp that fractured the bones in his arm, Blayd lay still, allowing Scarecrow the chance to dash after the errant Founder.

Haythem, however, was gone.

❧*❧

Though she would rather be looking for her daughter, making sure the child was safe, Neoma understood there was little she could accomplish in the dismal streets she knew so little about. She had never purchased nessies, had only entered a handful of vindis to replace clothing lost after the Coup and her confinement in Factory West 2 deprived her of her wardrobe. Any efforts she made to seek Ulynda would accomplish nothing. She hoped that Ulynda was being taken care of, not mistreated, and in the secret corner of thoughts she would never express, she had to hope that, if the girl had done this on her own, she was smart enough to go somewhere safe. To the Uppers, perhaps, places she had known her whole short life. She had to hope that Nanny would find her, or that Grainger or the bugorra would.

Admittedly, there was a part of her that hoped, if Ulynda had run away, that she was learning a valuable, if miserable, lesson and would come home to never doubt or disobey her mother again.

Ulynda was the future of Hebanthe Falls. Without her, the Kemway bloodline ended…unless Neoma, her escort, and the two people seated at this circular table in this posh club could come to an arrangement. Unless they could find Haythem before the city, the future, went to hell.

Neoma did not know the woman at Kal's side but she knew of her. She knew this was the woman's club. She knew it was the woman's family who produced the vintage in the two bottles on the table waiting to be poured.

Feena Wulfe.

She glowered at Kal, his face still bearing the marks of whatever unfortunate event he had been engaged in, in the hopes of gleaning information about the other woman's attendance. Vanderwall, who pulled out the empty chair for her, one of the few chivalrous acts he ever made, did not seem surprised to see Feena. Neoma wondered if he knew her too…and how.

"Please. Neoma…sit."

Kal's gesture of welcome made her hesitate, the rash resistance to granting compliance to his request, but since she did not want to stand for the duration of this summit, she acquiesced and settled into the chair as one of the club's staff filled four glasses with wine.

She did not want to be here but if she could gauge whether the Senior, the Voices, had both her husband and her daughter, then being here was what Neoma needed to do.

"What's this about?" grunted Vanderwall, snatching the first poured glass and drinking it quickly. He might prefer heavier spirits but he knew good quality alcohol when it was presented and he was not too picky to refuse.

"I think it is time we…" Kal began.

"It is time we find Haythem and restore the Founder to power," growled Neoma.

"Mam…or should I call you Neoma?" Feena's voice was warm, dripping with the sort of insincere honeyed emotion that Neoma could not stomach…because she was so adept at expressing it herself.

Neoma growled again.

Feena took that as an answer, smiled, and continued. "He is mad, is he not? You've seen him…to know it's true? Isn't it naive to think that returning him to power will change anything?"

Eyes narrowed, Neoma hissed, "With Haythem as head of the city and the Doctet in place again…"

"To subjugate us?" snarled Vanderwall as Feena said, "The Levs will not give up representation; the Doctet will never…"

"Ladies." Kal put hands on their wrists, intending it as a gesture of comfort. Neoma snatched hers away. Feena's withdrawal was subtler, covered by reaching for her glass. "We agree that a Kemway needs to be at the head of the city as has always been. There is no…"

"Suppose you heard the folly of another Kemway son?"

Kal cocked his brow, surprised that Neoma had heard the news and wondering when, and where, she had learned it. It was a revelation he was contemplating making in the public statement he had planned but had not yet made. He had thus far not had the time or opportunity to polish the recording. Wherever Neoma had heard the news, it had not come from him. Her knowing explained many things.

Vanderwall said nothing as he consumed a second glass of wine.

"Whoever we install," Feena started again, her voice still cool and level, "politics in the Uppers is going to do little for the state of things here…or Outside…while we fight amongst ourselves. We need an alliance. It is time for the brako feud to end."

Neoma understood then. Feena had brako connections. Feena was controlling the unmasked splinter faction of the brako. She stared at Vanderwall, wondering how much Feena controlled him too.

Ignoring her stare, Vanderwall spoke. "What do you propose?"

"That we let the others elect one of us as leader," Feena purred with a shrug, meeting the big man's gaze with languid ease, "and resume working together the way we used to."

"You were never…"

"You," Feena emphasized, "were never Second, Frankie. You muscled your way into…"

"I was appointed because they trust me…"

"You were appointed with her backing…not because it was what he wanted."

"You had him killed for what he wanted…" Feena arched her brow at the accusation before he added, "You gonna go out in the mask and assert dominance?"

The empty glass came down. "Of course a strong presence is needed, a strong arm…but so is leadership…"

Neoma, unnerved by Kal's unconcerned expression which proved he had been aware of the duality of brako leadership when she had not been, tightened her hold around her glass. This Vanderwall, the man she had appointed, was the only face she had ever seen in the original Vanderwall's company, the only one she had witnessed doing the brako leader's bidding. Learning that there had been another behind the scenes left a feeling of betrayal knotted in her stomach.

"They have leadership," she hissed. "Vander…"

"Me."

Angry that the woman had cut her off, Neoma snarled and leaned forward, "Our support, or influence, our ticks should go to…"

"This isn't about…"

"Leave the brako to Vanderwall and both of you," her heated gaze traveled between Feena and Kal, "stay out of it."

"The way you do?" countered Kal calmly.

"I am the Mam. I am the voice of the Founder until…"

"Ulynda has years to go before she will be ready to serve as Founder…if she ever is…and Haythem will never be…"

Neoma burst from her chair, her regal, stately figure towering over them. "Then we find him. Use him and the brako's strength to restore order to the madness, restore the city to what it could be again. Stronger. Stable. Better."

"Not just better for you," Feena muttered, slightly bored now, insulted by the command Neoma was trying to assert over this meeting, over the city. It did not surprise her.

Commanding was what Kemways did.

Kal was right. They needed a Kemway in place that they could manipulate, if not outright control. Neoma and her daughter, if mother continued to influence Ulynda as she did now, would never be that.

The madman or the dwarf it had to be. One or the other.

"Better for those who deserve it." Neoma tossed out before storming away, her assessment of whether any of those at the table had information about, or access to, her husband, her child, incomplete.

She made no mention of Ulynda. She would not allow Kal or Feena Wulfe the option or opportunity to use her child against her.

Feena had few doubts that the deserving few in the Mam's eyes would be those who pledged loyalty to the name Kemway. The one Neoma deemed the right and legitimate Founder.

Everyone else would suffer.

❧*❧

Ilya closed the door behind her with her foot, noticing the overall sparseness of the single resident flat before the man opening the door for her lost his footing. He would have fallen if she did not awkwardly catch him and direct him towards the sofa that had been pulled out into a bed. Contusions bled beneath the fabric of his undershorts and tee, his face and fists were swollen and bloody still, and his left forearm bore telltale evidence of bone breakage. She knew the life of a merc, like the lives of buggers, exposed them to frequent violence, but she had considered Blayd, before losing touch and coming back in contact again, to be a man capable of taking care of himself.

Blayd grunted and scooted to the edge of the bed so that she could sit beside him, open the medi kit, and begin to tend his wounds. Bloody gauze and a bottle of antiseptic already littered the nearby table, but his efforts to tend his injuries were hampered by his broken arm. He had not wanted to call her, given their recent communication failure, but it was either her or a medi…and though she was a bugger, he believed she would ask fewer questions about his condition than any medi would.

Besides, he had news she would want to hear.

"He had him. I tried to get him away…but this is what I got for the effort," he mumbled, forcing himself to sound intoxicated by pain.

"Who had who?" Ilya asked offhandedly, her focus on his injuries rather than his words.

"Scarecrow. He has Founder Kemway."

Ilya pulled back to look at him skeptically. "That makes no sense. Scarecrow wasn't there when he was taken. I know…I was."

"Maybe not, but he has him now. He did all of this." He looked at his broken arm and flexed his hand with a grimace.

Quiet as she worked, Ilya found the timing of this sighting to be peculiar now that the Mam's reward prodcast was legitimately airing. She had seen the SCAM footage placing Scarecrow on that low Lev stairwell during the recital, there with the captain's man Jaron, far away from the Founder. He had not been among those who had taken Kemway from his Upper's escort, but as Ilya had tried to argue, that did not preclude his involvement.

Maybe the groups had worked in tandem.

Maybe the image on the SCAM was a decoy, to give Scarecrow cover while he infiltrated the Uppers and took the Founder from beneath their noses.

But Scarecrow was a cautious man, and a cautious man would not attempt to move the Founder when he might be seen. If Founder, Scarecrow, and Blayd had been in the same location, there was something else going on.

"Where was this?" She would pull the SCAM footage if there was any. She could verify what Blayd told her.

Blayd shook his head. The truth would contradict his claim, if she saw it for herself, and he could not afford that risk. "Not sure what Lev I was on. Five? Six maybe?" He rubbed the back of his aching head. "It was dark, a street of flats…most of the lights were broken or missing. I wasn't paying attention until they were in front of me."

A street of unlit flats could be anywhere.

"Not paying attention?" That seemed unlikely. Mercs were required to be alert to their surroundings. It was the only way they stayed alive, the only way they could do their jobs.

"A lot on my mind," he replied with an evasive shrug and a sound of discomfort as she dabbed the antiseptic on his bloody knuckles.

"I'll see what I can find…and you should have this looked at." She splinted his arm but without a plast to set the bones, it would take weeks to heal. "Just don't mention this to anyone. The whole city's out looking for him now, and we don't want to stir things up by involving Scarecrow. We don't need him going after civilians. Keep this between us…and if you remember anything else, tell me."

As much as she hated the vigi, if Scarecrow did have the Founder, there had to be a damn good reason. He portrayed himself as a protector of the people. Holding the Founder hostage made no sense. But he had sheltered a parah child once. Might he be doing the same thing now for the Founder?

The only way to keep Kemway safe was to find him before someone else did. Before anyone else got hurt as badly as Blayd. A regular citizen confronting Scarecrow would likely end up dead.

"Not saying a word," Blayd promised. "Think I want people to know he bested me?"

To make Scarecrow's life hell, to force him into a public position with Kemway in his care, it was a promise Blayd was willing to break.

❧*❧

Having left his damaged gear in Tox's workshop, heavily secured and fortified after its discovery by the Crows before the Coup, Rhyd emerged into Vapors from the restroom dressed as if he was about to go on shift based on the cleanliness of his attire. His emergence garnered no peculiar glances. No one spoke to him or stopped him as he strode toward the front door with a nod at Pietro behind the counter. A familiar whistle in the mostly empty vindi drew his attention from his intent and sidetracked his exit.

He had not expected to find Skelter and Zara here, together, at this hour, but seeing them was a fortuitous thing. The others had to know what he now knew.

"Just getting in?" smirked Skelter, waving over a drink for the man who had joined him. The swiver knew what to bring.

"Kemway's on the streets."

Skelter and Zara looked at each other. "We've seen the reward…"

"I've seen him, near Jaron's flat. Mam's merc was after him, and I don't think he was intending to get a reward."

"What would he…?" started Zara.

"If he got clear of the Voices…with all the brako out there…he's in a mess." Skelter's voice was low. He knew now how the Founder had lost control of the city the night Skelter had fallen to his supposed death. He knew the man had suffered some unexplained health issues in the months since that rendered him unfit to care for himself or the city. And he had heard, as had everyone else, about the Founder's abduction by the Talkers the night Skelter had gotten free of the Core.

"You want us to find him? Get eyes out? If he's out there, I'm sure the Spinks'll…"

"This is going to be dangerous for anyone involved…once words out he's loose." Few knew, so far, but public sightings were likely to increase and there would be as many out there wanting him dead as there would be looking to bring him in for the reward.

On the other hand, with the reward prod having run for so many hours, the Spinks were already aware of some of the details. They were likely looking for the Founder to report to Scarecrow. Giving them additional information would not alter that.

The kidnappers would not likely make the same sort of public statement to find Kemway. Few were likely to believe the Founder walked among them even if that claim was made public. Asking the Spinks to keep their eyes open was not the worst idea. It might provide Scarecrow more information by the time he came off shift.

He nodded his agreement.

"I'll tell Ginna when I get back," Skelter promised, "and any Spinks I see along the way. Something I think you should know too."

The swiver arrived with the glass of Zaolei and Rhyd savored the burn, the way it jolted his weary senses. Not the ideal start of the day meal, but it would wake him up.

Once Pietro was gone, Skelter continued, "Been hearing off and on about something going down on Lev 1…along the southern wall."

Where they had come up from the river. Rhyd frowned. "Soaper?" Skelter shook his head no and Rhyd asked, "What sort of activity?"

"Haven't heard…haven't been there to see. None of my sources have been close enough to get a look. Don't think it's buggers…so brako maybe?"

With the soaper nearby, just because the activity did not involve the soaper itself did not mean the brako were not involved. The risk of running afoul of the brako around the soaper was reason enough for Skelter's reluctance to nose around.

"I'll take a look after shift," Rhyd promised. If someone had gotten wind of an entrance into the Core there, brako or bugorra, they needed to be dealt with before there was trouble.

He finished his drink, nodded as he stood, and asked as casually as he could, "Seen Jaron?"

Believing he expected something untoward, that he knew Jaron had spent time in her flat, Zara shook her head. "Stopped by for a look at the speecher; know he went on shift and was thinking he'd pull a double. You haven't seen him?"

"Gone before I left…and I haven't made it home. With the brako out there…he shouldn't be going about alone…"

"I'll check on him," Skelter promised. He sported his own collection of bruises from that last altercation, but he seemed no worse for wear. He did not appear to have been as badly injured as Rhyd.

No one, as far as Rhyd knew, was aware of his fight with Venn and the angry exchange of words he had shared with Jaron.

"Make sure he keeps clear of the brako until I take care of Vanderwall."

"You're taking on…?"

"Someone has to." If it was Vanderwall and the brako active at the south Lev 1 wall near the soaper, how convenient it might be for the brako boss to take an unexpected swim in the river that would chew him up on the jagged rocks and spit him out to sea.

❧Chapter 26❧

Kal did not trust her anymore. Feena never had. The desperation with which Neoma wanted to find her husband was a power-play from a woman beginning to understand that, without Haythem, she had no authority, no standing, no backing. Perhaps she did, if the child was allowed to use it or her mother chose to push her into the spotlight, but without yielding to the support of the Cult, Neoma did not have the influence necessary to manipulate public perception or to lift the Founder's only living heir into Hebenon's ruling seat.

Still, Kal knew Haythem Kemway must be found. It was in the city's, and Kal's, best interest, whatever condition the man was in. As long as he was unaccounted for, uncontrolled, he was an unpredictable liability. Whatever his state, the Cult and the Voices could use him.

While Kal agreed that the brako needed the might, muscle, and intimidation factor of a man like Vanderwall, either the previous fellow or the current one, he needed to be managed by someone with a head for that sort of business. Someone who worked in that arena without brute force but could wield force when necessary. Someone Kal could work with, since directing such force was beneath him. The first Vanderwall had been that. Feena was too. This recruit, a puppet whose strings Neoma believed she pulled, was not.

He might be willing to work with Neoma, or with Feena, but Kal had recognized a man with a mind of his own…and a plan…that did not include Mam Kemway or anyone else.

When this was over, when the Founder was once again under someone's care and control, his, Neoma's, Grainger's, or someone else's, Kal would see about shifting Vanderwall's loyalties. The voices had a lot to offer a power-seeking individual like Vanderwall, but only if the man was willing to work with him. If he could be swayed, if he could be made to see the logic and reason behind remaining the brutal face of the brako while Feena directed business from behind the scenes, Kal could use him.

If Vanderwall would not see reason, well, Kal would see that the brute met some end similar to his predecessor's.

He watched the live feed from the SCAM Feena had arranged for him, the feed that showed the brute in an office full of Echoes, and leaned forward, focused on what details he could glean. Whatever move he made next would depend on how the quest for the Founder played out…and what part Vanderwall had to play in it.

That move was intended to be his own public statement but since the Founder's abduction, Kal had left the daily Voices of Faith prods, which continued to run after the Coup, to others in the organization. His face had not yet healed after his encounter with Scarecrow and he wanted to avoid the questions that would undoubtedly arise if his abraded features were shown on every Echo in the city. He had thought to blame Neoma and her brako agents, but he had formulated no convincing means of doing so.

Under his hand, on the T2 he was using, the words of a brief speech had finally been polished to his liking but how to broadcast them was a dilemma he had to resolve.

He could not let someone else speak these words. They had to come from him if they were to carry any weight with Hebenon's citizens. He could not submit them as a text scroller; words on an Echo, either as a prod or as personal messages sent citywide, would be too easily ignored. Nor did he think the statement could wait until his facial injuries had healed, or had healed enough to be covered with concealer and prod makeup. It left one option. Some befittingly eye-catching imagery and a voice-over.

He set his staff to find suitable footage and began the painstaking task of rehearsing his words to his reflection in the Echo glass.

The words, his voice, had to sound honest. Had to sound sincere.

They had to sound right if he was to salvage the reputation of the Voices of Faith and Cult of the Founder.

❧*❦

She had the names now, names Oliver had grumbled about during their interlude, four men dead for an attempt to abduct the Founder. The dig for identities had required multiple algorithms and several backdoor bypasses and password decryptions, but her diligence eventually exposed two streeters, men believed long dead. There was another, a disillusioned fellow who had attempted to wipe himself from the Hub, the records not entirely expunged as he appeared in a single herpa census of clients housed. The fourth was a hemophiliac whose parents announced him dead in childhood after abandoning him to the streets. Nameless, faceless, the last had worked in the fisheries, undocumented, for whatever scraps anyone could spare. Two blurry images of his employment, and now his death record, were the only pictorial proof that he had survived a harsh childhood.

Only the undocumented status of the four connected them. They had nothing else in common. Not the Lev of their birth or residence, not their ages, not their families.

There was no good way to know if they had shared a common acquaintance, to know who had hired them, to know how Senior Kal, or anyone else, had selected them for this job. They were ghosts in Hebenon's streets, ghosts in the Hub. They were nobodies.

She sent the file after backing up the data and leaned back with an arm over her eyes. Nobodies or not, dead or not, asked to locate them or not, it was information the captain needed. What Grainger did with the information now was not Zara's concern.

She wanted Oliver to have closure. This was all she could give.

Poison.
Poison was the way to do it.
Poison did not have to kill. It only had to be potent enough to incapacitate him, when he was found, to get him safely off the street long enough to collect the reward ticks.

Switz was not a strong man. He could not bodily subdue anyone, even a madman like Kemway. But drugging him…he could do that.

He had narrowed down how to accomplish it before entering the pharma. The collection of herbs, tinctures, medical and cooking spices he requested were eclectic or common enough that those few rarer and potentially dangerous items would not raise undue suspicion as they would if purchased alone. Switz knew how to combine them to do what needed to be done.

First, he had to find Haythem.

He would protect himself, protect the Founder, by telling the truth, or a distorted version of it. He could claim he had been hired as Haythem's caretaker and eventually helped rescue him. Maybe he would name Blayd and claim it was Blayd's fault Haythem was on the streets. Maybe he would leave Blayd out. He was sure the merc would not protect him if it came down to it. Other than the man's name, and the location where the Founder had been held, Switz had little information to provide. It would be up to the buggers to figure out what had landed the Founder in that place in the Merc's possession.

What came after, Switz did not care, as long as he got those ticks.

❧*❦

The Ximenezes latest prodcast, the anonymous source who tipped them off to a fight witnessed between Scarecrow and a merc, a fight in which the Founder was said to have been seen in Scarecrow's custody, infuriated both Grainger and Ilya and set off a flurry of calls delivered to a bugorra message center ill-equipped to handle the demand. Scarecrow had been seen here. The Founder had been spotted there. Both were seen together somewhere else. Many of the messages contained timestamps that made it obvious the two men could not have been in so many places at one time. Reports claimed abusive treatment, reports of the two sharing friendly meals, claims of strange noises and fights and unusual behavior in this abandoned structure or that one. Each report, no matter how unlikely, had to be investigated, weighed for possible validity, and then re-examined by the already thinly stretched bugorra.

Grainger was right to investigate as many claims as possible, even if he did not believe Scarecrow was involved, even if some seemed too farfetched to be real. If any proved true, if the Founder, whatever his condition, had escaped his abductors, with or without Scarecrow's aid, in his company or not, then finding him became even more of a priority. If he was as Grainger had last seen him, he might harm himself, or someone else. He might require urgent medical treatment.

If Tamner's suspicions were accurate and Kemway had begun to regain his faculties, the man had to be located and brought in before he could begin pointing believable fingers at the person people already blamed his condition on, the man who had removed him from power and usurped it and sat in his place for the past two years.

Grainger did not know if he could spin the claims to be madness. It would depend on how lucid the Founder was when he was found.

It became increasingly obvious that the bugorra were not the only people looking for the Founder. It was expected after that reckless and ill-advised prodcast of a sighting, but with three reported run-ins between brako and his forces already, chiefly on Levs 1 and 2, as the buggers poked their noses into the hubs of brako business…places where the thugs felt the bugorra had no reason to be, Grainger knew their tactics needed to change.

Those conflicts came at the end of reports made to the message center. Someone was using the line to provide tips on the brako activities. Stolen goods, weapons stashes, and a host of contraband crates had been uncovered, confiscated, and brought to stations throughout the city for cataloging. Several arrests had been made. But their efforts were doing little good in the search for Founder Kemway.

Where had these tips been before? Why were so many coming now? As appreciated and necessary as they were, they detracted from the bugorra's top priority. And they were making the brako furious. The escalating assaults on patrolling buggers were evidence of that. Each bugger that ended up in a medi-facility stretched Grainger's resources that much thinner.

He felt justified in instructing his officers to ignore contraband stashes, unless they were weapons, and to ignore the brako's business as much as they could for now. Undoubtedly, those making calls would infer a lack of empathy, regard, or concern for Hebenon's citizens, but he needed his officers to find the Founder. Later, they would go back to focusing on the brako.

Ilya grumbled beneath her breath. This was Scarecrow's doing.

But the leak of information to the Ximenezes that had started off this second storm was not. He would not expose himself by calling in his activities to the prods. The tip had been anonymous, and yet it was one more instance where a secret bit of intel was leaked to the press…intel that only a handful of people had known.

Typically, Scarecrow witnesses came forward to praise him. If someone had seen the Founder, with a reward on the line for finding him, it was more likely that they would go straight to the Mam with whatever they knew.

Why report such a sighting to the prods?

There were only a few people who might gain from such a leak. Scarecrow. A glory-seeking archivist who had viewed SCAM evidence of the fight between Blayd and Scarecrow. Kal, if he wanted to redirect the blame of abduction. Or Blayd, if he hoped to use the chaos to find the Founder himself on Mam Kemway's behalf.

Scarecrow would never take the risk.

Archivists typically sent such sightings directly to the bugorra…or if seeking the reward would have sent it to Neoma.

Kal should not have known about this incident.

It left only Blayd.

Given the previous intel leaks, other details Blayd had known when there seemed no reason he should have, Ilya felt more convinced that the merc was at the center of this incident. Maybe he had fabricated it, as she had not yet seen any SCAM footage to back up his claim and the prods had not provided any either.

Could he have been involved in deposing the Founder two years ago? Could he have had some hand in abducting the Founder?

How? On whose behalf?

Why?

Mam Kemway was the only connecting thread.

Ilya had not been able to snatch more than a few minutes to sit and enjoy hot tea and half a sandwich in so many hours that she had lost track. One empty location after another, one bogus sighting or misidentified streeter, had kept her and the three officers with her on the run between the two Levs where Blayd claimed his Scarecrow encounter occurred. Assigning buggers to certain Levs made more sense than random runs around the city, and this section was the one she had specifically chosen to investigate.

No luck. No rest. Eventually, her team would have to stand down.

Few off-shift officers remained to fill their place.

So they pushed on, one given an hour break at a time to give them some manner of rest. Still, the desire not to give up until the Founder and Scarecrow were found was pushing against the harsh reality of human limitations. No one wanted to give up.

Not for the first time did Ilya consider that the law forbidding andi law enforcement officers was a bogus one.

From the increased activity in the streets and the Senior's public speech prod made over SCAM footage of a Marbordo sea sunrise, a speech denouncing the Founder's kidnapping, denying responsibility for it, and pleading for citywide cooperation in finding the most important person in Hebanthe Falls', it was obvious the Voices had their own agenda, their own agents on the hunt. Men and women in the robes of their calling traveled in pairs, perhaps following their own tips, perhaps moving at the Senior's direction. Despite the deepening doubts about Blayd's involvement, it made sense that, if the Senior was involved, he would publically deny it and be eager to have Kemway back under his control. To the Cult of the Founder, Kemway was, as the Senior said, the most important person in the city. They would want to protect the man at all costs.

The possibility of a reward and the desire to stir unrest explained the brako's heavy patrols. Most she saw, however, were spotted entering and exiting the system tunnels, leading her to think they knew something she did not.

There were no officers to spare to go in after them. The brako were too dangerous. The captain denied Ilya's request to send them in.

While those with her interviewed a pair of vindis about a claimed sighting, Ilya was distracted by a sighting of her own, her sister and a group of six children sporting the increasingly familiar black banda with the Scarecrow's adopted call sign. They were coming down a nearby staircase where a streeter huddled beneath, the stairs providing little protection from dripping moisture and keeping him out of the flow of street traffic. Ilya's hope that her sister had given up the dangers associated with the young scalawags compelled her to leave the officers to their interview and cut across the intersection to confront the younger woman.

"Ginna!"

Two brako emerging at the head of a nearby alley with access to the tunnels at the other end, watched her with expressionless, bird-masked eyes, assessing the threat level of the nearby officers.

From a pharma a few doors away, a little man emerged, tucking his purchases into the deep pockets of his raincoat.

Beneath the stairwell, the streeter turned at the call to see a woman in a law enforcement longcoat, an unmasked officer, striding in his direction. He saw the beaked horrors, saw the bug masked faces at a nearby vindi, and saw the face of the only person he had recently been able to trust. Seized by the sudden panic of being surrounded, trapped, he did the only thing his frantic thoughts allowed.

He erupted into the street from beneath the stairs, grabbed the little man by the arm with a shrill, "Save me!" and burst into a run through the crowd, dragging the staggering Switz with him.

It took the others, the buggers, the brako, the Spinks, long enough to realize what had happened, who had just appeared and dashed away, that by the time they reacted, everyone racing in pursuit, the pair had a reasonable headstart. While the fellow with the Founder did not wear the Scarecrow's face and, from Ilya's only direct encounter with the vigi, seemed too small and spidery to be him, it was a possibility. When she ran, it was as much after the Founder's companion as it was after the Founder himself.

Ginna piped off a series of whistles. The Spinks around her, the Spinks in the nearby shadows and within hearing range of her commanding call, knew what to do.

Summon Scarecrow.

Protect the Founder.

❧*❧

Forced to an extended shift due to the delays in his repair schedule created by the increased frequency of brako in the shafts, Rhyd did not get the message, scrawled in red spray on a wall outside the Shed's primary door, until long after it was left. Worried about Jaron, as uncomfortably afraid that the younger man had taken him at his word and returned to Grainger's bed as he was that the brako had found him, Rhyd's intention after his shift had been to go straight home. If Jaron was not there, had not been there, he intended to confront Grainger, pride be damned, if for no other reason than to make the captain aware that Jaron was a brako target and needed to be found, protected, whatever the differences were between the three of them.

The urgency he interpreted in the sloppily painted tag, however, drew Scarecrow elsewhere.

"What is it?"

The young woman poised on the steps where the Founder had last been seen, scrambled to her feet in reaction to the unexpected digitally manipulated voice from the shadows. It had been so long since they had sent word for him, she had nearly given up hope he would come.

If she stayed in one place too long, her sister would return. And Maemi would be cross with her tardiness.

Still, Ginna had waited.

"We've seen him. The Founder."

That was news worth the detour. "Where?"

"He was here…under the stairs," she pointed to the steps on which she had been seated. "There were brako…my sister, Lieutenant Young…some of her buggers…and Switz, from the tunnel. They chased him, him and Switz, that way." She pointed again. "Some of us followed, but we…all of us, all of them, lost him. Must have, cause the prods haven't reported him found and the reward's still running."

So was the periodically airing Voices statement Kal had released. Both only meant, thought Scarecrow with a frown, that if Kemway had been found, it had to be to someone's benefit to not make the news public. His condition, his health would be evaluated. Or maybe he had been killed and someone had to figure out a public spin for that news. He might have been taken directly to his wife and she had not taken down the reward to avoid paying out.

Scarecrow's options were weighed: follow the Founder's long-cold trail or return home to see if Jaron was safe. The risks of each, the doing and not doing, were tested before he finally said, "Tell the others we need to find the archivist…the one they took to the cat man. Tell Maemi at Vapors to get the doctor and the kaheao…tell them to be there at the cat man's. They'll know where to go, what to do."

"Yessa," Ginna chirped with an eager nod before bounding up the stairs in the specified direction. A message to Maemi from Scarecrow ought to win her a pardon for not arriving for her shift on time.

Scarecrow turned his head towards the dim street where Ginna had pointed. It would not hurt to take a quick look in the direction Kemway and the fellow Switz had gone. If they had found a good hiding place out of the eyes of the brako and bugorra, Scarecrow hoped he would be able to find them where the other seekers had failed.

If not, he would double back, check on Jaron, and as soon as he knew the younger man was safe, he would resume his hunts…for the Founder and for Vanderwall.

❧CHAPTER 27❧

At the first opportunity, when Switz paused to catch his breath beneath a covered overpass where no alglamps or neon vindi signs glowed, digging in his canvas sack for the morsel of food he had promised, Haythem ran. Out of Switz's reach, away from what he believed would be a weapon, the promise for requested food notwithstanding, he fled from both hunters and those who might help.

Though Switz might be considered an accomplice for helping him flee, the thin man was not the one people wanted. Despite his hunger, despite some level of recognition that, in his panic, he could not pin down, Haythem did not trust him.

He had seen her face on the flickering screens, had heard her voice, had heard her impassioned offer of ticks for anyone who brought him back to her, and although he did not know why he recognized her face, he knew he could not go back there.

He would not go back. He could not remember why he did not trust her either, except that in the fog of his jumbled thoughts, her face and Scarecrow's were one. If he stayed within reach of the masked faces, the birds and the bugs, he believed that, if they did not take him to her, he would still be subjected to an equally unpleasant fate.

It was better he took his chances in the city's shadows until his head cleared and he determined how to return to a place of safety that his conscious mind failed to identify but knew was there.

Every vindi corner he turned presented another Echo with her face. There was another voice as well, like a dream, the sun speaking to him, pleading for his safety. Haythem thought perhaps that voice, sincere and earnest and audibly caring, was one he could trust. But it was a voice without a face, without memory despite its fleeting familiarity, and so Haythem was left with no one.

Every staircase and alley threw more birds and bugs into his path, resulting in frequent changes of direction. Left. Right. Up. Down. He turned and turned until he had no concept of where he was or how much time had passed.

A few times he lashed out at hands that he was sure were grabbing at him from obscured doorways. A few times he struck at those who pushed him aside or whom he plowed into as his erratic, hasty steps dragged into the path of someone else. Here, where the Falls roared the loudest, where the mist billowed heavy and cold, Haythem was so disoriented that every face he passed looked the same.

They all looked like her. Or him.

Another, young and mop-headed, dark hair clinging wet to his face, crossed the alley where Haythem took refuge, heading towards the main path with quick, furtive steps. Haythem did not see him until they collided, an impact that brought the Founder's fist up to catch the fellow in the chin. The blow thrust the stranger back against the nearest structure with enough force to send shudders through the grate beneath their feet and then he slumped to the wet ground, blood trickling from his mouth.

Alive? Dead?

Haythem did not know or care or even think about it as he dashed across the alley in search of a place he did not know how to find.

❧*❧

She could not steal to eat, although the thought of doing so increased with each hour of churning in her long-empty belly. Having missed dinner, and then breakfast, at home, and uncertain how long she had been on her own, she could not guess how many meals she had missed. But stealing was wrong, it was an act unsuitable for the daughter of the Founder, and so she resisted the temptation.

When a kindly someone, swathed in so many layers of protection against the wet and cold that their face was not visible, offered her a pear, she gladly accepted. Later, she found a partially eaten basket of still-warm hempseed bread left by diners at an outdoor vindi; already paid for and destined for mulching, she rationalized that eating it was not technically stealing and so she took that too.

It had been many hours since either of those and now her stomach roared louder than ever.

Ulynda might have been able to endure more easily if not for the moisture that had long ago seeped through her inadequate clothing so that she shivered as she trudged tearfully away from the bowling vindi she had been chased out of.

"Pay or play," the vindi had demanded. Since Ulynda had no ticks, either to play or to buy a meal or cup of warming tea, she was once more in the dark, entertaining the thought that going home might not be such a bad thing. Her mother scared her, as did the host of possible punishments waiting if she went back, but at least home would mean a full meal, hot and fresh, a warm bath, and thick blankets to wrap around her shivering shoulders.

Once again face to face with her mother's visage on a street corner Echo, a reward made for her husband's return but no mention made of her absent child, Ulynda wondered if her mother missed her. If she knew, or cared, that she was gone.

Senior Kal's voice made her stop at a street Echo and allowed her to watch her first ever sunrise as she listened to him plead for her father's life. Peeling back her hood as if it would help her see and hear better, allowed the mist to gather upon her cheeks and mask the sudden eruption of tears. She missed her father. She was afraid for him.

Maybe, despite her doubts about his trustworthiness and her mother's doubts about his motives, the Senior did care about her father. Maybe he did want to help.

"Are you alright, maleni? Come…out of the spray."

Wiping her face with the back of her hand, which did no more than smear tears into the sheen of mist on her skin, Ulynda lifted her head, startled by the voice that interrupted the continuing drone of the Senior's impassioned plea. The round fellow beneath the herpa sign was the friendliest face she had seen since stepping into Hebenon's streets. Ulynda knew little about herpa, as they had not been welcome in the Uppers, but she understood that their mission was to help people without question or reservation. Behind him, through the open door of the hall, she could see a dirty rabble milling about with steaming cups and takeaway sacks of whatever food was offered.

None looked afraid. None looked wary, threatened, or threatening. While some bore the glassy-eyed expression of Heb use, most merely appeared weary and lost, grateful for something to eat and for the warmth Ulynda could feel bleeding through the open doorway.

"Come, sit by the radiator. I will find you something dry to wear while you eat and warm yourself." When she began to timidly shake her head no, her fear warring with her body's multitude of needs, he smiled, a sweetly innocent expression that reminded Ulynda of Flora, and held out his hand. "Come or go as you wish, maleni. You don't need to be afraid here. You will be safe, I promise you."

She bit her lip and looked past him again, at the others. "Do you…have books?" she asked through chattering teeth. The sudden notion of sitting in front of a radiator with a blanket, hot tea, and a book felt to be the most important thing in the world.

"I believe I do. Come, pick something out. Be content.

Content. That word was bait enough. She took the herpa's offered hand and forced a smile.

☙*❧

Three brako altercations later and the body trauma of bruised limbs and aching ribs to show for it, brought Scarecrow to his dark flat through the system grate he used more than his front door. He did not need to look around the living room, did not need to investigate the bedrooms or the bathroom as he wrestled the mask off and dropped it onto the dining room table, to know the flat was empty and had been since the last time he had been here. Jaron's lingering scent was flat, stale, too long unrenewed.

Everything looked as it had the last time Rhyd had been here.

One by one, as the pieces of body armor came free, the belts and straps and tools, the boots and gloves, Rhyd unconsciously put them where Jaron had previously placed them to dry, the emptiness of the flat gnawing at his nerves like rough paper as he berated himself for the last words he had spoken.

Jaron had taken his words to heart.

Jaron had not come home.

Rhyd frowned at that thought, how easily he had come to think of his home as Jaron's. The frown deepened as his thoughts kept returning to the same place, the only place that made sense.

If Jaron was not here, was not at the Archives or his flat, the only other logical place for him to be was with Grainger.

That possibility, coupled with the unsettling realization that he considered this Jaron's home, made Rhyd grind his teeth and limpingly stomp into the kitchen for a bottle from his cupboard stash.

A short three-thump of pounding on his door meant he never reached that destination.

Gods, he thought, even as he scolded himself for doing so, let it be Jaron.

He peered through the peephole, grunted, and opened the door though he would rather not.

He had to let him in. He had sent for the man after all.

Tamner looked Rhyd over in a long, sweeping glance, the black shorts hiding little of the excessive bruising, old and new, that his vigi lifestyle made him prone to. Rhyd met that gaze but then continued towards the kitchen with only an exasperated grunt for a greeting.

"You didn't show up for your appointment…and they said you wanted me," Tamner said with gentle sternness as he closed the door.

Rhyd grunted again and took the desired bottle from the cupboard, wincing as the muscles along his side stretched with a burning ache. Knowing the doctor would not leave until he had done what he had come to do, had learned what Rhyd wanted, he sat at the table, eased his leg up to prop it on the nearest chair, and took a long drink. The old bruising around the breakage site was melting into the fringes of the newer contusions gained during the last few nights' tussles.

"You seen Grainger?"

"Not today," Tamner admitted, grateful he had been able to see to his duties, his son, without multiple summons from the captain or the Nau. It was a state he knew would not last.

"Jaron?"

That question explained Rhyd's interest in Grainger and probably his purpose for summoning Tamner in the first place. "Not since his message to check on you. I got the impression, in his tone, you'd be at it again after I recommended…"

"I know my limits."

"Obviously not well enough." The hand scanner and the feel of muscles and bone beneath Tamner's trained touch made him nod. "Break looks good…but you're damn lucky you didn't break it again."

"Luck's nothing to do with it."

"Maybe."

Rhyd put the bottle down so the doctor could now examine his previously dislocated shoulder. "He's out there, you know…"

"Jaron?"

"Kemway. Dunno who took him…but he's loose on the streets with a little fellow called Switz…"

"How do you know this?" Tamner drew back to look at his face.

"Spinks…they've seen him." The name Switz might not mean anything to Tamner, but Switz was not the important part of the equation. "You said he's mad?"

"Occasionally. Manic mostly. Lethargic and unresponsive the rest of the time. Or he was before." Tamner plopped into the other chair after Rhyd moved his foot from it. "That night, I noticed things…coherency he'd not shown in two years."

"You think lack of treatment could make him better?" Rhyd did not know what manner of treatment Grainger had insisted on, what sort the doctor had recommended.

"Or worse." Tamner shrugged. "I don't know. I'd tried so many times to bring him back. Maybe I finally hit on a successful combination, or he just needed time to heal. If he's on the streets, running without supervision…no matter how much better he was doing, I don't think out there can be good for him."

"Why we need to find him…before Mam, or Kal, or the captain. Before the brako. Before he ends up in the wrong hands…or as fish food. I'm gonna track him down, but I need your help."

Wondering why Ballard included Grainger in that list but not asking, Tamner raked his hand through his hair. "What can I do?"

"Know any places he would go? Anyone he'd know?"

"Down here?" He shook his head. "Not in the Levs. Maybe some key business figures…but he avoided the Levs like they were Outside. Never came any lower than the arena to my knowledge. Last I saw him, he did not know anyone, not even himself. He wouldn't know where to go unless he'd started to remember, then I wager he'd go up. Where was he seen?"

"Lev 9, leading the buggers and brako on a helluva run I was told."

"They could've caught him…"

"Doubt it. Think we'd've heard something by now.

Tamner had to give him that point. If the Founder had been returned to the captain's custody, Tamner would have heard. The Mam or Senior would likely have made very public pronouncements if they had succeeded in getting him to safety.

Rhyd continued after several gulps that burned into his belly and along every nerve to dull the throb of bruising. "When I find him, sane or not, my usual methods won't apply." They would work, but he did not want to assault the Founder a second time. There was no reason, this time, for violence. "I don't have a buzzer or stinger…"

"I can give you a stinger." Some of those tasked with sentinel duty for the Founder had been armed with them and had returned the stingers. The tranquilizing agents used were still in storage in the lab, awaiting the Founder's rescue. Though it did not appear Ballard intended to go out tonight, Tamner doubted he could make it back with those things before Scarecrow resumed his hunt.

"In the meantime, I can give you this." From his medikit, he produced two hand injectors filled with a substance the color of old urine. "I keep it with me in case I need to knock out a Hebber."

Most Heb users never became violent, but it did occasionally happen in the late stages of addiction. That need, or the need to subdue anyone he was treating, made being prepared a necessity. "Can't guarantee it'll work…that it'll be strong enough to take him down, given the way he was, but it might slow him down."

Rhyd nodded and took both injectors. He would need to get close to use them, a hand-to-hand struggle with a potentially insane Founder he did not relish having, but he would make the most of any opportunity given.

Across the room, the ICD Rhyd he had abandoned in favor of the body armor began to buzz inside his tooler. Hoping it would be Jaron and not the troublesome captain who had left him multiple messages throughout the day, Rhyd pushed unceremoniously past Tamner to reach it before it fell silent. Wondering only now if Grainger's attempts to reach him were connected to Jaron…and if he should have answered those messages sooner, Rhyd's abrupt, "Yeah?", was breathless, eager, and a little bit guilty all at once.

The voice on the other end sucked his held breath away and filled his stomach with its previous ball of sour emptiness. "Ballard?"

"Grainger." If not for the need to know if Jaron was with him, if Jaron was safely out of the brako's reach, he would have cut the connection. "It's late."

"Doesn't sound like I'm the only one not sleeping. You didn't return my calls."

"Been busy. What do you want?" He imagined the big man smirking in response to the churlish question, an image that tugged the corners of Rhyd's scowl down further.

"I know you haven't accepted my offer…but there's something I need you to do."

Sucking in a breath between gritted teeth, his eyes squeezed shut against the images of Jaron and Grainger together that pushed into his head, he grunted, "What?" Helping the bugorra captain was the last thing he wanted to do. If this was Grainger asking a favor about Jaron, however, it would be worth hearing the captain out.

"Founder's on the loose…out there…in the Levs…"

"I know."

"You…?" Grainger's tone of annoyance was aborted by what sounded like a loud swallow that suggested the captain was drinking too. "You found him? Know where he is?"

"Looking. Haven't found him yet, but I've got resources…"

"Then you'll help."

"Not doing it for you. He's not safe out there. Lev's ain't a place for a man like that." Not for the deposed Founder. Not for a person unfamiliar with the Levs. Not for a possibly delirious madman. Not for a soul that so many in the Levs were now hunting.

His words did nothing to undermine Grainger's relief. "You find him, you call me. Call Tamner. Get him up here."

Again Rhyd grunted, side-eyeing Tamner as he did so. He might willingly convey the Founder's location to Tamner, as the doctor had proven to be trustworthy since their first meeting. But Rhyd had no reason to believe he could trust the Founder in the captain's hands. Grainger might have kept him alive for two years, might have seen to his care, but that did not mean he had Kemway's best interests at heart.

Rhyd could not think of anyone, other than Tamner, who might.

"Might want to look for a guy called Switz; think it's a last name."

"Switz?" Grainger paused. Rhyd could hear the sound of tapping on the line as the name was recorded. "Who's that?"

"Just…look for him. See if he pops on the SCAMs. He might be a link." He considered giving Grainger Blayd's name too, but that was a man Rhyd wanted to deal with himself…if there was any connection beyond a coincidental sighting and the hopes of bringing Haythem back to his wife.

"Got it. Anything else."

"Think I'm gonna do your work for you?" Rhyd scoffed. He hesitated for a moment to give Grainger the chance to speak again and then asked, "That it?"

"There's…I want you to keep your eyes open for…"

The pit of Rhyd's belly turned icy and his eyes darted towards Jaron's shirt that still hung over the arm of the sofa.

"Ulynda Kemway."

"Ulynda?" He choked in surprise.

"Neoma burst in here ranting about how you'd taken the girl because the vent in her bedroom was open. I assured her you had nothing to do with it…but she didn't tell me much."

"When?"

"Earlier today…when I first called you. Might have gone missing during the night. Neoma doesn't know. There was an incident with Tamner's son and your parah that may have precipitated her absence."

Again Rhyd caught Tamner's gaze, noted the doctor's sour expression, and frowned. He was exhausted. His body hurt. He was no good to anyone if he did not get a few hours of sleep. But a child alone on the streets, especially an unseasoned girl who had no idea how to survive in the Levs could not be ignored.

"No clues?"

"None we've found. Neoma refuses a public plea for assistance, something about not wanting their enemies to use the girl against her; if there's more to this, she's not telling me. If not you, she suspects Tamner…or Kal…but she's not talking, and for all I know the girl might be home now. I haven't heard from Neoma in hours."

"Find out and get back to me." The time Grainger spent reaching out to Neoma ought to give Rhyd enough time for an invigorating shower. A shower and another drink might be all he needed to get back out to find the missing girl."

"I will."

After a hesitant, pregnant pause that Rhyd believed was a prelude to more, he muttered, "What else?"

"What else?"

Rhyd snorted.

Grainger cleared his throat.

Silence.

There was a strangled, hesitant sound, swallowed words that Rhyd guessed the captain was reluctant to say or ask. Finally, after a heavy sigh, Grainger murmured, "He deserves better than either of us, Ballard. All I want is for him to be safe…and happy. I'm sorry."

The link went dead.

The words, to Rhyd, seemed proof of his fears, proof that his stinging admonitions had pushed Jaron back to Grainger. The captain was right about one thing. Up there, in the Uppers, Jaron was safer. Maybe not happy, but he was better off far away from Rhyd.

Nevertheless, despite the things he had said, back at Grainger's side was the last place Rhyd wanted Jaron to be.

Even if it was the best thing for everyone.

Clutching the ICD, still staring at the abandoned shirt, he asked out loud, "What happened with the Kemway girl?"

Tamner shrugged. "Cori and Agnys met her at the recital. They took it upon themselves to go for a visit without telling me…Neoma did not take kindly to visitors. She hurt them…not badly, but I've seen the bruises. According to Cori, she hurt Ulynda too. Never took the girl for a runner…"

But in the Uppers, there had never been any place for Ulynda to run to. A lot had happened to the girl in the years Tamner had known her. He had never had intimate dealings with the Founder's family, had not known any of them outside of polite, social interactions or business, but he knew how prickly Neoma could be. Older now, Ulynda was approaching her teen years, and after so much upheaval, perhaps the girl had decided she had endured enough.

Or as Grainger had hinted, someone had taken her.

Whoever had taken her husband, Senior Kal or someone else, would be the primary suspect.

Rhyd muttered something without looking at him, his fist still tight around the ICD. He needed to get word of this to Lash, to Enoch, to Skelter and the Spinks. They needed to look for the girl too. "Gonna shower. See yourself out."

The doctor, still seated at the table, listened to the retreating steps and the reverberating thump of the bathroom door. If anyone could find the Founder, could find Ulynda, it would be Scarecrow. Maybe Cori and Agnys knew something that would help. He would question them in the morning if there had been no success by then.

He did not believe Scarecrow intended to wait that long to act.

❧*❦

Molly had spent hours grumbling to himself about the order to take down his handiwork so soon. He was proud of his efforts, after having been out of practice for so long, and he had thought the Mam was pleased with it too. The order to transfer the vid to the prodcasting heads that came after the order to cease broadcasting, however, was the first time any of his work was officially shown throughout the city. He had not believed it would happen, had continued to lament his luck, until the prod showed up once more on every Echo in Hebenon. The unexpected success replaced his grumbling mood with a glow of pride.

It was not just the Mam's message being shown. It was Molly Netzer's production. His work, good enough not to be rerecorded, edited, altered, or retouched.

In time, he dreamed of securing a position in the prod studio alongside the likes of the Ximenezes and their ilk. A man like him. Living in the Uppers.

Wouldn't that be something?

It prompted him to seek other ideas, something he could piece together and air on the Mam's behalf without necessarily asking permission, something tasteful and helpful that would benefit her cause, help bring the Founder home, and prove his worth as both haikara and a prodcaster.

First, however, he needed equipment.

Vanderwall had taken most of the gear back but had allowed him to keep one Echo, the cam, and a couple smaller pieces of tech. It had been relocated to the flat he was given to live in, one with no suitable wall or background space for the type of prods he wanted to create. He needed another Echo or two, voice filters and modulators, additional lights. He needed a green canvas and a projector. He needed software and storage devices and additional Echo memory.

He needed more.

The need for those things at reasonable prices, now that his payment of ticks from the Mam had been spent on an additional stash of Heb tucked inside his coat pocket, eventually brought Molly to a kesfek next to a club that made his eyes light up with accomplishment.

Vapors featured prominently in the tales Skelter had told inside the Core. Molly had intended to find his way here after he settled and reintegrated into city life, after his first fix and his position with the Mam was secured. Skelter had made it sound like a good club to hang out in, one that would be, Molly imagined, the place to both score Heb regularly and track down the errant redhead.

Finding it today, on the trail of Echo equipment, was coincidental.

As was finding the man in question leaning on the kesfek counter talking to the brunette behind it. Molly waited to approach until the woman ducked through the doorway behind the stall counter as if looking for something inside, leaving the redhead alone.

"You got a promise to keep."

The ragged voice behind him was one Skelter had not thought to hear again, even though Enoch had told him the man was looking for him. He had not disliked Molly. He had rarely given the man thought if he was honest. They faced each other around the Spades table once each month for nearly two years, each waiting for the day the Ace chose them. Other than that, and random passings in the corridors of the Core, they had never shared more than pleasantries.

But Skelter knew him. During those years, if a Spades member showed reluctance to follow through with their selected destiny, it had most often been Molly who was there to see the pact through. Molly who arranged accidents, provided poisons, twisted the shank when necessary. It was not that he enjoyed killing or death.

Molly did, however, believe in vows kept.

"You made it," Skelter smiled with easy cheer.

"So did you."

Skelter ignored the sharp edge of Molly's voice. "Was wondering whose face I'd see first. Haven't seen or spoken with…"

"You made a pact."

"Doesn't apply out here. No need for dyin'. We're free to start life again. Hebenon's open…the whole world is…"

"Nothin' if men don't keep their word. Spades don't forget…"

Clasping the shorter man's shoulder, Skelter grinned, "Spades are gone, Molly. We're out. No need for anyone out here to…"

"The pact…"

His argument was cut off by the return of the kesfek with a wrapped bundle that she handed to Skelter across the counter.

"Thanks, sorella," Skelter said to her, leaning to kiss her cheek before heading away with only a "See you around, Molly" given over his shoulder with barely a look back.

Molly's fists balled at his side but his expression remained impassive. He was not a man prone to fighting, particularly if it was a fight he thought he would lose. He considered following, forcing Skelter to uphold the pact he had made. But he could not force the man to take his own life without the other Core Spades to back him up, and he had nothing on him with which to see that the promised life was offered to the Ace as it should have been days ago. A failed promise put the world out of balance. Molly saw it as his responsibility to make sure that balance was put right.

But not today. If the kesfek had the items he wanted, for prices or payment terms he could afford, Molly had work to do.

The next time he met Skelter, the outcome would be different.

❧Chapter 28❧

Not a single person, brako or otherwise, prevented Grainger from his exploration of the area where SCAM footage had shown Vanderwall's fall. The captain could feel them there, eyes in the shadows, behind bird masks he could not see, as he ran his hand over the wet grate, long ago washed clean of evidence. From where he squatted, the tails of his longcoat fanned out in the damp, he looked up at the staircase, the place where Jaron had met Scarecrow, had helped him to the level above, to a place of safety as yet unidentified.

There were many empty structures here, hostels, storages, and vindis damaged in the Coup, unrepaired and unoccupied because the population hit during those too long yet too brief days had created no need to do so. He imagined, as he straightened and wiped water from his unshielded eyes, that with the opening of Outside, many of these places would never again be needed except by streeters for temporary shelter, and brako for their illicit ventures. It would take several generations for the population to recover, and now that there was a new world to explore and expand into, Grainger steadfastly believed that those new generations would migrate more and more beyond Hebenon's walls until there was little need for the city in the falls.

Only people like himself, like Ballard, would remain. People unable to move on. Unable to let go.

Within the stone of the earth, beneath the East Factories, the work to clear the Core entrance and investigate what lay behind it continued. The ongoing salt protests needed to be addressed and if appeasing that need meant reopening the mines, their structural integrity had to be assured. Those other explosions, those that had come after the opening of the mine door, were yet to be explained. None of them had been Grainger's doing but he could not risk that their cause, their effect had created destabilizing damage.

If there was evidence of historical relevance inside, damning or otherwise, Grainger wanted to know that too.

If the mines were to reopen, he wanted to be certain it was safe, for the miners, for the Factories, for himself. A new source of labor had to be coordinated, a potentially more difficult task than clearing debris, for those with mining experience were either dead or free of their forced obligation. Some of those might agree to come back as overseers, but Grainger would not condemn another person to that life.

He doubted many would choose it willingly.

For now, that was a problem he chose not to dwell on as sounds behind him announced Lieutenant Young's arrival.

"Anything?" He might have asked Ballard, asked Scarecrow, to help find the Founder, but that did not mean he had relieved his officers of the duty. The bugorra had been seeking the Founder since his abduction and would continue to do so until he was located. Seeing to Kemway's safety was imperative though the news that he was now freely roaming the streets was limited to only a few.

Maybe the fellow Lieutenant Young had seen relocating the Founder to a different prison could help. His face, called up from the Hub, had been sent to all of the officers too. The little fellow had been a murderer after all. It was reason enough for the bugorra to seek him without asking too many questions. It was more likely they believed he was being sought in connection with the missing child.

"No, sir. No sign of the Founder or the girl yet. We've searched the structures in the vicinity where I saw him…where we lost him." Ilya hated that word but it was accurate. "I'm widening the search street by street. If he's there, we'll find him."

"The fellow with him?" She did not seem to realize that the face of the man connected to Kemway belonged to the man Grainger had asked them to also locate.

"Didn't get a good look, but I have spotters combing the SCAMs, hoping one of them caught him. I believe it was Scarecrow."

"Scarecrow?" Grainger snorted with annoyed disbelief.

"Out of uniform, but yes. The reports that the Founder was seen in Scarecrow's company…that Scarecrow was with him…that Scarecrow is the kidnapper…"

"Lieutenant…"

The scolding prompted her to continue. "We know he wasn't there for the kidnapping, but this one? Who else? Who else could disappear into the shadows and escape us like this? I trust my source."

Or at least she wanted to.

Ballard said he was aware the Founder was missing, said he was looking for him, but what if he was lying? What if his words were intended to misdirect the manhunt away from him? Grainger could think of no reason why Ballard would find, and hold, Kemway and not return him to safety, but that did not mean there was none. However, he sighed as he glanced again at the stairwell, Scarecrow had not been the kidnapper. That much he was certain of. He had seen the proof.

"He didn't do it." He pointed at the stairs. "He didn't do any of this. You've seen the evidence…"

Multiple what-ifs ran through Ilya's head but as they were only theories without evidence, theories she clung to because of her belief that the majority of Hebenon's troubles stemmed from the vigi's unchecked activities, she kept her thoughts to herself.

"Doesn't mean he doesn't have him. We should put out a…"

"No." Grainger had already heard the whispered gossip as he traveled to Lev 1 to investigate the rumors of people moving outside of the city's shell. He had hoped to find the Founder, the kidnappers there, connected to that movement, but he expected to find the brako. He had not made it there yet, but so far all he had found was the bubbling and sloshing of the churning river over his feet on the grate that produced the city's lowest footpath. Nothing but river and rumors.

People were already too uneasy about the Founder's absence.

"Too many want him dead or want the reward. If he's out here…"

"If people think Scarecrow has him…"

"We don't know who has him and further speculation is going to get someone killed. I don't want that on my conscience." He already carried too many burdens and did not want to add the Founder's death, or Scarecrow's, to them. "If he's in Scarecrow's care, I suspect he's safe enough."

Ilya scowled. "You're willing to bet the Founder's life on someone who doesn't obey the laws…just because he hasn't killed anyone? You want that on your conscience?"

When he glared at her for challenging his authority, Ilya closed her mouth and looked towards a metallic clatter that proved to be cart wheels over the grating at the crossroads behind them.

Satisfied she would not contradict him again, Grainger nodded with a grunt. "I am. For now, we keep looking…for Kemway, for his daughter, for the fellow Switz. Not a public word to anyone about either, is that understood? Put a team here. I want to know where Vanderwall came into the frame…trace him back if possible…where Scarecrow," and Jaron, he thought, "was going…what happened to the body. I want to know how a dead man is still alive."

This time, Ilya nodded dutifully. She had heard that Vanderwall had resurfaced too, despite his rumored death. If the brako boss lived, who had died here? If the brako boss lived, they needed to know.

Before Vanderwall and the brako got their hands on Founder Kemway or his daughter and Hebanthe Falls paid the price.

From the shadows he saw him, black and looming in his peacekeeper's coat, without a veneer to hide behind, without the need for a Crow's beak or Scarecrow's mask. Bigger than the florid mountains that haunted his dreams beneath bloody skies, a towering thing that filled the breadth and scope of his vision and blocked out everything else around him. A man with pricking barbs like a legendary quill beast, barbs that brought oblivion and forgetting to everyone he sank them into.

Scarecrow.

Kemway knew it, knew the fear of death, the taste of it that followed in the air as his nemesis was left there alone. Holding still, breath sucked in and held so that he made no sound that might alert Scarecrow to his presence, he waited, he watched, and he tried to count the seconds it would take for the deadly shade to be gone.

One. Two. Three. Eight. Four. Nine. Five. Seven. Six.

The numbers jumbled, the words in his head failing to correspond to the order he thought they should be in, and with that confusion came the harder, louder, pounding of his heart.

A sharp crack, a nearby window springing open on broken coils, made him jump. It also drew the maskless, black-skinned Scarecrow's attention towards the sound, allowing Haythem the chance to sprint for freedom in the hopes that the only flapping to follow was the tails of his own coat in the swirling mist.

❧*❧

Those rumors, validated by the brute called Vanderwall when Molly sought him out in hopes of another audience with Mam, gave Molly the fodder needed for a second prodcast. He spent hours on the footage, digging through the archives for the material he wanted, tweaking the voices, the visual imagery, the light and shadow, before again hacking the Hub to upload his masterwork for Hebenon to see.

He did not know that Vanderwall did not wish to share those rumors with the Mam. He did not know why the man's minions had worked him over for stepping into the office without invitation. He did not know why Vanderwall sat silently by and watched, nor why he was forbidden to see her again. He did not know if it was her order or if the decision was Vanderwall's.

But Molly was damn sure the Mam would demand to see him as soon as she saw what he had done. She would demand the truth and Molly would give it. He would not hide it from her the way Vanderwall did. Molly would prove himself loyal and trustworthy and in doing so, intended to win his place at the Mam's side.

A single press of a button and it was done.

Vanderwall and his brako were never going to rough him up again.

❧*❧

It was the perfect bait. The perfect trap. She trusted her officers, those few the captain had informed about the stakes they were up against, not to breathe a word to anyone. There was one person, however, that she did not trust despite her desire to believe in him. This could be an ideal test of fidelity. The effort might cost her status, might cost her job, might cost her a friend, but if she could present the mole to the captain, perhaps learning in the process the true identities of the Founder's kidnappers, she believed she would, in time, be forgiven for her mistakes.

One sentence.

'The Founder's loose in the Levs.'

Then she returned to duty and waited to see what would happen.

Grainger's call irritated and upset Neoma, prompting her to pace from one side of the flat, into Ulynda's empty, unchanged bedroom and back. He was likely right and should be permitted to inspect the untouched room for details Neoma was too emotional to see, but allowing the captain or any other bugorra into her home was a violation she could not stomach. They might plant evidence to implicate her in Haythem's kidnapping. They might arrest and hold her the way they had done her husband. She remembered how she had felt when Haythem demanded a search of every space in the Uppers when seeking an intruding parah girl…the same girl, she learned, who had been in her home before Ulynda vanished. That experience had made Neoma feel sick and vulnerable, violated and anxious, feelings that returned now with a vengeance.

She hated feeling vulnerable.

There was a link to that parah. There had to be. Perhaps the parah had absconded with Ulynda through the vent. But that would require more intelligence and cunning than Neoma believed parah possessed.

Playing with the parah was no different from playing with a pet.

Outside might be livable, but the parah were uncivilized, unnatural beasts. Ulynda was surely bright enough not to follow one into the vents, regardless of Cori Tamner's unfortunate connection to one.

There was that name Grainger had mentioned, someone called Switz, but the name meant nothing to Neoma and Grainger refused to tell her whether that individual was connected to Haythem's kidnapping, Ulynda's absence, or even to Kal. She tried to remember every person she had ever met as she paced the room in the hopes that name, or a face to go with it, would come to her.

Pacing brought her nothing.

Regardless of his public statement to the contrary, made through all the right channels thus lending credibility to his words that perhaps her hackcasts did not have, she did not believe Kal's innocence. No one else could have successfully kidnapped Haythem from beneath Grainger's nose. It could not be done.

Minutes echoed past into pacing hours, the drone of the late-night prod ads selling moisturizers and cooking products and the latest fashions erasing the passage of time like so much white noise, ignored, barely recognized as meaningful sound.

Until she heard the name Kemway.

The footage was a tasteful, respectful compilation of snippets gleaned from a lifetime of Founder material shown to the citizens of Hebanthe Falls. His ascension. His marriage. Family gatherings and speeches, silent still images supported by the underpinnings of his favorite sonata and overlaid with a soothing, genderless voice continually repeating the same phrases.

The Founder is in the Levs.

The Founder is alone.

The Founder must be found.

Help him.

Neoma's hands began to shake.

Alone in the Levs.

Had Haythem taken Ulynda?

As quickly as that thought came, she crushed it between grinding teeth and stopped pacing in front of the Echo long enough to send the first message that came into her head. Kal had refused to come clean with her, but her screeching demand of "How could you let this happen?" was evidence that she refused to believe his innocence.

A second message, first met with an out-of-service code, added to her fury. She had dismissed Blayd from service, but she had not believed he would cut all communication with her. She tried again, this time reaching his message box, and though she wanted to speak to him, not leave a message he might never hear, she growled her request into the comm and then slammed her finger on the button as if the act would make her feel better and take away her frustration.

It did not.

Then a third, the only message she could think to send in the only way she knew. Desperate for someone to help where the brako, the bugorra, and even the Voices were failing, Neoma opened the front door, stepped into the falling mist and water, and screamed.

"SCARECROW!"

❧*❧

Neoma's message, coming as it did during his efforts to meditate and clear his head, went unanswered. By the time he listened to her screech of outrage, Kal had seen the newest prod and was watching it again with steepled fingers and brows knit in consternation.

Either she was furious about his public plea…or about this one. The Founder. Free and unaccompanied in the Levs.

That was a dangerous thing.

How? Why? When?

Kal had no answers. Undoubtedly, he would be blamed for this as well. The Founder kidnapped and sought was one thing. The Founder on the loose, if the stories of his madness were true, was much worse.

Surely Neoma did not believe he would be so foolish as to risk Haythem's life by letting him go…if he'd had him in his care…or by publically revealing an escape to a city as likely to ignore or kill him as they were to return him home for treatment.

He thumbed the comm button on the desk, beckoning one of his assistants to his office. There could be no delay. The parameters would change, but the search would continue. Kemway would be found.

It was time to pay the dwarf another visit.

❧ * ❧

"Again?" Exasperated, Grainger snapped at the empty air and turned the Echo off, having seen more than he cared to at the start of another day of unresolved crises. The ongoing string of prodcast hacks was grating on his nerves and he had no idea how to prevent them.

The city prod-staff failed to do so or did not care to try until he ordered it done. He needed someone like Zara to shut down such disruptions as soon as they popped, someone to upgrade the systems to prevent such hacks from occurring. Maybe if Zara, or someone like her, was on his permanent staff, he would wake up each morning without those hostile prod takeovers greeting him with bad news.

He was reluctant to reach out to her. After the way he had left her, silently as she slept without a kind word, without gratitude, without a message, he anticipated she felt used, betrayed. She probably believed he was embarrassed by their association or his own weakness.

The latter would not be far from the truth. He should not have been there, should not have stayed. He had not sought her company, but he had accepted it when he should have remained strong.

He was a user of people after all, but he was determined never to do so again. Instead, he instructed the Ximenezes to shut down all prods until further notice, shut the entire system down until it was protected against this sort of intrusion.

It would not last. People would demand their laughies, their news, their mindless drivel, and the Hub would provide. But for a few hours, perhaps, there would be blissful silence.

A summons to an interview room, where one of his officers believed a captive had something important to say, kept Grainger from turning the Echo back on to verify that his order had been obeyed.

❧ * ❧

"Where would your daughter go?"

The knock brought Neoma to the door in the hopes that Ulynda would be there, or Blayd, or even Kal or Grainger with news about her daughter, her husband, or both. There was no one to be seen when she stepped onto the walkway, however, neither left nor right on the path. The damp quickly soaked through her thin blouse and trousers as she looked up onto the rear balcony of the residence above and then below to the balcony there.

Perhaps the knock had been her expectant imagination or the vibration of a knock on another door nearby.

"Where would she go?"

The voice, the question, came from a narrow space between structures across and a half-Lev above where she stood. The alley was barely wide enough for the recycle and rubbish bins it contained on each side, with space enough for a person to squeeze between them. The bins she could see.

The speaker she could not.

She had heard that modulated voice before. It was not difficult to guess who the speaker was.

"If I knew where she…"

"Tell me what she knows. Places she would be familiar with."

Neoma nearly cried, 'nowhere' to the vexing voice, but instead, having summoned his help and knowing of no one else to turn to, she swallowed her outrage and snapped, "Nanny already looked there. The vindis for nessies. The dek. The only other places she's ever known are Up. She's never been anywhere else."

She should not be having this conversation in public. The neighbors would hear. The family to the left, however, the woman and her three children, were out, school and work having taken them somewhere else. If there was a family to her right, she had never seen or heard evidence of them. No one could be seen on the nearest walks, the nearest stairs, but that did not mean they were not there. She should have kept this conversation private.

But she could not invite Scarecrow in for drinks.

If she wanted his help, she needed to take what he offered, even if that meant talking to the public darkness.

They agreed, without it being said, that shopping for nessies and dek visits, had occurred in the nearest district. Most city residents rarely traveled further than they needed to through the damp. They also agreed that if Ulynda had gone to the Uppers, someone would have found her. Grainger would have been notified and would have, in turn, told Neoma. The child would already be safe at home.

"I will look for her."

"How do I know you don't have her? That you're not using her for…?"

But Neoma had offered no reward for her daughter as she had for Haythem. She had told no one she was missing except for Captain Grainger and she doubted Nanny would have done so. The matronly woman was too desperate for the income security of her position in Mam's household to betray her by speaking out of turn. Though Neoma's earlier bellow had been meant to draw the vigi to her door, the only way he could have known about Ulynda was if he had her, had seen her, or if the captain had told him.

So there was a connection between Grainger and the vigi.

That could be useful knowledge.

"Why else would you call for me?"

"A trap?" She paused with a sigh. "How do you know I…"

"I have resources." He had been in the shafts investigating the point of Ulynda's disappearance when the cry rang through Hebenon's streets. Rather than respond immediately, he took the time to follow the minute traces of torn fabric, the scuffs of street shoes on the shaft floor, the little things that revealed the direction Ulynda had traveled. Into the heart of Hebanthe Falls. It did not narrow down her location, but it suggested where she was not.

"What do you know?"

"Someone came through the shafts and took her."

"Why?"

"How should I know?"

"Who?"

"If not you or Kal," she snorted, "it would have to be the brako."

"Vanderwall? What's your connection…?"

"They've divided," she replied flippantly, with a dismissive wave into the air in the direction of his voice. Anyone paying attention would have realized this by now, and she assumed Scarecrow had already noticed. "Anyone threatening their power has to go. They're looking for Haythem, I imagine, and Ulynda and I are part of…"

"Then why offer a reward for him if you're afraid of them? Why not offer one for your daughter?"

Riled by questions she deemed unnecessary and self-explanatory, she snapped, "Because no one is doing their cazzing jobs! How hard can it be for so many officers to find…and now he's alone out there…"

Uninterested in her rampage, regretting the question, assuming Grainger had informed her of the Founder's latest predicament without having seen the latest prod-hack, Scarecrow growled and cut her short. "I will find her."

She did not know about his interest in finding Haythem. She did not need to know he was already looking for the man who continued to elude the bugorra. Scarecrow had never been publically interested in pursuing anyone except Crows and brako. His interest in the Founder might be suspect. Finding a missing child, however, would fit the sort of heroic act his public persona was known for.

"I will find her…and you will never lay a hand on her again."

A small sound tailed on the end of that unvoiced threat, the tremor of metal beneath feet, and he was gone.

If not for her missing daughter and Scarecrow's accusatory words, Neoma might have smiled.

Yes, Grainger had a link to Scarecrow. She wondered what it was.

෨*෫

"That guy who was here?" Tox smoothed the fabric she was working with and pressed the button on the laser line torch that lay on one side of the table. The tip of the torch, the only thing he knew of that could penetrate this particular material, began to glow deep red. He had never seen her work with the material she used exclusively for Rhyd's body armor. He assumed she was working on creating some new piece for Rhyd. Despite their previous discussion, he did not think she would waste this precious fabric on him. It was too hard to produce, too hard to come by.

It was her free day, but even on free days, Tox could be found in the backrooms of her vindi, tinkering, building, repairing, crafting. It was as much a creative passion as it was a paying job. It was why Skelter knew where to look when she was not at the counter. It was a relief that some things, in the time he had been gone, had not changed.

"Molly? Yeah…ripe piece of shit he is. Can't let the past be the past. Thinks I should stick to Spades' creed and die because I drew the fotzing ace on the inside."

"Dunno why you did that," Tox scoffed without looking at him.

"Seemed necessary at the time…the thing to do." It had been easier to gain people's trust by pretending he had nothing to lose, by keeping up the charade of a man living on borrowed time just as they were, while he regained his strength and health, gauged the Core's resources, and concocted a plan to get out. He had cut that effort short, events inside the Core conspiring against him, but it had worked out well enough. He, Otta, and Colyx were alive.

Unfortunately, so was Molly. Of all the possible survivors of that skirmish, Skelter had never imagined Molly would be one of them.

"Seems harmless."

"Mostly…but I wouldn't be the first he knifes…or poisons…for not following Spades' protocol."

"Scarecrow can jolt some sense into him."

With a crooked smile, Skelter said, "Maybe, but until then, I'd feel better if you could spare a bit of that." His hand gestured over the worktable. "Safer from him, from the brako bastards who want my head. They all think I'm an easy target." He patted the eye patch and thumped his walking stick on the floor. "I'd like to prove 'em wrong. After all the trouble I went through to get out…"

Tox looked up then, the torch in her hand white-hot for cutting. Only her eyes moved as she studied him and then she nodded. "Fair enough. Been working on other stuff for you, but I'll see what else I can do. I'll try to get you something by the end of the day."

"Wasn't meaning for today; not trying to rush you. Just…soon as you can, you know?"

"Don't worry, Ivan…I've got this. I'll take care of you."

"I'll repay you; you know I'm good for it."

He was one of her primary sources of customers, for resources, for gadgets and trinkets to repurpose and sell. He rarely asked for anything. Just as he did for his best clients, he did what he did to be repaid in kind later. He understood this was Tox's way of giving back, but he felt obliged to offer something significant. This material she had designed was not cheap.

Another supply of the resources necessary to create more would be in order.

"Stay alive, keep Rhyd alive, and we'll call it good."

"I'll do my best," he promised with a grin and a bow.

❧*❦

He could not open his eyes.

Or maybe they were open and he was blind as well as mute.

Or he was in a room so dark there was nothing to see.

Every muscle, every joint, every nerve ending screamed in such pain that he was afraid to move for fear it would make it worse.

His jaw, his mouth, felt stiff…swollen.

He was cold. He was wet.

And though there was little awareness of his surroundings except for a damp rotting plant smell that filled his nostrils and settled on his tongue with pungent bitterness, he knew something else.

He was utterly alone.

No one would ever find him.

❧Chapter 29❧

White-attired figures, white from hats and hoods to banda, to gloves and boots, crept back and forth beneath the folded metal sheeting designed to protect Hebenon from the world. No longer needed, the four mist-wraiths worked with their questionably gotten tools to cut away more of the barrier, peel it back, set Hebanthe Falls free. No one came, not bugorra, not brako from the nearby soaper, not the curious, as if the sounds of their efforts were pre-approved, pre-ordained, accepted as inevitable.

The citizens of the city in the falls had been captive too long.

The Igraci believed it was time for that captivity to end.

❧*❧

Two messages awaited Blayd when he stirred from the tranquilizing stupor the healing meds had dropped him into several hours ago. The first, from Ilya, was only surprising because it confirmed what he already knew.

The Founder was loose, unmedicated, alone in the Levs. The brevity of her message did not explain her knowledge, whether Kemway had been seen, if he was alive. The message did not ask for help and gave no clues that would help him find the Founder himself.

Unless Switz had reported the Founder's absence, a stupid thing if he hoped to protect his involvement in Kemway's captivity, it meant that someone else had seen him.

He had not been, Blayd guessed, in Scarecrow's company.

It left too many questions, too many ramifications of the man's status, for Blayd's pounding head to process.

Ignoring the second message, one he was more surprised to see, he struggled from his bed, filled his kettle in the sink, and set the pot to boil. He needed to get back out on the streets, find the Founder, before Switz or anyone else did and claimed the reward he believed he was entitled to, having been the one to abduct and protect the Founder to implicate Senior Kal as Neoma wished.

As he waited for the water to boil, he leaned his lower back against the counter and turned on the Echo to see if the prods offered any updates on the hunt for the Founder that he needed to be aware of. The monotonous voiceover that announced the Founder's newest predicament made him scowl and forced him to play the second message on his ICD. If she knew enough to make that hack, he expected her to be belligerent. If someone else had made it without her knowledge, he expected her to be furious.

Instead, it was a demand, couched in the tone of a request, summoning him to a critical meeting as soon as he was free. She sounded frantic, an unusual tone for her but an expected response to the running hackcast and he allowed a moment of hope that she felt eager for his return to her side, his employment, for some crucial duty only he could undertake.

What he did not hear that would make those things reasonable, was an apology. No apologies for the insults she had hurled, none for the lack of trust in his work, no apology for firing him for doing the duty she had tasked him to do.

Closing the message without replying as the kettle began to screech, he grumbled beneath his breath. He ate a small meal, drank his tea, and dressed, trying to work the kinks out of his aching muscles as he did so. The Echo continued to drone in the background. The medi's care had given him the strength to do what he needed to and he was eager for it.

Neoma be damned. He did not need her likely petty mission. To hell with her smug, disrespectful attitude. She claimed she did not need him the last time they had seen each other.

In his opinion, she did not need him now either.

If the entire city knew that Haythem was alone in the Levs, Blayd had something more important to do than cater to the ungrateful Mam.

❧*❧

Without needing to discuss it, to be asked or told, Zara knew the latest prod-hack, the stylized edited footage of Founder Kemway overlaid with the masked voice revealing the Founder as an escaped fugitive in the streets of Hebenon, irritated Oliver as much as it did her. Since her work at the start of the Coup, no one had dared try to hack the prods, or if they had, they had been unsuccessful. Until now. Within the span of a few short days, the system had been twice hacked with prods about Founder Kemway.

It appeared, from the duration each ran, that the city's staff was powerless to weed the haikara's work from the system, that they were powerless to prevent it. They could have been responsible for it themselves, she knew, or else they felt no reason to take it down.

Such a disruption stirred the people. Drew attention to the prods. Increased their ratings. Annoyance or not, it was good for business.

Having turned the sound off so the annoying, droning voice would not rub her nerves raw, Zara considered offering her services to build a more defensible, less easily hacked prod system. Doing so would impede her work on Rhyd's behalf, however, expose her other areas of expertise, and potentially endanger Oliver.

She decided against making the offer.

Instead, she poked around in the Hub long enough to identify the same digital footprint in the last two hacks. The haikara, whoever it was, used outdated, almost primitive, coding, but they were a master. One did not have to be up to date to be effective. She respected the craft with which the haikara produced such intricate, intimate work with outdated methods. It made her curious who they were.

The disadvantage to such methods, however, as she quickly input code and streaming bits of data, was that someone like Zara, adept with both newer and older languages and the Hub system itself, did not need long to disable the prod and block all further attempts made with that haikara's digital signature. She returned the controls to the prod director in the Uppers and shut down her system.

All without a word to, or from, Oliver.

He might not know it was her work, she thought with arms folded across her chest, but it did not matter. Such inflammatory prods would make it harder for Oliver and Rhyd to do their jobs.

Zara was satisfied to offer some service to help them.

❧*❧

His contacts with the Spinks, the best source to track an out-of-place child, eventually led to Lev 1 with tales of an unfamiliar girl seeking refuge with the herpa there. Herpa establishments were scattered throughout the Levs in their ongoing efforts to extend outreach to as many of the suffering, the undesirables, the lost, as possible. With no reliable direction as to which herpa hall on Lev 1 to choose, he was left to guess.

There was no guarantee she would still be there.

Sounds of construction greeted his descent. Having chosen to start as far from the site of his captivity and torture as he could, the sounds reminded him of Skelter's report of peculiar activity at the city's edge that he had not yet investigated. The need to find Founder Kemway, to confront the brako, to find Jaron and the missing girl, had pushed that matter out of his head, preventing him from investigating potential trouble he should have seen to sooner.

But those matters had brought him here now.

At the site of Skelter's rescue, he was surprised to find several lower panels of corrugated metal removed from Hebenon's shell, exposing the skeletal infrastructure to the splash and spray of the river. The four in white halted their stripping efforts and stared warily. Though they were masked, he could read the sudden spikes of fear in their eyes, sense the quickening of their heart rates, and the increase in the temperature of the air around their bodies revealed their anxiety.

Igraci.

"You shouldn't be here," Scarecrow began as one of the four slipped the restraining grasp of the others and charged, his pry bar raised to strike.

Mindful of the rail and the river, knowing its power firsthand, Scarecrow ducked the blow, caught the attacker's other arm, and pinned him face-first against the city's slippery skin.

"Drop it…or I'll break it."

The pry bar clattered on the grated walk.

"You're not supposed to…" he began again.

"This is not your concern, Scarecrow," countered the only woman in the group, her words crisp and succinct.

"Stopping people from destroying our city…"

"Needs to be done. People need to know the truth. It is time we leave this place."

"There are better ways than tearing Hebenon apart. Isn't safe here; the river's dangerous. Tearing down the city's dangerous. Take your things and go, or the bugorra will learn what you're doing."

Scarecrow and the woman stared at one another; though she could not see the vigi's eyes behind the protective enhancement of his eyepieces, she knew he was reading her. Eventually, she gestured to her companions to gather their tools, relenting to his demand. The Igraci knew they were no match for him.

The tilt of his head discouraged any of them from striking as they slunk past. Only when two of the four were once more inside the city's perimeter, with the woman standing at the opening through which they had come, did Scarecrow release the man he had pinned to the wall.

"I know you'll be back," he grunted, "but when you do…the bugorra will know it too."

With a sound like a chuckle, the woman gently urged the last fellow back into the city and then ducked inside as well. Scarecrow followed as far as the opening, watching and listening to be certain they left and would not immediately return, squatting in the shadows out of the way of the occasional brako going in and out of the soaper.

This sort of activity was a first, as far as he knew, for the Igraci. From the number of panels missing, they had been at this effort for several days. Typically, they were protestors, harbingers of doom, not domestic terrorists. They had never taken physical action, undertaken any form of physical destruction of property, to prompt people to vacate Hebanthe Falls.

Until recently, however, there had never been a place to vacate to.

Scarecrow ran his hand over the exposed metal edge of the sheeting, the fabric of his glove undamaged by its knife-like sharpness. He wondered if something specific had prompted this change…and if perhaps the Igraci were right.

Perhaps it was time for mankind to leave this place.

Scarecrow, however, was not going anywhere. Hebenon was his home…and he had work to do.

❧*❦

Hours passed without word from the captain, without word from Scarecrow, without news of her husband or her daughter. She knew such things took time, but it was not time she was willing to accept or give. Hebanthe Falls was a big place, with miles of walkways and shafts and hundreds of homes, vindis, manufacturing, recycling, cleaning, and food production and processing buildings. While Neoma did not believe Ulynda would go far, Haythem could be anywhere.

If Haythem had been taken, Ulynda could have been too.

Either would be lucky, she would be lucky, to be found alive.

Without them, without Blayd…who had yet to respond to the message she had finally been able to send, Neoma realized how alone in the Levs she was. How alone in Hebanthe Falls she was.

She considered making amends with Blayd if it gained the merc's support, support she reluctantly admitted she needed, but a man like that would see through the smokescreen of such efforts, her lack of sincerity and be reluctant to grant it.

A man like that, however, eager to rise in rank and status, might also accept her efforts to make peace as his ticket to power.

She believed he would.

None of that belief, however, no amount of support from the merc, or Kal, or anyone else, she thought with a sigh as she sealed the wine bottle and drank the glass she had poured, was going to bring her husband or daughter back.

❧*❧

Dressed in thick trousers with a waxy sheen that repelled moisture, water boots that did not fit but kept her feet dry, and a heavier canvas jacket that was both warmer and more water-resistant than her own had been, Ulynda left the herpa's protection while most of the others were asleep. Her focus on finding her father, her uncle, was foremost on her mind though she did not know where to begin. Not knowing what questions to ask anyone that would not endanger her, afraid that someone would take her back to her mother if her questions gave her identity away, she had eavesdropped as she ate, listening for details that might tell her what she needed to know.

The only useful snippet was one gleaned from the prodcast on the herpa hall Echo.

Her father had escaped captivity. Her father was somewhere in the Levs on his own.

Her father needed her.

Mistrustful of everyone, all Ulynda could do was wander, watching those faces not hidden by rain cloaks, listening to those conversations she could decipher, focusing on every voice she heard in the hopes of finding a familiar one.

It had been two years, but she was certain she would know her father's voice if she heard it. How big could Hebanthe Falls be? Eventually, she had to cross paths with her father.

Time after time she escaped the attention of the brako, the Talkers, the bugorra, ducking into alleys, hiding beneath vindi counters or behind carts and recycle boxes. She avoided the children with marked bandas over their mouths and noses, whenever they made eye contact and tried to approach, who then filled her ears with bird whistles as she slipped away. She guessed the sounds were akin to the made-up language she used to share with her siblings, but she did not understand it.

The symbol on their bandas had to have meaning too, but only later, when it jumped to her attention from a graffitied vindi wall, painted in brilliant yellow with the words, 'help us', did the meaning begin to clarify.

With growing hope that it could lead her to the one person most likely to help her find her father or uncle, the next time Ulynda crossed paths with two banda-wearing children slightly taller than herself, she held eye contact as long as she dared and forced herself not to move when they curiously approached.

"You're her…aren't you?"

Without knowing what the thinner of the pair of children meant, Ulynda swallowed and asked, "That…?" She pointed at the symbol on their bandas. "Is that for Scarecrow? Can you help me find him?"

The stockier child, with rosy round cheeks and eyes that sparkled to match the grin she could not see behind the banda, nodded and said, "Spinks. Yea…he's told us…he's lookin' for you."

"For…me?" Ulynda began to tremble more. Maybe he worked for her mother. Maybe he worked for the bugorra and Captain Grainger had spoken to her mother. Why else would Scarecrow be looking for her? Or did he know she was looking for him too?

Did he intend to take her home?

"I…it's not…I'm not…I'm nobody…I just…"

"You said…"

"I need to find my father…my uncle…" She wanted to trust these children but she did not know if she could. "I thought he could…"

From somewhere further up the street, out of the line of sight of where the three stood at the top of the stairs near a spener's Shed, a chaotic chorus of whistles erupted, causing other children on the street to scatter. The thinner Spink grabbed Ulynda's arm to pull her along as the other child ran in a different direction. Ulynda, frightened by the stranger's intent, yanked away hard enough to fall and almost tumble down the stairs where the first Spink had vanished. In the distance, near enough to identify but too far away to be an immediate threat, six beaked brako emerged from a side-street, armed with Crow-issued poppers, buzzers, and thumpers.

Finding Scarecrow was temporarily forgotten. Heart hammering, Ulynda tried to scramble to her feet, lost her footing on the wet grating, and tumbled down the steps, each bump and thump adding bruises to her already aching body. With the Spinks no longer nearby to help, to direct her to shelter, to take her to sources or places of protection, she ducked behind a collection of goat carts at the lower base of the spener Shed. The animals skittered, bleated at the startling interruption, but quickly resumed munching their meal of hemp stalks without giving further indication to passersby that Ulynda was hiding there.

She waited to watch the brako pass. When they started down another set of stairs and went around the corner away from the Shed, not far from where Ulynda hid, she forgot the Spinks too.

She forgot everything except fear. Panicked, she ran.

There had never been a reason to visit Maemi's hostel before, as the woman had not lived there in the years Zara had known her. Now it was the home Skelter had set up for himself with Otta, Colyx, the rescued children from the Core, and several of the youngest Spinks who possessed fewer survival skills than many of their street-wizened counterparts. She might find herself here more often if she could get over the awkwardness of nerves she felt as she approached the door. She had resisted the errand Tox asked of her at first, reluctant to face Otta should Skelter not be home. But she was curious to see how Skelter lived. Amidst too many thoughts of Oliver of late, reminders he represented of people lost and chances not taken, she realized she missed having Skelter in her life.

This visit had to be made if it was to be the first of many. A simple delivery to a friend. No ulterior motives. If Otta read more into her gesture, if Skelter did, that reading would be on them.

Although that reading would not be entirely wrong.

"Zar!" Skelter greeted her with his usual tight embrace as if nothing between them had changed. The woman behind him, seated on the floor building a bench from a collection of materials scavenged from the nearest Levs, looked up and nodded without a trace of upset, jealousy, or annoyance.

She was secure in her relationship with Skelter; Zara could see it. "Come in."

"I can't stay; I have to get back to Vapors. But Tox asked me to bring you this."

The unwrapped, wide-footed walking stick, better designed for Hebenon's grated streets than the stick Skelter had been using, sported an intricately carved fanged adder's head as its handle. When twisted, the cane separated to reveal a narrow blade hidden inside, the sort of weapon Skelter had imagined possessing in his efforts to regain the regal, old-world appearance he had once sported. It complimented the embroidered frock coat and long-sleeved, lace-collared shirt recently acquired and made him grin madly.

From the wrapped bundle Zara offered, he removed two more items. The undervest, lined with soft treated hemp to prevent chafing, was fabricated from the material Tox used for Scarecrow's body armor. There was no elaborate detail to the design and it would not protect his limbs, his neck, or his head, but it would protect his vital organs from any torso assault the brako or Molly chose to aim at him.

"She's working on more," Zara said as he studied the vest. "This is the best she could offer on short notice."

"It'll do," Skelter assured her, setting it down and leaning nearer to kiss Zara's cheek again. "Anything that keeps me alive."

"Alive is preferred," she agreed, resisting a glance at Otta in case she took offense at Zara's earnest concern or Skelter's look of rapport.

The final item from the package was a leather-encased monocle adorned along the strap with an array of silvery grommets, rivets, and stylized metal threads that barely masked the tech between the layers. He removed the patch he had worn in the core, secured the strap of the monocle around his head, and whistled low in appreciation.

Whatever Tax had done between the leather layers, he could see more clearly through his injured eye and, if he focused, he realized he could see details around the room he had not noticed before. On the periphery was a digitized display of temperature readings, distance and height figures, and an unexpected blinking that began as one of the children crossed the room behind him.

The display was distracting, but he could imagine the usefulness such information might have in the dark streets.

Scarecrow used such tech all the time.

"This'll do. This'll do real good," he said with murmured awe and a nod. He began to say something else but changed his mind. "If you can wait a few, I'll join you. Need to speak with Maemi anyhow."

He preferred to thank Tox in person for the short-notice gifts. Accompanying Zara to Vapors would allow him to make that stop and test his new toys.

It might even give him the chance to put Molly in his place and be done with that particular threat.

❧*❧

Despite the decision not to respond, to allow Neoma to stew in frustration and regret her decision to fire him, Blayd found himself in the woman's living room, the flat silent except for the bustling sounds of Nanny in the kitchen. The servant had welcomed him in, had said the Mam would be with him shortly, and then left him without any indication where Neoma was or when she might arrive.

He should have called, told her he was coming. But showing up at her door had been a spur-of-the-moment choice when his hunt for the Founder brought him close to this flat.

He was here, but his limited patience would not allow him to wait for long. Only knowing that coming unannounced was his doing allowed him to wait at all.

"Blayd!" He could not tell, when Neoma came through the door, her coat dripping and her arms full of purchases she seldom made herself, if the word was an exclamation of surprise, of anger, or joy and relief. Maybe it carried all of those emotions bound together. To be polite, he offered to take some of what she carried and set the packages on the sofa table as she put hers down and removed her coat and boots. But he did not speak until she finished, turned, and offered her hand. "You came."

Her hand was icy when he clasped it. She had been outside for some time. "You asked me to meet you. Said it's important?"

His gruff tone, despite the handshake, reminded her of the unfriendly terms on which they had parted, and reminded her that, whether she had slighted him or not, he had failed in his duty and she would not tolerate failure.

Dispensing with small talk, without the offer of a drink as she typically led business transactions with, refusing to give him the satisfaction of an apology or some appearance of groveling and kowtowing, Neoma flipped her head so that her hair fell again into place before saying, "I want you to find my daughter."

Blayd studied her, gauging her sincerity, wondering what had happened to Ulynda, what Neoma would offer in return, or how she would reciprocate such a favor.

Finding his silence unpleasant, she added, "She has been missing for more than a day. Captain Grainger has failed to locate her."

She did not mention Scarecrow. It was a detail best left out.

"You failed to bring me Haythem or Kal but surely you can…"

"No."

"…find one child. Your position will be open if you…no?" Her brain caught up to the single word he uttered. Eyes narrowed, she stalked across the distance between them until she stared icily into his face. Blayd did not move. "What do you mean no?"

"Exactly that. No." No, he would not take his position back, regardless of how tempting the offer was. No, he would not be responsible for finding her daughter, although he had nothing against the girl and did not wish harm to come to her. He would continue his search for Haythem because he had lost him to Scarecrow, because he had a score to settle with Senior Kal, because he had been the one to take him and for the reward she offered. If he found Ulynda in the process, he would make sure she was safe. Afterward, however, he would be done with Neoma and the Kemways.

Not so many days ago, he had been willing to do anything for her.

Now, for reasons he did not entirely understand nor care to think about, he wanted no connection to her.

She was not the only path to power. Everything around them was changing and it was time to forge a new path.

"I've got things to do. If I see her, find her, you'll get her back. Or I'll let you know where she is. But I've got more important things…"

"I'm not paying you a reward for bringing me Haythem," she hissed. "Not when it was your responsibility to protect him from…"

"That's just it," he hissed, jaw clenched, fists curled at his side. "You're not paying me anything."

He moved around her and opened the door, allowing a cold swirl to push inside that mirrored the chill of her words and his that followed. "I don't need you or your reward, Mam…and you're not the only one looking for him. Whatever I find…whenever I find him…I've no obligation to bring him to…"

"You wouldn't dare."

Be it brako, bugorra, or Senior Kal, Blayd had options. Neoma's brashness only removed one of them.

"I would…and I will."

The words hung in the air as the door slammed between them.

"Scarecrow ain't nothing."

Jonner turned in his folding chair to eye the speaker, noting in doing so that Eido was staring at the robust fellow with the cool annoyance of a parent losing patience with their interrupting child. He had heard references to Scarecrow bandied about on the streets, a vigi who fought on the side of the oppressed, the sort of man Jonner would like to meet. A group like the Igraci that encouraged people to bigger, greater achievements ought to be the sort of organization such a vigi would support.

In this instance, Jonner agreed with him. Shutting down the dismantling of Hebenon's shell was the wisest course of action.

"Southern wall's there to keep the city together, protects us like a clam shell," he muttered, expecting Eido to give him, the neophyte in the group, the same cool, side-eyed glance. "Take the shell away and it destabilizes everything. He's right. Can't take it down while there's people in here. We risk bringing down the city, killing everyone."

The first speaker scoffed. "Some sheets of metal aren't gonna…"

"Still don't know how the plan's going to encourage anyone to leave," interjected someone else.

At least a dozen heads throughout the room packed with white attired Igraci bobbed in agreement. For a first proactive action to encourage mankind to evacuate the Fall City, the idea of stripping the shell away and exposing the interior to Outside did not seem logical to many and seemed the perfect solution to others.

"Did you do a survey? Look at the city plans? Look where the load points are before you started to…?"

"Suppose you know how to…?"

Jonner shrugged. "Know a thing or two. Enough to say that if you want to tear Hebenon down, you gotta empty her first."

Eido, who had not interrupted Jonner's takeover of the dialogue, shifted her crossed legs so that her entire body turned towards him. With an elbow on the back of her chair and her chin on her fist, she asked, "How do we accomplish such a thing? Little steps, little exposures, little failings…encouraging a few at a time…?"

"Why not wider?" Jonner looked around the room at the array of discontented faces. Having just escaped one prison not of his making, he was eager to escape the prison of Hebanthe Falls too and he was willing to help as he had helped those inside the Core.

He wanted to encourage Maemi to move out into the world too.

That was not going to be easy.

"Any of you been outside?"

Not quite a dozen hands lifted into the air, including the young woman who had introduced Jonner to Eido.

"How many of you have even seen it?"

More hands went up, people who had made it to the open doors or to public spaces in the Uppers with windows to view the outside world. They had not, however, dared to step beyond the city's shell despite their belief that going out was what mankind needed to do.

How could they coax others out if they had not been there themselves? For an organization encouraging human expansion, Jonner had expected the numbers of both groups to be higher.

"You seen the rivers?"

Heads bobbed.

Once more looking at Eido, Jonner shrugged. "Hebenon needs the Falls. For power. For food. It would take time…but we could do it. Enough of us together…far enough up the rivers so the parah don't see. We stop the water…and everyone here will have to go."

It would only take one person discovering their activities, some well-placed response to counteract their efforts to restart the flow. If they tried such a thing, they would have to take care not to flood the farmland and homes, to kill anyone already living outside of Hebanthe Falls. His suggestion might not be practical, with four rivers to dam without anyone being aware of their efforts, but it was primarily intended to encourage the others to think in broader terms.

Eido nodded with a thoughtful expression as the talk in the room devolved into one preposterous idea after another. The ideas themselves did not yet matter. With Jonner's influence, the Igraci could evolve from a talking organization into a doing one.

By the end of the meeting, he hoped they would have a half-dozen potentially viable actions they could take, thorns they could lodge beneath Hebenon's skin to prompt its citizens to action.

Eido, Jonner could see, appreciated his influence.

❧Chapter 30❧

The floor beneath Grainger's feet shuddered. The walls shook. The room swayed with a force he had never felt and the domed windows overhead creaked and vibrated to the explosive sound that pulled him around in his chair to the sight of black smoke billowing from one wing of Factory West 2.

"What is that?" he roared as he leaped to his feet, hoping that at least one member of his staff was near enough to hear him, knew enough to give him answers, even though the event had just occurred and was unfolding before his eyes. In the corridors outside his office, the clatter of running footsteps added to the tremors. Face and hand pressed to the window as if it would allow him to see more clearly, he caught an eruptive flash at the periphery of his line of sight, somewhere amidst the solar array on the dome of the city.

Then, other than the sunlight beaming in from the blue, cloudless sky, the lights in the room flickered, dimmed, and went out, taking the Echosys and the hum of Hebenon's systems with them.

People scattered and scurried, the bi-monthly fire drills falling immediately into effect as flames devoured the storage facility door and began to lick at the contents behind it. What was burning, what they stood to lose, was at the bottom of everyone's list of concerns.

Lost supplies could be replaced, perhaps at the expense of productivity or a shortage pinch the city would feel, but replaced. If the fire spread beyond the storage area, if it made it into the west factories, the potential economic devastation would be overwhelming.

Other boots scrambled elsewhere, those familiar with the solar power systems donning the harnesses that allowed them to work on the dome without fear of falling. Gone was the need for protective haz suits and breathing equipment. Hatches opened, workers poured out like ants across the ground to determine the location of the failure that had plunged a significant portion of Hebanthe Falls into darkness.

꙰*꙰

Ilya stumbled out of her shower, tripped on the lip that kept the water from splashing across the floor, and narrowly missed cracking her head against the sink as she fell, knocked down by the shaking of Hebenon's many levels and the unexpected shock of darkness. There was a shot of pain up her arm where it struck the sink, and up from her elbow to her shoulder as she braced her fall with the other. There were likely fractures there, but she had no time to think about it.

There was no emergency lighting as she fumbled for the door and dragged herself through it, still wet and soapy, into the bedroom. Without power, the shower had ceased running behind her. She moved by rote memory of a flat that had changed little in all of the years she had lived in it, until she found her uniform, her utility belt, and then the buzzer hanging from it which, by an adjustment of the settings switch, allowed for a flickering but functional light source.

She set the buzzer on the dresser long enough to swipe the bedsheets over her damp skin. As she began to pull her uniform on, fearing some city-wide emergency that would prompt a summons from the captain, the lights in her bedroom, the kitchen, and in the bathroom where she had been, popped back to life.

The water system's failsafe prevented the shower from turning on.

The now feeble glow of primary lighting, barely half of what it normally was, told her that something was very wrong.

꙰*꙰

"Stay calm," Maemi called from behind the bar, the sudden blackout a startling thing even to those accustomed to the semi-dark world of shadows in the Levs. Alglamps continued to glow but the world of neon was at the mercy of the power grid.

So were the circulation fans and the sound system.

"Anything I can do?" asked Jonner from across the counter, nursing his drink in both hands as if afraid that an effort to set it down would result in it dropping into his lap or allow someone else to swipe it. His voice sounded nervous, frayed, and his gaze strained to find the only person in the club he knew.

Only a faint hint of light from an alglamp outside the beaded curtain gave her face illumination.

No wonder he seemed troubled, Maemi thought as she busied herself. After the tails he had told, she imagined he had known more than his share of darkness in the Core. She shook her head though doubted he could see the gesture easily. "No. No worries, mpenzi. Quakes happen, take the power with them sometimes." Though never, she admitted with swallowed anxiety, for quite this long. "Just a few more minutes…ah…maintenance fell short no doubt…or the shake loosed something they have to fix. Happens sometimes. Here. Here it is. Lights will be back on soon."

She flipped on the portable lantern found beneath her bar, kept for instances such as this. It illuminated the counter, reflected off the mirrored surface behind so that it thrust an additional glow into the room moments before a hiss and sizzle in the neon tubes around them brought the lighting back to life.

The lights were on, startling multicolored brightness in the black. The filt and air systems wheezed back on but the sound system did not reinitiate. It took little effort to realize, however, that the world around them, even with the lantern upon the counter, was dimmer than it had been before.

Colyx blocked the door, disallowing anyone from coming or going, his eyes, as though he had been able to see in the dark, barely leaving the man seated at the bar.

❧*❧

Grainger's breath of relief, when the flow of power switched from the split hydro and solar system to lay the burden entirely on the hydro generators, was met with a beep on his wrist, an incoming ICD message he hoped would bring answers and better than expected news. This was not the first time power issues had arisen in the city. It would not likely be the last. But each time it occurred, it came with the fears that the city's age had finally caught up with it. Following as it did on the heels of the fire that continued to belch smoke where there were no doors or windows to permit its proper release into the outside air, however, was worrisome.

"Inverter's failed, Captain," said an unidentifiable voice over the comm, the sound muffled by background dialogue and a sounds so recognizable as burning electronics and wiring that Grainger could almost smell melting plastic and metal contacts.

"Then replace it," he barked. "Hydros won't carry us long."

Once upon a time, they might have, when the city was young.

But not any longer.

"We're on it."

A second beep. A second voice. Storage fire. Unknown origin or source. Impossible to determine the damage until the flames were knocked down.

Grainger was still on his feet but there was nothing he could do to help in either location. The best thing he could do was field the calls that flooded his Echo, the citywide requests for information he did not yet have. He could not provide information but he could assure everyone that things were under control.

And he did.

Even though they were not.

❧*❦

"Keep 'em in."

"You shouldn't be out alone…"

The main room of the hostel, transforming gradually into a communal living space for the evolving family as Skelter brought back objects and materials to create furnishings with, was filled with the comforting sounds of children pecking at their morning meal and squabbling amongst themselves as if they had always been siblings. The room was lit by the gentle radiance of an alglamp on the table, allowing those in the room to see despite the power hit. The now dark Echosys and the diminishing glow of the burner beneath the kettle, and the fading shudder of the city's metal bones, continued to announce what had happened and though the children looked up with the sudden loss of sound and light from the Echo, they resumed eating, laughing, and teasing each other.

The children from the Core were used to frequent power outages. The street kids, used to a dim world, barely noticed. They were less troubled by what was going on than the adults were.

"Wanna take a look." Skelter did not expect to see anything, especially as the burner beneath the kettle began to glow again. The Echo did not turn on by itself, but the filt systems did. Turning the Echo on when he awoke was an old habit, an old routine from before the Coup, before the Core, when beginning the day with prodcasts required by the Founder and Doctet was expected. For Otta, the rescued children, and the Spinks, the luxury of an Echo they could watch without standing in the cold was a marvel.

"And I've got clients." He kissed her mouth and fingered the bangs that dropped forward on the left side of her face, blue now and longer than the buzzed short cut on the right side of her head. "They aren't gonna wait, power out or not. I'll take care of business, take a look and be back. Shouldn't take long."

Otta grunted. She was used to fighting for her survival, for what she needed, used to fighting for him. Now her fight was of a different sort, protecting a multitude of inherited children and the one she carried. She needed to be here but felt she belonged at Skelter's side, particularly since others were looking to take his life.

She was not happy, he knew as he went out, to be left behind.

☙*❧

Rhyd felt the shudder of Hebenon's skeleton as it coursed through the enhanced sensors of his body armor, felt it shimmy into his sore bones moments before the power drop registered in the systems humming around him. Here in the shafts, where it took power to manage heating, water, waste, airflow, and dehumidifying systems, anyone trained to tend those things learned to hear the subtle differences that came with blockages and changes in power. Such drops were not uncommon as parts failed or required maintenance that necessitated a switch between generators to complete.

This time, when the power was restored, there was a noticeable whine, a strain in the system, an increased draw on the hydroelectric units as they struggled to meet Hebenon's power demand.

Shaft lighting was dimmer than before.

The power buzzing through insulated wiring, while flowing harder, was not sufficient to support each system, to meet each draw request, at full capacity.

There was little chance to ponder it as the pair of brako met in this shaft charged again. They were not looking for him but rather for Founder Kemway, but no brako would pass on the chance to remove the vigi scourge that plagued their business activities.

Half a dozen punches later, without having to resort to his thumper, their crumpled bird-masked forms lay scattered on the metal floor. At the mouth of this particular shaft, a cluster of Spinks watched the fight with awed expressions of delight and when the battle was over and the brako lay still, the Spinks waved Scarecrow closer.

With his little army scouring the city on his behalf, he hoped their summons meant they had news he could use. Every minute that passed with father and daughter in the streets meant one less they had to live. Though he knew of no one specifically who wanted the Founder dead, he knew some would twist that to their advantage. Any child out here, without a streeter's experience, was prey for all manners of depravity.

"There's a girl," started one.

"Looking for you," piped another.

A third, "We found her on Lev 4 by the recycle, but the brako came and she ran."

"She asked for you, said something about her father and uncle…"

Behind the mask, Rhyd frowned. Did Ulynda know about Enoch? Did that mean Neoma did as well?

He did not believe that would be to the dwarf's benefit.

The Spinks continued. "She didn't give her name…"

"…but she's not one of us…"

"…seemed cazzing lost…"

Another child elbowed that one in the ribs for swearing and he hastily mumbled an apology.

It had to be Ulynda. Agnys would know where to find him, who to talk to if she needed him.

"I know where it is," he said with a nod about the recycle station on Lev 4. Perhaps the girl would not be there by the time he arrived, but it was the first clue of a location he had been given. It would be easier, he hoped, to track her from there. "Keep looking; find her. Send for me when you do and keep her safe. Whistle. I'll come."

He did not know their birdcalls, but he had identified which sounds meant brako, which meant bugorra, and assumed that, by following the whistles, he would trace it to the summoning Spinks.

"We will," one of the kids promised.

"And the Founder," swore another.

"If you see brako, stay clear of them. Don't let them catch you."

"They never do," the boy who swore earlier said cockily before the group scattered back into the street.

Scarecrow remained in the shaft. While he would continue to cross paths with the brako here, the more he incapacitated the fewer he would have to contend with when he emerged into the street. He could reach Ulynda's last known location faster in the shafts and with luck, she would not have gone very far.

❧*❧

"Prime inverter's fried, Captain…"

"Then fix it!" Grainger barked at the stoop-backed man who followed on Lieutenant Young's heels to make his report. Tamner was seated on the other side of the desk, there to view the anonymously received data about the four unidentified men killed during the abduction of Founder Kemway; he looked up at the exchange with a scowl but did not speak.

"They can't, sir. The explosion in West Factory storage burned two vaults…the ones with the supply of solar panels and equipment," Ilya said grimly, not having realized that the news she bore had any relation to the power issues in play throughout the city. It had taken nearly three hours to suppress the fire, make certain no hotspots remained, and ascertain what damage had been done, what goods had been lost. Power in the Factories, supplied by their own solar arrays and systems, had not been affected but if the Uppers were running dim on reduced power, the Levs were too.

The panel worker frowned. "That's not…all of it?"

"Unless there's more stored elsewhere or any of its salvageable," Ilya replied.

"What?" huffed Grainger. If there was more bad news, he preferred to hear it, not guess.

The worker wiped his red nose on a square of checkered cloth that he pushed back into his pocket as he nervously shrugged. "A lot of data, the diagrams and schematics, for the arrays, was lost in the Hub crash. We've been working on recreating everything, but we lost a lot of our best minds too…and it's been slow. Having backup units and parts in storage…there hasn't been a rush to…"

His apologetic tone did nothing to offset the rising annoyance and outrage on Grainger's face. "Obviously, there should have been…"

"Obviously," the worker agreed. In hindsight, they should have done a lot of things differently.

"There's no one who can…?"

"I might know someone." Tamner rubbed his hand over his face. What he was about to suggest was risky, but if the manpower, the skill to repair the array was lacking, there were few other options.

Grainger barked, "Who?"

"He was a solar engineer and tech under the…years ago. One of the most brilliant men I know. He's…retired." It was the easiest way to explain the man's precarious position. "If anyone can recreate those schematics or work without them, I think he can. If I talk to him…"

Grainger did not need a name, a face, an identity. He only needed the repairs made before the city lost all power and he trusted Tamner to know what he was talking about. "Talk to him; get him on it. Whatever you have to promise him. The hydros aren't meant to sustain the city. If they go down, we'll lose everything."

Tamner was already out of his chair with a nod, contemplating how best to present this responsibility to the man in question, whether he could find him fast enough to make a difference, whether he would be willing to help.

"And you," Grainger pointed at the panel worker, unable to recall if the fellow had given his name, "re-evaluate what we need, what we've got, what we can scavenge…what's wrong with the array…so this engineer will have what he needs when he gets here."

Echo images being discussed with Tamner forgotten, Grainger got up with a growl. "Lieutenant, reinforce the Lev units as best you can, make sure they have the support they need." He did not need to monitor the flood of incoming reports to anticipate that the brako would take advantage of citywide power problems. While he knew Ilya wanted to try her hand at sorting out the cause of the fire, with so much else at stake, that was a job best left to the fire experts. Her fellow officers needed someone to lead them. Grainger was still recovering from his injuries and was going to have his hands full here.

It left the situation in the Levs in Lieutenant Young's care.

"Do I have permission to conscript off-duty Factory personnel?"

"I'll have word with the foremen and get you what you need." He would also need to discuss operations in the factories because of the fire. If they needed to suspend production to prepare for the emergency fabrication of solar parts, they needed to begin doing so now.

It was also, he decided, a good time to discuss the temporary suspension of all other Factory operations and the rerouting of power into Hebanthe Falls. The less demand there was for power in the Uppers and Levs because of it, the less draw there would be on the hydros and the longer the city could function. It was not an ideal solution, but it was the only one Grainger had.

Delegating a debate to the Nau for answers would take too long.

＊

As Skelter wound his way to the stairs that would take him to Vapors, he passed through clusters of neighbors outside of their flats, around those seeking shake damage or damage to the power systems visible outside of their homes. People wanted an explanation for the noticeable dimness of the light levels, the slowing of fans the reduction of warmth being bled into their homes and vindis, the trickling flow of water in sinks and showers. As was often the case in times of power cuts, non-essential Echos remained dark and deks shut down.

The outage lasted less than two minutes but the decreased power, when it returned, was a concern that filled each gathering with gossip.

Had there been another explosion like those rumored to have occurred during the recital? If so, where had they happened? There was abundant suspicion, for the captain and Nau had remained cagey with their explanations of that night's events. Was this another quake, one strong enough, after the previous shaking, to damage the power grid? Were the brako to blame? The bugorra? The parah?

On those same street corners, fanning the flames of fear, the Igraci gathered. The curious, the bored, the fearful, clustered to listen.

Hebenon was deteriorating, they said.

Hebenon could no longer sustain humanity.

Hebenon was telling them it was time to return to the world. Time to move into the world, to cease relying on the artificial and begin life anew where they were meant to live.

The loss of the Founder was an omen. The old order was dying so that a new one could be born.

The role of Hebanthe Falls in the annals of history was at an end.

Paranoia, Skelter thought with a shake of his head. There were always those willing to feast on it.

Until he rooted out some official word, he was not going to buy into what they said.

He had not escaped the Core to have his city collapse around him.

❧*❧

The maintenance systems of Hebanthe Falls, incorporated during the primary building phase of the city, had run continuously since before the doors closed a selected cluster of humanity inside the great metal shell. As the rivers carved deeper into the earth, layers of city were added above and below and the access to Outside shifted. With each adjustment, the systems adapted to provide clean air, water, and a steady supply of power to every facility the city housed. The Four Falls provided an ongoing influx of hydroelectricity, a resource working in tandem with the abundance of solar arrays across the city's dome and the rooftops of Factories East and West.

There had been glitches. Equipment failures as parts aged and weakened, lighting strikes and breakage resulting from blowing debris, dust, wind, storms, and other acts of nature. People were trained from the first day of design to meet these challenges, to repair the equipment, correct issues, and manufacture and install new parts as necessary. Tech evolved, was upgraded, and repair capacity changed with it.

Such maintenance took time. Men and machines could only work so quickly to replace or repair broken parts and non-working units. But the Founder and Doctet had always made certain there was a supply of both on hand to do these things without significant delays.

The matter of repairs and maintenance had never crossed Grainger's mind. He was a peacekeeper, a law officer, not a city planner. Like so many others, he daily took for granted that the systems ran to keep the city functioning, without thinking about how they did so. And like many members of the Nau, he had assumed there were parts on hand and time to build more as necessary. Compared to restoring order to the city and stabilizing production after the loss of so many lives, rebuilding the Hub database, reconstructing schematics and city plans, had seemed less imperative than establishing stability after the Coup.

It was easy to assume all was well.

No one anticipated that a storage fire would destroy every piece of solar equipment on hand.

Grainger frowned as he watched the man studying the SCAM footage taken of the failed array by the crews who had been outside inspecting it. He had seen the long-haired man before, seated at a table in Vapors with Ballard, Zara, Jaron, and others. He assumed that Tamner, therefore, also knew those people and he wondered, after a glance at the doctor who was likewise studying the schematics over the engineer's shoulder, how many other secrets Tamner kept.

There had never been a need to know. Before the Coup, they were nothing to one another. With a grunt of annoyance, Grainger realized that until now, Tamner's life had been none of his business.

He did not know the blonde man's name, his history. As thin as he was, the way his leathery skin seemed to be sliding from his frame, Grainger could not imagine he had ever been a solar engineer or tech. Dressed in dirty trousers and a hempleather vest, his stringy hair tied back from his face, he looked more like a streeter than a man of learning and science.

Retirement, voluntary or forced, must not have been kind to him.

"That's not right."

Blinking at the oddity of the man's speech, the stilted quality that barely masked his impediment, Grainger asked, "What's not right?

"That." Lash pointed at one of the still images after enlarging it to better study the damaged area. "Can't think of one cazzing thing that could sheer or burn a board like that…nothing natural at least."

The stooped tech leaned across Lash's back to more closely examine the damage he had seen with his own eyes when he had recorded those images.

"Someone sabotaged the inverter?" the tech croaked. Sabotage simultaneous to a fire in the solar storage did not sound coincidental.

"Saying it didn't happen by itself." Perhaps an exceptionally strong wind had sheered the unit, or some airborne animal or windswept debris had generated the failure. Lash could not place blame or point fingers, but he knew it had not failed on its own.

"Lieutenant," Grainger snapped into his comm. "Get me all SCAM footage of the dome, starting today and working back. I want to know if anyone other than our crews has had access to the array…when our crews were out there last. Same for the storages."

He did not give Ilya a chance to reply before glowering at the man beside him. "Can you fix it?"

Lash shrugged. "It'll take time…I can redraw it…redesign it…but with this," he tapped the leg that was the cause of his limp, "going up would be a struggle…"

"Do you need to redraw it first to fix it?"

Brow cocked, Lash side-eyed the captain. "I can fabricate a fix without schematics, something that should be enough to take the strain off the hydros while I draw things up and new parts are fabricated. I can talk someone through replacement…"

"Do it. Whatever it takes. Whatever you need. He'll take you…"

Lash's irritated expression stretched thin. He never thought he would be in the Uppers again after the way he had been expelled. He trusted his qualifications and skills, both to make the repairs and to rebuild the database, despite the years since he had last had to do so, but did he want to?

Wanting did not matter. He had been asked to try. The city needed the best. The city needed someone. Needed him. But he would not go out on the shell again. That would be suicide.

"I know the way."

Knowing the way to restricted areas was not the same as having access to places where he had once freely worked. After glancing at the tech, a face he did not remember, he nodded as Grainger said, "He'll get you tools, parts…anything you need."

"Give me a workspace," Lash relented, "and stay out of my way. Let me work."

Grainger growled.

Lash held his gaze steady, defying the captain to challenge him.

With a huff, Grainger eventually snorted, "Tell me when it's done," before stomping out of the room.

If the man did his job, he would not need to tell Grainger anything. The evidence would be there in the brightening of the city lights.

Grainger had forgotten Tamner was there.

❧Chapter 31❦

Patrons produced a variety of P1 and T2 Echos operating on battery power to provide additional lighting in Vapors while Colyx glowered by the door at anyone wanting to enter who looked interested in causing trouble. Shouts and cries of fear and the sounds of physical altercations reverberated through the maze of Lev streets as those with ill intent took advantage of the reduced lighting. Brako roamed past the club in twos and threes, turning their heads to peer towards Vapors door without making an effort to enter. The hulking man with the braces on his legs was satisfied that he was the deterrent that kept them at bay but perhaps they had somewhere else to be. There were certainly a lot of them.

He and the other patrons would see that there was no trouble here. Rather than risk the tumultuous streets with its uncertain security, they chose to remain where they were. They were safer here than they were out amongst the unseen troubles they could hear through the roar of the falls now that the sound system in the club had shut off. The restoration of power was not enough to allow for the sound system, a secondary, non-essential power draw the straining systems did not need to endure, but someone took the initiative to play music on their T2 and the andi dancers mingled with the guests, dancing and chatting with the patrons to keep the mood calm.

"Takin' 'em long enough. Maybe I should go see…"

Maemi swiped her rag over the sticky bar, turned the nearest P2 so that it illuminated the counter, and snorted. With no prods running, there was no news about either the shaking or the power issues.

"I'm sure everyone else has the same idea," she scolded the speaker in a friendly tone. "It'll right itself soon."

Another patron, waiting for a swiver to refill his glass, snorted and asked, "Think if you say it enough it'll be true?"

"They're trying to drive us out of our homes," said a woman's shrill voice from his other side. "Want us to go into the poisoned…"

"Not poisoned," grunted the taller of a pair of men who looked to be brothers as both plopped empty glasses on the counter for refilling. "Bet you haven't even seen…"

The woman huffed and tipped up her nose. "Don't need to see it. The Founder said…"

"poq Gai," the shorter brother countered. "Kistama is a cazzing fotz. Lies…all lies…"

"We're safer in here…"

"I've seen it," the shorter brother continued despite the interruption. "I've been there. Think it's 'bout time we all go out."

His brother agreed. "We're not made to stay here forever…not meant to be trapped. It wasn't what the first Founder…"

"Komeada," she spat, pushing him away with more than adequate force. "You'll kill us all with your…"

A throaty growl cut her off as Colyx's shadow loomed over them, ending the bubbling hostilities. As empty glasses were filled, the patrons drifted back to their tables, but Colyx did not move until only Jonner remained. Though the bouncer's stern gaze did not waver, Jonner made no effort to move. He had been in that seat before the argument had ensued, had not participated in it, and he expected Colyx to see that he had no ill-intent or inclination towards trouble. He had not been one to cause trouble inside the Core. He intended none now.

Colyx growled again and thumped away.

"May be right though," Jonner eventually murmured.

Maemi did not ask what he meant as she sighed, topped off his glass, and put the bottle back on the shelf. "I know…now that we can. But," she shrugged, "she's not the only one not ready for the change. Been so much in the last few years…of course they're afraid."

Jonner sipped his drink and looked at the struggling neon lights above the bar mirror without shifting his head. "Might not have a choice. May come down to that one day."

Maemi met his gaze and nodded.

Hebenon without power, if it came to that, would be a world no one could live in. It would mean abandoning the city…or die. She, like so many others however, was not ready to make that decision.

❧*❧

Her heart hammered, the temporary darkness reminding her of the night she lost her father, the night she was locked away in a Factory with her mother and siblings, the night the world she had known had ended. More pressing than the darkness, however, was the heavy steps of braco, men she was sure had seen her, who continued their pursuit despite the dark as if their eyepieces allowed them to pierce the veil to permit movement even without light. They might be able to see her, but except for the feeble glow of occasional alglamps here, she could not easily see them…or find her way through the city.

She could only hear them, their ponderous steps, their mechanical breathing. She could only listen, terrified, as she pressed herself flat against the wall in the crevice where she had hidden with the hope that the clatter her feet made when she stepped over rubbish and recycle bins would be mistaken for a rat or cat. She prayed they were not looking for her, were only passing by.

When the slow glow of neon again warmed the air and misted the streets with the evaporation of accumulated moisture, she could see how near the braco had come. Too close. With her pounding heart stealing her breath, she leaped from her inadequate shelter and ran.

She lost track of where she was. How many stairs and streets and alleys she had run down, climbed, turned through. What Lev was she on? Her vision had tunneled to what was directly before her and her ears tuned out nearly every sound except for her heartbeat and the thump of braco boots.

There were voices in the distance. Many voices, chanting and loud. Hurried steps charging up nearby stairs. Perhaps the person on the stairs would distract the braco. If she reached those voices before the braco reached her, the crowd might afford her protection. She had to find shelter long enough to catch her breath. She had to find safety long enough to make a new plan.

Enoch could not have anticipated being in the streets, summoned to the Lair by the woman who had yet to commit to a job arrangement with Skelter, when the city disappeared into darkness. The stretch of street he was on had no functioning alglamps, so for several anxious heartbeats he remained still, breath held in straining lungs, listening to the Four Falls, the river, and somewhere on the Lev above him, the anxious voices of a gathered crowd trying to decide what to do next.

He was not afraid of the dark. His tunnel in and out of the Core had always been dark and the Core had often endured blackouts when equipment failed or it was deemed crucial to conserve their meager resources. In Hebenon, however, one wrong step in the dark could mean a fall to one's death and Enoch had better plans for his life than dying from a tumble onto a roof or into the river.

The churning of the hydros picking up the additional output load brought with it the burning faint glow of neon and the skittering murmur of dragging feet in the gloom. Someone was following him. If they had been there before the power loss, he had not noticed. Or maybe it was someone exposed when the lights came back on who decided to retreat. A glance to his left caught the perceived shape of a beaked shade withdrawing into a nearby alley.

For several moments, Enoch did not move as he waited for the threat to reemerge. None did. On the off chance that it was waiting, watching, just as he was, he decided that the meeting he was scheduled to attend was not worth the cost of his life.

Let her come to him.

He preferred to avoid death at the hands of the brako as much as he did the pounding of the river.

He rushed on, twisting through the streets, shimmying through spaces too small for a normal man to fit. But he realized he lost one tail only to pick up another, until he was certain the brako, if that's who they were, were relaying his location and route to one another, herding him through fear to someplace they could trap him without anywhere to run. Unable to elude them forever, he decided to get off the street, to find shelter somewhere they might be reluctant to go.

Vapors.

He usually felt safest there.

Another course change brought him up the nearest stairway as something whirred past his head and clattered against the building next to him. Enoch did not see it, but from the ringing sound the strike made, he wagered the projectile had been sharp, pointed…a stinger of some sort. He reached the platform, ran half a dozen steps towards the lift midway along the street, and ducked sideways to avoid a second projectile and the youngster who darted across his path away from gloved hands that might have been reaching for her or, judging by the beaked silhouette, might have been after him.

He drew up short in surprise.

Duty was duty. Duty had brought her here with only one officer at her side. Her forces were stretched too thin to lay a blanketing presence of order and law, to reassure the people of their safety and discourage the brako from their already obvious increase in activity. A reported salt protest on the Lev she was on was something Ilya thought she should investigate, as any sort of gathering in this atmosphere was likely to erupt into violence as it had done two years ago. She hoped to disperse the crowd quickly, if not for good then at least until the power crisis was over.

She emerged from the lift, facing the sound of the throng to her left, but was drawn around by the clatter on the stairs. A girl of perhaps twelve darted out of an alley, across the path of a wide-eyed dwarf.

She was followed by a beaked brako with a yellow band tied around his arm.

"Vanderwall."

Scarecrow emerged from the shaft system as near to the location the Spinks had indicated as he felt comfortable being, knowing from experience which shafts emerged into alleys, into streets, into vindis, homes or abandoned structures. A power outage and change in lighting when it was restored had not affected his vision, but the straining of the electrical and filt systems was a distraction he did his best to tune out. Those were not things he could do anything about.

When he emerged in the alley, he crouched, listening to his surroundings, the sounds of a protest in the distance, feet on the nearest stairs, the rattle and clunk of the lift stopping, and the hiss of pneumatic doors sliding open to deposit the identifiable thump of two pairs of bugorra boots, as well as two heavier sets of following steps.

Brako.

The decision to act was an instinctive impulse, unplanned but necessary if the streeter who emerged from the alley across from him was to escape the encroaching brako. Scarecrow leaped from the short alley into the perfect position to snatch the child away from the hands that had nearly closed around her. It was also the perfect position to shield the smaller man from the popper pellet aimed at his head by the second brako to emerge from the side street. In that instant, as his headgear deflected the popper pellet, Scarecrow registered a smattering of important, surprising details.

Enoch was the target of the popper fire…and of another three brako chasing from a fair distance behind on the Lev he had just fled.

Lieutenant Young and another bugger had exited the lift.

The child bore no immediately distinguishing clues that should mark him, or her, as a brako target.

And the man directly in front of him, the one who had nearly laid his hands on the fleeing child, wore the yellow band of the brako boss.

That detail struck as the lieutenant said his name, as Vanderwall, in his attempt to claim the child he had accidentally stumbled upon, in the hopes of reuniting her with her mother, swung his spike-gloved fist at Scarecrow's head.

"Scarecrow!" Ulynda cried, stumbling into the dwarf's path as she was yanked beyond the brako's grasp. The dwarf kept her from falling and ducked to one side to avoid the melee. The cloak hood covering her head fell back, exposing her frightened, wide-eyed face.

Ilya saw Scarecrow too. The bane of her existence. They both were, Scarecrow and Vanderwall. Two men she was equally resolved to bring to justice. Behind them, as the brako accompanying Vanderwall charged, Ilya also recognized the dwarf from the club…and the child he was trying to shield. "Get out of here! Run!"

Scarecrow's fist came up beneath Vanderwall's chin. He dropped, rolled beyond the man's reach, doing his best to keep himself between the boss and the dwarf and girl, while trying to maneuver the group into a position where Enoch and the child could make it to safety. His research told him who she was. She needed his protection. The alleys were dead ends for anyone unfamiliar with the shafts. The stairs were blocked by the trio of brako nearly at the bottom.

Their only hope for exit was the lift, or to flee down the walk and lose themselves in the group of protestors he could hear but not see.

Ilya wanted to rescue the Founder's daughter. She wanted to arrest Scarecrow. She wanted to take Vanderwall out of play. But Ilya and her sole accompanying officer were outnumbered with the arrival of the other three brako. They could not hope to accomplish all three agendas. While the bugger with her continued to wrestle with the brako who had engaged him, she let off a volley of stingers, striking two of the three approaching brako.

One dropped quickly.

The other continued to stagger sluggishly to his boss's aid.

There were obvious differences in fighting styles between this Vanderwall and the last. This man was heavy-handed. Brutish. This man was left-handed.

This was not the Vanderwall Scarecrow had fought before. A bilger, heizer, or other systems worker, yes, but not the man who had been thrown down the stairs to his death by the thrust of Jaron's boot.

This might be Vanderwall, but this was not the same man.

The spiked glove struck him in the side, at the base of his ribcage, and though his body armor protected him from the spikes' bite, the power of the blow forced the air from his lungs and sent a snapping jolt of pain up his spine. Scarecrow dropped to one knee, clutching his side, and groaned.

"Get her to Tamner," Scarecrow hissed over his shoulder before jumping up for another sparring exchange with Vanderwall, forcing an opening for the dwarf and child to run through. "Go!"

Enoch did not question the command. Taking the lift did not cross his mind. He grabbed the girl's hand and bolted past the pair of bugorra and away from the brako boss and his men, narrowly skirting another brako who emerged from the other side of the lift unseen.

Another brako. A lone figure focused from the moment of emergence on Enoch and the girl. Favoring his ribs, trusting the bugorra could handle Vanderwall and the two brako now with him, one staggering as the injector's sting sped through his bloodstream, Scarecrow charged the new arrival.

Stopping Vanderwall was important. Protecting Ulynda and Enoch was more so.

The injector spent, it clattered to the walk and Ilya fumbled for her buzzer as the dwarf and Kemway girl fled for cover. If the dwarf was an acquaintance of Jaron's, Ilya chose to believe Ulynda would be looked after so long as they escaped this fight. Buzzer in hand, she turned, intending to drop Scarecrow, hoping that, if he was out of the action, she could focus on Vanderwall and bring in both men at once. The sizzling, electric end of the buzzer missed its target as Scarecrow pushed past, a coward leaving the fight, and instead burned against Vanderwall's thigh.

The fabric was an inadequate shield against the jolt. Vanderwall lurched backward and roared.

The milling throng of protestors, Igraci, and others with signs bemoaning the ongoing salt shortage…and more hastily made ones decrying the power cut some deemed to be intentional, reached the intersection a Lev and a half above the fight. Their movement was aimless, noisy, but with three red-eyed functioning SCAMs at this junction, they settled on this place to make their political stand. Thanks to those SCAMs, if they were functioning in this time of reduced power, Captain Grainger and those in power would be sure to see and take notice of them.

They chanted. They cheered. They circled and swarmed like irritated bees so that their mass was ever moving, ever-shifting. It was the place, Enoch judged, to lose themselves. He and Ulynda reached another set of stairs at a run and stumbled up them, hastily intent on finding shelter in the chaos.

Catching a low hanging awning to swing himself several feet away, Scarecrow planted both feet in the newest brako's back. The man pitched forward and fell facedown onto the walkway. His head slammed into the grating with a crack, his beaked mask twisting sideways at an awkward angle.

Enoch and the girl disappeared into the protestors, safe now with no brako in pursuit. The drugged brako finally lost his footing and slumped against the lift door.

Only Vanderwall remained.

Breathless with each sharp stab at the base of his rib cage, Scarecrow thought it prudent to make his retreat. It was a one-on-one battle now between Vanderwall and Lieutenant Young and surely a well-armed bugorra could take him.

He could see she was no longer armed. The buzzer had been knocked away, the injector dropped and kicked beyond her reach. If she carried either a popper or a thumper, Scarecrow could not see them. She had skill, but Vanderwall had the advantages of size and strength. He looked to be gaining the upper hand. Scarecrow knew the lieutenant wanted his head too and would not hesitate to come after him if she could, but as he watched the fight for a few more moments, he knew he could not leave her at Vanderwall's mercy.

Together they could take him. Maybe she would reconsider her opinion then.

He turned and plowed into the unsuspecting man's lower back.

Believing herself left alone to face Vanderwall, her other quarry having fled, Ilya was determined not to go down easily, despite the blood dripping into one eye, the fractures she felt along her forearm where his gloved fist had smashed and torn her protective bugorra coat, and the pain in her knee suggesting strained or possibly torn ligaments. Her efforts to land blows while avoiding his, her attempts to turn the fight so that she could retrieve either of her dropped weapons, were continuously twisted to Vanderwall's advantage. He was manipulating her into a place where a tackle, a kick, a push, would force her down the slippery stairs.

Her efforts to avoid that position were failing.

His maneuvering, however, left his back open to the blindsided, unexpected assault of Scarecrow's return. Ilya saw the attack coming in time to sidestep a fall down the stairs, expecting that Vanderwall would tumble down them instead.

Vanderwall, however, brought his hands out to catch the rails on either side of the landing; he did not fall but his body snapped awkwardly in the repercussion of the slamming force behind him.

He bellowed. He spun. Scarecrow's fist caught the side of his head but failed to knock the mask free as Scarecrow had hoped it would. Another blow, directed at Scarecrow's already cracked ribs, was averted when Ilya brought her reclaimed thumper down across Vanderwall's shoulder. Scarecrow leaped back to avoid Vanderwall's direct blow and the brako boss twisted again. He caught the thumper and Ilya's wrist and pushed her back with enough force that she collided with Scarecrow, knocking them both to the ground.

Vanderwall jumped, caught the lip of the nearest building's roof, and with unexpected agility, hoisted himself onto it. Once there, he began to run.

Straight towards the crowd of protestors.

"Take the stairs!" Scarecrow shouted, his distorted voice unrecognizable. The angle of his point, towards the path Enoch and Ulynda had taken, made the intent of cutting Vanderwall off from two directions an obvious one. He used the walkway rail, an alglamp post, and the edge of an awning to take him onto the roof where Vanderwall had gone.

Ilya neither wanted to take direction from Scarecrow nor work with him. But to take down the brako boss before he hurt innocent bystanders in that crowd, this time she decided it was better to work with Scarecrow than against him. Swiping blood from her eye as she climbed to her feet, smearing the crimson like a mask across her face, she ran in the direction the others had gone, watching Vanderwall's progress and Scarecrow's above her as she followed below.

❧*❦

The flotsam at the repair crew's feet, connectors and adapters, coil springs and clips, lengths of conduit wire, were what remained of the damaged inverter, along with the array of tools used to remove it. Lash watched the effort through the techs' headcams, directing them through the process of undoing the damage crippling the city. The impaired unit had been replaced with a power board Tox had provided and other electronic bits Lash had gotten from Zara before sending the crew onto the dome. Neither woman knew solar systems the way Lash did, but they understood their areas of expertise, electronics and computers for Zara and mechanical and engineered systems for Tox.

Able to communicate with techs and his friends through comms once used by those who had done this job in years past, when it was believed the Outside was poisonous and deadly…they worked to cobble a temporary fix for Hebenon's primary solar inverter.

In place now, interfaced with the visually undamaged portions of the system, the lead tech gave a thumbs up to the other working with him and Lash began the count.

One.

Two.

Three.

The switch was thrown. The current rerouted.

There was a spark.

❧*☙

Curious onlookers gathered around the stairs directly in their path, those interested in the spectacle of protest, those wanting to join it, those wanting to catcall and ridicule the troublemakers. With little time to consider their options, unaware if the brako were still in pursuit, Enoch and the girl thrust into his care ducked into a lift as its occupants, wanting to reach the intersection crowd, stepped out.

"Where are we going?" Ulynda asked as the door closed. She was breathless, alarmed, but not afraid of the dwarf acting as her protector. The brako seemed to want him as well. To her, that made them allies.

"Somewhere safe." Scarecrow had advised taking her to Tamner, but there were several Levs between them and Outside, between them and the Uppers, and Enoch was not confident about their chances of reaching either without being intercepted by brako or bugorra.

His route to Vapors blocked by protestors, Skelter was too stubborn to go around. The intersection was not so big that he could not elbow his way through. Doing so would take more effort but less time, he hoped. He was late as it was. He did not bother to retrieve his rain hat when a fist-pumping dissenter knocked it from his head. There were too many stomping feet; the hat was already ruined.

Vindi lights went dark again but Skelter kept moving, walking stick tucked beneath his arm.

Another power outage was not going to stop him.

Through the glass sides of the lift, Enoch spotted Vanderwall disappearing into the gathered protestors.

Scarecrow was not far behind.

Enoch scowled and started to speak.

The lift yanked to a stop.

"I didn't touch anything!" stammered Ulynda, stepping away from the control panel, certain she would be blamed.

The neon around the crowded intersection went dark with a pop.

"We can't stay here." They had passed the Lev platform near the intersection full of protestors but they remained near enough to it that Enoch thought they could reach it and get safely out of the lift if they could get the doors open. He was not about to be trapped inside until the power came back on. The pneumatic lift doors had bypass switches to force them open manually, should the steam systems fail or become blocked, but those still required power to operate. It might take their combined strength to pull the doors apart without power, particularly with the lift stuck between Levs, but it was the only choice unless they wished to remain trapped here.

From his coat pocket, Enoch drew a short switch knife he had begun to carry with the onset of so many people's interest in him. Ulynda shrunk away, wide-eyed and frightened.

Enoch swallowed his initial response, wondering what sort of things the streeter had endured to result in the brako's interest and a belief she was about to be attacked. The streets were never easy for anyone, especially kids. The brako had made things worse.

From the plumpness of her cheeks, however, Enoch did not think she had been a streeter for long.

"Not for you. For the door. Here; when I pry it enough, we get our fingers in and pull the doors apart, you on that side, me on this side."

Fretfully watching him wedge the blade between the panels and fight to force them apart, she croaked, "They won't crush my fingers?"

"No." Once the doors were several inches apart there would be no chance of them springing closed.

Ulynda watched. When there was space enough for the dwarf to wiggle his thicker fingers between the panels, he did so, and Ulynda anxiously followed his lead.

"What's your name?" Enoch hoped a little friendly banter would put her at ease as she struggled to pull on the second door panel.

"Ulynda."

Enoch coughed and almost lost his grip on the door.

A little further, the panels lurching in resistance to their straining, and he dropped the knife to use both hands. The exertion took his mind off of details he did not want to dwell on right then.

"What's yours?" she asked when he did not volunteer it.

Instead of replying, he grunted, "Pull…harder."

Ulynda obeyed without questioning his failure to answer.

His quarry had led him here but the crowd had quickly swallowed him, leaving Molly stranded among strangers, his quick eyes scanning the heads of those around him.

Just like the Core door. People oppressed, wanting their needs met, wanting to be free.

He felt at home in this mass of bodies. He felt as one with them. He felt ready to fight again.

He felt ready to see the Spades' pact fulfilled the way it should have been.

Molly squinted through the dim blue-green glow of sporadically distributed alglamps and the neon of the Igraci's signboards.

The red hair ought to stand out.

His palm itched around the grip of his stolen popper.

Scarecrow heard the crackle in the electrical circuits, the prelude to another drop in hydropower output. The noise was like needles across his skin, making his nerve endings crawl. It was distracting enough at that moment that he lost sight of Vanderwall.

His foot pushed through the gap, and then his body, until the lift doors were open far enough that both dwarf and child could pass through, one at a time, to get out of the unmoving lift. So far the neon lights had yet to come back on.

"There…good. See the ledge? Can you jump to it?"

Ulynda began to shake her head no, but then her eyes narrowed stubbornly and she took another long look at the gap between the lift and the platform and the lift support stanchion that separated that distance. It was no further than the maze of furniture and cushions had been when playing 'the floor is the river' with Cori and Agnys. Not once during that game had she fallen into the 'river' even without something like the stanchion to steady her. The platform was wide enough, the cross rails high enough, that she could jump, land, and roll without falling off the other side.

"I think so."

"Good…because I'm going to need you to do something." He unfastened his cloth belt and worked it through the lip of the lift at his feet. His legs were shorter, his ability to leap that distance less certain, but with a little effort from Ulynda, the distance could be diminished by three or four inches, enough to make Enoch's jump across more likely to succeed.

"I'm looping this here, this way. Hold it; jump when you're ready. Once you're across, wrap this around the rail, like this…" He showed her how on his arm. "Then you'll have to pull, hard as you can."

She paid close attention to his instructions, to his example, and nodded when he finished. "I can do that."

Again she judged the distance, judged the height of the rails, the best place to make it across, and after a nerve-steadying gulp, she jumped. Her skidded stop on the walkway yanked the fabric belt out of her hand and the end fell and dangled between the lift and the platform. Falling to her hands and knees, her face pale, her expression mortified in the barely discernable glow of the nearest alglamp, she peered over the edge.

"I'm…I'm sorry. I didn't think it would…" she stammered.

"It's okay. It's okay, Ulynda." He was not certain it was okay, that he could still make this work without risking a leap he did not think possible, and so he fished up the loose end and knotted it to give the fabric weight enough that she might be able to catch it.

"Catch this…wrap it like I showed you. We'll try again."

She nodded eagerly. "I will. I'll catch it."

Three tries later, amidst frustration and disappointed tears from the child who had never had to try anything like this in all of her short life, and the knotted fabric was finally held tight in her fist and wrapped around the rail as Enoch had directed. Clutched like a prize between her hands, she strained to pull as hard as she could.

The lift budged on its pulleys, moving only a little nearer to the destination Enoch hoped for. Ulynda's feet, planted on the mist-slippery grate, began to lose traction.

As Enoch thought she would slip and be pulled over the ledge, her strength not great enough to realize what he had hoped, as he called, "Let it go, Ulynda. Let it go…it's okay…" long arms and big hands reached over her small shoulders, caught the fabric belt…and pulled.

❧Chapter 32❧

Haythem was afraid of the dark. It reminded him of a soft-walled room, a fettershirt, being trapped inside a mind that would not heed his bidding. He was afraid of the loud throng of people not so far away, with its instinctive sense of being hunted. Not by anyone specific but by everyone, for reasons he could not deduce or fathom. Something to do with her. Something to do with the black, with beaked masks, with the word Scarecrow that kept banging around in his head but which currently held no meaning. Something to do with the little man he had twice knocked out, twice escaped, who pretended to be his friend but was not.

Did he have a name? Was that Scarecrow?

Haythem was not sure.

What he was sure of was the voice, a girl's voice from a face he could not see straining at the end of a length of fabric tied to the open lift's frame. He knew that voice; from somewhere in the murkiest corners of his befuddled, hole-ridden memory he knew it. There was no concrete memory of a wife or children, although there was a hazy recollection of an icy-featured face guiding three small forms somewhere…accompanied by a sense of duty and despair that he would never see them again.

That sense was wrong, proving to him that the memory was wrong, confusing him further. He saw this girl and as the soft soles of her shoes slipped again on the wet street, her struggle to bring the little man to safety, risking her own, Haythem knew he had to help her.

He believed he had failed her once, somehow, letting go as he had.

Though afraid of the noise and dark, he would not fail her again.

He left the protection of the abandoned vindi where he had taken shelter the first time the power had gone off, looking left and right for the threat of a dark-skinned man or the woman whose face had appeared on city-wide Echos...whose face was now intertwined with the child's, and slunk across the street to help her.

He reached over her shoulders. Beyond her. He took hold of the cloth to which she clung and pulled on with all of her young might…and he pulled too, ignoring the screaming pain in his wrist and thumb that shot up his arm and made his eyes squeeze shut.

Enoch stared. Ulynda could not see who was behind her, heaving on the fabric belt with one hand and did not look, focusing instead on helping her new friend to safety. Enoch was looking straight at him, meeting the surprising man's gaze with a mix of emotions that made his chest ache as though his heart would explode behind his ribs. Rooted in place, barely hearing Ulynda's plea of encouragement for him to jump, it was not until the other man's hand reached for his and the stranger spoke that Enoch shook off his daze.

"Take my hand."

Not the words or voice of a catatonic madman.

The offer accepted, the distance between the lift and platform reduced, the supporting strength of the stranger's grip brought Enoch to safety. He teetered. He trembled. He looked into the face of a brother he had never met…speechless.

ↂ*ↂ

The stolen Crow mask should have made the tall man an easy mark in the middle of the protestors. His height and girth alone should expose him, should allow Scarecrow to find him as he skirted the edges of the crowd, sticking to the shadows so as not to draw attention to himself. Scarecrow was a thing of shadow, not of the masses.

Neither, he thought with annoyance, was Vanderwall.

There were tall men, big men, strewn throughout the intersection, raising fists and signs and voices in protest of things they believed were unfairly denied them by the whims of those in power. None wore the age-old protection of the Crows. None pushed through as though to escape the crowd or escape pursuit. None looked suspicious. Without knowing Vanderwall's face, without knowing what the brako boss wore beneath the stolen Crow coat, there was no sure way to identify his prey among the sea of possible targets.

Until he noted one particularly rough-featured bald fellow near the center who was scanning the fringes of the gathering, the side alleys and streets, the rooftops and doorways of corner vindis as if looking for something.

Looking for him, Scarecrow mused with a predatory, hidden grin.

He noticed something else as well as his gaze swept across the group and locked on to his primary suspect. Skelter, sliding through the throng, pushing to reach the other side, was not an immediate concern. The smaller fellow following him, however, moving with stalking focus like a cat after a rodent as he popped his head above the crowd again and again, as if standing on his toes, was obviously in a pursuit of his own.

Scarecrow did not know the man but he knew suspect behavior when he saw it.

His target was, or should be, Vanderwall. But he could not leave Skelter exposed to risk after having undertaken so much to save him from the Core.

Another glance at his primary target, committing that face to memory and to the SCAM memory built into his hood, and then Scarecrow changed direction, hoping to reach Skelter before the squirrely little fellow following him did.

"We have to go."

Enoch could no longer see Scarecrow, could not see Vanderwall or any brako intermingled with the protesting throng, but they had to be there. The brako did not give up that easily. With the brako hunting him and everyone in Hebenon looking for Founder Kemway, standing here in the open was the worst thing the trio could do.

Ulynda turned, now that Enoch was safe, to thank the stranger who had helped them, and gave a surprised squeak before throwing her arms around the man's waist. "Papa!"

She had abandoned the dubious security of home to find Scarecrow, to find her father, to find a mysterious, unknown uncle. Finding two of those three was good enough and one of those, whose scent she recognized despite the damp city smells permeating his clothes, was the most important of all.

Papa.

Haythem stiffened, alarmed by the unexpected affectionate gesture, alarmed by his impulsive reflex to stiffly put his hands on her shoulders, alarmed by the influx of disjointed memory snippets that side-showed behind his wide-eyed stare in the echo of that word.

☙*☙

Being caught in the protesting crowd had not been Switz's plan. After losing the Founder a second time, his head still pounding from the blow that had robbed him of consciousness, he had wandered the streets without aim or purpose for several hours, again seeking clues to find a man who was proving to be more trouble than he was worth.

Honestly, he thought with annoyance as he allowed the protestors to bump and push him along, he should forget the notion of finding the Founder, of seeking the reward ticks, and focus on getting on with his life. He had hoped that serving Blayd, that returning the madman to his wife, would provide a secure future, but realistically that pursuit was giving him nothing but headache after headache and leaving him nothing to show for his efforts except injuries and empty hands.

He was a free man. He did not have to answer to anyone anymore. He could make his own prospects, forge his own future, without relying on Blayd, the Kemways, or anyone else to provide for him.

Maybe he should try his luck Outside. If not in the village said to be there, if not at farming for which he considered himself ill-suited, there was a whole vast world to make his own. He had always been a survivor. Surely he could be one Outside too, in a place where no one knew his name, his face, his history.

The ticks Kemway's capture could provide, however, would make the likelihood of survival, either in Hebenon or Outside, much easier.

He climbed onto a cluster of recycle bins to escape the press of those taller than him, using the vantage point to scan above their heads to determine the best path out of the chaos. He could breathe easier there as well, escape the sweat and wet fabric smells created by those pushing and jostling past. It was there, from that elevated place, that he saw them.

Enoch.

A child.

Haythem Kemway.

Switz growled and leaped down. There was no way he would allow the dwarf to take what he had worked so hard for. Enoch did not need the reward ticks.

Not as much as Switz did.

❧*❧

"Isn't safe here; we have to go."

The continuing growth and movement of the crowd meant their gradual absorption into it, despite Enoch's efforts to propel those with him to a further distance away. He could not tell if the Founder recognized the child clinging to him, but Ulynda recognized him. This was a family reunion that needed to wait until they escaped the swirl of protestors and the lingering persistence of brako.

It would only take one person recognizing Founder Kemway to turn the protest into something more dangerous.

Jostled and bumped, Haythem looked from the top of the girl's head, a single word forming in his mind, in the back of his throat, as he glanced sideways into the crowd. He saw the people of Hebanthe Falls, frightened, small, frantic little beings, in a way he had never seen them before. He smelled their desperation, tasted their anger for what it was, something aimed at an intangible power he knew he had once been part of…even though he could not piece those memories together. He heard their voices, the cries for help, help he, he understood, had been born and destined to give them.

It was his duty. His birthright. His place to be here and offer hope and security and a future it seemed he had failed to provide, just as he had failed the child clinging to him now.

"Ulynda." He murmured the word with uncertainty without looking at her.

"Papa." She looked up with bright eyes brimming with joyful tears, respect, admiration, and love.

He heard those things and it drew his gaze to her face. In acknowledging them, his features set in stern determination. That was the look he needed. The belief he needed. Words and emotion he needed to deserve. To have them again he knew what he needed to do.

"You will be proud of me. You will be strong. You will remember that I love you."

Haythem did not know what that word meant, but he understood it was true.

For a moment he met the dwarf's gaze too, the little man suspiciously judging him as if not trusting his perception. Haythem's head cocked to the side, a burning sense of something eating at him that suggested he should know this man though he could not recall from where. How could he? Dwarfs were not allowed in the light. This fellow could not have been part of the warmth of life Haythem recognized had been part of his own somewhere back before the dark, disjointed thing the world had become.

Not so disjointed. Not anymore. He had purpose. He knew what duty was, what it demanded.

He gently pried the girl's arms from his body. "Take care of her."

The dwarf knew duty too. Haythem saw it in the way the man caught Ulynda's hand to hold her back, even as he reached for Haythem's with the other.

Kemway eluded the touch as he turned and pushed into the mob.

"Papa!"

The girl's wail of dismay drew Scarecrow's focus away from Vanderwall, away from Skelter, away from the rat-like man he intended to cut off. His shifting gaze never reached the girl's face, for there, charging through the crowd with the same blood-born arrogance he had exuded every time he had spoken to the people of Hebanthe Falls on the Echo screen, Founder Kemway passed without hindrance, the mass parting for him without full awareness of who he was or even that he was there.

Along the edges of the crowd, in the shadows where few could see or sense them, Scarecrow noted other movement.

Brako.

Bugorra.

The threat of exposure to the masses was set aside. Scarecrow chose to trust that this new draw of the people's attention would keep both him, and Skelter, safe.

Protecting the deposed Founder was Scarecrow's only goal.

The hush of awe turned Skelter to face the mob too. In his line of sight, he missed the familiar face of one man and focused on the two Talkers in ceremonial dress shoving others aside in their haste to reach the figure spearheading towards a low platform from which a woman with a loudhailer led the chanting in continual passionate cries.

Skelter could not believe what he saw.

Ilya, frustrated with the loss of both Scarecrow and Vanderwall, heard the girl's cry, sought its origins, and though she located both the dwarf and child she believed had safely escaped the brako, movement out of the corner of her eye demanded her focus.

Founder Kemway.

Talkers.

Brako swooping in to pick at the carcass of the carnage Ilya instinctively recognized was about to erupt.

Her fellow bugorra, those here to contain the mob if the protest spilled over into violence, recognized it too.

And pushing through the crowd without concern for his safety or anonymity, Scarecrow targeted the Founder as well.

Ilya whistled. Signaled. Her officers moved as one into the throng as she began to elbow the tightly knit gathering aside with the intent of reaching Kemway before Scarecrow, the Talkers, or anyone else had the opportunity to do so.

The whistles brought others. Every Spink within hearing distance took up the call.

Unaware that people knew his face, unaware of the hush that fell over those around him, Haythem climbed onto the platform and unceremoniously took the loudhailer from the woman using it. He cleared his throat and began to speak from his befuddled heart, his disjointed soul, from the tails of thought that he could grasp hold of but barely string into a coherent stream of words.

"Fear isn't the world! I was like you…afraid of change…afraid of being without."

He wiped his hand over his forehead, sweeping sweat and mist back into his unkempt dark hair, and began again, his frantic pacing taking him from one edge of the platform to the other.

"Respect people lesser than you. Don't let the world say you can't…you can! Anyone can! I didn't think it was true! For a long time, I thought I knew. High. Low. Light. Dark. I thought I knew!"

He made a choking sound as his body began to shake, unfamiliar, incoherent emotions strangling his efforts to reach those who stared at him with blank, perplexed, or rapt expressions.

How many times had he spoken to them? Hundreds, he was sure, though never had he seen their faces when he read the pre-arranged words on the scroller.

A Talker, dressed in the robes of his office, reached the platform and Haythem skittered as far from the reaching hand as the platform allowed. Those at the front of the group surrounded the Talker as though he was a threat and absorbed him back into the crowd.

"The sky is blue! The world is new!" Haythem cried, wild gaze darting side to side as the ghosts of his horror began to take shape in the crowd outside of his nightmares. His eyes lighted on a little man, a man he sensed had given him a fleeting sense of security though he did not recognize him now. He pointed at the fellow and shouted, "Don't focus so on a dream that you cannot see what is there. What is real! There is no meaning…except to live!"

Switz, feeling cornered and singled out by Kemway's gesture, froze in fright. Some around him looked at him but their attention did not linger. With the brako and bugorra closing in, he pulled out the injector he had been saving for later use from his coat pocket.

The Founder's audience did not perceive him as a threat.

Switz was certain Kemway did.

If he did this, he would only get one shot.

"Experience," Haythem continued. "Grow! Know! Go! Go out and see! Don't let her stop you! Go now…before she kills you all! Don't let her stop you!"

Scarecrow stopped moving, thinking the direction of the Founder's sweeping gesture was meant for him. Scarecrow was no her, however, and no one paid him any more attention than glances of surprise that Scarecrow was there among them.

Scarecrow they knew. Scarecrow was no oddity, despite this unusual, unexpected public mingling. What they wanted, instead, was to listen to the rambling, nonsensical words of their Founder, a man believed lost, mad, or dead. He was speaking to them directly for the first time, without the filter of an Echo and a multitude of Levs between them. Seeing him here was more amazing than rubbing elbows with Scarecrow.

"She doesn't know! She doesn't know! What she wants…what she will give you if you let her…is death!"

With his red-glazed eyes dragging across the crowd to Ilya's position, she swallowed and hesitated as if his words were a spear driven through her soul to pin her to the street.

But his gaze was off again, showing no recognition of her bugorra uniform nor any of the threats in the shadowy forms steadily encroaching on his position.

Enoch recognized what was happening without thinking about what he was seeing, without attempting to understand the words he doubted would ever make sense. Scarecrow. Brako. Bugorra. Talkers.

A scurrying cluster of Spinks, led by Ginna, emerged from the shadows, some of whom swarmed protectively around Enoch and the girl while others moved into the crowd. Protected by the streeter children who shuffled along with them, Enoch tugged Ulynda's hand, hoping to reach secure shelter before the world went to hell.

Ulynda, however, resisted, reluctant to leave the father she had just regained. Her mother was wrong. Her mother did not have him hidden away. He was alive. He was safe…although she did not think, given the plethora of buggers, brako, and Talkers around them, that her father would remain safe for long.

Only, she thought desperately, if Scarecrow reached him first did he stand a chance.

"Papa!"

His words made no sense to her. She barely heard them as she fought to reach his side and take his hand again.

"Papa!"

"When you come back…don't be driven by fear! Be driven by choice…to know…to make a difference…to live and experience and give others what no one gave me!"

Again Haythem's eyes focused on Scarecrow, the nightmare man now nearly at the corner of the platform. Lieutenant Young was at the other. His gaze was penetrating, with a degree of clarity his words did not possess, piercing as though he could make contact with Scarecrow through the vigi's tinted eyepieces.

Skelter sidestepped those nearest him for a better line of sight.

When he spoke again, shaking a furious fist at the people who stared as if they did not know him, it was with a tone of sadness that undercut the anger in eyes that refused to leave Scarecrow's face. "I know you! All of you! We've been blind! All blind! But not you! I know now! We were wrong…wrong…but you knew. You were the one! Crows took my eyes so we could see…gave a gift in that thievery…but do not be afraid! Don't make him take them too…to make you look. Open them! Open your eyes and see!"

Brako moved.

Bugorra pushed towards the stage and Ilya's side.

The Talkers lurched to mount the platform, to intercept those who aimed to take their Founder away from the Cult that had supported the Kemway family for hundreds of years.

Switz shuffled to the side and aimed.

Molly saw his opening.

The pneumatic crack of popper fire pierced the air.

The Spinks dogpiled the dwarf and the girl in their midst.

Skelter lurched and clutched his burning shoulder.

A second popping split the air right next to Scarecrow's head, the shrill volume making his ear ring as he and Lieutenant Young cut off the Talkers' efforts and rushed to Founder Kemway's side as he slumped to the platform between them.

The whole of Hebanthe Falls shuddered from the dome above to the river below…and Scarecrow's glove came up with blood on his fingers as he met the lieutenant's gaze, both thinking the same thought.

What in the name of Hebanthe Falls and the Founder had just happened?

THE END

(The Scarecrow will return…)

❧GLOSSARY❦

algtea: algae tea

andi: androids; artificial humans made most often for the sex trade and as dancers. Sometimes used to perform other undesirable duties.

bilger: those who work on dehumidifying systems

bozhe moy: my god

brako: thugs

bugger: nickname for new law enforcement due to the new breathing apparatus having a bug-like appearance. Also called bugorra or gorras

bugorra (bughat): nickname for new law enforcement due to the new breathing apparatus having a bug-like appearance. Also called buggers or gorras.

buzzers: tasers used to stun victims.

cazzing: fucking

chrono: watch, time-telling device, often with built-in comms

Crows: police/military force, someone not to be trusted; a snitch

crosser: those who have moved outside of the city; also those who work outside but live inside

deks: holodek suites used for recreation/vacations, since there is nowhere else for those in the City to go.

denki: those who work on heating systems

Doctet: Hebanthe Fall's Council of 10 that used to run the city in conjunction with the Founder

Echosys (also XCO/ekso/echo): computer; Current model is the 237 as they are frequently redesigned and built over 5 to 10 years. There are four basic models:
w (home view screens)
d (public view screens)
p1 (personal Echos)
t2 (portable tablet echos)
All are linked to the city's Hub at the time of manufacture. They are customizable and can be, illegally, removed from the Hub network.

fettershirt: straitjacket

ficken mich: fuck me (German)

filt: breathing filtration system

fotz: bitch (German)

gorra: nickname for new law enforcement due to the new breathing apparatus having a bug-like appearance. Also called bugorra or buggers

haikara: cybercriminal, hacktivist, hacker (Punjabi)

Hebenon: 1) name of the drug produced by official sources, intended as population control for use by the Crows but long ago made available to the public after its addictive properties became known; 2) The nickname Hebanthe Falls gained after the rise of the drug in the streets. The word Hebenon was taken from the Shakespeare play Hamlct duc to thc similarities in side effects experienced by its users.

Heb: the injected form of the drug Hebenon.

Hebbies: the drug Hebenon in pill form

heizer (also denki): those who work on heating systems

herpa: (from Japanese for helper) pastors, men of religious faiths outside of the Church of the Founder.

hijo de puta: son of a whore (son of a bitch)

hook: either **a** prostitute or the act of prostitution

Hub: the central broadcasting & computer system in the city.

ICD Images: still images captured with an ICD by passersby.

ICD: Interpersonal Communication Device

Igraci: The Players, (Bosnian in origin) group determined to move mankind out of Hebanthe Falls now that the city is open.

injectors: air guns that fire needles laced with Hebenon

kiomonga: from the Maori 'kiora mahanga, rat trap, a rundown room, home or business space

kaheao: one who dabbles in many trades; has their fingers in many pies

kef: marijuana

keffer: marijuana cigarette

kesfek: a tinker, a repairman, one who repairs things

kype: steal

Levs: refers to any of the lower 20 city levels. Houses most businesses and most of the population of the city.

malakes: from the Greek, plural of malaka(s); literally masturbators but as slang used as a curse word similar to asshole or idiot.

maleni: little one, child (Bosnian)

Marbordo: Seaside/Seacliff; what the parah call their village

mierdita: little shit
moka: mooch (Samoan)
moking: mooching
mpenzi: Swahili, darling
Nau: The Nine, the group that replaced the Doctet; potentials are selected by the whole of the city, but posts appointed by Grainger. Some were members of the original Doctet, most were not (because they were locked in the factories for so long and some died) No longer a lifetime or hereditary appointment but set for a term of five years. Can repeat service at Grainger's discretion. 1) material production; 2) distribution; 3) news/programming; 4) SCAMs and computer systems; 5) medical sciences, research, and care; 6) technical systems (including life support systems); 7) food production & distribution; 8) outside/inside relations (also monitors religious activities); 9) construction, city maintenance and upkeep (including life support systems)
parah: a corruption of the word pariah, used for those 'humans' who are living outside of the Hebanthe Falls in the world polluted by mankind's failings.
parah (2): refers to those born on the outside, although now sometimes used to refer to those who have moved outside as well.
poppers: air guns, firing small synthetic pellets.
poq Gai: "Go die in the street", general-purpose swearword (Chinese)
prodcast: broadcast productions aired through the Echosys, ranging from news, to sports, to entertainment and educational subjects.
prosser: those who have moved from the outside into the city; also those who work inside but live outside.
SCAMs: security cams used for monitoring public behavior. there are no SCAMs on the Uppers.
schweinhund: pig dog (German)
scroller: a prod consisting of scrolling text over a photographic or video backdrop, either silent or read.
Shed: facility out of which shaft crews work.
sikuea: squatter; one who resides in empty, abandoned buildings. (Samoan)
Soaper: where Hebbies are made by the brako on Lev 1
sorella: sister (Italian)

Source: the center of all material goods and food distribution.

speaks: speakers

speecher: digital implant units, typically in three parts, that allow mute individuals the ability to speak. One unit is located over the larynx, the other two at the temples, allowing electrical thought impulses to be converted into computerized speech.

spener: those who work on plumbing

streeter: those living on the streets

svodnik: pimp

swiver: someone who owns a food/beverage serving establishment or who serves food or drink; a bartender, waiter, waitress

Talkers: priests of the Voices of Faith established religion.

thumper: police stick used for beating prisoners to subdue them.

ticks: currency points used for the acquisition of food and supplies and services. Distributed by the Doctet on a predetermined scale.

tinger: someone who takes things, thief, vagrant living off of others

tinging: begging

trick: work as a prostitute

tupik: lockup (Russian)

Vapors: Maemi's club/bar

varon: man (Spanish)

vigi: vigilante

vindi/vind: venders, shops

Voices of Faith: the 'religion' supported by the Founder and Doctet which supports the Kemways divine right to run Hebanthe Falls; they produce prodcasts angled toward religious faith, community cohesiveness, and Kemway support.

XCO/ekso/echo: computer; current model is the 237 as they are frequently redesigned and built over 5 to 10 years

w (home view screens)

d (public view screens)

p1 (personal Echos)

t2 (portable tablet echos)

Zaolei: algae whiskey

About the Author

With fantasy and sci-fi as her passions, Tamara has written multiple novels to date, including the five books of the Kestrel Harper Saga, two installments of The Blood Wild Chronicles, and the stand-alone novel Suspicion's Gate. Cozenage is the third book in The Scarecrow Trials series

When not indulging in her love of words, Tamara relaxes in the company of her pack of Papillions, her horde of cats, and an ever-growing collection of films.

Learn more about Tamara's work at www.agdhani.com

www.ingramcontent.com/pod-product-compliance
Lightning Source LLC
Chambersburg PA
CBHW071524120726
47907CB00012B/268